Praise for *This is Just E*

A Finalist for the 2010 Fla

"As convincingly as Perry swift-paddles ~~the perilous waters of love,~~ he just as ably limns male comaraderie in all of its bantering rawness. [He] brings it all to life in such remarkably pinpoint, hilarious, and convincing fashion that you revel in spending more than three hundred pages here. It's difficult to come across a sentence, let alone a word, that doesn't smack tone-perfect and also refreshingly colloquial, candid, real. . . . The rough and tumble of men and women trying to make sense, eye-to-eye, toe-to-toe never leaves our view. The novel's final collision sparks operatic." —*The Boston Globe*

"Husband and father Jack Lang is on a mission: There's something out there that will fix things, but only he will know what it is, and he won't recognize it until he sees it. He tells himself that against all odds, all he needs is 'a patron saint of lost causes, or damaged ones.' . . . A deadpan, uproariously funny first novel about a young couple whose marriage has collapsed." —*The Atlanta Journal-Constitution*

"Jack Lang has trouble planning ahead, which is how he has ended up as the owner of two houses. His wife Beth has left him and his autistic son Hendrick to move in with Jack's closest friend. In the course of the book all three of them confront the things that you can control— and those you can't—and start to figure out what to do about them." —*The New York Times*

"Most poignant are Jack's tender, if bewildered, interactions with his son, Hen, a six-year-old savant. . . . Jack's good intentions don't quite pave the road to hell, but they do mastermind the construction of a 'backyard sidewalk tricycle racetrack' for Hen, accented with fiberglass crustaceans rescued from a defunct mini-golf course. Ultimately, Perry's debut is as charming, as touching, and as odd as Jack's magnum opus." —*The Oxford American*

"About once a chapter, Jack finds himself pondering why he operates the way he does and where's he's going from here. I really enjoyed this book, as much for its dialogue, which is really natural and occasionally really funny, as for these parts—where Jack tries to work out how he can do better by himself and those in his life."

—*Chicago Tribune*

"This is a richly imagined, beautifully written, and completely absorbing work of fiction. I found myself spellbound, turning pages well past my bedtime. What a fine, fine book." —Tim O'Brien

"Hilarity in the face of autism and infidelity may seem inappropriate— but not in Drew Perry's edgy new novel. From its madcap title to its choice chapter headings to its clueless males and their capable if baffled women, the book is a triumph. But not because of any of the above. The novel soars because of a six-year-old boy named Hendrick, who happens to be autistic. . . . It is Hen who gives Perry's book soul. . . . In fact, all of Perry's characters are unforgettable."

—*The Buffalo News*

"A finely tuned character study and a compelling read which deserves all the attention it gets . . . Perry has managed to create in Jack Lang the kind of original character a reader can admire in the pages of a novel—a Don Quixote, tilting at windmills." —*Seattle Post-Intelligencer*

"A terrifically accomplished study of character and motive, and a deeply personal tale of life with an autistic child, all carried off in a narrative voice that is winning, funny, and true. I loved this book. It moved me. I recommend it to anyone who has ever had, been, or known a troubled child." —Mark Childress

"Perry has nailed some key observations about modern life, like the tiny, compulsive gestures we make to convince ourselves that we still have some control. He notes the complexity of marriages and romantic relationships that never really end, especially when a child is involved. . . . In the process, [he] manages to say a lot about the state of the twenty-first-century human heart. This is just exactly the way a lot of us are." —*StarNews* (Wilmington)

"Drew Perry's wonderful debut will hold readers spellbound from beginning to end—think *A Midsummer Night's Dream* set in a small college town, plus a dog named Yul Brynner. The estranged grown-ups switch partners and dance back and forth with some of the liveliest dialogue I've read in years, all while struggling to come face-to-face with reality. And at the center of this often comical, sometimes tragic chaos is that reality—a child, Hendrick, brilliant and autistic—with the power to ultimately pull this cast of memorable characters back into the light of day and give them new perspective on what is most important. Perry is a gifted writer, and this novel, with its wit and warmth and wisdom, is an absolute winner."          —Jill McCorkle

"A striking debut novel about a man whose responsibilities haven't yet overcome his ambitions . . . Out of these tales of ordinary madness, Perry constructs a riveting familial drama. . . . A charitable and bleakly funny portrait of the American dream gone off the rails."
                                                   —*Kirkus Reviews*

"First-time novelist Perry tells a story that, in summary, seems like a rehash of a Lifetime movie-of-the-week. But what Perry does with this seemingly paint-by-numbers story is anything but predictable and melodramatic. . . . Perry doesn't shy away from looking closely at the how and why of the crumbling marriage, but lightens the mood with witty writing reminiscent of Tom Perotta."          —*Booklist*

"A beautiful rant against the so-called sane majority. And very funny: a dead-on, hilariously sad account—without a scintilla of sentimentality—of raising a brilliant autistic child in a marriage gone mad on account of it."          —Brad Watson

"Like all the very best novels, *This Is Just Exactly Like You* will make you first forget your own life and then reevaluate it. Drew Perry has written a beautiful and riveting book about the relationships that won't let us go, and the heartwarming human comedy that we call love."
                                                   —Nina de Gramont

ABOUT THE AUTHOR

Drew Perry holds an MFA in creative writing from the University of North Carolina–Greensboro and currently teaches writing at Elon University in North Carolina. His short fiction has been published in *Black Warrior Review*, *Alaska Quarterly Review*, and *New Stories from the South*. He lives with his wife in Greensboro, North Carolina.

DREW PERRY

# This Is
# Just Exactly
# Like You

PENGUIN BOOKS

PENGUIN BOOKS

Published by the Penguin Group
Penguin Group (USA) Inc., 375 Hudson Street, New York, New York 10014, U.S.A.
Penguin Group (Canada), 90 Eglinton Avenue East, Suite 700,
Toronto, Ontario, Canada M4P 2Y3 (a division of Pearson Penguin Canada Inc.)
Penguin Books Ltd, 80 Strand, London WC2R 0RL, England
Penguin Ireland, 25 St Stephen's Green, Dublin 2, Ireland (a division of Penguin Books Ltd)
Penguin Group (Australia), 250 Camberwell Road, Camberwell,
Victoria 3124, Australia (a division of Pearson Australia Group Pty Ltd)
Penguin Books India Pvt Ltd, 11 Community Centre, Panchsheel Park, New Delhi – 110 017, India
Penguin Group (NZ), 67 Apollo Drive, Rosedale, North Shore 0632,
New Zealand (a division of Pearson New Zealand Ltd)
Penguin Books (South Africa) (Pty) Ltd, 24 Sturdee Avenue,
Rosebank, Johannesburg 2196, South Africa

Penguin Books Ltd, Registered Offices: 80 Strand, London WC2R 0RL, England

First published in the United States of America by Viking Penguin,
a member of Penguin Group (USA) Inc. 2010
Published in Penguin Books 2011

10  9  8  7  6  5  4  3  2  1

THE LIBRARY OF CONGRESS HAS CATALOGED THE HARDCOVER EDITION AS FOLLOWS:
Perry, Drew
This is exactly like you : a novel / Drew Perry
p.  cm.
ISBN 978-0-670-02154-3 (hc.)
ISBN 978-0-14-311860-2 (pbk.)
1. Marital conflict—Fiction.  2. Marriage—Fiction.  3. Parents of autistic children—Fiction.
4. Parenthood—Fiction.  5. Autistic children—Fiction.  6. Parent and child—Fiction.
7. Suburban life—Fiction.  8. Domestic fiction.  I. Title.
PS3616.E7929T47  2010
813'.6—dc22    2009042562

Printed in the United States of America
Set in Joanna    Designed by Francesca Belanger

For Tita

# Contents

But the dog says, Let's go make a sandwich.
Let's make the tallest sandwich anyone's ever seen.
And that's what they do and that's where the man's
wife finds him, staring into the refrigerator
as if into the place where the answers are kept—
the ones telling why you get up in the morning
and how it is possible to sleep at night,
answers to what comes next and how to like it.

—Stephen Dobyns, from "How to Like It"

Oh help me, please doctor, I'm damaged—

—The Rolling Stones, from "Dear Doctor"

# This Is
# Just Exactly
# Like You

# ONE

# Patriot
# Mulch
# & Tree

From the half-insulated attic—a space he's been wanting to carve out as an office if he can ever even *get some goddamned drywall up at least, Jack, please*—he calls over there. Lets it ring. His big plan: Run bookcases down the sides, replace the windows in the two gable ends, put a desk under each window. Maybe set a couple of upholstered chairs out in the middle, and a rug, and it'd be nice up here, a place they could sit in the evenings, have a drink. She'd like that. Ice in glasses, sprigs of mint. Coasters on little low tables. *How was your day, dear?* That'd be just grand as hell. It rings. Six times. Eight. He's calling to tell Beth that he needs to come by to drop Hen off. It's Canavan who finally picks up.

"Hey, Jack," Canavan says. He sounds sleepy.

"I wake you guys up?" Jack says.

"You're calling for Beth," says Canavan.

He doesn't feel any real need to answer that. "No jobs this morning?" he asks. Canavan cuts trees down. Likes to call himself a tree surgeon, like there's a medical degree that goes with it.

"Not till later on," says Canavan. "Slow Friday."

Jack can hear sheets and blankets, and then also what sounds like dishes, like plates. "You two eating breakfast in bed?"

"No," Canavan says. "It's dinner."

Jack checks his watch. "It's eight in the morning."

"Yeah, I know. It's from last night. Beth made us soup and bread. Campeloni."

Somewhere in the background, Beth says, "Cannellini."

"Cannellini," Canavan says. "Apparently."

"Beth made you soup and bread," says Jack. Beth is not a huge cook.

"Cannellini," he says again, as if it's some kind of explanation. "Tomatoes in it. It was pretty good."

Jack holds the phone out in front of him, like he'll somehow be able to look in there through the little array of holes and see them in bed, his wife and his excellent friend Terry Canavan and all the plates and bowls from soup and bread. At least she doesn't have a suitcase with her yet. Every time he's come back home this week he's checked the closets first thing. All the suitcases are still right there. And her clothes, too, he's pretty sure, or most of them. Which only means she's probably over there wearing some old sweatshirt Canavan's found her, or his Carhartt fucking jacket he's so proud of, the one with the zip-off arms. Zippers everywhere. That's how Jack pictures her, then, little panties and the unsleeved vest of Canavan's jacket. Hair all in knots. "Gimme Beth," he says.

"Yeah. Hang on." Canavan puts the phone down and Jack hears them talking, but can't make out the words. Then Beth picks up.

"Hey, Jackie," she says.

"Hey," he says back, and just stands there. In their attic. He doesn't know why he came up here to make the call. Sometimes he does things like this. Now he feels a little like zipping his own arms off.

"You called me," says Beth.

"Yeah," he says, recovering some. "I need to drop Hendrick by. I'm going in to the yard."

"I have a class," she says. "Summer session started yesterday. You know this."

The way she says it, like he's a kid. *You know this.* "You couldn't take him with you?" he asks her.

"What, to my class? I don't think so, Jack. And anyway, why can't he go with you? He went with you yesterday. And Wednesday."

"Fridays are crazy," he says. "Plus with the weather like this, the line'll be out off the lot. We probably won't even get to break for lunch." He picks at the windowsill, can't really believe he's having this conversation. "It's not like I'm dying to come over there and, what, help you two clean up your dishes from last night, maybe straighten the covers for you, put a mint on your pillow—"

"Stop it, OK?" she says, her voice gone all brittle. Just like that. "I'll figure something out. I'll take him. Let's not do this right now."

"Hey, I know: Let's not do it at all."

"Jack," she says, and then quits.

He waits for her to start talking again. A piece of someone else's conversation breaks in on the line, then disappears. On her end, there's something like the sound of Canavan rearranging the dressers in the bedroom. Or bowling. "I'll be by, then," Jack says finally, to fill up the space. He checks his watch again. "In half an hour." And instead of waiting for more quiet, he hangs up on her, stabbing at the button on the handset a few times, which just makes him feel a whole lot better. *Bitch,* he thinks, and right away feels sorry for that, or stupid about it, or both. One more thing done wrong. He puts the phone in his pocket and goes downstairs to find Hendrick. Whatever else there is, there's this: She will have been gone one week tomorrow.

❧ ❧ ❧

The weather's been perfect, actually, like it's spiting him somehow, the end of May into June and cool weather hanging on after a

weird warm winter, the seasons all out of whack. He's got windows open all over the house still, breeze blowing in from everywhere. It's been fiercely sunny, daylilies coming in, everything
greening over, everything in bloom. It's not even supposed to make
it much past 80 degrees today, a kind of Chamber-of-Commerce
forecast, which means by ten o'clock the line will be out to the
highway, pickups and trailers and minivans bumper-to-bumper
back behind the Shell station next door, past the Dumpsters and
down the gravel side lane the county put in for them on 61. Everybody taking Friday off to buy flowers and soil and mulch. Hardwood, pine, dyed pine, pine bark, pine needles. Everybody in a
fight against weeds, against the hot and the dry that's got to be
coming. He'll have been doing this four years this fall—hard to
take in that it's been that long—and they've got it to where the
thing will almost run itself. A day like this, and Butner and Ernesto
could have moved sixty yards of mulch and soil by the time he gets
in, maybe more. Butner: His right-hand man, his heavy lifting, his
lot manager. He's been with him nearly the whole time. Ernesto's
been on a year and a half, conduit to the Spanish-speaking landscape crews, a genius with the plants. He can bring anything
back to life. Last summer he grew peppers in a plot next to the
greenhouse—hard little orange things the size of golf balls, wrinkled green witch hats, ten or fifteen other kinds. Jack had no idea
there were that many varieties of pepper. Butner grows heirloom
tomatoes, has every year. The two of them sold produce out of the
office all last season. One more way to bring in money.

Patriot Mulch & Tree. Butner named it. The first week after he
hired him, Jack deep in the red and already paying bills out of their
savings account, Butner took him out there, stood him in front of
the old sign that said HIGHWAY 70 MULCH SUPPLY, said *Here's your problem right here. Go get you fifteen American flags and run 'em across the front of
the property. Rename it something patriotic and people'll buy whatever you sell.*
Business doubled in six months. Butner and the flags and the loca-

tion. It's on the same lot as the Shell station, in Whitsett, on the only real road that's not the interstate anywhere nearby. Twenty minutes east from where they live in Greensboro, ten minutes west from where Beth teaches, Kinnett College. PM&T sits just up from the Holy Redeemer International Church of Whitsett and the First Whitsett Church of Jesus Christ Our Only Lord, both prefab metal buildings, built right next to each other. International flags on poles around the Holy Redeemer, competing semi-apocalyptic sign marquees out front of each: IF YOU THINK IT'S HOT HERE, JUST KEEP ON GOING. GOD ANSWERS KNEE MAIL. PREVENT TRUTH DECAY——BRUSH UP ON JESUS. Bible verses, threats, prayers for the living and the dead, for storm survivors, for soldiers. Ride a few hundred yards past the churches, and there are Jack's fifteen American flags, Jack's two yellow loaders, his red dump truck, his low gray office shed, his small mountains of pine bark and gravel and leaf compost. The little world he's made for himself.

He finds Hendrick downstairs right where he left him, sitting in the kitchen on the half-finished tile floor, fully into his morning routine. He's in front of the one cabinet they've left the guards off of, opening and closing it, rocking back and forth, humming the tune to the WXII NewsChannel 12 evening news. He knocks his forehead against the cabinet door every second time he gets it open. He's got a good rhythm going. Jack watches him do that a while, stands there and looks at their kitchen, tries to see what Beth sees. This is something she asks him to do. So he looks. He ran out of tile at the hole where the dishwasher is supposed to go eventually, and when he went back to the flooring place the next week, they were out. Evening Mist had been discontinued, they said. *But why wouldn't you have bought it all the first time?* Beth wanted to know. No good answer, like most other things. He goes ahead with projects without planning them all the way through first. It makes her crazy. He knows this, does it anyway. Gets excited. Which is why there's plywood running one entire wall of the kitchen: Jack knocked a hole through the back of the house in February, planning a little 8x8 breakfast nook with a bay window. Something Beth might enjoy. She was out of town, at a conference in Chicago. He had dreams of getting it roughed in over the course of the weekend—ambitious, he thought, but possible—except he hit the water line trying to dig out trenches for the footings and foundation. When the city came out to turn it off, a good-sized geyser Hendrick got a kick out of watching, they shut him down. No building permit, nothing to code. Now he's supposed to get actual licensed plumbers and electricians. Plus an architect. He's got to get drawings approved downtown. He's done none of that. *How was Chicago?* he asked her at the airport. *How's the house?* she said, knowing already, somehow. Expecting. She took it well at first, or pretty well, but it was what he'd have to call a mitigating factor in her leaving. Last week, during her meltdown: *And I've had a goddamned plywood kitchen for six months!* Jack wanted to point out that really it was just the one wall, and that it had only been four months, but she'd already moved well past that and on to his most recent sin, his most grievous, the one they'll surely send him up the river for: That he'd *bought, Jack, for chrissakes, the house across the street.*

Which was an accident. He'd never have done that on purpose. Nobody would have. They woke up one morning at the end of April to an auctioneer working his way through a series of end tables and sofas and riding lawn mowers all set up in the yard over there. The old man, somebody they'd known well enough to wave to, had died, and his kids, in from out of town, were auctioning everything they weren't keeping. The auctioneer had a microphone and a podium. Jack took Hen over to watch, to stand in the crowd of old men wearing camouflage ball caps and listen to the guy work his way through *ten, ten, gimme ten, can I get ten? Ten! How 'bout fifteen? Gimme fifteen, gimme fifteen.* He had a high, thin voice that rode out over the top of the crowd. Up for sale: Boxes of old *Field and Stream* magazines. Shovel handles. Mini-blinds. Light fixtures. Shotguns. Trash cans full of shotgun shells, bags and bags of shot. The old man must have been preparing for an invasion. When the auctioneer got around to the house itself, the bidding stopped thirty thousand dollars below what Jack had bought his own house for last year, and there it was: The exact same house, same floor plan, same everything, one more house in a neighborhood full of postwar ranch houses built all the same by the same builder, and it was too simple. He could not help it. Didn't even really think about trying to. He raised his hand.

Beth couldn't believe it, kept saying that over and over. *I cannot believe you did this to us.* It was easy money, he tried to tell her: Open up a couple of walls like they'd done, pull up the carpets and redo the hardwoods like they'd done, replace the stove and fridge like they'd done. Coat of white paint top to bottom. Sell the place in two months. Easy money. Beth wanted to know how in hell he thought he could do all that across the street *when you can't even finish a tile floor in your own kitchen.* Wanted to know *what on earth, Jack, could have gotten jammed inside your skull that would make you do a thing like this.* Last week, after they'd railed through their own house at each other for a while, Jack went across the street while she stuffed her toothbrush and whatever else she could find into a plastic grocery sack. He sat on the steps, identical to his own steps. Concrete. Iron railing. He watched her come out their front door, watched her get into the car and back down the driveway, watched her drive down the road. To Terry fucking Canavan's house, of all places. If he'd known that—if he'd known where she was going—he might have thrown himself under the back bumper while she was leaving. Or stood in the street and lit himself on fire. Or something else that might have gotten her attention, or his.

Open, closed, open, forehead, closed—Hendrick bangs his head on the cabinet, hums a little louder. Jack refills his coffee and runs his toe along the place where the tile ends. At least Hen's dressed today. This is a minor triumph. He hates textures right now, hates his sheets and clothes, likes to be naked a lot. Two weeks ago at the post office Jack looked up from checking whichever square it is that allows delivery without signatures, and there was Hen, walking the row of PO boxes, naked but for his socks and shoes. He had one hand out to the side, for balance, and he was hanging onto his little pink dick with the other. He kissed each keyhole as he passed. What Jack couldn't figure out was how he'd managed to get his pants off over his sneakers, how he'd done it so fast. A logistical miracle, hugely impressive. People in line whispered to each other, staring, not sure what the protocol was for a situation like this, not sure if this was the sort of thing allowed in government buildings post-9/11. Nakedness, shouting, repetitions, astonishments: These are the things Jack's all but used to, finds a little funny sometimes, even. They are the sorts of things that freak Beth right the hell out. Sign after sign after sign that Hen's not getting any better. The difference is that Jack doesn't really expect him to—not any time soon, anyway. At the post office, he picked him up and put him over his shoulder and headed for the door, Hen going fully limp in his arms. Jack stared right back at the people in line. Made eye contact. He left the pile of clothes and the mail and everything there on the counter, drove back home.

*What do you mean you left his clothes there?* Beth wanted to know, Hen standing naked in the hallway, spinning in circles, making his noises. *Bup-bup-bup-bup-bup.* She asked him again: *How could you just leave them there?* He wanted to tell her that it had all been pretty simple, actually, but instead he went and sat at the kitchen table, flipped through the stack of credit card offers and bills: Reward miles and bonus points, the first mortgage payment due across the street. Beth made a big show of piling into the car and then came back in half an hour, mouth set in a thin line that meant victory, holding the clothes, and holding Jack's overnight envelope, too.

Hen switches into the Patio Enclosures song. It's his favorite TV commercial right now. *Someone you know knows something great: It's Patio*

*Enclosures.* He does it falsetto to match the voice of the woman in the ad. The people in the ad are deeply moved by their new glass sunrooms. Glass sunrooms are the cure for cancer, for erectile dysfunction, for our dependence on foreign oil. All that is missing from your life is a new glass sunroom from Patio Enclosures. Hen sings it again and again. It's the background music of Jack's life— jingles, the full texts of radio commercials, state capitals, state birds, state flowers, the entire sides of cereal boxes. All from memory, everything in perfect recitation. *Montpelier Montgomery Albany Sacramento Carson City. This is Budweiser, This is Beer. The cardinal, the dogwood. We've gone C-R-A-Z-Y here at American Furniture Warehouse,* and then, word-for-word, the monologue that the guy, decked out in his flag tie or his gorilla suit, delivers as he sprints the rows of recliners and daybeds. Hen's a genius, if a broken one. He could read at two and a half. Getting him to talk *to* them, though, instead of at them, or at the television—that's something else altogether. There have been so many doctors that Jack's long since quit counting, and anyway, they all say the same thing: Hendrick is autistic. Some of them say he's high-functioning, and some of them don't. They stand or sit behind their desks in their candy-colored pediatric doctor coats and generally want to talk about *where he falls on the spectrum. Autism is what we like to call a spectrum disorder.* Jack always finds himself picturing something actual, Hen splayed out on a big blue mat, having fallen *onto the spectrum* from some significant height. The doctors have cartoon animals on their coats. Baboons. Gazelles. Hendrick sits over by the box of toys and lines up the blocks in identical, regimented rows, probably pointing to true north.

There are good days. There are days when they go to the post office and nothing happens, or not much happens, days where Jack does, in fact, go back to trying to believe in what one of the first doctors told them, a guy with a biggish mole over his lip. *Could still be nothing,* he'd said, fingering the mole. *No need for alarm.* He soothed them. Jack sat in the highback chair on the other side of the desk, and Beth sat on a sofa with Hendrick, straightening his hair with a wet finger. They felt soothed. The doctor's degrees hung on the wall behind him. *Boys develop more slowly,* he told them. *He could still grow right out of it.* They nodded along, eager. *Language acquisition comes at different times, and in different ways. We'll see where we are in a couple of months. We can run some tests then, maybe do a little blood work.*

A little blood work. It was like they were in a movie about going to the moon, or tunneling to the center of the earth. Any amount of blood work seemed like too much. They waited the couple of months, then another couple. And now he's six. He's not growing out of it. This morning, like any morning, Beth gone and impossibly moved in with Canavan or not, Hen is disappeared deep into his secret set of notes, his rhythms and maps, marking time with his forehead on the kitchen cabinets. He could as easily be watching the ceiling fan spin, or reading—he'll read anything they put in front of him—and touching the same sentence on the same page of the same book again and again for hours at a time. At the grocery store Wednesday night, he started pulling soup cans off the shelves one by one and throwing them down, yelling *Alexander Haig! Alexander Haig!* as each one hit the floor. He'd been all week in the H encyclopedia. *He actually hates Secretaries of State,* Jack said to the mothers standing there, watching. He picked cans of Cream of Mushroom up off the floor, put them back on the shelf.

Nobody at home to tell that story to. He and Hen came home to their plywooded, half-tiled kitchen, and made dinner, two men in the house. Macaroni and cheese for Hen, a little thin steak in the pan for Jack. Can of beer. Beth had already been gone three days. What spooks him is that it's starting to feel familiar. He's getting to the point where he's not looking for her in the bed when he wakes up. At work, Butner and Ernesto can't believe she left Hen with him. It doesn't make any sense, they say. She'd at least have taken him with her. Jack tries to explain that actually it does make a kind of sense. That it's fucked up, but it makes sense. That yes, she's always been the paranoid one, and yes, she's the one who's got the *CPR for Kids* and *The Pediatric Heimlich* placards stuck up on the fridge. She's plugged the primary and backup numbers for emergency rooms and urgent care centers and the Ear, Nose & Throat guy into their speed dial. She's put poison control magnets on every metal surface in the house, she's covered over all the sharp edges on everything, she's filled every outlet with the little plastic protective tables—but the thing is that Hendrick, for all of that, for all her readiness, has never really been hers. If he's ever been anyone's, he's been Jack's. It's Beth who finds and drags them to special parenting classes, and it's Beth who records the afternoon talk shows any time there's going to be anyone on there with a special-needs child, but Hen chose Jack, or he chooses him—smiles, when he smiles, at Jack, aims his few brief cogent moments generally in Jack's direction. It rubs at her every, every time. She doesn't understand it, doesn't know why she can't be the one to unlock him, or why he can't be unlocked—and then she hangs another choking hazard list on the pantry door, sticks another awareness bumper sticker on the back of the car.

For his part, Jack wants none of the peripheral bullshit that arrives with *the autistic child*, has never wanted it: He hates the passing sympathies he gets in the stores, the caring looks, the whispering. He doesn't want anybody else feeling like they get to weigh in on the subject. No ribbon magnets. No Differently-Abled. No special summer camps with psychopathic overstimulated teenagers running on about how *Y'all, I've just always felt so called to help the less fortunate, you know? We are so blessed for this opportunity. We are going to have a super-fun time.* None of it. No more magazines, no more pamphlets, no more instructional videos. He just wants Hendrick, wants to be with his son without being told by sloganeers how to feel about it. He does not want to have to hear any more human interest stories on NPR. He doesn't want to listen to somebody's soft, caring voice asking somebody if it's hard. *How hard is it? Is it so hard?* It cannot possibly get any harder.

He's never wanted anyone, under any circumstance, to *reach out to him*, or to *be there for him*, and the way he's got it working in his head is that Beth must have finally started to feel that way, too. That it maybe got to the point where even she couldn't, in all her freaked-out glory, record one more show about kids in helmets. That what this has to be for her is a vacation, a sabbatical. She's checked out of it for a day, a week, for however long this is going to take. Just checked out of her marriage, of her son. Because she can't be over there at Canavan's going through her same routine, watching Oprah walk somebody through the stations of the cross one more time. *And when did you know for sure that your son was different from all the other children?* He can't picture her over there surfing the web obsessively, trying one more time to find the right diet combination to sync Hen's mouth back up with his brain. He can easily enough, though, picture her over there fucking his best friend, which makes him want to drive nails through his own shins. That's another thing they can't believe at work: That of all people she'd have gone to Canavan instead of somebody from the college, or somebody from another part of her life, or anyone else from anywhere else. And he tries to explain that, too, to them, to himself. That even that part might make its own sick sense. Because of course she'd end up with a friend. Even an old boyfriend would have been too strange for her, too unfamiliar, someone too much from another time. There would have been too many things to explain. How much easier to land with someone, even if it is Canavan, who already understands about Hen, about her, about everything. Right?

The dog, Yul Brynner, gets up, clicks his way down the hallway, stands in the kitchen and asks to go out. Another country heard from. He's got a wide bald scar on his forehead from where he was hit by a car when he was a puppy. Or so said the shelter people, anyway, when Jack got him. He predates Beth by two years, which makes him ten. He's aging a little, going white through his muzzle, slowing down just enough for Jack to notice. What he'll do when the dog dies, he has no idea. Evenings, after he gets Hen down, he's been taking Yul Brynner out on the porch and listening to the radio, listening to a call-in show run by a woman who keeps saying that *everything happens for a reason*. It's a break-up show. Jack sits there with the dog and drinks beer and women call up and say *I just want to dedicate "Keep On Loving You" to my boyfriend Bryan, and I just want to say, Bryan, I really mean it, OK? I'm going to. We were meant for each other. I just know it.* And the woman who runs the call-in will say *That's right, Stephanie. You just keep on going the way you're going. You take care of Stephanie first. He'll be back. And if it doesn't work out, then it wasn't meant to be. Am I right?* Stephanie always tells her she's right. Confession, absolution, REO Speedwagon. *Brought to you by.* Sometimes Jack thinks about calling in, thinks about what he'd say. Yul Brynner, for his part, lies there and waits for Jack to get near the end of his beer so he can lick the bottle.

The dog heads out into the yard, finds a good spot, shits, smiles while he does it. He pants and squints into the sun. To be that happy for ninety seconds in a row. Then he comes back in the house and settles down next to Hendrick, who is, of course, still working the cabinet door. Open, closed, open, forehead, closed. Jack tops off his coffee, starts in on Hen's breakfast, on their day. Beth at Canavan's house: Alexander Haig, Alexander Haig.

❧ ❧ ❧

Getting Hen into the car—getting him anywhere—goes like this: Get him dressed. In anything. If he'll pick out clothes, let him pick out clothes. Shorts and flip-flops in December? Doesn't matter. Whichever combination of shirt and pants and shoes does not in any way matter so long as he will let you put a shirt and pants and shoes on him. Get him dressed, and then get him whatever it is that has become the sacred object of the week or month. Whatever it is that holds Most Favored Nation status. Right now, it's the glossy 300-page catalog from Lone Oak Tree Farms that turned up in the mail at PM&T. Jack gets vendors of all stripes asking him to carry specific kinds of double impatiens or faux terra-cotta urns or bagged river rock. The Lone Oak people sell serious trees, trees that come in on flatbeds. Jack has no room for that kind of thing. The trees of Patriot Mulch & Tree are fruit trees in five-gallon buckets. But the Lone Oak operation seemed impressive, so he kept the catalog, and Hen found it, loves it. He's read it cover to cover and back again so many times that the edges of the paper have gone soft and grimy. He carries it with him to the grocery, to the bathroom, to dinner. He sleeps with it. Always and forever make sure that you have the catalog.

And do not, under any conceivable circumstance, leave the house without the Donald Duck sunglasses. The Duck. Without The Duck, there is disaster. Without The Duck, as soon as he registers he's outside, there is the immediate walking around in small, tight circles, the repeated touching of the eyes with the first two fingers of each hand, the noises. *Bup-bup-bup-bup-bup.* What generally follows is that he'll throw himself down onto the ground, cover his eyes with his full palms, start screaming in earnest. The books say autistic kids have *increased sensitivity to light*, but that's not all it is. He just loves the sunglasses. Once he wore them three days in a row, inside the house and out. Jack sometimes isn't sure how much of any of this is *on the spectrum*, and how much of it might simply be Hendrick being maybe more human than everybody else, more sensitive to his own cravings.

Jack gets The Duck and gets Hendrick dressed and out the door and aims him toward the dump truck—since Beth's got the wagon, he's been driving the truck, a custom hydraulic bed on a heavy-duty Chevy pickup frame. He puts him in his booster seat, belts him in. There's no backseat, so the front has to do. Beth gets on him about this, but there aren't any airbags, either, so they're safe. Hen starts saying *certified AMS meteorologist Lanie Pope with weather* over and over. *SuperDoppler* 12, he says. In his glasses, white plastic with Donald Duck on the edge of each lens, he looks like a tiny Elton John. Jack gets in over on his side, and Hen stops talking, holds his left hand out in the air. He pinches his thumb and forefinger together, sticks his other three fingers out to the side: *A-OK.* "What's that you've got there?" Jack asks him.

"A dust," Hen says, and for the moment, there he is, looking dead at Jack, a six-year-old kid like any other. "I have got a dust," he says again.

Jack holds his own hand out in the same way, pinches at the air below the rearview. "Me too," he says, but Hen's already back down and in, playing with the glove compartment. Anything that opens and closes. These are the flashes they get, where it seems like he's in there for sure, like he's capable of registering any single thing in the whole damn world. And then he's gone again.

Jack cranks the engine and backs down the driveway, out into the street a little too far, clips the mailbox over at the auctioned house with the back of the truck. It makes a good-sized bang. He's leaned it over about halfway. This is good, he thinks, pulling back forward. On balance, this is good. Something to fix one of these nights when he gets home. Bag of cement and the post hole digger and a beer or two. Something to fill up his evening. He's been having trouble filling his evenings. He aims the truck for Whitsett, for Canavan's house, for PM&T, adjusts the windows so the air blows in the way Hen likes. Get it right.

❧ ❧ ❧

It's not just that Canavan would be familiar enough for her, or only that he would be. Canavan also and on top of everything tends to be a generally decent guy, funny, a quick ally at the dinner table.

He defends Beth's wall-to-wall safety placards, explains Jack's end-less projects. *He'll have the sliding glass doors back up in a week, right?* Or: *What's so bad about having phone numbers close by when you need them? You're just organized, is all.* He's helpful, courteous, cheerful, five or six other points of the Boy Scout Law. And now he's a prick, too, to go with that.

When Jack pulls up, Canavan's out in his carport, sitting on a big blue cooler and doing something to a chainsaw. He's got the arm off the saw and he's working the blade, link by link, through a ruined white towel. There's a can of gas next to him, and a little plastic bottle of oil he keeps upending into the towel. He doesn't look up until Jack cuts the engine off. It's the first time Jack's seen him since Beth moved in—Canavan's sent guys to the lot a couple of days to drop limbs and branches back at the chipper, but he himself hasn't come by. Hen plays with the door lock. Canavan looks up and waves, and Jack gets out of the truck, and there they are.

"How's it going?" Jack says. He feels like an idiot, but doesn't know what else to say. He's not going to challenge him to a duel or anything—though maybe he should. Limb saws at dawn.

"Good," says Canavan. "It's going fine."

"How come no early job?"

"We've got one midday out in Burlington. Big maple overhang-ing a garage. Delicate. Gave Poncho and Lefty the morning off hop-ing they'll be sharp for it. Probably they'll just be hung over." Poncho and Lefty is what Canavan calls anybody who's working for him, no matter how many people he's got on at any given time. Right now it's three rail-skinny white guys, tins of chew in their back pockets. Canavan puts his chainsaw down. "Give me a hand a minute?" he asks.

"Sure," says Jack.

"There's a header I'm trying to get put up on the toolshed out back. Putting a tin roof on, a little overhang, so I can get the door open when it's raining. It's too big for me to pick up by myself."

"Sure," Jack says again. He sticks his head back in the truck to check on Hendrick, who's making his noises and working through the catalog, touching the pictures of Red Oaks, available for sale in various sizes. There's a Lone Oak Tree Farm employee in most of the photos, a little fat in his tan coveralls, standing next to the trees, presumably to give some idea of scale. The trees are taller than the fat man. That much is clear. Jack tells Hen to stay put, follows Canavan back through the carport to the shed in the back yard, where he's got two ladders set up. Has he already asked Beth to help him, and she couldn't do it, or did he know Jack would help, regardless?

It's simple enough: They get up on the ladders, carry the beam up, and Canavan tacks in his side with a couple of screws. He passes the drill to Jack, who does the same. It's three minutes, but still. It's a favor Jack has done him. Another favor. "I can get the rest later," Canavan says. "I just couldn't lift the thing on my own."

Jack comes down off his ladder, then asks him, "Is it dead or alive?"

"What?"

"Your maple. Today. Green?"

"Dying," Canavan says. "But if we split it sometime later this month, it should still be good by November." To sell as firewood, a sideline business at the yard. His and Canavan's, specifically. They went in halves on a log splitter last year. Forty dollars a pallet for stacked and split. They're partners: Canavan drops off limbs and logs, they split them for firewood. Canavan drops off branches, Jack chips them for mulch. They went in together on the chipper, too.

"How tall?" Jack asks him.

"Eighty or a hundred feet."

"Good money on both ends," Jack says, running rough numbers in his head.

"Yes indeed," says Canavan.

Jack looks at him. "That's how you talk now?"

"What's how I talk now?"

"Indeed?"

"That's how I always talk," he says, not quite looking at Jack. Or at anything, really. He seems embarrassed to be talking at all, which Jack appreciates, given the situation. Also he seems healthy, seems fit, which Jack appreciates less. He's taller than Jack by a couple of inches. Skinnier. He maybe shaves a little more regularly. Canavan walks back through the gate, back to his chainsaw project, and Jack stands in the back yard, looking at the back of Canavan's house, at his patio, his grill and chairs all set up. His grass is too long, and there are seedlings growing up out of his gutters, but the house is in good shape, is pretty well taken care of for the most part, has fresh paint on some of the window trim. It's a bungalow, a mill house, little easy projects all over the place. Canavan needs to, say, re-screen his side porch. He might think about digging out one or two dying shrubs here or there. Jack needs for the kitchen place to magically get his tile back in stock so he can run it the rest of the way across the floor. He needs a dishwasher in the hole where the dishwasher is meant to go. He needs a new breakfast nook rising of its own accord from the mudpit that's left from the water line disaster. And then he needs all of that across the street, too.

He goes and finds Canavan in the carport. He says, "Beth's inside?"

Canavan says, "Beth is inside."

"How's that going?"

"It's going," he says.

"You guys making each other happy in there?"

Canavan looks down his driveway at the street, then goes back to whatever he's doing to the chainsaw. He says, "Listen, Jack, you should know that none of this was really my idea."

"From here it seems like it was a little bit your idea."

"You know what I mean."

"What I'm saying is, you look like a willing participant."

"Well, maybe I am, then. I don't know. Jesus." And Canavan's phone rings and saves them both and he answers and gets up and walks around the side of the house, saying *Yeah, we can do that, we do jobs like that all the time. Now: Let me ask you a couple of questions.* Jack looks up and catches Beth in the window of the side door. She's wearing a white shirt, has a white mug in her hand. Her hair's down in her face, a mess of curls, the way he's always liked it best. His wife: He doesn't think of her that way very often, tends to think of her simply as Beth. But there she is, his wife, right there. She's waiting, in Canavan's house, for him to come up and ring the bell and present her with her son.

&#8531; &#8531; &#8531;

This was all coming, is the thing. Or maybe not this exactly, but something like it. He knew that much, knew something had been out there on the horizon even before he'd added a second house to his vast real estate portfolio. So: Last week, when Beth started banging around cups and plates and the mail and anything else she could move or slide or pick up and shake at him, he wasn't wholly surprised. It'd been in the water. Rena, Canavan's girlfriend, had left him at the beginning of the spring semester. She teaches with Beth at Kinnett, both of them in art history. This is how everybody met, how they ended up at the dinner table together once or twice a month for the last several years, one big happy family. Rena packed up in February, moved downtown, was living *for a little while* in a condo that belonged to somebody else over at the college, some corporate communications associate dean or associate-associate dean who was on fellowship somewhere for the semester. Canavan played, to the letter, the fucked-up boy. Drunken and spurned. Beth and Jack were *there for him.* They went over to the house a couple of times, ate pizza out of delivery boxes and drank beers on the frayed screen porch, him telling them how *This is just temporary, this is just until we can work a few things out.* Beth and Jack got gently drunk with him and agreed as much as possible. *She'll be back, Terry,* Beth told him. *How could she not?* Now Jack wonders when Beth started plotting her own move into Canavan's house. If, on those nights, she was sizing up where she'd throw her shoes after she came in the door. She had him fooled, though. They'd ride back home down 70, lights on high to watch for deer, and she'd reach across the seat for his hand. They were thankful it wasn't them. That's what he thought they were. Thankful.

Canavan. What he'd figured was that she'd probably go downtown and crash with Rena for a few days—three or four, tops. Because he could see that easily enough: The two of them set up in the little swanky downtown revitalization condo together, drinking wine out of souvenir downtown wine tasting festival glasses, sitting around and listening to pirated underground Sri Lankan hip-hop some intentionally edgy student of Rena's had turned her on to. They'd crank that up on the out-of-town dean's stereo and grade papers and let their blue collar men hang out in their respective houses and *get their heads together.* It'd be good for everyone.

Instead, she chose Canavan, which will break everything into pieces, of course, will put a fairly permanent dent in the diplomatic ties between everybody. His friendship with Canavan's in the shitter, and he can't see Rena and Beth drinking wine together out of any glasses, souvenir or not, any time soon. Butner sits with him after work, says, *This is pretty goddamn fancy, what she's up to here. I don't know what the hell she thinks she's doing over there, but this is something, I'll tell you what.* Jack tells him things were fine before the house. Or more fine. Butner shakes his head, says, *I don't know, man, I don't know.*

It's not just the house. He knows that. Knows it doesn't help, didn't help, but knows it isn't the house, the money, nothing easy like that. It's no one thing. They eat well enough together, sleep well enough, talk about school and the mulch yard. *I had another one today*, she'll say, walking in the door, hanging her bag over the back of one of the dining room chairs, a paper in her left hand. *Listen to this: "Our father, who art in heaven, hollowed by thy name." Hollowed! Can you believe these kids?* Or: He'll come home late on a Tuesday, pine needles in his boots and sleeves, and they'll sit on the front porch until dark, watching the hummingbirds come to the feeders. Her hobby. She brews sugar syrup, has all these red plastic flower-shaped feeders strung from the trees. If they can get Hen set up in front of The Weather Channel, they have an hour or two to themselves.

But something underneath all that got wrinkled. The small, stupid fights had been getting a little more frequent, a little higher-pitched, the both of them at each other too often about whose turn it was to run out to the store for dog food, for yogurt for Hendrick. At first he'd pegged that to her tendency to drift away from him at the end of semesters anyway, to shrink back into herself, into her job, papers piling up, the whiny GPA kids wanting to know what they could do for extra credit. He'd had all that, too, knew what November and April could look like. Jack had taught at Kinnett as an adjunct, taught the freshman humanities series all the students have to take. General Humanities—GenHum—I & II. Fall: Mesopotamia to the Renaissance. Spring: DaVinci to Nixon. The real job was hers. They hired her right out of Carolina, tenure-track, and the dean found an adjunct gig for Jack. She negotiated it for him. But he timed out after his four full years—a college rule that got bent for some adjuncts, and not for others—and with no permanent slot in history opening for him, that was it. It was Canavan, actually, one night over enough beers, who suggested something like a landscaping service. *It'd be easy*, he said. *Couple of pickup trucks and an ad in the Yellow Pages. We could work together.* Rena was all for it, said it was *such a good idea. Try it for a year*, they all said. Even Beth. He'd done it in high school and college, but Jack didn't want to mow lawns again, didn't want to rake leaves. Then they hit on the mulch yard. Plants for sale out front, like a little nursery. *You know,* Canavan said, *people do want cheap pine nuggets.* There was the vacant lot out on 70 between Burlington and Greensboro. Beth could stop in afternoons on her way home from the college. It all seemed almost romantic. He had to do *something.* Why not this? He liked the idea of watering pansies and petunias and azalea bushes. Liked the idea of selling people dirt. He got his loans, bought his yellow loaders, bought a sign.

And once he hired Butner, and once Butner was all but running the show, on the slow days he could be home with Hendrick. In a lot of ways it was easier than teaching. When he was at Kinnett, Jack had drawn all the time slots nobody else wanted, eight in the morning and five-thirty in the afternoon. This was better. This was people pulling up in trucks wanting a few dogwoods, wanting four yards of mini-bark. He could do this. In two years he was making what he'd made as an adjunct, and after three, last year, they moved, bought the little house in Greensboro. Good school district for Hendrick, an elementary school with a fully integrated curriculum. Hen in with all the other kids. Jack was for this. Beth wasn't sure, wasn't sure he was ready to be with everyone else. But she went along. The water heater failed the first week, flooded the den. They knocked the couple of walls through. He's got his plans for the attic, for the kitchen. The A/C doesn't work so well. The house is a plain rectangle. He's working on that. She wants him to work faster.

What she really wants more than anything, she says, is to have things *finished,* to have the trim finished and the paint finished and the tile finished. She wants the kitchen cabinets back up on the wall so she can have places to keep everything, so she'll *know where everything is. I need a calmer life,* she says. *I need places where things belong.* Jack keeps telling her to wait until *I've got it fixed up. Wait until we clear out that back room. Wait until we've got the office roughed in upstairs.* She shakes her head, doesn't want to wait. Last week she walked the halls, straightening the pictures, crying. *I can't live like this,* she said. *Not right now. Not this week. I can't do this like this any more.* He knew she meant the house, but he knew she meant everything else, too. She meant him. She sat at the table, head in her hands. *I have to get out of here for a while,* she said. *I'm sorry. I am. But you'll be fine with him. I know you will. I need—* *You've got to get this house cleaned up. You've got to finish the floors in here. The upstairs. You've got to finish all of this. And the wall, Jack, goddamnit, and the house across the street, another whole house—*

*I'm trying,* he said. *I'm trying to make it nice for you.*

*How is this nice?*

*It will be,* he said. *It will.* But then she was gone, out the door, and she was calling him twice, three times a day, making him lists of things he'd need to do for Hendrick, things to watch out for, things he already knew, things she knew he knew. *You're finding him new books to read? You're making sure he has snacks in the afternoons?* Same old CPR-poster Beth, now from a distance. She's been coming over once a day, or meeting them out for lunch, or just taking Hen for an hour. She's left him, and she hasn't. And Hen's handling it, is bearing up: He's his same old self, working through his same old routines. That first call, though, the first night, Saturday night, when the little light-up display showed Canavan's number, Jack did not handle it so well. *Where are you, exactly,* Jack wanted to know, already knowing, because there it was, right there. *About that,* she said. *Now, Jack, don't flip out.* He flipped out a little bit. Yelled a little bit. He hasn't really yelled that much since then. He's not sure what he's supposed to be doing about it. Something, though. He's supposed to do something. He's sure he is. He just does not know what.

❧ ❧ ❧

Canavan comes back around the side of the house, waving his phone in the air. He grins. "Rainmaker," he says, talking to Jack like Beth isn't and never has been standing in the door. "Lady's kids want a stand of pines taken out of her front yard. Over by Kinnett. Right almost on campus. Huge trees. I've driven by the place. Pretty easy job. But big. Five grand, maybe more. Plus, if we cut it right, if we can get it shredded, there's got to be fifty or sixty yards in it for you. So another thousand right there."

"That's great," says Jack.

"Yeah," Canavan says. "It could be."

"It's just all coming out perfectly for you, isn't it?"

"It's money for both of us," Canavan says.

"Outstanding," Jack says. "Really."

"It's just business," says Canavan, putting his phone back in its holster. He has a holster for his phone. He stands there, hand on his belt, king of the castle. "Listen," he says. "I don't know, OK?"

"About what?" Jack says.

"About I don't know. About anything."

"OK," Jack says. "Great."

Canavan points at Hen. "You want to take him inside?" he says.

"I guess," says Jack. In the truck, Hen's reciting the progression of oak trees from the catalog—he's saying *Sawtooth Oak, Pin Oak, White Oak, Swamp Oak.* Jack knows them, too, knows the list, finds himself mouthing the names along with him. This was a dumbass move, bringing him over here. He sees that now. He can't do this. He can't leave him here with Beth at Terry Canavan's sweet little tumbledown house. He can't leave him here while Canavan goes off to bid his million-dollar pines and Jack goes into the yard to watch soccer moms paw over the marigolds, watch dads in deck shoes stand there and approve of the way Butner drives the skid loader. What was he thinking? Hendrick stays with him. That's how it has to be. Hendrick says, *Live Oak, Bur Oak, Overcup Oak.* He says, *Post Oak.*

"Something wrong?" Canavan asks.

Jack says, "You know what? I think I'll probably just take Hen in with me after all."

"To the yard?"

"Yeah. I thought it would be easier this way, but I changed my mind."

"Yeah?"

"I think so," Jack says.

Canavan runs a finger in his ear, checks to see if he got anything. He says, "Are you sure?"

Jack says, "I am, actually. I'm pretty sure."

Canavan says, "OK."

"OK," says Jack. They're not looking quite at each other. They're nodding a lot. Everything is very OK. He sees what's next. "So I'll go tell Beth?"

"OK," says Canavan, nodding.

Jack's known him long enough to guess that Canavan's going through several loops of what to say. Hen rocks himself back and forth in the truck. He looks at Canavan, then at Jack, and says, "Zero percent for qualified buyers." He says, "For a limited time only." He says, "Chinquapin Oak."

"Willow Oak," Jack says.

"Water Oak." Hen pronounces it carefully, exactly, his mouth round as a ball on the O.

A woman walks by in the street trailing a huge red dog. Jack and Canavan wave. She signals back with a stick. "OK, then," Canavan says, and opens the passenger-side door of the truck, hauls himself up into the cab alongside Hendrick, looks at the catalog with him.

Hendrick flips a few pages. "All oaks are deciduous trees with toothed leaves and heavy, furrowed bark," he tells Canavan. "The fruit is, of course, the acorn."

"Of course," Canavan says. Jack heads for the front door. *I changed my mind*, he'll tell her. *I'm keeping him with me*. This may not go well. She will have already figured out what to do with him during her class, won't want Jack changing her plans again. She opens the door before he can knock, and she's tall there in the doorway, somehow, taller than normal. Maybe she's grown. She looks good. Her eyes look clear, like she's been getting sleep. She says, "Hello, Jack."

"Bethany," he says, which is not her real name. It's just Beth. Sometimes he calls her Bethany. Can't help himself.

She says, "Would you like to come in?"

"Not, you know, a whole lot, I have to say."

"Don't start in," she says.

"Start in on you how?"

"For God's sake," she says, and moves out of the way. "Don't be a jerk. I didn't even say *on me*. Come get some coffee. You look like shit." She squints out at the truck, at Hen and Canavan. "How's Hendrick?" she says.

"He's good."

"You're keeping him on the yogurt?"

"Yes."

"And half a granola bar in the afternoons?"

"Jesus. Of course. Yes, OK?"

"Come in, Jackie," she says. "Just come in."

And he does go in. Because what else is there? He hasn't gone to Wal-Mart to buy a rifle. No shooting sprees here, negotiations by bullhorn, Chopper 5 live on the scene. Instead: Coffee. Maybe some toast. Suddenly, he wants toast. He follows her in, but he can't figure out how or where to stand. He leans awkwardly on a wall, watches her at the coffeemaker, pouring him a cup. "You look like you know where everything is already," he says.

She smiles at him, a little half-sad smile, brings him the mug. She touches him on the arm.

"Don't do that," he says.

"OK," she says. "You make the rules."

"I don't want there to be rules."

"I don't want you to be angry," she says.

"I'm not here to ask you to come back home."

"I know that."

He sips his coffee. It's pretty bad. "I'm taking Hen in with me. I'm not leaving him here."

"I figured."

"You're not pissed off?" He shouldn't give a damn about that, but there it is.

She sits down on a sofa, a huge blue reclining thing with actual cupholders in the arms. It's leather, or fake leather. It's ridiculous. Jack wonders if there's a cooler in it. It's new since the last time he was here. Maybe Canavan won it in a sweepstakes. "I'm not pissed off," she says. "I'm not much of anything, I don't think."

"What does that mean?"

She looks up. "It means I've got a class at ten-thirty, and twenty papers coming in about Modernism." She plays with a seam on the sofa. "Eight pages apiece. So, you know, other than that, I'm not much of anything. That's all that means."

"Fine," he says.

"Fine?"

"How the hell do I know?" he says. "I don't really know what's happening here."

She doesn't say anything back. The ceiling feels low. There are snapshots of Canavan and Rena running along the mantel, pictures of Rena standing in front of national monuments, on hills over Mediterranean cities. One shot of the two of them with a very large bird, an emu, maybe, or an ostrich. Canavan and Rena in a restaurant. Canavan and Rena on a lake. Canavan and Rena next to a huge riverboat named, in red cursive lettering, *The General Beauregard*. This is all awfully fucked up. If it'd been him, Jack thinks, he might have put the pictures away. There's an empty bottle of wine on the coffee table in front of Beth, two glasses. Jack says, "I still can't believe it's you and Canavan."

"It's not 'you and Canavan.'"

"You know what he's doing right now?"

"No," she says.

"Running trees with Hen in the front seat of the dump truck."

"What do you want him to be doing? Ignoring him? Letting him play in the road?"

Jack looks out the window. Hen's explaining something to Canavan, and Canavan's listening hard, asking follow-up questions. "I could use him acting like a little bit more of an asshole out there," he says.

"It's not his fault."

"It's his fault," Jack says. "Some."

"It's everybody's fault," Beth says.

It's been like this at lunch, too. She'll come by to get Hen and it's short like this, a kind of half-assed truce interrupted by these exploratory cannon rounds fired at each other. Feeling each other out. It's all wrong. Everything's wrong. They should be yelling at each other. He should be dragging her out of here by her hair. He should be hitting Canavan in the face. "Do you want toast?" he asks her. "I want some toast."

"No," she says. "Thanks."

He goes into the kitchen, finds the bread, shoves a couple of slices into the toaster. He opens up a few of Canavan's kitchen drawers, looks in at the knives and forks and spoons. They look like anybody else's knives and forks and spoons. "I read in the paper that they found a stand of chestnut in Georgia that had survived the blight," he tells her. The toaster's not working. He bangs it on the counter a couple of times.

She comes in and leans on the counter. "It's the switch there, on the wall," she says, pointing. He flicks it, and the toaster comes right on. "What blight?" she asks.

"The chestnut blight," says Jack. Why's he telling her this? "There used to be ten million trees. Or ten billion. I can't remember. It was in the article."

"And then the blight."

"And then the blight," he says. "In the nineteen-hundreds. Early, like the thirties and forties. I think it was million. Ten million. Anyway. They found some in Georgia. This old stand of trees."

"Wow," she says.

"Yeah," he says. He's got nothing more for her on the famous chestnut blight. She's standing there, waiting for him to do something else. The shirt she's wearing is too big for her, and he realizes it has to be Canavan's. Perfect. He looks at the tendons in her neck, her thin collarbone, the freckles on her skin. "You look good, you know," he says. "You look good to me."

"You look good to me, too, Jackie," says Beth, rubbing at her forehead. "Even if you do look like shit."

"You keep saying that."

"Well, it's true. Are you sleeping?"

"Some," he says. He stares in at his toast. His face feels hot. "I'm not asking you to come back home here," he tells her again. "You decided to leave, you decide to come back home."

"I know that," she says.

"I don't want this to be over," he says.

"It's not over. And I don't either."

"You and Canavan," he says.

"It isn't like that."

"How is it not like that?"

She flicks something off the countertop. She says, "You know what? I don't have any idea what it's like."

"How long are you going to stay here?" he asks her.

"I don't know."

"I mean, what's your plan?"

"I don't know that either."

"The dog misses you. He can't figure out what the hell's going on."

She says, "Did you call the vet about getting his summer shave?"

"Yes," he says, lying, trying to make a note to himself to actually remember to do that. "Next Wednesday."

"What about the bug guys?"

"You come home, you can worry about bugs in the house."

"I don't like bugs."

"Houses have bugs," he says.

"Not this one."

"Ours does," he says.

"I know," she says. "I know."

He'd like very much for his toast to catch on fire in the toaster, give him some minor emergency he can take care of. Anything. *Stand back, ma'am.* "So you're fucking him, then?" He hasn't asked her this at the lunches.

"I really don't feel like we need to talk about that right now."

"In front of all their pictures of all their fabulous vacations? Their whole lives right here in eight by ten? Are you fucking him in here on his big blue sofa? Or just in the bedroom?"

"I said, Jack, I don't want to talk about it."

"Does Rena know about this? Have you told her?"

"Have I told her? When would I do that?"

"At school," Jack says. "You'd tell her at school."

"She's not teaching summer classes."

"How about when you go over there to see her? Are you going over there to see her?"

"No," she says. "Not right now."

"Isn't she going to wonder where you are?"

"Probably," Beth says. "She probably is."

"This just gets better," he says. "Doesn't it?" His toast does not catch fire. It pops up, and Jack eats it dry, like always. All he can hear is his own chewing. He needs to get out of here, get away from the sofa, from Beth in Canavan's kitchen. He's got to go to work. He refills his mug, picks up his other piece of toast. "I have to go," he says. "I'm taking this mug with me."

She looks at him like she feels sorry for him, and says, "Fine."

"And I'm not fucking asking you to come home."

"Fine," she says.

"You stay over here for six fucking years if you want to," he says.

"I'm not staying six years."

"This isn't right," he tells her. He wipes toast crumbs off his face. "This is not right."

"Maybe not," she says. "But it has to be. For now, it has to be." She looks at the floor. "I know it's not fair, Jackie, but I don't know what else to tell you."

He could do things right here. He could club her over the head with a lamp, carry her unconscious body to the truck, drive her home and chain her to a tree in the back yard. Or he could beg her for something. He could make her some promises. He could lie and tell her he's finished the tile floor. Instead, he steals the coffee mug, goes out the door without saying anything else to Beth, walks to the truck and climbs up into the driver's seat and waits for Canavan to get out of the cab. Doesn't say anything to him, doesn't look at him. Just waits. This hasn't quite been the victory lap he had in mind. Somewhere back there he fucked this up, he's pretty sure. Somewhere back there he may have made things worse. Canavan gets down, and Jack starts the truck, drops it in gear a little too quickly, lurches down the driveway. Canavan watches him go. Jack looks dead ahead. Hen looks dead ahead. He doesn't open or close anything at all.

❧　❧　❧

At PM&T, there is chaos. The line of cars is out to the highway, and there's a little crowd of people standing at the office shed. Waiting to pay, probably, but it's hard to tell. Jack parks the truck in front of the pile of crushed gravel and it's only after he gets the brake kicked in that he sees what the problem is, why nobody's doing much of

anything: Butner and Ernesto have managed to roll one of the skid
loaders over on its side. Full bucket, of course, so there's half a yard
of red-dyed pine washed out across the middle of the lot. Also, the
loader looks like it's leaking fuel. Butner and a kid who can't be
much out of high school are standing next to it, pointing at it and
then back at what seems to be the kid's truck, a Nissan pickup
jacked about five feet up off the ground. Ernesto is tying lengths of
chain off to the front bumper of the pickup, looping the other ends
around the loader's roof, around the bucket. Jack gets out and jogs
over there.

"*Jefe*," says Butner. He's proud of picking up Spanish from Ernesto. Slow days on the yard, Butner will sit there with him asking
what individual words are, one by one. *Ernesto, what's "help"? What's
"dump truck"? What's "pussy"?*

"Just tell me you didn't hit anybody on the way down," Jack
says.

"It was Ernesto, actually."

"Damnit, Butner, he's not even on the insurance—"

"I know. But you weren't here yet, and things started getting
crazy."

"There's still no way you should have let him drive."

"It wasn't so much 'let,' " says Butner, "as me talking him into it.
We were pinched. I'm sorry." He shrugs. "Anyway, this is Randy,
my buddy's little brother. He brought over the chain." The kid
reaches out his hand, and Jack shakes it.

"Thanks," Jack says.

"No problem," Randy says.

"How's Ernesto?" Jack asks. "Is he OK?"

"Cut his arm some," says Butner. "Cherry came out and patched
him up." Cherry works behind the counter at the Shell most days.
"He went over real slow. And I had him strapped in there pretty
good. I made sure. He couldn't have done any real damage."

"Other than crashing the skid," Jack says.

"Yeah," says Butner. "But we'll have it back up in a second." Randy drops his cigarette on the ground, grinds it out with his toe, then lights another one. He's got what looks like a tattoo of a litter of kittens on his arm. Butner says, "Once we've got it all rigged up, Randy'll just back up real slow until the thing sits up on its own. Shouldn't be much."

Ernesto finishes with the chain, comes over to stand with them. "I'm sorry about all of this, Jack," he says. With his accent, it comes out *Chack*. Sometimes Jack wishes he had an accent, too.

"It's Butner's fault for putting you in there," Jack says. "How's your arm?"

Ernesto holds it out, some gauze and tape wrapped around it, a little blood seeping through in a couple of places. "It's fine," he says. "It really is."

"You don't need to get it looked at?"

"I think that would probably be a little much."

From the line, someone honks a few times, and Butner waves at whoever it is. He always seems to know. He points at the over-turned skid loader, holds up his hand. *Five minutes.* The guy honks again, two little taps. *OK.* Butner turns to Jack. "We should proba-bly go on and do this," he says. "You OK with that?"

"I guess so," says Jack.

"Well, let's try this thing," he says, and then they're all moving, Ernesto toward the office and Butner toward the chains and Randy up into his pickup, gunning the motor. Butner checks everything, gives him the thumbs-up. Jack backs up a few steps and the kid's already going, easing the truck back, foot by foot, until he gets some tension in the chains. This is the kind of thing Hen would want to see up close, Jack's pretty sure. He should bring him over here. "Hang on," he says, and Butner holds his arm up in the air. Randy stops, holds where he is, waiting. Jack goes to get Hen.

"Good idea," Butner yells to him.

"What?"

"Good idea," Butner says, coming toward the dump truck.

Jack has no idea what he means. "Hendrick?"

"No, man, drive the truck over here. We'll tie off to it on the other end. Keep the skid from flipping over the other way."

"Oh," says Jack. "Good."

"Yeah. That'll work, I think." Butner sticks his hand in through the window to Hendrick, palm out, wanting a high five. "How's the brains behind the operation?" he asks him. Hen doesn't move. "No?" Still nothing. Butner rubs him on the head. "That's OK," he says.

"Hello," Hendrick says.

"Hello," Butner says.

"Hello and welcome to another edition of This Week in Baseball," Hendrick says.

"Awesome," says Butner. Then, to Jack, he says, "Come on, man, let's get this show on the road. You got customers waiting."

Jack drives the dump truck over near where the skid's lying on the ground, puts it in gear and shuts it off. Butner ties one more length of chain from the skid to the dump truck, pulls on it to make sure it's right, gives his sign, and Jack's only barely able to get Hen out of the cab before Randy starts back again. He hangs onto Hendrick, and the skid drags along on its side a little bit before the chains start to pull it up, but pretty quickly it's leaning up into the air, and Butner's right next to it, checking everything, giving more hand signals, telling Randy to *stop, stop* or *try a little more*. The kid gasses the truck back in little leaps. Finally Butner tells him *go, go*, and the Nissan jerks back and the loader lifts up off the ground the rest of the way all at once, rocks upright, holds at the top of its arc for a second or two, and then starts heading over the other way. Hendrick reaches out into the air like he might be able to catch it. The chain running to the dump truck does it fine, though, like Butner said it would, goes taut as a wire, and then it snaps the bumper right off the front of the truck, a huge shearing bang. But it does stop the skid. It stays up on its wheels. The kid shuts off the Nissan, and the crowd over by the office claps. Hendrick covers his ears, squirms free of Jack, marches in place.

"Well, fuck me twice," says Butner, looking at the bumper. "Tied the chain wrong. I did worry about that."

"You did?" Jack asks.

"Yeah. I let it pop too hard. Should have stopped it right at the top. I thought we'd be OK." He nudges the bent chrome bumper with his toe. "Shit."

"Why didn't you say something? What else broke? Do you think anything else broke?"

"Don't worry about it," Butner says, squatting down to inspect the damage. He sticks his head in underneath. "Minor. Cosmetic. This thing's straight as an arrow otherwise. I'll fix it this afternoon." He picks up the bumper, sets it on the hood of the truck. "At least we're back up and running."

"I guess so," says Jack. He's not so sure.

"Seriously," Butner says. "Good as new. This afternoon." He points at something under one of the headlights. "Just need to weld a couple new bolts on there." Randy gets down out of his pickup and Butner tries to give him some money, peeling tens off a reel of cash he pulls out of his pocket, but the kid shakes his head, laughs, starts unhooking the chains. Butner shrugs, gets in the dump truck, backs it out of the way. He tries the loader next, which, amazingly, cranks right up, and he drives that over to the side of the lot. A woman in a huge red duelie starts toward the pine bark, but Butner waves her off, holding up both hands. *Wait*, he mouths at her. He pulls a book of matches out of his pocket, gives Jack a quick grin to let him know what's coming. Jack wraps his arms around Hen again, pulls him back. Butner strikes the match, tosses it into the puddle of fuel from the loader, and there's fire five feet tall. Jack can feel the air being sucked into it. Hen shrinks into him, away from the heat. They watch it flame out, smolder a little. Some of

the spilled mulch is on fire. This all just dangerous as hell. If Beth
had been here to see this, she'd have beaten him to death with the
broken bumper. Hen's talking into Jack's arm, saying, *It's gonna be a
scorcher, folks.* He's saying, *Your local forecast is next. Weather on the ones.*
Butner starts waving to the woman in the red truck now, saying
come on, come on, come on, and while she backs up against the mulch
pile, he gets the loader going again, sending the bucket deep into
the bark, coming back out with a full load, turning, tumbling it
into the truck bed. It's choreography. It's air traffic control. It's everything all at once.

Jack walks Hendrick over to the office and gets him set up—
they've got a couch in there, a little mini-fridge, a radio Hen likes
to play with. Ernesto's ringing people up. Fifteen dollars. Fifty.
Thirty-two. "Thank you so much," he's saying. "Please come and
see us again tomorrow." Hen watches him key in the prices, en-
thralled. He loves the register. Jack stands in the doorway, just out
of the sun. Randy drives away, taps the horn on his way out. The
lot smells like fire, like cedar, like fuel. Jack thinks about Canavan
up in some tree, about Beth over there rinsing out her cereal bowl,
her coffee mug. He wonders whether they're taking showers together or one at a time. Out on the lot, Butner's gotten hold of a
guy in white slacks, is showing him the three kinds of compost
they have. Jack turns to make sure Hen's still watching Ernesto run
the register, tries to clear his head, heads out onto the yard to help
whoever's next.

&#8478; &#8478; &#8478;

They go like hell all day. They're selling everything on the lot. After
her class, Beth takes Hen to lunch, drops him back off again.
*Where'd you eat?* Jack asks her.

*We just went to Mike's,* she says. *We had sandwiches. He had most of a
PB&J. He'll need something later.*

*How was it?* Jack asks Hen.

*Right now*, Hendrick says, *a forty-year-old nonsmoker qualifies for a $500,000 life insurance policy from Colonial Penn for just $19 a month.*

*The TV was on*, Beth says. She frowns, looks around the lot, watches Butner toss bales of pine straw into a truck. *I guess I better get back*, she says. *Be careful, OK?*

*We always are*, Jack says, and she drives away before either of them can say anything that matters. Midafternoon, a landscaper who comes in two or three times a month to do business specifically with Ernesto buys every rose they've got, twenty-two plants. Four hundred dollars right there. A couple buys a boulder that's been out front for a year and a half. Somebody even buys the lighthouse he and Butner had a bet about. Five feet tall, wooden, black and white barber pole stripes, electric lights inside. Meant to go in your front yard. Jack doesn't know why. An old German guy from McLeansville showed up one day asking them if they'd buy it for $75. Jack said no, but told him if he left it on the lot he'd try to get $100 for it. Like a consignment. He felt bad for him. Butner laughed and laughed. *A hundred dollars*, he said, over and over. *A hundred goddamn dollars. That motherfucker will be sitting right there when you die.* And it was a young guy, standing in front of it toward the end of the day, frowning, looking a little desperate: *Well*, he said, *I guess this is what she was talking about*, and bought it. A hundred, cash. Butner stood in the shed and stared. Ernesto hit the cash register bell several times after the guy was off the lot and down the highway, the lighthouse sticking out the back of his trunk like the head of some dead animal.

Hendrick's been happy all afternoon, easy, even, spending his time running between the rows of plants and shrubs, arms outstretched like a plane. *He doesn't look sick at all*, Ernesto said. Hen rode with Ernesto on a couple of late-day deliveries. Jack stood on the lot, watched the truck pull out onto 70, Ernesto's left arm hanging out the driver's side, Hen's arm poking out the other window, tiny, pale. Then they'd come back, Ernesto grinning away and Hendrick serious, concentrating on riding, staring straight ahead through the windshield.

Six o'clock. Jack flips the sign from OPEN to CLOSED. Hen gets up immediately from the sofa and flips it back, then takes it down and starts playing with the WILL BE BACK AT clock arms on the CLOSED side, spinning them around and around. Butner drives both loaders to the back of the yard, parks them up against the mulch piles, walks over to the Shell station. Jack gets a cottage cheese from the fridge for Hendrick, locks the shed, and he takes Hen, his catalog and the OPEN CLOSED sign in hand, back to the greenhouse. They keep a few lawn chairs back there. Jack's got nowhere to be, feels like sitting a while. Hen eats his cottage cheese in a hurry, carries the container and the plastic spoon over to a trash can, carefully drops everything in. When Butner comes back, he's got a six-pack with him. He tosses a beer to Jack and another to Ernesto, who's coiling up the hose against the side of the greenhouse. Ernesto pitches his back. "I can't," he says. "I need to go home."

"You sure?"

"I am," he says. He turns to Jack. "Nine o'clock tomorrow?"

"Good enough," Jack says.

"I'm sorry about the loader. It won't happen again."

"No problemo," Jack says, careful not to use any accent. Ernesto thinks the way he massacres Spanish is hilarious. He walks away, smiling, calling them gringos.

"Same to you, Paco," Butner calls, and from his car, a little silver Toyota, Ernesto flicks them both off, then waves, the bandage on his arm a white flag.

"Don't let him drive the skid any more," Jack says to Butner, once he's gone.

"Yeah."

"I mean, something happens, nobody would ever insure us again." Butner nods. Jack knows he's not telling him anything he doesn't know. "At least get him out here some Sunday and teach him not to turn it around with the bucket up," he says. "Do that, and I'll add him to the insurance."

"OK," says Butner. "Will do."

A helicopter flies over, low, headed in the direction of the interstate. "Big day," Jack says, once it passes and it's quiet again. "We lit the lot on fire."

"Only for a second," Butner says. "And anyway, we had to clean it up somehow." He scratches his arm. "I'm not gonna kill us, boss man," he says. "Or anybody else. Don't worry."

"Fair enough," says Jack. "I'll try not to."

They sit and drink and slow their clocks back down and the beer tastes good, cheap and cold. Jack works on enjoying himself, on relaxing. It feels like forever ago that he was in Canavan's driveway. Like it might not have happened, even. Like he might just wake up out of this and find Beth at home, complaining about the kitchen wall. Hendrick's doing something with the black plastic pots Jack's been saving to start a few seeds and saplings in. He's got them lined up in a long half-circle, keeps going back to adjust the middle ones. It's a calendar, maybe, or a way to make contact with aliens. "I was surprised the loader still ran," Jack says. "Once we got it back up, I mean."

"Yeah, but it was running rougher. Something's probably knocked loose. I'll tear it apart some time next week and make sure all the hoses and wires are still good."

"When you do the bumper," Jack says. It's leaning against the office now.

"When I do the bumper," Butner says. "Sorry again, man."

"It's OK." Jack eyes the dump truck. They were too busy to get a chance to fix it, but he's actually starting to like the look of it like that.

"I'll get it fixed," Butner says. "I'll get it back on there."

"*No problemo*," Jack says again, flicking the pop tab on his beer can.

Butner runs an auto body on the side, nothing official, just cash under the table from his friends and their friends. He's been saying he wants to do the dump truck, front to back, if Jack will let him. Says he wants to hammer all the dents out, repaint it. Jack's not convinced, not sure he doesn't like all the bangs and scratches, which is why the missing bumper's been growing on him. He's always liked that the doors are rusting out at the bottoms. Thinks it gives everything an air of authenticity. Beth says that's because he likes pretending he's some kind of cowboy, rolls her eyes at him, drives off to work or to the store in the wagon, safe and sound in all weathers.

A huge tractor pulls up to the diesel pump at the Shell. Jack and Butner raise their beers and the farmer waves, gets down, runs the pump hose into the top of the engine. "We ought to get ourselves something like that," says Butner. "We could take out all these pines back here and disk in an acre of tomatoes."

"We need something else to do," Jack says.

"I bet that thing cost a hundred grand."

"You think?"

"Easy."

Hen looks up from his pots—he loves trucks, trains, bulldozers, anything big and motorized—and watches while the guy fills up. When the tractor pulls back out again, flashers behind the driver's seat blinking away and the big engine rumbling, Hen goes back to his project.

"Hey, Hen," Butner says. "Hendrick." Hen looks up. "What's that you're up to over there?"

Hen says, clear as anything, "It's buckets."

"Oh," Butner says.

"It's buckets," he says again, and then starts working his way through the tags for each of the radio stations he knows. B 98.3, *the Triad's Oldies Station. 100.7 The Jackal, with Rob and Red in the Morning.*

*Country 104, Your Home for Today's Best Country Hits. Be caller one-oh-four
and you're on your way to see Faith Hill at the sold-out Philips Amphitheater.*

Butner pretends to dial the station on his open palm, but Hendrick keeps right on going. *105.5, The Hammer.* "Damn," Butner says.
"I never win those things."

Hen gets up, picks up a piece of a pole from what will be the second greenhouse whenever Jack can get the time to build the thing,
and starts walking the back wooden wall of the mulch bays, hitting
each post a set number of times. A lot of times. Seventeen, eighteen.
Butner watches him go. "He never stops, does he?" he says.

The sun's dropped behind the trees across the street, and it's
coming through the branches like glass. "Not really," Jack says.

Butner shifts in his chair, opens a new beer for each of them.
"You know," he says, after a while, "I guess I don't care what she
told you. For my money, there's not enough excuses in the world
for her to have moved in with Fucknut." Fucknut's what he's been
calling Canavan since Jack told him.

"I know," Jack says.

"Do you?"

"I went over there this morning," he tells him.

"What in hell for?"

"I was going to drop Hen off with her for the day. I figured we'd
be so busy over here. But I changed my mind."

"Hell yeah, you did. Fuck busy, man. You bring him here every
goddamn day for the rest of your life if you want to."

Jack's not sure he needs Butner's permission, but he appreciates
it anyway. "Thanks," he says.

"You're welcome," Butner leans forward. "Now. How about we
finish this beer and go sugar that motherfucker's tanks? Make you
feel better."

Jack likes the thought of Canavan's three or four green trucks
sitting dead on his lot. "Let's set them on fire," he says.

"Arson'll put you in jail too long," Butner says. "That's an actual crime. Vandalism's better."

"Useless anyway," says Jack. "While I was standing there this morning he bid out a job that'll give us fifty yards of pine."

"You're not gonna cut him loose?" Hendrick comes back down the row of bays, moving faster, hitting the posts fewer times. *One two three four five.*

"He's not even mine to cut loose any more, is he? Half of the log splitter's his, and half the chipper. He brings in too much business." People call in and ask if Jack can do a job, limb a tree back, and he says no, that's not what he does. *But I've got a guy who can*, he tells them, farms the jobs back out through his regular commercial customers. Ten percent cut. Everybody happy all the time.

"I still think we ought to do some damage," Butner says.

Jack watches Hendrick, who's added a few taps on his own knee-cap to his routine. "She looked good this morning," he says. "Over there, in his house. And today, when she came to get him."

"I always did think you'd done well for yourself there."

"Oh, yeah. Just perfect."

"She'll be back, boss man. And you know what? If she doesn't come back, then just fuck all the bitches."

Jack looks at him. "That's your philosophy?"

"That," he says, taking a deep breath, "is my philosophy." He nods, agreeing with himself, it looks like. "Listen," he says. "Rachel's making pork chops tonight. Y'all are both welcome if you'd like. I can just call ahead and tell her to make more."

Jack thinks about that, considers becoming a refugee in Butner's house for the evening. Thinks about sitting out in his garage with him after dinner while he sands down the fiberglass fenders on whatever he's working on now, Hendrick asleep across the dump truck's bench seat. Butner could tell his stories about *all the pussy I got in high school*, and Jack could sit there and imagine a younger, skinnier Butner choosing which of the girls he would backseat that weekend. But it's a little too much for him, the idea of having to make conversation with Butner and Rachel and the kids at the supper table, the three little Butners knocking their sodas over into their food all night. "Thanks," he says, "but I should probably just get Hen home, get him fed, get him to sleep."

"You sure?"

"Yeah," Jack says. "But thanks."

"Offer's good any time," Butner says.

Jack goes to corral Hen. "I'll just see you tomorrow," he says.

"Not if I don't see your ass first." Butner drains off most of the rest of his beer, folds up both chairs, leans them against the greenhouse, and they walk back around to the front of the yard. There's a couple standing next to a Lincoln, looking at the compost. Jack didn't hear them come in. "We'll be open tomorrow morning," Butner tells them.

The woman says, "How much for your dirt?"

"Thirty-eight a yard," Butner says. "Best you'll find. We compost it ourselves. Nightcrawlers all through it. You could make a stick grow in that shit." It's thirty a yard, not thirty-eight, but Jack doesn't say anything. "How much you need?" Butner asks. "How many yards?"

"Do you guys deliver?" asks the man, older, gray at the temples.

"We absolutely do," Butner says. "Forty dollar fee." It's twenty-five. Jack gets Hen squared away in the truck, belts him in, starts it up, taps the horn, pulls out onto the highway, and stops at the light. In the rearview mirror, he watches Butner lead the couple from one pile of mulch to the next, and then over toward the plants, closing down another deal. The light changes and Jack heads for home, to check to see if the suitcases are still in the closet.

∽ ∽ ∽

He's been thinking about being the kind of person who owns two houses. Because what he is now is a card-carrying member of the

aristocracy. He explains this to Hendrick, who says *Aristophanes*,
*Aristophanes*. No, Jack tells him. Go back a few entries. Evenings,
he'll stand on his front porch, look out over his yard, at his house
across the street. That it's his doesn't really feel real. He keeps waiting for someone to move in over there, U-haul half in the driveway and half on the lawn, rugs and lamps going in through the
front door. Instead, it just sits there. His. He's owned it seven weeks
and done nothing to it except to empty it some, to bring the dump
truck home a couple weekends, fill it with shit from the garage or
the attic, take it all away. Everything that didn't get auctioned got
left behind. *Yours to keep*, the auction people told him. Like it was a
prize. He finds himself now the owner of the world's worst yard
sale and ammunition dump. He's still turning up shotgun shells
everywhere.

The mortgage payments will add up soon enough. He knows he
ought to be more worried about that. He can go a few months, but
the math isn't complicated. This is not money they have. He's got
to get that thing on the market. Get it cleaned up, get a sign in the
yard, get it sold, show her the thirty thousand. It's still a good bet.
It's still easy money. Even if he does nothing to it, he can get what
he paid for it, probably more. But for right now, anyway, more
than a little part of him is starting to like having two front porches
to choose from. He likes the mirror image across the street. Likes
surveying his lands. Beth, of course, does not like it, does not like
that he likes it, has decided to survey Canavan's house, has decided
to survey Canavan.

Nights: Jack works on getting pissed off, which he can manage
easily enough, but then he gets lonely, which only pisses him off
in new ways. He feeds Hen, works his way through the evening
routines. He tries to get everything right, tries to leave Hen's bedroom door open the requisite five inches, tries to leave the radio on
at the exact correct sanctioned volume, drives to three separate
stores to find the right *shape* of bulb to replace the burned-out night-

light. Without Bethany's help, it's three times the work. Once Jack does get him down, once they've taken one last lap through the house, Hen knocking twice on the top of every faucet with his toothbrush—including the water shutoffs under each sink and toilet, and the emergency hot water runoff in the closet by the water heater, each recently discovered and thus toothbrush-knockable—after all that, once he's got him down and sleeping, that's when it's been getting worse. That's when he looks out the window. That's when the house goes dead damn quiet.

He's been sneaking out the front door and going across the street to stand in the dust and wallpaper and shotgun shells and look at the empty rooms. Or he'll stand in the garage, depot for everything left over, staring at open boxes of wire shelving and kicking at the pedals on a broken exercise bike. Or he'll sit on the front steps over there and watch his own front door back across the street, waiting for it to open up, waiting for Hen to stand in it, screaming. Or silent. He'll crack a beer open—he's keeping beer in an ancient fridge he moved from the garage into the kitchen—and tell himself one more time that she'll be back soon enough, that she'll be the one apologizing.

School's been out two weeks, which means he's been sitting out there and listening to the high school girls down the street giggle in the dark in their tiny jean shorts and call each other endlessly on their cell phones and their cell phone walkie-talkies. Their friends pull up in their parents' minivans and play music until someone from inside the house tells them to turn it down, shut it off. Then they all talk on their phones about how this is bullshit, this is complete shit, and they pile into the van and head for someone else's house, somewhere they can play their music as loud as they want. Jack tends to go back across the street after that, turn the 10:30 ball game on, and make himself a drink, maybe two, watch the thing on mute. He loves a game he doesn't have to care about, loves watching the Royals at the Mariners, San Diego at Arizona. Pull for

whoever's behind. And then it's 12:30, 1:00, and he's a little soft
around the edges from the booze, and he goes to bed because he's
got to be up by 7:30, because that's when Hen wakes up. If it's not
anything else, he thinks, lying in bed in the white wash and roar
of the attic fan, it's a routine.

When he was four, what Hendrick loved above all else were the
Dodge Truckville commercials. *It's better in Truckville. Grab Life by the
Horns.* When one came on, he'd stand directly in front of the set,
touching the screen, singing along with every note of the jingle.
Jack and Beth made it a game, invented a whole other life for themselves out there in Truckville. An alternate existence. Jack spent his
days loading I-beams into the back of his one-ton, baling hay, calv-
ing, standing around at sunset in a flannel shirt and pointing out
sections of the fenceline they'd have to mend tomorrow. Beth, in
her half of the dream, drove the kids to wherever Truckville kids
went in their new Dodge Yeti, leather seats and leather cupholders
and a full-size movie screen that rolled out of the ceiling. Then
she'd come back home to chink the cracks of the log cabin they
built themselves from trees they cut down with a saw they black-
smithed in the shop out back.

And who's in Truckville now? Fucking the goddamned mayor of
Truckville? That's what plays on a loop in Jack's head through the
weekend, a little louder each time she comes to pick Hen up, each
time she brings him back, to where Monday night, after the girls
tear off in their minivan, Jack decides he's got to do something
other than sit here on one or the other of his porches. Because he's
earned that much, hasn't he? A change of scenery? That's all he
wants. A little half-assed escape for a few minutes. He gets up, goes
across the street, looks in on Hen. He's left him alone before—
quick runs to the grocery, to the bank. It's not like he'll be anything other than right damn here when he gets back. He puts the
TV on mute, though, on The Weather Channel, just in case. If Hen
did get up, he'd camp out in front of that, no problem. Jack pats

Yul Brynner on the head, tells him to keep an eye on things, tells him *good dog*, and sneaks out his own front door, even lets the truck coast a few houses down before he turns the ignition. He's out and gone.

He can hear her no problem: *Alone? You left him alone? Are you out of your mind?* But here's what she doesn't get, won't get, even with her safety magnets, her phone numbers: Nothing's going to happen to him that hasn't happened to him already. He's not going to jump off the roof, because he'll never make it out there. Instead, he'll stand in front of the window, throwing the lock back and forth for seventeen hours. She thinks she can help him, can fix him, by treating everything like it's an emergency. By being prepared for any possible situation. They have two fire extinguishers. Smoke alarms in four different places. They live two hundred miles from open water of any kind, and last fall she made them a hurricane kit. It's in the front hall closet, in a waterproof box. Batteries. A radio. Granola bars. Pop-Tarts for Hendrick, the only thing he'll eat some days. Jack told her she ought to put a few miles of extension cord in there, a toaster oven, some fish sticks—Hendrick's favorite meal. *I'm serious about this,* she said. *Jesus Christ,* he said. *I can see that.* He should call her up right now and tell her where he is, where Hendrick is, see if she calls out the State Patrol or the National Guard. He makes a couple of turns. What he ought to do first is see where *she* is right now, check in on things. So he aims for Canavan's house. Not to go in. That's for assholes. He's not going in. He's just going to drive by, to see what he can see. And after that, who knows. Whatever he feels like. He rolls down his window, finds the bluegrass station that comes in from Galax if the weather's clear, rides east.

He shuts the engine off at the top of Canavan's street and coasts down in front of the house, because now he's James fucking Bond. They've got the lights on out back. Which means they're probably out there under Canavan's spanking new tin roof, sitting in chairs on the little concrete stoop in front of his workshop, listening to some music. Canavan's proud of his record collection, owns vinyl pressings of obscure concerts, pays a hundred bucks a pop to buy these things off the web. It's where he spends his money. When they'd be over there for dinner, he'd make a big show out of choosing the right records for the right night. Jack can't quite see Beth going for this part of his personality. But what the hell does he know? Maybe she gets off on his forty-five minute speeches about the difference between the way they recorded bebop in New Jersey and New York. Maybe she wants to have the conversation stopped so she can listen to that right there. You hear that? You hear that? Or maybe right now she'll take anybody who's not Jack.

He picks at the steering wheel, jingles the keys. It's not oysters and champagne and strawberries back there. He knows that. They're probably not fucking each other on a handmade quilt while the last known vinyl copy of a session at the Montreux Jazz Festival 1973 spins on the turntable. It's probably just chairs they've dragged over from the patio. Canavan's got a few beers in a bucket of ice. Classy. They've had dinner, or they're just finishing up a late one. She's on adult time again. Not one part of her evening rigged toward getting Hen his fish sticks by 6:45 so that he can eat them one by one and be done in time to watch the seven o'clock rerun of Murder, She Wrote. They don't know how he found it, or why anybody would still be showing it, but there it is, every night, Angela Lansbury putting the pieces together one more time. When it's over, he reads the encyclopedia, and then he goes to sleep. By eight-thirty or so, you get your own life back for a while.

They'll have Canavan's freezer-burned ice cream for dessert: It's fine, she'll say to him, and it is, sort of. It tastes old, but it tastes like ice cream. They'll finish that off and have one more beer, or a martini, maybe, Canavan producing an antique shaker and making some show about the first martinis of the summer. Cheers, he'll tell her, and then bounce up again and switch the record to something else,

something he finds in the closet, blows the dust off of. *I haven't lis-*
*tened to this in forever,* he'll say. *Perfect.* And she'll be sitting there, not
thinking about what any of this means, not thinking of moving
her things in. She will just sip her martini, which will have too
much vermouth in it. Outside of her lunches with Hendrick, she's
in some alternate universe, somewhere she can basically cease to
exist for a while. She'll go in and teach Summer I and then come
back home. She'll sit under Canavan's new roof. She'll sip her drink
and say to him, *Listen to this. I had some kid use the term "escape goat"* in
*an essay today,* and they'll laugh about that, and they'll go inside, and
they'll go to bed. Jack's plenty jealous of Canavan in all the ways he
knows he's supposed to be, wouldn't mind it if something fell on
him or if he caught leprosy, but the kicker is that it turns out he's
getting jealous of Beth, too. It is Monday in her life. She hasn't had
to make a single decision about anything.

She's up for tenure in the fall, and she'll get it. Which means
they're here forever, which means he's tied to PM&T. Which is fine.
He's proud of having made something, of having dropped a fully
functioning business onto a gravel lot. Soon, the two of them will
be making enough money to where they'll be able to pay the bills
without having to keep close track of the bank accounts. He'll sell
the house across the street. He'll go to work. Pine needles, pine
bark, chipped pine pallets. Christmas trees in December, fruit trees
in the spring. Marigolds, impatiens, pansies. *Yes, we deliver. Yes, we'll*
*be sure not to block the driveway.* Maybe they'll hire a third guy, someone who can manage the greenhouse. Someone who can grow the
bare-root mail-order stuff, send their profit margin through the
roof. Mulch for the rest of his life. And Beth will end this thing
with Canavan, will come back home. She'll have to. Everything
will work out perfectly, perfectly fine.

Jack cranks the engine, drops it in first, and edges the truck up
onto Canavan's lawn. What's called for here, he's suddenly pretty
sure, is something on the order of the grand gesture. You can't just

sit in your truck in front of your wife's boyfriend's house. You have to do something. You have to be a man of action. So he drives across the yard, cuts the wheel, and rumbles slowly along the front of the house, taking out the line of shrubs Canavan's got planted there. Azaleas and boxwood. A couple of hydrangeas, which he feels a little bad about. But he puts it in reverse, backs up to make sure he got them all. If he's going to do it, he's going to do it right. The branches snap under the wheels. It doesn't take long. He's careful not to hit the house itself. Vandalism only. At home, Hendrick's probably dreaming the list of Deputy Secretaries of Housing and Urban Development, or of prime numbers spooling endlessly across reams of paper. On his way back out, looking for something extra, a grace note, Jack lines up the mailbox, drives right over the top of it, over the top of the garden Canavan's got going there. No lights come on in the house. No one comes flying out the front door. No one starts in yelling at him, asking him what the hell he thinks he's doing. Nothing happens. Jack, his wife somewhere back there in Canavan's back yard, drives away. He's done what he needed to do. He puts the truck through its gears and heads for 70, for a little bar out there that's on the way back into Greensboro. After all this hard work, he's pretty sure he deserves a cold beer.

❦ ❦ ❦

The Brightwood. It was the old roadhouse and inn back before the interstate came through. A low-slung brick building, a gravel drive they've got the contract on. Thirty yards of crushed gravel every eighteen months. Six or eight trips in the undersized dump truck. There are two dead Pontiacs, one on blocks, off to the right of the door. Roosters live, seemingly, loose on the property. Neon sign on the roof, all caps: BRIGHTWOOD. A smaller one hangs on the brick front wall: SIZZLING STEAKS.

Inside, the place is small, shotgunned, smoky, a rectangular room that runs front to back with the bar set along the right-hand side. A TV hangs off a mount that drops from the ceiling at the far end, tuned to one of the forensic crime dramas where things get solved because someone sneezed and forgot to cover his mouth. A pube on the carpet, the half-moon of a fingernail. This is how they'll get him for Canavan's lawn: A single fiber from his shirt. There's another room on the other side, a dining room, from the days when the Brightwood was a supper club. It's closed down now, tables stacked on their ends. There are pictures everywhere on the walls. Lieutenant Governors, baseball players, Elvis—signed. And back behind the bar, on built-in shelves that run the length of the room, more pictures: Sears store family portraits, school pictures of kids in braces. Alongside those: Incomplete sets of china, stuffed animals, dolls, scaled NASCAR die-cast models, crystal wine glasses, decorations from all the major holidays. An electronic Santa that's always on, always waving. A few bottles of liquor crammed into a corner. Souvenir shot glasses. Baby spoons from national parks and monuments. Beth gets uncomfortable in here, says the craziness of it makes her nervous. Jack loves it.

There's a couple in the round booth in the corner, smoking, holding hands. She's in a yellow tank top, drunk, skinny, laughing at everything her date says. Two women are sitting at the front of the bar, heavily made up, mid-forties, maybe fifties, drinking something orange out of stemmed glasses. He's the only other person there. He sits down a few seats away from the women and far enough away from the TV so the sound doesn't feel like it's in his skull. The bartender, an older woman, short, the same woman who's been here every time he's ever come in, brings him a menu and a napkin, says, "What'll you have?"

"A Miller's," he says, thinking of his grandfather, who called all beer, regardless of brand, a Miller's.

She nods, purses her mouth, reaches into the cooler and then opens his beer for him, something he's always liked. She sets it on his napkin. "Anything to eat?" she says.

He's earned himself a snack, he figures. He orders a cheeseburger.

"We make all our own ground beef," she says. "Right here."

"Yes ma'am," he says. She leaves to put his order in, and he watches the TV. The crime scene is poolside, the suspects girls in white bikinis. The detectives are swabbing the bikini girls' mouths with Q-tips. There is shock and outrage and surprise and the cops look serious, vigilant, preternaturally beautiful. Jack sips his beer, considers the facts: Canavan's probably out in his lawn by now, assessing the damage. Beth'll be telling him all about how this is why she moved out in the first place, because Jack's *nothing more than a god-damned overgrown child.* She'll be telling him to go and get his log splitter off the lot at PM&T. She'll be saying *he's crazy, he's crazy.* He's not crazy. He was just stopping by, leaving a note. *Sorry I missed you.*

The show goes to commercial. When it comes back on, the action has shifted to other bikini girls at another pool. One of the ladies at the end of the bar is explaining something about a house fire to the bartender. Something about money burning up, about having kept money in coffee cans in the house. "You just don't ever know," the woman says.

"I know," the bartender says.

Jack orders a second beer when his cheeseburger comes out, and a third, eventually. He watches the end of the cop show. It was one of the bikini girls. Long shot of the bikini girl in the back of a cruiser. Justice. The ladies down the bar are talking now about somebody's son who has to go to jail for a month. The local news comes on. The anchor's name is Neil McNeill, which has always seemed impossible, but there it is. *That can't be his name,* Beth said, the first time they saw him. *Why not?* Jack wanted to know.

*He must have changed it.*

*You think he changed it to that?*

*I don't know,* she said. *That just can't be his name.*

She'll hold onto things like that, worry them through. She wants to push at the world. It's something he likes about her, something he admires—that she feels she's owed some kind of explanation. Jack's often enough content just to drive the truck over the top of Canavan's landscaping, see what happens.

He hangs on for one last beer, for the weather and sports. In minor league action, the Bulls and Grasshoppers and Warthogs all win. Smiles all around the anchor desk. At the round booth, the tank top woman gets up on her knees, pulls her shirt up in the back, shows her date a tattoo. *Don't that look just like a world globe?* she's saying. *Don't it?* Jack looks, but not too long. It's time to go. He pays his tab, leaves a big tip, walks out into the parking lot. He feels better. A burger and a beer. A night on the town, a calling card. He's feeling better.

He knocks some of the mud from Canavan's lawn off the front tires, climbs up in the truck. Maybe it was a half-stupid thing to have done. Maybe somebody who had it together better wouldn't have done that. Doesn't matter. It was at least a fierce goddamned show of force, is what it was. It was an update with scores and highlights. He gets the truck turned around without hitting anything, and drives out past a huge display of mahogany furniture sitting in a mowed field. There's a long yellow banner that says REAL MAHOGANY. There are tables, some dressers, a four-poster bed, something that looks like a throne. It's all been out here at least a year. Jack's never once seen anyone looking at it, never once seen anyone who looks like he might be selling it. It just sits. Furniture in a field. He rolls down his windows, finds what he wants on the radio, drives home with the volume cranked up. On the way by PM&T, he slows down and takes a look. Everything's still right where he left it: His plants, his office, his piles of mulch.

❧ ❧ ❧

Beth's sitting on the front porch, drinking coffee, when he gets home. Shit and shit. Yul Brynner's out there, too, and the both of them look disappointed. And pissed. Jack hasn't called about getting him shaved yet. Another failure. It'll be 95 degrees soon enough, and the dog will lay around panting, miserable. Jack gets out of the truck, reminds himself one more time to call the vet.

The porch light's on across the street. He moves slowly, buying time, trying to make every move look like he's doing it on purpose. He does like her back over here, sitting on his porch. Their porch. She's chewing on a strand of her hair. It makes her seem like a kid. He climbs up the steps, and Yul Brynner watches him. Beth doesn't. Jack nods at the dog on his way by.

Inside, the house is quiet, but bright, all the wrong lamps on. He checks on Hendrick, who's sleeping on his side, just like they taught him. *First, push your hand down on the bed. Like that. Push and roll. Great, honey, that's great. That's perfect.* Every new movement had to be taught, had to be broken down step by step. Regular kids don't have to be taught to roll over. At the yard last week, Butner said, *He runs like a goddamn marionette, you know.* Jack didn't know for sure that Butner knew what a marionette was. He grabs the last four of a six-pack out of the fridge, brings that back out on the porch with him. Might as well keep going. Yul Brynner's staring out into the yard. Beth is, too.

"Beer?" Jack says.

Beth shows him her mug, says nothing.

"Don't mind if I do," Jack says, opening himself one. He sets the other three back behind him, up against the house. He scratches Yul Brynner behind the ears. "What's he looking at?"

"I don't know," she says, her voice something dug out against him. "It's out in the trees. It's been out there a while."

Sticks snap in the little stand of shrubs and ivy in the side yard. Yul Brynner starts to shake a little, vibrate, his version of being battle-ready. A possum comes wallowing out from under a bush, sits up, stares at them. It seems anti-climactic. It seems fat. Yul Brynner whines, then barks a couple of times, and it runs away.

"Possum," Jack says.

"He looked smart," says Beth.

"Smart?"

"Like he was looking at us," she says.

"He *was* looking at us."

"You know what I mean."

The dog works his way through a series of more whines and growls. "Good boy," Jack says, rubbing his ribs. "Good boy."

"Put him on his lead," Beth says.

"What for?"

"What do you mean, what for? I don't want him going down there, chasing after that thing."

"He's fine," says Jack. "Isn't he?"

Beth gets up, gets the rope from its peg by the door, hooks one end to the porch railing and the other end to the dog.

"He's not going anywhere," Jack says, and Yul Brynner promptly gets up and runs for the shrubs, the rope trailing behind him. Beth steps on it some right before it goes taut, slowing him down enough to where he won't hurt his neck, a trick they've learned from enough evenings out here with him. She looks at Jack a long time, proving something. Then she dumps out her coffee, reaches for a beer, pours half of it in the mug. She says, "Jackie, what in the hell is it with you, anyway, do you think?"

"What do you mean?" he says. He knows what she means.

She aims her mug at the truck. "How about this, for starters: What is that all over your tires?"

"Mud from the lot, I guess," he says.

"Mud from the lot. That's your answer."

"Sure," he says.

"You know what?" she says. "We heard you out front before you even did it. We heard the truck, Jack. We got up and came and stood in the window and we watched you do it." She sits up straighter. "I didn't think you'd do it. I told him you wouldn't. But then you did." She doesn't sound all that impressed.

Jack reels Yul Brynner back in, hand over hand on the lead. The dog's still staring out into the dark. A car horn goes off a couple of times out on the larger road. "I think the first time I saw a possum was in kindergarten," he says. "They found it in one of the trash cans outside. Stevens Kindergarten. I was a Cardinal. Or a Bluebird."

"What are you talking about?"

"They had us grouped off, named for birds. Maybe I was a Robin. We had Robins one year."

"Was Hen still asleep when you went in there?"

"Of course." He gets the dog the rest of the way back up on the porch. "They took us all out there to see it. Lined us up and brought us out there. I don't know what they were thinking. That thing could have come up out of there and bitten somebody."

"Why are you telling me this?"

It's a fair question. Maybe because he's supposed to be telling her something, and this is what's coming out. "Because of the possum," he says. "It was a mother possum, in the trash can. With babies. I remember we looked in there and saw she had babies. She could have given everybody rabies." Beth's shaking her head. "Rabies babies," he says.

"Jack."

"What?"

"Are you drunk?" she says.

"I don't think so."

"Where've you been?"

"What?"

"Where were you? What is it that made you think you could just leave him here?"

"Because I could just leave him here. I didn't think it. I did it. He's fine. He was fine, right, when you got here?"

"That's not what I meant."

"He was fine. You know he was."

"That's not the point—"

"Nobody could figure out how she'd gotten them in there," he says.

"Gotten what in where?"

"The possum babies. They got the county extension or the nature preserve or something to come out and get them. They pulled up in the truck and we all watched. The guy got them out of there with this metal pole with a noose or something on the end of it."

"The nature preserve came out to get possums?"

"Maybe it was just an exterminator, and they lied to us," he says. "I don't remember." The idea that it could have been an exterminator brings a sadness down on him. Maybe he is drunk.

"Maybe it was one of those catch-and-release places," she says.

"I've never believed those places actually do that. I always imagine them clubbing everything to death once they're back at the shop. Like baby seals."

"Jesus, Jack."

"I'm sorry."

"They don't do that. They don't club them to death."

"They might."

"They don't," she says. "And anyway, it doesn't matter." She slides a little away from him, stares at her feet. "Are you done?" she asks.

"What do you mean?"

"With your possum story. Are you done?"

"Yes."

"Then is it my turn?"

"Sure," he says.

"OK." She leans against the railing. "Listen to me," she says. "I've been here an hour and a half. What I'd like to know is, where have you been?" The dog rolls over on his side, offers up his belly. She says, "I mean, after you tore up Terry's yard. I know that part of it. I want to know what it is you did after that."

"I'm sorry about that."

"No, you're not," she says.

"OK," he says. "You're right."

"You know what he's doing right now?"

"Not you, I'm guessing."

She ignores that. "He's out there with all the lights turned on, with his car parked in the street with the headlights on, and he's trying to see if there's anything you didn't destroy, trying to see if there's anything he can salvage."

"I didn't plan it," he says. "Really. It just sort of happened."

"Why don't you try that with the police? I tried to talk him into calling the police, but he wouldn't do it."

"What a stand-up guy your boyfriend turns out to be."

"Jack, you want to know what's going on? With me? With us? It's this. This right here. The way you do things, the way you walk through the world and don't pay attention to anybody else, ever. The things you're capable of—"

"Wait," he says. He'll take some of this from her, but he's got to draw a line somewhere. "You wait. How about let's maybe not talk about what I'm *capable* of. Because between the two of us, you're the one who looks a little bit more *capable* of something right now—"

"Not to mention that you left him here alone, Jack, *alone*, for what, two hours? Three hours? What if something happened? He's six years old!"

"I don't need you to tell me how old he is, OK? I know how old he is."

"Do you?"

He can feel the both of them starting to lose hold of the conversation. "What the hell is that supposed to mean?"

"What if something had happened to him?" she says again. "What if—"

"What is it you think could have happened?"

She looks straight at him. "Do you want me to make you a fucking list?"

"Yes, I do," he says. "Go right ahead. You tell me what it is you've got in your head that could have happened to him."

"Anything, you imbecile! *Anything!* He could have turned the stove on. He could have electrocuted himself when he decided he needed to touch the dryer outlet seventeen times. He could have crushed his head in the garage door."

"He could have drowned in a teaspoon of water."

"Oh, fuck you, Jack, alright? You know what I mean." She says it again: "You know what I mean."

"But that's what I'm telling you. He didn't do any of that. That's what I'm always trying to tell you. None of that happened, because he was already down. Because I got him down. Because we went through the whole fucking thing, the whole song and dance. Just the two of us. We've done it every night. Every night. The faucets. The nightlight. The catalog. And he's doing the windows in the French doors now, by the way. He has to run his finger around the inside of every single pane, which takes half a goddamned hour by itself. Here's what we did tonight: We lined up the shoes. We read the stories. We did the doors. We did all that, and then he went to sleep, and that was it." He reaches back, gets himself a new beer. "He was *down*."

"You left him alone." She says it slowly, quietly.

"To sit at the Brightwood for an hour and have a beer and think. That's all." He stands up. "*He. Was. Down.*"

"The Brightwood," she says.

"Yes."

"You couldn't think here?"

"Who the hell are you to ask me that? You can't do whatever it is you're doing here, either, right? Right. Because Canavan's not here to do, is he?"

"Do you think I wanted this?" she says. "Do you think this is the way I wanted my life to be?"

"Well, what do you want me to say, Bethany? I mean, Canavan? Fucking Canavan?"

"That's not what this is about," she says. "How many times are we going to do this? You know it's not about that. You know it."

"How is it not about that? In what way is any part of this possibly not about that? I swear to fucking hell," he says, tensing, feeling like his head is about to come off his body, and without thinking it through, without thinking about it at all, he turns around, and from the bottom of the steps—he's ended up out in the yard, somehow—he throws his beer through the living room window.

She's up then for sure, coming at him, wild. She throws her mug at him, misses. It lands behind him in the yard. Lights come on next door. Something very definite is happening between them right here. Here is a discrete moment. He thinks she might try to tackle him, but she stops right in front of him, stands facing him, breathing hard. They stare at each other. After the crash of the window, things suddenly feel very quiet. Very still. She says, right into his face, "What in the hell is the matter with you?"

He doesn't know. His arm hurts from the throw. He can't really believe the can went through. He stands there in his front yard at whatever time it is, midnight. His window's broken. He'll have to fix it, have to tape something over it tonight. Cardboard. He picks her mug up, hands it back to her. "I'm sorry," he says. Then he says, "I love you." It just comes up out of him.

"Oh, shit, Jack, I love you, too," she says. "But—" She stops, her voice catching.

"But what?"

"But nothing," she says, backing up. She sits down on the bottom step.

"I didn't mean to do that," he says.

She pulls at her hair, looks out at the street. "I don't think you ever mean to do anything," she says.

"That's not fair," he tells her.

"I don't care," she says. "I don't care. I don't have to be fair." She sounds quiet now, small.

"I mean to do things," he says.

"Like the house?" she says. "Did you mean to do that? Have you done anything to it?"

"No. Not much."

She runs her finger around the inside of her mug. "Are we broke yet?"

"We're not broke."

"Are you sure?"

"Pretty sure."

"Great," she says. "Superb."

"Yeah," he says.

"Jack," she says, "maybe it'd be better—"

"You can't have him," he says, cutting her off. He saw this part of it coming when he parked the truck, found her on the porch. There's no way he's letting her pack him up and take him out of here.

"What?"

"If that's what you're doing here. You can't have him. You can't take him."

"I miss him, Jack, OK? I miss him. And if this is the way you're planning on taking care of him—"

"I'll take you to court," he says. "You left. You're the one who left. I'll take you to court, and I'll find some way to win. If you want him, you come back here. You come back home."

"I think you'd do just beautifully in court."

"I think maybe we both would," he says. "In fact, why don't we just take this shit on the road? Sell tickets? Bring Canavan along? We can parade all of this in front of a judge and let him—"

Yul Brynner gets up to greet Hendrick, who's all at once standing there in the screen door, naked except for a T-shirt, which he's
wearing on his head like a veil. He's marching in place, very carefully picking up one foot and then the other, very carefully putting
each back down again. He'll be great in marching band, Jack suddenly thinks, picturing him wearing a xylophone in a chest har-
ness, playing "When the Saints Go Marching In." And all the fight
goes out of him. Beth too, he can see. A little truce drops down on
them. Hendrick, the great and powerful common denominator.

The streetlight flicks off, then on again, and Hen starts breathing
heavily through his nose, which is never good. What tends to come
next is the *unarticulated screaming*, something that can go on for hours.
A few months after he'd started it—long openmouthed wails, no
tears, only stopping to breathe, and even then going on for what
seemed impossibly long stretches, so long that at first they worried
that he might suffocate himself—once they'd gotten used to it, or
as used to it as they could get, they started betting on how long
he'd go. A dark little game that helped them last it out. He'd start
in screaming, and they'd each put a dollar on the counter, write a
number of minutes on the face of it. 15. 40. 70. The kind of thing
they wouldn't share with regular parents in line at the checkout,
but the kind of thing that eventually helped them survive. Hen's
breathing harder now, and Beth's at the bottom of the stairs, pushing on her forehead. Jack gets a dollar out of his pocket, writes 0
on it, hands it to Beth. He's got one trick left, this last trick, something new, something she hasn't seen yet. She takes the dollar,
looks at him like she'd like to know what it is he's got in mind.

He walks up to Hendrick, opens the door. "Arizona," Jack says.

Hen grunts a little, still trying to decide.

"Arizona," Jack says again, eyeing Beth. They both know he
should be at full blast by now.

Hendrick looks up at him, marching, planetary green eyes, little
pot belly. "Tempe," Hen says, measuring the syllables. "Phoenix."

"New York," Jack says, squatting down to his level.

Now he answers right away. "Binghamton Albany Bridgeport Buffalo Cooperstown."

"Georgia," Jack says.

"Macon Albany Valdosta Augusta," Hen says. "Atlanta Kennesaw." He's calm.

Beth walks up the steps. "How did you figure this out?" She hands him his dollar back.

"He's been in the road atlas some this week. At work. He likes to do the cities. Butner quizzes him."

"What, like he's some kind of toy?"

"No. Like he's some kind of kid who likes place names. Montana."

Hen wipes his nose. "Missoula," he says. "Helena."

"It works," Beth says.

"Yeah."

"I can't believe that really works."

"Yeah."

"Bozeman," says Hendrick.

"I'm not coming back yet," she says. "Just so you know."

He stands back up. "That's what you came over here to tell me?"

"No. I came over here hoping I could bring fucking Child & Family Services down on your head."

"OK."

"I'm not coming back yet."

"That's fine. But you still can't have him."

"Jack—"

"What?"

"Jesus. I don't know." She gives the porch railing a shake, rocks it back and forth. "I tried to get him to call the police. He wouldn't do it."

"Cut Bank," Hendrick says, almost whispering.

"I'll replace it all," he tells her. He's not sorry, but he can help put it back together. "Tell him to come by the lot tomorrow and take whatever he wants. I'll even send some guys over to replant it for him. I can find a crew. We've got better shrubs on the yard than what he had in, anyway."

"It's not like that fixes anything," she says.

"It fixes some of it, doesn't it?"

"He had tomatoes by the mailbox. Tomatoes and basil. When I left he was out there trying to get the vines back upright. He was wrapping electrical tape around the places where you broke them."

"I've got tomatoes going in the greenhouse. Butner does. They're huge. He can have as many as he wants."

"I'll tell him that, I guess," she says, going to retrieve Hendrick, who's walked down into the flowerbed. He's drawing lines in the dirt with his finger. She shepherds him back up onto the porch. "Don't do that," she tells him. "Daddy's having a hard enough time keeping track of you as it is."

"How about I put him to bed," Jack says, trying for something. "We can have another beer. We can sit out here a while."

"No," she says. "No way. I'm leaving." She watches Hen. "I'm going to go ahead and leave."

He can't tell what he wants here—whether he'd like her to change her mind, to stay, to drink beer out of her coffee mug for a while and then maybe go to bed with him, or whether he might actually want her gone, away again, the house back to its quiet awful rhythms of men. Regardless, he realizes, it worked. He trenched Canavan's lawn, and it worked. She's here. Whatever he meant it to mean, it did.

"I could put him to bed," he says again, "and we could sit up. We could sit right here."

"I have to go," she says. She looks at Hen. "Maine," she says. "Have you done that one yet?"

"Have you done that one yet?" Hen repeats.

"Maine," she says.

"Maine."

She tries one more time. "Maine."

"Bangor," says Hen, slowly, squatting down, his penis hanging like a comma. "Portland. Bar Harbor. Bar Harbor, Maine."

"That's terrific, honey," she says. She might be crying. He can't quite tell.

"Get him to come by tomorrow," says Jack. "Tell him to come take whatever the hell he wants."

"Bar Harbor, Maine," says Hendrick.

"I'm going," Beth says. "I'm sorry." She says it to Hen, too. She leans down, holds his face to hers. "I'm sorry," she says. "Mommy's really sorry." She tries to hug him, but he backs up, starts marching again.

"Maine," he says.

She's definitely crying now, and Jack's pretty sure he wants to do something to hold her here, but he can't think of what that would be. She stares at Hen a while longer, and then she turns around and walks to the car, gets in, backs it down the drive. Like that, she's gone again. He wonders whether or not she'd stop if he chased her down. If he got in the truck and chased her to the next traffic light. But what would he say? He'd pull up next to her, roll the window down, and he'd have to have something to tell her. He watches her headlights sweep across each front yard until she turns at the end of the block. He thinks about those possums down in the bottom of that metal trash can. He opens the last beer, takes Hen back inside, runs him once more on his loop around the house, toothbrush to each faucet head, gets him down again. Then he sits outside with Yul Brynner, listens to the night birds and the crickets. Across the street the porch light has timed off, or burned out, or something—he's not sure—but the house over there is so dark it's like no one has ever lived there. He gets a starkly clear picture of Beth sleeping not in Canavan's bed tonight, but on his blue sofa, downstairs, bath towels for blankets. Bar Harbor, Maine. Except for it being in Maine, Jack has no real idea where that is.

࿇ ࿇ ࿇

Tuesday morning. His head's full of Beth on the porch, and he takes Hen in early, thinking they might have the lot to themselves for an hour or so. It's good when it's empty. But Butner's there already, and so's Ernesto, and they've got the radio tuned in and blaring, coffee going in the little cheap coffeemaker, doughnuts set up on the desk next to the register. *It's a no repeat workday on 94.1 FM*, the morning guy says. *Your home for the hits of the eighties, nineties, and today. Up next, a Mr. Mister rock block.* Butner leans forward on the sofa, mouth full of doughnut, greets them as they come in the door. "It's the little man and the big man," he says, stuffing more food in his mouth. "You remember dancing to this shit in middle school? Like at your middle school dance?"

"No," Jack says.

"I wasn't talking to you," Butner says. "I was talking to Paco. I danced with Jenny Resnick. She had a terrific ass, even in eighth grade. And a huge rack." He offers Hendrick a doughnut.

"He can't," Jack says, intercepting. "Blood sugar. He's not supposed to eat them." He gets a yogurt out of the fridge instead, pops the top off, hands it to Hendrick with one of the spoons he keeps in the register drawer, in the slot reserved for fifties.

"Jenny Resnick," Butner's saying. "Eighth grade could be the high point of ass. The assal high point." He's making motions in the air, drawing it out for Ernesto. "After eighth grade," Butner says, "they start eating cheese doodles. Then it's over."

"That's lovely," Jack says.

"I had this on tape and on vinyl," says Butner, nodding his head at the radio. "Both." He starts singing along in a kind of terrible high whine.

Ernesto shakes his head. "I hate this shit," he says. "American music." He goes out to water the flowers, mumbling to himself.

"Paco's in a bad mood today," Butner says. "Isn't talking to me much."

Jack watches Hen playing with his yogurt, stirring the fruit in patterns. "Maybe if you didn't call him Paco all the time."

"I think he likes it, actually."

Jack looks up at the whiteboard. "Any business?"

"Hundred and twenty bales of wheat straw to Greensboro. Guy called this morning."

"Do we have a hundred and twenty?"

"We do," he says. "Barely."

"It's late to be planting grass," says Jack.

"Hey, man, do the math. Five hundred bucks free and clear. What do I care what time of year it is?" He takes another doughnut. "That's my week right there. You paid me in the first fifteen minutes this morning. Plus fifty delivery."

"Just make it twenty-five for everybody," Jack tells him. "People talk to each other."

"Not these people," says Butner. "But it's your show, boss man." He gets up, walks out on the lot. "Hey, Paco," he yells, heading for one of the loaders. "What's 'delivery'? How do you say 'delivery'?"

Hen looks up from his yogurt, looks at Jack, touches the end of the spoon to his mouth twice, and says, "*Entrega.*"

Everything gets a little brighter right then. The phone rings and Jack lets it go. His head feels squeezed. This is not something that's possible. He stares at Hendrick. He says, "Say that again." Hen says nothing. He eats his yogurt. Jack sits down next to him, takes his arm, says, "Hen, say that again."

"*Entrega,*" Hendrick says. Easy, simple, clear, perfect. "Delivery. *Entrega.*"

Jack goes to the door and yells for Ernesto to come in, but he's already on his way, jogging, to answer the phone, which is still ringing. "Patriot Mulch & Tree," he says, in a hurry, so it comes out *Patriomulshantree*.

"Hang up," Jack tells him. "Jesus Christ. Hang up."

Ernesto shakes his head no, gives him the thumbs-up sign. He says, into the phone, "Hardwood is thirty. Pine will be twenty-seven." Neither of those is the right price. Ernesto says, "There is a forty-two delivery charge."

"Please," Jack says. "Hang up."

"*Entrega*," says Hendrick. "What's 'delivery'? *Entrega*."

Ernesto smiles, nods at Hen, gives him a thumbs-up, too, like nothing of any consequence has occurred. Jack feels like the world might have come to a full stop, might now be spinning around the other way. "Very good," Ernesto says, "three-thirty will be perfect," and hangs up. "Ten yards of pine," he tells Jack. "Delivery." He shakes the phone at Hendrick. "Hen," he says, without pronouncing the H. It sounds like *Eng*. "*¿Qué es eso?*"

"*Es un teléfono*," Hendrick says.

"*Sí, bueno.*"

Not one doctor has ever told them to look for anything like this. "You taught him to speak Spanish?" Jack asks. "He speaks Spanish?" He cannot process this.

"Sure he does," Ernesto says. "We've been learning. In the truck."

"You taught him to speak it?"

"Not all of it," he says. "*Solamente un poco*." He holds his hands close together. "A little bit. A few words."

"Like what words? Which ones?"

"You know, vocabulary. *Arboles. Hamburguesas. ¿Y qué es eso?*" He holds up a pencil.

Hen looks. "*¿Y qué es eso?*" he says quietly. And then he says, "*Lapiz*."

Jack watches him say *lapiz* again and again. "Does he—"

Ernesto stands behind the desk. "Does he what?"

He's got to ask. "Does he talk to you?"

Ernesto smiles, shakes his head. "No, not much. We just do the words. He doesn't care for much talking. Not to people. You know."

Butner comes back into the office, takes a Coke out of the mini-fridge. "Paco," he says, "there's some dudes out there wanting to talk to you."

Ernesto gestures at Butner, says, "And I can't really blame him, you know?"

"Stop calling him Paco," Jack says, but it's like somebody else is saying the words. He's floating above the office now, watching himself watch Hen.

"Sorry, Paco," says Butner. Ernesto flicks him off, heads out the door.

Hen starts singing the Patio Enclosures song. In English. The switch flipped back the other way. *Someone you know knows something great: It's Patio Enclo-o-sures.* Butner looks at him. "We could use one of those in here," he says. "Little sun porch, some rocking chairs. Do this place up in style."

He speaks Spanish. He speaks Spanish. Ernesto walks out toward the men, who are standing around a light green pickup. The lettering on the door says TRIAD LAWNSCAPES. The number of landscaping crews they get in here just because they know they'll see a familiar face: He ought to give Ernesto a cut. "What are they needing?" Jack asks, trying to bring himself back down, trying to hold it together.

"Hell if I know," Butner says. "A lot of jabbering and pointing. Talking in Spanish."

"They wanted Ernesto?"

"They did. Stroke of genius hiring a Mexican, there, boss man."

"Guatemalan."

"Whatever."

"Maybe lay off him a little bit?"

"Yeah, yeah, OK." Hen says *Paco, Paco, Paco.* He's opening and closing the fridge. "Little man's letting all the cold out," Butner says.

Jack says, "Did you know he could speak Spanish?"

"Sure, *jefe.* You didn't? Ernesto's been teaching him. For like a month now." Butner starts flipping through a catalog for sprinkler systems—they've been talking about setting one up so all the watering would be automated—and Jack stands in the doorway, his bilingual son now knocking his forehead against the refrigerator, and watches Ernesto sell the guys some mulch. How could he have missed this? It's like he's learned Hen can do surgery, can play the oboe. Ernesto points at the skid loader, and there's a flurry of discussion, and finally one of the guys from the landscaping crew gets in it and starts loading hardwood into the back of the pickup. Christ on a stick. If he rolled it and killed himself he'd put Jack out of business. *Adios.* Hell, even if he just ran a tine through the side of the pickup it might put him under. But Jack stands in the door and watches it all go on anyway, his whole life a buzzing wire, Ernesto smiling and leaning against the side of the truck, all of them reaching over into the bed and smoothing out the pile when it starts to get full. *What's delivery? Entrega. Language acquisition comes at different ages, at different times. Mr. and Mrs. Lang, your son may be severely impaired. Pervasive Developmental Delay.* They had to teach him to eat, to swallow. They had to teach him, all over again, to fucking sit. He'd fall asleep nursing, and they'd have to wake him back up. And now he speaks Spanish. He is the Boy Wonder. *For my next trick.* He'll grow up to be an interpreter, a public defender, a dentist to the immigrant communities of the eastern seaboard. *Entrega. Lapiz. Abierto. Cerrado.*

They finish loading the pickup and the three guys give Ernesto some money and drive off. He should call Beth right now. That truth he knows to be self-evident. He should call her and he should hold the phone out to Hendrick and he should have Ernesto ask him what things are. What's this? What's this? *¿Y qué es eso?* But he doesn't do it. He's not ready to talk to her today. He doesn't want to go back through everything from last night. Plus, he realizes, even as he's sure this is what she'll hold against him forever once she knows, he's not sure he wants to share this just yet. Here's something that's his—only his—for the time being. And Ernesto's, and Butner's. But still. Ernesto comes in, opens the drawer, puts the cash in the register. Hen gets up, wanting to play with it, wanting to punch in the numbers and make the drawer ping open. Ernesto lets him and the machine rings and whirs and the tape spools out, purple numbers that mean nothing other than that the books won't be right for today—except that Ernesto draws a little red mark on the tape at the place where Hen started messing around, and Jack gets a good hold one more time of how easily all this might go on without him, or in spite of him. A huge tandem dump truck pulls onto the lot, backs up against the pile of topsoil, dumps more out on top. Butner must have scheduled the delivery. *Entrega.* The driver waves to them, pulls back out on the highway. In and out, not even five minutes. Ernesto holds up the phone book. "Eng," he says. "*¿Qué es eso?*"

"*Libro,*" Hen says.

"*¿Qué tipo de libro?*"

"*Libro de teléfono.*"

"*Claro, bueno,*" Ernesto says. "*Ven aquí, mi amigo.*" He holds his hand out, and Hen takes it, Hen who hates to be touched, and the two of them head out toward the hoop greenhouse and Ernesto's plot of peppers. Butner mumbles to himself about timers, about sprinkler heads, starts making notes on a yellow pad. He's getting it all figured out. At least somebody is. "*Claro, bueno,*" Hen's saying as they walk away. "*Claro, bueno. Ven aquí.*" This is not possible. It just is

not. He should call Bethany. He knows that. Hen keeps talking,
keeps saying words, and Ernesto, still holding his hand, says, "Sí, sí.
Perfecto."

◌ ◌ ◌

Jack hates the therapists they're seeing right now, can't even begin
to imagine what they'd have to say about this little arrangement,
about Beth camped out at Canavan's. Leave aside that Hen suddenly, magically speaks Spanish: Bethany's banging away at Canavan. Or was until last night, until Jack trenched his lawn. Now
she's either quit that, or redoubled her efforts. That's the stuff of
therapy right there. *Now, Jack, does that make you feel frustrated?* These
ones always want to know what frustrates him. *Everything,* he wants
to say. *I am never not frustrated. I don't really remember not being frustrated.*
*How are you not frustrated?* He liked the last woman, the one before.
She would set Hendrick up on the floor with an enormous box of
toys, all outdated, toys Jack remembered from growing up—the
plastic tree house with the hand-crank elevator in the trunk—and
then she'd sit there and just *talk* to them. Like they were people.
She'd give plain, practical advice about how to get him to eat
lunch. How to get him to make choices. *Whatever you need him to do,*
*say that last. Ask him, Do you want to wear the red shirt or the blue shirt? He'll*
*say "blue shirt."* But Beth switches therapists every six or eight
months, always looking for some silver bullet. Hell, Jack thinks,
for that, just leave him with Ernesto for a few days. See where that
gets us.

Jack's been calling the new ones the Beanbags, which drives
Beth bonkers. *Don't call them that. Why can't you ever take anything seri-*
*ously?* But: They have huge beanbag chairs all over their office, and
Jack feels like they're going to sessions in some middle-schooler's
basement. Yellow and orange and green Naugahyde beanbag chairs.
Dimmed halogen lights on poles in the corners, Japanese paper
lanterns hanging out of the ceiling fixtures. Some kind of music

always on in the background, some recording of migrating whales playing in the Gulf Stream. They go every two weeks, should have gone yesterday. He doesn't know if Beth called to cancel or not. She hasn't said anything about it. Doesn't matter: Let them sit over there on their beanbags and listen to *The Sounds of the Temperate Rain Forest* and flip through their day planners. Let them eat their healthy snacks. They keep a big bowl of raisins in the waiting room, for Christ's sake. Little domino-sized individual boxes of raisins.

PM&T is slow, even for a Tuesday, but what does come in is big orders, so they do alright. Hen rides along with Ernesto on the wheat straw delivery. God knows what words he'll know now. Wheat straw, for one. While the lot's quiet, Butner builds in more caging for the tomatoes he's got in the ground. They're starting to take off—he'll have fruit by the Fourth of July. Jack pulls a few plants from the greenhouse, Better Boys and Cherokee Purples and one Butner's been swearing by, something called Mortgage Lifter, to give to Canavan. To replace what he took out last night. He's feeling bad about that part of it now. He should have let those be. You shouldn't go after somebody's food crop. The shrubs would have been enough.

They get a call for fifteen yards of river rock for next week. A guy in a beat-up Chrysler comes in and buys out the last twenty or so bales of pine straw they've got, takes them home in three trips, tied into his trunk and across his backseat. Beth comes by around one, and Hen's still out with Ernesto. She says that's OK, says she'll call later, says maybe she'll take Hen for an early dinner. They don't talk about last night. He doesn't mention anything about the Spanish. He tries to get her to take the tomatoes. *I don't think so,* she says. *I think maybe you two boys should work this out.* He stands there and looks at her. *How's it going over there?* he wants to know. *Don't,* she says. *OK? Just don't.* He thinks about that. *OK,* he says. As she leaves, he almost reaches out to touch her on the hip. Muscle memory. Reflex. Instead, so he'll have something to do, he goes to talk to Butner about whether they ought to price down the annuals yet—it's getting late to put flowers in—and Butner says he thinks they ought to wait a couple more weeks. Ernesto and Hen come back, go out again. At the end of the day Jack flips the sign in the window and Ernesto goes home to his family and Butner walks across the dusty lot to the Shell, comes back with two tall boys. They sit in the back and Hen does his buckets and the light gets long and Jack unties and reties his shoes and he realizes: This is what it will be like if she never comes back.

The birds start coming back in to roost in the hanging baskets they've got for sale up under the trellis. Butner's in charge of the birds, too, knows which ferns and Wandering Jews have nests in them, won't sell those. He'll take them down to show anybody who wants to see, always saying *Careful, don't spook the nest*, as though the nest itself was what was so fragile. Wrens and sparrows, mostly, and a nest of towhees in a big trailing petunia off to the far side. *Ma'am, I can't sell you that one now*, he'll say. *Come back in a couple weeks after they fledge, though, and we'll give it to you for half off.* He's explaining something about the towhees that Jack's not really listening to when Canavan pulls into the lot. "Shit and goddamn," Butner says. "It's the motherfucking prize patrol. What the hell's he doing here?"

Jack's body goes tight. "I trenched his yard last night," he says.

"Good for fucking you, man," says Butner. "How?"

"With the truck. I took out the shrubs up by his house. And his mailbox."

"No shit?"

"I got pissed," Jack says. "I got a little pissed."

"Well," Butner says, holding his can out, "it's about fucking time. You grew a pair. Congratulations."

Jack sits there, congratulated, while Canavan pulls his rig—a fourteen-foot panel truck he bought from U-Haul and cut the back door off of, so it's an open box with a trailer behind—back past the greenhouse, toward the pile of branches and limbs they chip once a month. Maybe he's just here to make a point. He's a free man: He can drive by the lot whenever he likes. The truck and trailer are both loaded with maple. He's painted the truck dark green, hired a kid from Kinnett to logo the side. AN HONEST TREE, it says, in block letters. SERVICE is outlined, but not painted fully in. There's a picture of a guy with a chainsaw next to that, and it's a pretty good likeness. The arms are a little out of proportion, but it looks like Canavan. Canavan's actual arms may be out of proportion. He says he didn't mean for it to look like him, acts like it was some big screw-up, but Jack's pretty sure he secretly likes it. Likes driving a truck around with a life-sized painting of himself on the side. He's got his other trucks, new pickups and a flatbed, perfect condition—but he drives this thing most of the time. Jack and his bumperless dump truck, Canavan and his cut-up U-Haul. They're the goddamned same person. Jack chews on which one of them he ought to hate more.

Canavan starts unloading the wood by himself. It looks like he might have as much as two cords, plus the branches. Jack can't figure out why he wouldn't have brought somebody with him to help. There's no way he loaded all that alone. "I'm not going over there," Butner says.

"Nobody's asking you to."

"Good."

"Good."

What Jack intends to do is just sit a while longer, get his bearings, and then he can give him a hand. He can apologize for the tomatoes. Tell him he's got some replacement plants for him. Tell him the maple looks good. But not yet. Let him go for a while. He's in a good rhythm, anyway, and pretty soon he's got most of it off the trailer. There's still more in the truck. He pulls a chainsaw out

of the cab and starts in on some of the smaller branches, sizing
them down for the chipper. The gas-oil smell of the engine drifts
over.

"Maybe I should go help him," Jack says.

"We covered this already," says Butner. "Fucknut can cut every
damn inch of it himself, as far as I'm concerned. It's enough, him
just fucking showing up here in the first place." He looks around.
"Hey, where's the little man?"

Jack looks at the lineup of buckets, and Hen's not there. He's
not at the hose spigot, and he's not in the greenhouse. He's not
anywhere. Jack's up and out of his chair, imagining, what, the
sound of air brakes locking up out on the highway, Hen disappearing under the bumper of one of the medical supply trucks
that drive up and down. Or drinking diesel out of the pump over
at the Shell. And Beth will have been so right about him, about
everything. She'll make him explain it again and again to her: *No,
we were just sitting there. Yes, I was watching him. I don't know how.* She'll
make him explain it to everyone at the goddamn funeral. *And he'd
just started speaking Spanish.* But Jack comes around the mulch bins
and of course there he is, Hendrick, right there, because where
the hell else would he be, except fine, unscathed, squatting at the
foot of the cedar pile—he's lining up long pieces of cedar, each at
a ninety degree angle to the last, a staircase, a calculator, a Spanish-
to-Hendrick dictionary. He's choosing each piece carefully, ex-
amining it, touching it to his lips, then laying it in place. And he's
whispering. At first Jack can't pick it up over the noise from Canavan's chainsaw, but when he leans in, he recognizes it—it's the
lead to one of The Weather Channel storm retrospectives. A show
about the history of weather. They've seen it twice this week.
Hendrick chooses another piece, looks up, and says, *The remnants
of Tropical Storm Allison march toward the city, dumping as much as thirty
inches of rain in two days.*

Jack's heartbeat starts coming back down. He's listening to the trucks on the highway headed east and west without having to run over his son to do it, so it takes him a few beats to register that there's something else now, another something, a new thing wrong—that Butner's yelling for him, that the chainsaw motor has stopped. He looks up, and across the yard Butner's standing over Canavan, who's on the ground in a pile of branches. Butner's waving, yelling something Jack can't hear. He picks Hendrick up and starts over there. Hen keeps right on through his litany. How much of this has he got memorized? *Let's go to Jim Cantore in the Weather Center for a look back*, Hen says, over Jack's shoulder. *Jim?* Probably all of it. He probably has the whole thing. As they get closer, Jack can see how much blood there is, and he starts to hurry.

Canavan has put the chainsaw all the way through his leg, Jack thinks at first. His jeans are soaked in blood and he's sitting there in the leaves, both feet out in front of him. There is blood down in the dirt next to where he's dropped the saw. Everything smells like sawdust and saw oil and sweat. He looks sick. His leg's still attached. So not all the way through. His face is pale, and he's not screaming, not grabbing at his leg, not doing much of anything. He's staring at his truck, at the painting of himself there on the side. "Call an ambulance," Butner says. Gently, almost. And that's what Jack does. That's certainly what's called for here. He puts Hen down and pulls the phone out of his pocket. It's the first time in his life he's ever called 911. Hen's staring at Canavan's leg, whispering *At three-thirty a.m., the storm drains in the downtown neighborhood of Campus Reach fail. And at Mercy Hospital, nurse Gloria Arroyo prepares her patients for a possible move to higher ground.* He's even got the intonations down. It takes five rings for anyone to pick up, and when they do, the line's bad. Jack can't tell if it's a man or a woman on the other end. He can't tell for sure if he's even connected. He just starts saying his name and address. "Jack Lang," he says. "Patriot Mulch & Tree, 7144 Highway 70, Whitsett." He says that three times. Canavan looks like shit.

The phone goes perfectly clear, and the voice on the other end says, "Sir, what is the nature of your emergency?"

The nature of his emergency. Jack bites on the inside of his mouth. He says, "Somebody cut himself with a chainsaw. Terry Canavan. Somebody we work with."

"Does anyone there know first aid?" asks the voice.

"I do, a little bit," says Jack. "From Boy Scouts." He feels absurd. He remembers learning how to carry somebody out of the woods, how to boil water to purify it. He remembers that if one kind of bear charges you, you're supposed to throw yourself on the ground, and if it's the other kind, you're supposed to run. He doesn't remember which is which. He remembers a kid at Scout Camp actually getting his eye poked out because he was running with a stick. Jack Lancaster. The kid who poked his eye out. The mothers must have loved that story.

"If you can put a clean cloth over the wound and elevate it, that would be great. Can you do that for me, sir?"

Jack says to Butner, "Can you put a clean cloth on it and elevate it?"

"Where the hell is a clean cloth?"

"Hang on," Jack says to the 911 operator, and puts the phone on the ground. Hen picks it up and says, "Patriot Mulch & Tree." Jack pulls Hen's shirt off over his head. He gives it to Butner, who presses it against Canavan's shin. Canavan wakes right up after that, comes out of his trance screaming and kicking at Butner with his good leg. Hen says into the phone, "At Bob Dunn Ford, We're Dealin'." Jack gets a log off the back of the truck, rolls it over to Canavan, and he and Butner elevate his leg. There is a lot of blood. A lot. Hen's shirt soaks through. Hendrick says, "We're the Little Cheaper Dealer." A cartoon chick, the Little Cheaper, pops up on the screen during that ad, and Jack half-expects it to appear here, now, in the yard. Butner wipes his hands on his own jeans, on Canavan's jeans. Canavan goes quiet again, lays back on the pile of branches, groans some. Jack wonders if he's going to pass out. He takes the phone from Hendrick and says, "What if he passes out?"

"Try to keep him awake for me, sir, OK?"

"But what if he passes out?"

"Sir, just try to keep him awake, and somebody will be there in a few minutes. We've called fire and ambulance for you."

"Nothing's on fire," Jack says.

"Sir, fire is generally our first responder."

Butner's got Canavan sitting back up, is behind him now and holding him, his arms around his chest. Hen's squatting next to Canavan, shirtless, rocking, whispering. Things seem blurry. Jack stands there and holds his phone. Beth will find some way to make this his fault. The line goes bad again, and he takes a few steps in each direction to try to get it clear. The voice on the other end says, "Sir, they're about five minutes out now, OK? Sir?" Then the line goes dead. Butner shifts behind Canavan some, trying to make him more comfortable, and blood spurts up and out of the gash in his shin. It hits the back of the trailer, the license plate, drips down. Butner gets up and takes his own shirt off, tears it into a long strip, ties it tightly around the cut. As he's doing it, Jack sees bone, sees where the saw has cut well down into the bone, sees the stark white of it, and that does it for him: He turns around and vomits. Hendrick says, "Side effects may include nausea and diarrhea."

He wipes his mouth off and stands up, tries to do something, to find something to do. He's dizzy. Do something fatherly, he thinks. Act like you own the place. He pulls Hen back away from Canavan and Butner a little bit, runs over to the office, where they've got a first aid kit. He brings that and a bottle of water back, tries to hand the water to Canavan, who waves it off.

"You gotta drink," Butner tells him, and opens the bottle, pours some water in Canavan's mouth. He spits it back out again, but then motions for more. Butner pours, Canavan swallows. Jack tries not to look at Canavan's leg, at the little pile of shirts soaked in blood. He opens up the first aid kit. There's only ace bandages and gauze. Nothing that would really do anything more than what they've already done. He hands the gauze to Butner. "They said they'd be here in a minute," he says.

Canavan says, "You called somebody?"

"I called 911," Jack says, showing him the phone.

"Oh," Canavan says. "OK."

Butner puts the gauze on Canavan's leg, and Jack takes one of the red tie-downs from Canavan's trailer, hooks one end through Hendrick's belt loop, starts tying him off. He doesn't want to lose track of him again. "Listen," Jack says, finishing the knot. "I'm sorry about your yard."

"Don't apologize for that," Butner says.

"Why not?"

"His leg's cut. He's not dying. Get your shit together."

"Thanks," Canavan says.

"How'd you do it?" Jack asks him. "What happened?" It only now occurs to him that Butner might have done it, might have walked over here and taken the saw and sheared his leg right open. It is vaguely possible that Butner would be capable of something like that, Jack thinks. *He was always real quiet, a good employee.*

"I'm not sure," Canavan says. "I was cutting all this to length, and I guess the saw jumped on me. Should have been wearing guards. Stupid."

"It could have happened to anybody," Jack says.

"I was hurrying," says Canavan. "That's all. I'm sorry."

"You'll be OK," Jack says.

"How much of this am I going to have to listen to?" Butner says. "You two should be clusterbombing each other's houses. Instead you're asking each other to dance. Fucking pussies."

Jack wonders whether Beth's at school or at Canavan's house right now. Maybe she's taking a bath. Or she's at the grocery, buying a sweet little dinner for two. "I pulled some tomato plants for you," he tells Canavan, because otherwise he'll have to ask where Beth is. "From the greenhouse. I'll drop them by."

Canavan nods. He's sweating pretty hard. "OK," he says. "Thanks."

Hendrick leans against the radius of the tie-down, playing with the circle it gives him. He's making airplane noises, arms out, when the fire truck pulls into the lot, bouncing through the potholes. There's no siren, but the lights are going. The driver hits the horn on his way in, and that about does it for Hendrick. This is enormously exciting. He starts turning in circles, gets himself tangled, and Jack spins him back in the other direction, wonders what the Spanish word for exciting is. Some of the firemen are off the truck before it stops. They take the whole scene over right away. Two of them know Butner. They talk with him while two more firemen look at the shirt tied around Canavan's leg, hold fingers up in his face and ask him to tell them how many there are. He gets it right, mainly. Everything seems much more professional now. The firemen get him laid down on what looks like the kind of board that beach patrol lifeguards carry, and one of them pulls some bandages out of a big black first aid kit and ties a tourniquet around Canavan's leg just under the knee. That same summer at Scout Camp, a kid tied a tourniquet around his penis and couldn't get it undone, had to go to the infirmary to have the nurse do it. Hendrick spins himself into the tie-down again. One of the firefighters who's talking to Butner says, "Is that kid on a leash?"

"No," Butner says. "He's autistic."

"He's what?"

"Like Ronnie Dorchester. Remember him? Tenth grade?"

"I think so," the fireman says. He's wearing his helmet backwards. He says, "Is he this guy's?" He nods at Canavan.

"No. He's his. The guy who owns the place."

"Kid like presents?"

"Sometimes," Butner says. "Depends."

The fireman takes his helmet off and walks over to Hendrick, holds it out to him. Jack runs his tongue across his teeth: What's possible here is that Hen takes it, and everything goes well. He could also launch into orbit, throw himself on the ground, scream for seven hours. The other firemen are still working on Canavan. Hen blinks a few times, takes the helmet, and stands still. He holds the helmet out in front of him. Then he puts it very gently on the ground. The fireman turns to Jack. "I'll tell the chief it fell off the truck," he says.

"Thanks," says Jack.

"Blood can be a tough thing for a kid to see," he says. "A lot of people don't know that." Jack wonders who doesn't know that, then registers the fact that he's actually tied Hen in place there in front of all of it. Fair enough.

An ambulance comes in from the other direction, siren off, lights off. It stops just past Canavan's truck, then backs up, reverse warning beeping. Hendrick stares. Two EMTs, a man and a woman, get out and talk to the firemen, load Canavan and his lifeguard board onto a stretcher. A third EMT stands by the ambulance, watches. Supervises. They inflate something around his leg, a sleeve to stop the bleeding, maybe, or just to protect him, and they wheel him over the gravel toward the open back doors of the ambulance. One of them gets on the radio, and the other, the woman, comes over to Jack and Butner and the firefighters.

"We'll take him to Moses Cone, in Greensboro," she says. "Better trauma unit, almost as close."

"OK," Jack says. Hendrick picks the helmet up, puts it on, then takes it right back off again. It's much bigger than his head.

The EMT says, "You guys know him, I assume."

"Yes," Jack says.

"Is there maybe someone you could call, tell somebody where he is?"

Butner's getting ready to say something, but Jack says, "I can do it."

"OK," she says. "Terrific."

"Do you know how bad it is?" Jack asks.

"It doesn't look awful," she says. "I mean, it's bad, but I've seen uglier. Looks worse than it is, probably. More blood than anything. It's kind of a messy cut."

"Messy?"

"Chainsaws are bad. Knives are better. The edges are smoother, easier to patch up. Chainsaws are a pain in the ass."

"OK," Jack says.

"Moses Cone," she tells him again, like she thinks he won't remember.

"He's got it," Butner says. "He's got it."

"We should go," she says.

"Yeah," Jack says. "OK."

They get ready to load Canavan into the ambulance, and Hen starts freaking out, starts doing his noises. Something's touched him off. Everybody stops what they're doing and watches while it gets worse, while he starts shrieking in short, staccato bursts. He's out at the very end of the tie-down, pulling hard on it, leaning. Jack goes over to him, tries to calm him down, tries to hold him, tries state names. Arkansas. Kansas. It doesn't work. He's really ramping himself up now, kicking and screaming, spinning back into the strap, and Jack unties him, trying to make it so he can't get too tangled, at least, and that turns out to be all he was wanting: Once he's free of the tie-down, Hendrick runs over and stands next to the stretcher, silent. He stands eye level with Canavan, who's not talking, not moving. There is blood on the stretcher. Hendrick leans in and kisses him on the arm. He actually kisses Canavan on the arm. *Some children with autism have difficulty showing affection of any kind.* Hendrick kisses Canavan, and he says, "These member sta-

tions." He says, "NPR is brought to you by this and other NPR stations, and by contributions from listeners like you." He says, "By
the Ford Foundation, and by the Lila Wallace Reader's Digest Fund."
He says, "Archer Daniels Midland, Supermarket to the World," and
then he steps back, having said what he needed to say, and the
EMTs get Canavan loaded into the ambulance. Jack puts his hands
on Hen's shoulders. One of the EMTs gets in the back with Canavan, and the other closes the doors, hits them twice, gets in up
front and they pull away, lights flashing now, but still no siren.
Butner walks over to the Shell to talk to Cherry, who's come out to
see what all this is. The firemen start loading back up, and Hendrick's talking again, saying something else Jack can't figure out, a
garbled mess of half-words and sounds, or maybe just sounds. Secret code. The ambulance is around the big curve and out of sight
by the time Jack gets it figured out, gets hold of what he's saying,
which is *ecnalubma, ecnalubma*. He's read the backwards printing on
the front of the ambulance. A brand new word, yet another language. Ecnalubma. Hendrick sits down in the dust and puts the fire
helmet on again. In it, he looks like he's the wrong size for the
world.

&#8487; &#8487; &#8487;

"I don't know," he tells Beth again, standing on the yard. He's
called her at Canavan's. "I wasn't looking. I was chasing Hendrick
around, and when I looked up, he was down."

"What do you mean, 'he was down'?"

"I mean," he says, "I found Hendrick over by the cedar, lining it
up, and when I looked up again Canavan was down, and Butner
was shouting."

"You found Hendrick? Was he lost?"

"He wasn't lost. He just got away while I was sitting with Butner. He was ten feet away."

"So you don't know what happened."

"That's what I'm trying to tell you. Nobody does. He just cut himself. The EMT said it didn't look that bad. She said she'd seen worse."

"Of course she's seen worse. She's an EMT."

"It wasn't that bad. I only puked because of the blood."

"You threw up?"

"Only a little."

"Did he cut anything off? Like toes or anything? I mean, should you be going to get a bag of ice or something from the gas station and looking for toes?"

"He didn't cut anything off," Jack says. "I think he just let the saw slip off a branch, and it nicked him."

"You don't ride in an ambulance for a nick, Jack."

"You know what I mean."

"Have you looked for toes?"

"The cut's on his shin. I saw it myself, remember? You want me to look around anyway?"

She sighs on the other end. "No," she says. "I guess not." Then she says, "There was a lot of blood?"

"Yeah," Jack says. "There was."

"How's Hendrick?"

*Well, he's fluent in Spanish, and he kissed your boyfriend.* "He's fine," Jack says.

"Where is he?"

"He's right here."

"He's not lost again?"

"He's right here." He's sitting on the step up into the office, tapping on the fire helmet with his yogurt spoon. "He's got a fire helmet now."

"What?"

"A fire helmet. One of the guys gave it to him."

"One of what guys?"

"The firemen, obviously."

"Why were there firemen? Was something on fire?"

"Fire's usually the first responder," he tells her. He's an expert now.

"There was a fire truck?"

"Yes."

"Jesus Christ." She's shuffling papers or something. "Look," she says. "Are you going to the hospital?"

It hadn't even occurred to him. "I guess so," he says. He doesn't want to, but it happened on his watch. "Maybe I should."

"So I can see Hen there, at least," she says.

"Yeah," he says. "Sure." And just like that, he's going.

"Fine," she says.

"Fine."

"You really have no idea what happened?"

It's something about her tone. "What are you saying?" he asks.

"I mean, Jack, just tell me you didn't—"

"Tell you I didn't what?"

"Nothing," she says. "Never mind. I'm sorry."

"Are you asking me if I did it? As in, did I go over there and take the chainsaw and just slash him across the shin?"

"No," she says. "No. I don't know what I mean. I know you didn't do that. I'm sorry. I'm just—I don't know what I am."

"It doesn't matter," he says. He rubs the back of his neck. "For a second I thought the same thing about Butner."

"You don't think—"

"No," Jack says. "I really don't think so."

"You would have seen that."

"I might have paid to watch it," he says.

There's a long pause on her end. "Do you have to be that way?"

"Probably not," he says. He should figure out some other way to be. He can hear well enough that she's not entirely OK. And he can't blame her. Things are now worse than they were before. Simple as that. Whatever else Canavan is to her, he's now also wounded, and headed for the emergency room. Neither of them says anything for a long time, and then she finally asks him, *Moses Cone?* And he tells her *yes, Moses Cone*, tells her they'll meet her there. Before they hang up, Beth says, "Jack?"

"Yeah."

"Someone should probably call Rena."

Rena. In her little borrowed condo downtown. View of future redevelopment, of parallel parking, of men picking up after their dogs when they walk them in the evenings. "Probably so," he says.

"Maybe you could?"

"Better me than you, I guess," he says.

"That's what I was thinking."

"I don't have her number here," he says.

"Hang on," she says. "I think it's somewhere in here." He hears her walking through Canavan's house. There are so many things not right with this. "Here it is," she says, and gives it to him. He stands there on the yard, the sun so low it's behind the piles of mulch now, and he doesn't write it down. He doesn't want to call anybody, doesn't want to go to the hospital. He wants to go home, go back to before any of this happened at all. "Did you get that?" she asks him.

"Yeah," he says. Then he tells her, "No."

"No?"

"I didn't have anything to write with," he says, and slides past Hen into the office. "OK," he says, and she tells him again, and he writes it up on the big delivery whiteboard.

"So you'll call her."

"Yes," he says.

"Moses Cone," she says.

"Yes," he says.

"OK, then," she says, "I'm hanging up now."

"OK," he says, and she does. This one thing's probably true: If she didn't sleep on the sofa last night, she will tonight. Canavan's not going to be able to do anything for her with a cut like that. The sun catches the clear plastic of the greenhouse, lights it up. Hendrick moves the fire helmet to a new, better position on the step. Jack stands there and looks at Rena's number.

ভ    ভ    ভ

Butner said he'd clean up the blood, he'd finish limbing the rest of the branches, he'd figure out how to get Canavan's truck back to him. *Come in tomorrow whenever you need*, he said. *Me and Paco can work the lot pretty good. Call in the morning and we'll let you know when we need you.* Butner leaned in through the truck window. *It's OK you're going*, he said. *Just don't stay long. Show your face and then get the hell out of there*, he said. *Doesn't need to be you sitting there all night just so they can tell you it's seven hundred stitches or however many it turns out to be. Get out of there and take the little man somewhere good. Take him to one of those pizza places where there's skeeball and go-carts and all that. Slides and shit.* Jack can't imagine Hendrick inside a place like that. At school, or at the park, Hen stands in the center of all the kids while they run around. He likes the playground, likes to watch, but it doesn't occur to him to play. He doesn't really have any friends his age, doesn't really know how to act around other children. It's like it doesn't ever occur to him that he's one of them, too.

Jack and Hen drive 70 back into Greensboro. He's gotten him into a new shirt, from an extra set of clothes he keeps at PM&T just in case. It's got a cartoon character on it Jack doesn't recognize. Beth must have bought it. They pass the Elks' Club Lodge, where the sign says DEFEND OUR TROOPS. A couple of miles later, the L&M Clutch and Transmission sign says SIRLOIN $7.99. No explanation for why they'd be selling meat out of the clutch shop. They come in through the ragged neighborhoods outlying this side of Greensboro, long brick apartment buildings and old Sears houses half-rotting into the ground, the occasional house fixed back up, a pineapple flag out front and a neat little lawn. Then a clear-cut neighborhood of doublewides, Saving Grace Homes. On the scalped land the houses look like growths, like something that might have to be taken off. At Gentry Used Auto Sales, there's a huge inflatable eagle on the roof, face airbrushed on. That's a job. In another life he could have been an airbrush artist for promotional balloons. He points it out to Hendrick. Hen says, "Pin Oak."

"Eastern Red," Jack says right back.

Warehouses and a warehouse that's been turned into a wedding and special events hall and a few more churches and he's there, north on Elm and the half-mile up to the hospital. He parks the truck off on the edge of the lot, leaving himself room to turn around. It's been a couple of years now since they've been to the hospital with Hen—long litanies of EEGs and tests for metals and yeasts and physical therapy—but he still knows all this by heart. The small signs, the calm lettering: Parking. Outpatient. Maternity. Even EMERGENCY, even in its capitals, seems demure. As if every situation here might still be equal. It's all sort of sickly familiar, like knowing the words to a song mainly because it's eternally on the radio.

He has not called Rena. He couldn't understand how the conversation would go. So. Beth moved in with Canavan. Right. I know. Also, there's been an accident.

The emergency room is empty. Theirs is apparently the only emergency today. There are no kids who've fallen out of trees, no dads who cut hornet nests out of hedges. No pellet gun accidents, no head wounds, no meningitis scares. Jack gets Hen set up with the tree catalog and his fire helmet, sits him next to an enormous fish tank. There's one huge yellow fish, and about a hundred glittering silver-green ones the size of nails. Hen puts two fingers on the glass, takes off The Duck so he can see better. Jack walks up to the desk. Find out how he is, get the hell out of here.

"May I help you?" the nurse says. She looks exhausted, looks like she could do without one more emergency.

Jack says, "I'm a friend of Terry Canavan's. Acquaintance. I work with him. Terrence Canavan. He should have come in about a half-hour ago? Maybe a little less? Chainsaw cut on his leg?"

"Yes, sir," she says. "Are you family?"

"No. He works with me. For me. He works for me."

"Well, sir, unless you're family, I don't think they'll let you back there. But I can check."

"That'd be super," he says. She vanishes through a set of doors. Jack walks back over to Hendrick and the fish, thinking *super, super.* All of this is super. "Are you watching the fish?" he asks Hen.

"I am watching the fish."

"Are you hungry?"

Hen hits the sides of his thighs with his fists: *Yes.* Jack digs in his pockets for change, for dollar bills, and takes him over to the vending machines. "No candy," he tells him, and starts pointing to the sleeves of crackers, orange ones, brown ones. Something with peanut butter in it, something with protein. "These?" he asks, pointing. "These?" Hen shakes his head no, then no again, makes his noises. *Fnh. Fnh.* He finally settles on the orange ones, square, salt shining in the light of the machine. Jack taps in the letter and number and the package spirals out and down, thudding into the bottom. Hendrick discovers the flapping door and sits down in front of the machine, in front of the door, pushing it open, reaching his hand in, taking it back out. A new entertainment. Jack opens the crackers, eats one himself, sits down nearby to make sure Hen doesn't get his head stuck in the door. Though if he did, they'd be in the perfect place for it. Jack wonders if you can have emergencies in the emergency room. Who you call.

The one time they went to the hospital for any real emergency—the only time it wasn't appointments or Hen with the flu in the middle of the night—Beth had almost cut the end of her thumb off slicing onions. He was in the back of their old house, the rental in Burlington, putting Hen down in his crib, and she'd called to him. *Jack?* She was so calm. *I think I just cut myself really badly.* They were making chili. He got to the kitchen and there was blood on the cutting board, on the counter, on the floor, small drops tracing her walk to the sink, where she was running her thumb under cold water, the sink draining pink beneath it. He remembers thinking, *We're going to have to cut new onions.* He remembers being hungry, being frustrated with her. Wondering when or if they'd eat. He turned the heat off under the pot, threw the onions away, told her to hold her hand over her head. *I am,* she said, sitting down, leaning against the cabinets. They kept wadding paper towels against it, kept checking every few minutes, probably kept reopening the cut. They tried ice. Jack cut a T-shirt into ribbons, tried tying off the base of her thumb to slow the blood down. Nothing worked. After an hour and a half Jack gave up, decided to take her in. *Here,* he said, giving her a bowl of cereal. *Eat this.* He poured one for himself. *I don't know how long this'll take.* She had her thumb wrapped up in a dishtowel, blood coming through. Jack couldn't believe she was still bleeding, that so much blood could come out of her. Was this the kind of thing that would have killed prehistoric man? With no hospital, did those guys cut the shit out of their thumbs and just lay there at the mouth of the cave and bleed out? She never cried, even when the doctor told them the cut was too close to the end of her thumb for stitches, that she should just bandage it tightly and go home. This after two hours of watching cable news in the waiting room, Hendrick asleep across two seats between them. They just went back home.

She bears up under things like that better than he does, holds it together, doesn't yell at the doctors. She'll yell at him fine, holds her patience for the things she can't control. He remembers her calmly asking the nurse for an epidural during Hendrick's birth, saying thank you, telling Jack everything was going the way they'd planned. It all seemed so animal, so wild, and then there was Beth above it all, hovering, almost, giving directions, explaining. He can't always reconcile this side of her with her hurricane kit side, doesn't understand it, isn't sure it makes any sense. And then sometimes he's not at all sure he's supposed to be able to, that in fact this is what life with her means, these places where he will not know, will have to navigate for himself. He loves her. He does. He just does not always know how to do it right. And now neither of them seems to know.

Bethany comes in the front door of the ER, all business, walking fast. It's a disaster, somehow, seeing her this way, seeing her here— though lately it's a disaster seeing her almost anywhere. She aims straight for the nurses' station, says something to them. *Are you family?* he hears a nurse ask.

"Yes," she says, turning around to look at Jack. "I'm his sister." Smart Beth. The woman gets up and disappears through the same doors Jack's woman did, and Beth comes over. She squats down next to Hendrick, who has found a squeak in the arc of the vending machine door. She says, "Hey, buddy." Hen says nothing, squeaks the door. She looks at Jack. "Tennessee," she says.

Hen stops. He says, "Memphis Murfreesboro Sevierville."

"Hi," she says.

"Hi," Hen says.

"How are you?"

"I am fine."

"Good," she says.

"Good." He goes back to the door. Another flash where he's right there with them. Maybe, Jack's starting to think—maybe— something's shifting in there. Maybe the diet and the meds and the therapist parade are starting to jiggle things around. There have been moments this week when Jack can almost imagine having a conversation with him about, say, the merits of sending doors back and forth on their hinges. Maybe in Spanish.

"Hi," Beth says to Jack.

"Nashville," he says. "Knoxville."

"Very good," she says, sitting down next to him. "What's left? Chattanooga?"

"Yeah," Jack says. "Chattanooga." He's hugely tired, all of a sudden, would maybe sell a few of his own toes for a bed, for crisp white hotel sheets.

She fishes around in her purse for a Tylenol, pops one in her mouth. Just one, no water, like always. "I'm not mad at you, by the way," she says.

"For what?"

"For any of this," she says. "I've thought about it, and I'm not mad."

"Well, that's great," he says.

"You're mad at me, though," she says. "I wish you weren't mad at me."

"How do you want me to be?" he says.

"I don't know," she says. "All I said was I wish you weren't mad."

He doesn't say anything. Announcements come on over the hospital's PA: Please report to oncology, to pharmacy, to inpatient. He has told no one other than Butner and Ernesto about Beth leaving, about any of this. He has not told his parents. Her mother hasn't been calling the house, so he wonders if maybe she knows. When his parents call, he tells them she's fine, that she's at the grocery or the gym. When anyone else calls, he lets the machine pick up. Her birthday is in August. Hen's is, too. Something's bound to shift by then. She'll be back home, or maybe she'll have decided she needs some rest of a different sort, will have checked herself into some facility somewhere where people sit around in groups, drawing pictures of their feelings. Or there is the chance—and he starts to get hold of this right there in the waiting room, feels for maybe the first time the full shape and size of what might have landed in his life—there is the chance that she will actually leave him for Terry fucking Canavan and his newly chainsawed leg.

A doctor comes out of the doors, walks across the room and stands in front of them. He's tall. "Mrs. Canavan?"

A good-sized firework goes off in Jack's head. "No," she says. "Mrs. Lang. I'm his sister."

"Mrs. Lang. My apologies." He's got a hint of an accent. Something European.

"It's OK," she says, and the doctor stands there. He's not wearing a nametag.

"Would you like to speak in private?"

"No," she says. "We're fine. Jack works with Terry. They're friends. He saw it happen."

The doctor says, "Very well. I'm pleased to tell you that Mr. Canavan is doing fine. I've just finished stapling his leg."

"Stapling?" Beth says.

"It's a superior method to stitches. The healing time is quicker. Though there are a few stitches at each end of the wound." His accent makes all this sound slightly more complicated than it might actually be. "There was damage to the bone," he says, "but technically there is no fracture. When the cut begins to heal, we can determine whether or not he will need further measures."

Beth's nodding along to all of this. "So he's OK?" she says. "He can walk?" Jack thinks, *But will he ever be able to play the piano again?*

"He'll be on crutches for at least a week, perhaps two," the doctor says. "That is just for the wound. Again, as for the bone, we won't know until later." He smiles, holds his hands out, delivers his benediction. "These things take time."

"Can we see him?" Beth asks.

"You may," he says. "He is awake, but he is medicated. Just so you know."

"So we know what?" Beth asks.

"So you know that he is on medication. He will be groggy."

"Will he be here overnight?"

"Oh, no," the doctor says, smiling. "Just another hour or two to make sure the bleeding is arrested. Then he may go home."

"Oh," says Beth. "Good." It's clear she had in mind staying the night here. The stoic woman in the waiting room, the late-night talk shows, the terrible vending machine coffee. That he's hurt, but not quite hurt enough, feels like some odd victory.

"He is in room 271," the doctor says. "I will be by once more to look at him. Everything went very well," he says. "Very well." And then he walks away. He doesn't take them to room 271, doesn't ask if they have questions. He leaves them there in the waiting room and they watch him go through the double doors, disappearing.

"Well," Beth says.

"Yeah," Jack says.

"It's good he's OK," she says.

"It is."

"It's good the bone's not broken. That's what he said, right?"

"He said they'd have to see," says Jack.

"But he said it wasn't fractured."

"Right."

"So," she says, and as she says it, as they're standing there in the emergency room, he sees, clearly, that it was a mistake for him to come here at all, knows already what she's getting ready to ask, knows, too, with what feels like relief, that he's going to have to say no. That he's going to be able to. He can't be part of this. Not this way, not any longer. "Should we go back there and see him?" she says.

"No," he says. "I don't think so. At least not me."

She looks at him. "What are you talking about?"

"I can't go back there," he says. "I don't feel like it." They'd be standing there together at the foot of Canavan's bed, asking him if it hurt a lot. "I don't want to do it," he says.

"Why did you come here, then?" she asks.

"I don't know," he tells her. His stock answer, and the truth most of the time. "Because I watched them put him on the ambulance. Because you just assumed I would. So I did." He looks over at Hen, at the fish tank. There's a treasure chest with bubbles coming up from it, a pirate who pops out of it from time to time. "And he's OK," he says. "The doctor said he's OK, so I'm going."

"You're going."

"Yes."

"You came here just to sit in the waiting room."

"I guess so."

"He's not OK. He has staples in his leg."

"And you should go back there and see him," Jack says. "You should go take care of him."

"What does that mean?"

"It doesn't mean anything," he says.

"Should I tell him you were here?"

"Sure," he says. "Tell him whatever you like." He's suddenly in a pretty big hurry to go. He wants away from all this, from Beth, from Canavan, from Beth and Canavan. He wants the truck, wants his front porch with the cardboard taped over the broken window, wants the quiet and the noise of his street. And he feels untied, telling her this, feels freed, feels like somebody's opening up a door and letting him out. He does not have to go back there, does not have to watch Beth minister to the gravely injured Terry Canavan, and so he's not going to.

"This is ridiculous," she says. "Come back there with me and see him. He's your friend. He almost cut his leg off."

"I'm not sure he's my friend," he says.

"Come on, Jack, we can talk about all of this later, we can work—"

"Work it out?" Jack says. "How I live in our house and you live in his? Maybe the three of us can come to terms," he says. "We can work out how much longer you'll be there. We can all of us make some kind of deal." He walks back over to the rows of chairs, gets the catalog, gets the fire helmet, gets The Duck. He gives Hendrick the rest of the orange crackers. He says, "I don't think so, OK?"

"Jack."

He looks up. "What?"

She zips her purse closed. She bites on the inside of her mouth. He's got her on this one. He knows he does. "I'll tell him you were here," she says. "I'll tell him that you came by."

"OK," Jack says. "Good. Thanks." And then—what comes next is that he sees himself holding his hand out to shake hers. It's like his body is rebelling against him. There's his arm, his hand. Her face changes as she reaches out, takes his hand. Something unbends. This will be one of those brightly lit moments they'll have no problem remembering. *The time when.* He is shaking hands with his wife in the emergency room. He's not sure he's ever shaken her hand before. Surely he has. Joking around about something. *Pleased to meet you.* She looks like she can't figure out what to say to him now. She probably can't. He lets go, puts The Duck on Hendrick, and walks him out the automatic glass doors into the parking lot and toward the truck. The first time he turns around, Beth's standing right where he left her, looking confused, watching them go. The next time he looks, though, she's gone.

&#8483; &#8483; &#8483;

Back home. He gets Hen in bed, late—tomorrow will probably be hell—and sits on his porch for a minute. The girls down the street are really at it, standing out in the yard and smoking and laughing and yelling at each other to *shut up, shut the hell up, oh my God.* He goes across the street, turns a light on in one of the back bedrooms, comes back and sits in his own house and watches the glow. It's cool again tonight. He turns the attic fan on low, drags air in through the windows, listens to the enormous hum, feels the floor vibrate. He's hung the fan just wrong enough to shake the whole house. Eventually, he'll have to get back up in the ceiling with some foam or something, put that under the edges of the fan, see if that might cut down on the shaking. He gets a beer, clicks The Weather Channel on. Rain in Portland, 106 in Phoenix. Storms in the Midwest and in Kentucky. Nothing in North Carolina. Maybe showers later in the week. A woman in a pink suit shows the radar loop of a thunderstorm moving through Austin over and over. She's new. He doesn't think he's ever seen her before. She's pointing to the storm, then spreading her palm wide like she's wiping something off the rest of Texas.

Hendrick is asleep. The house hums and bounces. Bethany is either still at Moses Cone, waiting, or she's driving Canavan back to his house. She'll stop at the grocery, offer to buy him whatever he wants. *Peach ice cream? Chips? Nothing? Are you sure?* She'll get him back home, get him set up in the bed or on the sofa, leg elevated, glass of water, fancy pain pills. He'll fall asleep and she'll walk the house, trying to figure out what to do now.

How pissed off he is comes and goes, which worries him, because he feels like here's one more thing he's getting wrong. He feels like anybody else would be over there trenching his yard every night, would be slashing their tires, would be standing in the driveway screaming at her, demanding things. *Stella!* Anybody else would have stood there in the hospital and asked her to end it, to come home, finally, would have said *Isn't this about enough?* He's not talking to a lawyer, he's not asking for a divorce. He doesn't go to strip clubs, doesn't go home with the woman at the Brightwood with the tattoo of the world globe. He doesn't tell Hendrick that his mother is a stonehearted bitch, doesn't even tell Butner that. Because she isn't. That's half his problem right there.

He watches more radar, runs a checklist of what he's got to do before he can get a sign in the yard across the street. Get the house sold, or ready to sell, and that'll help. Prime and paint. Sand the floors. They hired the floors out over here, but he watched the guy do it, thinks it might be something he could do himself. The weather goes to commercial. Toyota, allergy medicine, a gun show coming to the Coliseum. The local forecast is supposed to come on next, but the feed's all wrong, and instead he gets loops of the visible satellite for the Pacific Northwest, for central Canada. His doorbell rings, and he looks at the clock on the microwave: It's ten-thirty. Yul Brynner goes apeshit, comes flying down the hall, barking, puts his nose right up against the door. It's way too late for it to be anybody trying to convert him to anything. It could be the police. It could be Bethany, ready to apologize, ready to help him figure out just what it is that they've done to each other. He gets hold of Yul Brynner, opens the door, and it's Rena. The dog stops barking, wags like crazy. She's standing there holding two bottles of red wine. She's been crying. She says, "Hi."

He says, "Rena." She's wearing jeans with holes in the knees and a thin T-shirt that says ORE-IDA OVEN CRISP FRIES on it.

She holds up the wine. "This is the best I could find at your quickie mart down the street."

"Did you dye your hair?" he says. It's blue at the ends.

"Yeah," she says. "I thought I should try it. You know—kid stuff. While I was out on my own." She looks at him, looks behind him into the house. "What have you tried? Since you've had the place to yourself?"

"Nothing," he says. Her hair looks good. Strange, but good.

"Too bad," she says. "Guess what? Terry called me from the hospital. Seems my boyfriend has sustained an injury. I think I've got most of the story now."

"I was supposed to call you. I'm sorry. I just didn't know what to say."

"What's there to say? Let me in your house. Let's drink all this wine."

"OK," Jack says, and he lets her in, follows her into his kitchen, watches her dig through his drawers, watches her work his shitty wine opener into first one cork and then the other. She opens both bottles. She's got little ropes of muscle in her elbow. He gets them a couple of tumblers out of the cabinet, sets them down on the counter.

She fills each glass almost to the brim. "Cheers," she says, picking hers up, holding it out.

"Cheers," says Jack.

Rena looks at the tile floor, at the plywood wall. "Well," she says. "I love what you've done with the place." She takes a long drink from her glass, smiles. The attic fan is rattling the dishes in the cupboard. Rena says, "Tell me all about your day, dear."

And he does.

# Olives
# in the
# Street

Jack Lang. Always the kind of name Little League coaches latched onto without any problem whatsoever, rolled in the mouth and shouted across the diamond: LANG! Like that. WATCH IT IN, LANG! HERE WE GO! LOOK ALIVE OUT THERE! SHADE HIM TO THE RIGHT, LANG! YOUR OTHER RIGHT! YOU PAYING ATTENTION, LANG? BE A HITTER, NOW, LANG, BE A HITTER! YOU COULDN'T HAVE HIT THAT WITH A CANOE PADDLE! HOW YOU GONNA HIT IT WHEN YOU'RE SQUEEZING YOUR EYES SHUT? WHEN YOU'RE PULL- ING YOUR HEAD OUT? PRETEND THERE'S A STRING BETWEEN YOUR LEFT ELBOW AND YOUR RIGHT FOOT, LANG! HOLD THE BAT LIKE IT'S AN EGG, LANG, AN EGG YOU'RE TAKING HOME TO YOUR MOMMA! NOW YOU'RE READY, LANG! HERE WE GO, NOW! LET'S GO, LANG!

His last coach, though, was not a yeller. Forrest Adair. His Pony League coach, his last serious baseball, thirteen and fourteen years old. Coach Adair drove an ancient silver-blue Cadillac, blue crushed velvet interior, spoke hubcaps. He kept all the practice equipment in the trunk: Extra gloves, a bag of baseballs, old splitting sack bases, a metal fungo bat he used for practice. Miss Fungo. *Here, Lang. Carry Miss Fungo for me.* Stood there and smoked while he hit pop flies one-handed with that skinny, strange bat, muttered at his players around the side of his cigarette. *Get under it, Lang. Two hands, now. Two hands. Fundamentals.* You struck out, you let a ball between your legs: *Fundamentals.* Knee in the dirt, eye on the ball. They worshipped him. On uniform day he'd come bouncing over the speed bumps, springs and shocks creaking, park across two spaces, hand out jerseys from his trunk, smoke cigarettes one after another. *Lang, which number you want? Five? Good. Five's a good number.*

Jack quit baseball in high school. By then almost everybody was bigger than he was, taller—not that height and weight mattered nearly so much as being able to hit a curveball. They could, he couldn't. He was never what anybody would have called a *natural athlete.* He played hard—he *hustled,* coachspeak for having no idea what else to say: *HUSTLE, LANG!*—but he was not going to get recruited to play for some college somewhere, was not ever going to get drafted in the late rounds by the Royals. It was never going to be a matter of *how much you want it, Lang.* He could set challenges for himself all day long and give the full 110 percent and he was still going to be a little slow, a little clumsy, at least compared to the Lee Swearingens of the world. Lee was the kid on that Pony League team a step or two ahead of everybody else on the puberty curve, six feet and change at fourteen, already shaving every day, a mystery to all of them. He was the kid who could hit the ball over the trees past the right field fence and down the hill into the Mercedes dealership. The pissed-off salesmen would come up to the practice field, shiny gray suits and black shoes, holding baseballs, wanting to know about *damages.* Coach Adair would shrug his shoulders, smoke his cigarette, say to them, *I don't know, boys, I just don't.* Grinning. *I can hardly tell the kid where to hit it, can I?* Not the sort of man with a whole lot of time for Mercedes dealers. They'd leave, and he'd go back to pitching batting practice, serving up fat ones for Lee, hoping like hell for another blistering shot over the pines in right.

Jack did play softball, though, in college, at Georgia, for an intramural coed team, the Early Modern British Women. He was majoring in history—liked the line of it, the same wars in the same places, the same hordes sweeping across the same plains. He played shortstop for the Early Moderns, batted cleanup for the first time in his life. This was more his speed. His senior year, the team made an improbable glorious run to the coed quarterfinals, but was crushed by a team one of the sororities put together, the Delta Force, full of pretty thin blonde girls in tiny shorts, plus huge ringers from the baseball team's practice squad. Those guys gave 110 percent. They strove all over the place. The game was called after four innings, the Delta Force leading 17–0. Mercy rule.

Jack the historian graduates and goes on to Carolina, to grad school, to get officially certified as smart, as the man who sees it all now, his undergrad in American and British, his Master's/PhD track in something he'd tell people at parties was going to be a kind of history of land usage. He'd stand on someone's run-down front porch in the middle of the night, half-drunk, and say, *You know, a history of the United States through the lens of the way we use the land*. The *lens*. He'd loved that word. Thought it made him sound like a thinker. He was drunk a lot in grad school. They all were. They'd go to long afternoon classes, and then out to the bars, yell at each other about whether John Crowe Ransom ought to be as significant a figure as he was. Or Sinclair Lewis, or Upton Sinclair. Jack had a big book in mind. Everybody had big books in mind; everybody was going to be on *Charlie Rose* or *Meet the Press*. His master's thesis was on the Linn Cove Viaduct, *the most complicated bridge ever built*, which cantilevers itself around a mountain in western North Carolina. 1,200 feet long. 153 segments, 50 tons each. *Only one segment is actually straight*, he'd tell anybody who would listen. *Only one. They built it in the air, hung one section off the last. Supreme technological achievement*. He'd been out there several times to take pictures, had 8x10s up all over his apartment. He was expanding his work for his dissertation. Each Wednesday afternoon, when the History and Philosophy faculty and grad students would take on Chemistry and Physics—there was a softball game—his advisor, Dr. Dunst, would tell him that he was under no circumstance to use the phase *one of the marvels of the modern world. Goddamn it all, Lang,* Dunst would say, lacing up his cleats. The man wore cleats for faculty softball. *We've seen enough marvels, don't you think? Aren't you tired of marveling?* Jack played left field, made long diving catches when he didn't really have to. He hit OK.

He meets Beth this way: At a party, cheap can beer on ice in a plastic tub, somebody out on the sidewalk grilling chicken legs and corn on a big red kettle grill propped up on cinder blocks. He half-knew who she was already, had seen her at TA orientations. Sharp chin, green eyes. Art History. She was one of a gang of grad students who all lived on the same street, rented from the same landlord, haphazard apartments cut three and four and five at a time into a handful of slouching Victorians. They had cookouts a few times a year for all comers. She walked up to him at the party, said, "I'm Beth. I know you from somewhere. Do you need a dog?"

"I can't," he told her. "I've already got one." The first week he was in Chapel Hill: Registered for classes, got a dog from the pound.

"What's your name?" she asked.

"Jack."

"Right. I thought I knew you. Are you sure you don't want another one? Another dog?" Her lip was sweating. Her hair was tied up in something. She had barbecue sauce on her shirt. He liked all of that. "Tanya's dog had puppies."

"Who's Tanya?"

"She lives down the street. French Lit. Not my thing, but she's pretty into it."

"I can't get another one, I don't think. Yul Brynner would be pissed."

"Isn't he dead?"

"Is he? Kojak?"

"That's Telly Savalas," she said. "Isn't it?" Telly Savalas. It came down on him. An historical blunder: He'd named the damn dog after the wrong bald guy. Too late now. She leaned over, did something to her sandal. "Anyway," she said. "That's your dog's name? Yul Brynner?"

"He's got a big scar on his forehead," Jack said.

"That," she said, "is excellent."

Deep into the party somebody produced a wooden baseball bat, and they drew bases in the street with chalk, played baseball with the leftover ears of corn. If somebody hit it just right, the thing would disintegrate in a spray of kernels and husk. When the police drove by they'd apologize, get out of the street, wait a few minutes, start over.

He meets her again at the yearly Halloween party the art department throws. It's famous. There's plastic taped to the floor, wall to wall. People come dressed as historical figures, as time periods, as abstract ideas. Beth comes as someone's inner child. Little red polka-dot dress, braids, roller skates. She skates through the door, hits a threshold between the kitchen and the living room, falls, hits her head on the floor and knocks herself out. Jack's one of the ones who picks her up, puts her in a bedroom, unlaces her skates. He goes for ice, and by the time he gets back she's awake, holding her head, crying a little, laughing. "Thank you," she says.

"You're welcome."

"What are you dressed as?" she asks him, taking the ice.

He's glued flags and rocks to a torn windbreaker he found at the Goodwill. He's carrying a Molotov cocktail that he's using as a real cocktail, is drinking out of it. "Sectarian Violence," he says. He's proud of it.

Easy enough after that. Dinners at her place, mostly, a green garage apartment behind one of the Victorians, a tiny, rickety deck off the back of it. And they take the dogs to the lake: Yul Brynner, who she loves immediately, and Austria, hers, an ancient German Shepherd. White around the muzzle and all the way back to her ears. Yul Brynner will run off, disappear for half an hour at a time. Aus stays glued to Beth. *You don't worry when he's gone like that?* she asks him. Jack says he's gotten used to it, but he worries every time. *Why art history?* he wants to know, over glasses of wine, over chicken casserole, over coffee in the mornings. *I don't know,* she tells him. *I just love it. I don't think I could imagine doing anything else.* Jack's been starting to worry that he might not feel that way about his own work: He likes history in his own way, likes the Viaduct still, but he's half-ready to admit to himself that all that's mainly owing to the fact that he's good at it. That it's maybe more like a hobby for him. He's not sure any more that he loves it the way his classmates seem to, knows he's probably supposed to. He can imagine doing something else. He just doesn't have any idea what that might be.

Beth is steady, she's funny, she's not crazy. He's comfortable. He's happy. Austria dies, thirteen years old, and they bury her at the lake. Jack moves into the garage apartment. They get married in her parents' back yard in Knoxville. Dr. Dunst gives them a first edition *Rivers, Aquifers and Watersheds of the Southern Appalachians,* leather-bound.

Beth finishes her dissertation and applies for a job at Kinnett that fall *just to see what happens,* because *it'd be perfect for a couple of years. You could still drive in to Chapel Hill. We'd have enough money to live. You'll finish up and we'll both apply for jobs for real.* They didn't think she'd get it, and then she did. Burlington, North Carolina. Maybe forty-five minutes west of Chapel Hill, an old mill town, dying since the early eighties because all the socks and pillowcases get made in China now. And Kinnett's not even in Burlington. It's in Kinnett College, North Carolina, which sits right next to Burlington. There's a town hall and a fire station and a little run of storefronts, all owned by the college. And there is the college itself, immaculately landscaped—

botanical labels on every tree, flower gardens anywhere possible. Beth scores Jack an adjunct gig and they move, rent a plain brick box of a house on the west side of Burlington, close enough to bike to campus. A couple of miles. Beth is the second of two art historians. Rena's the other one, and they're joined at the hip right from the start. Rena invites them over for dinner, and soon enough it's every couple of weeks all fall, all year, all the time. Rena and Beth and Jack and Rena's boyfriend, Canavan. They sit up late into the night yelling at each other about Kinnett politics and general politics and eventually Canavan the tree surgeon will work himself toward some kind of proclamation about whether or not Bradford Pears are too fragile for landscaping, or about how to cure green wood. It becomes, simply enough, a life.

Jack teaches the freshman core classes. It's easy, teaching—at least the rhythm of it is, comfortable, back to work in the fall, summer vacation right as you get too tired to do it one more day. And he likes the crazy GenHum courses, basically the history of everything. Art and culture and geopolitics. What amounts to an excuse to roll in there and go for an hour and a half about whatever's happening in the world. Floods. Gaza. High-fructose corn syrup. He gets approval from Chapel Hill to postpone his dissertation hours. He has six years, they tell him. Finish when you want to. Dunst tells him it's a solid first job, says it'll be good for him. *Take it where you can get it, Lang, believe you me. Write your bridge book when they fire you.* By now he's fully afraid he'll never write his bridge book, that he might not have it in him. So he takes it where he can get it. He teaches.

The year Beth is pregnant with Hendrick he starts going to Rookie League Burlington Indians games with Canavan. He's a little in love with Canavan, because they all are, and for Jack it's because Canavan's plenty smart enough, but has no real time for all the bullshit that comes with being smart. At least not how it goes over at The College, anyway. That's what Canavan calls it. *The Col-*

lege. Now I don't know how y'all would do it over at The College, he says, and
then he'll go on to explain how half of them over there wouldn't even know
how to fire up their own weedeaters without some kind of panel discussion on the
ontology of the string pull. Canavan's probably the only person Jack
knows well outside of school, outside of the academy, someone
who never says pedagogy or learning strategies or goals and objectives. He's
someone who just wants to go to ball games with him. Rena and
Beth come along once or twice, but it's mainly Jack and Canavan,
cheap beer, cheap hotdogs, bad baseball. Games end up 12–10. Er-
rors everywhere. Most games, a woman who's got season tickets
right above the visiting dugout gets up and sings along with "Green
Acres" when they play it over the loudspeakers. Top of her lungs.
The visiting team looks up at her and stares. The crowd cheers
while she belts it out: Darling I love you but give me Park Avenue. Jack and
Canavan give her a standing ovation every time.

When Hendrick is born, it's Rena and Canavan who come to the
hospital in Greensboro, who are the first people who aren't Jack's
parents or Beth's mother to see Beth. No one sees the baby, not yet.
He's four weeks premature, is whisked off to the ICU immediately,
the doctors serious and frowning but saying Don't worry, it's just a
precaution, we'll bring him back, we'll bring him right back. It is hours before they bring him back, and when they do, he's in a little glass
case, tubes running into and out of it. He had some trouble breathing, but
he's doing fine now, breathing on his own. In his glass case, Hen looks like
something from a museum, or something for sale—a leg of lamb,
a bolt of cloth. His hands and feet are blue, and this is what Jack
focuses on, keeps asking the nurses if his hands will be that way
forever. That's perfectly normal, they tell him. The more honest ones
say It's really nothing to be concerned about, this sometimes happens, he should
be better later tonight or tomorrow. Rena and Canavan wait until the doctors say they can come back to see the baby, see Hendrick, named
for Beth's grandmother, her maiden name. They tell Beth he's
beautiful. Jack realizes as Rena says it that he hasn't said it yet,

apologizes again and again after they're gone. *I just forgot. I'm sorry. In all of that, I forgot.*

Rena and Canavan are also the first people who aren't Jack's parents or Beth's mom to come to the house after Hendrick comes home. They arrive with groceries, cook the meal, clean up when they're finished. Jack has not once in his life imagined that he could be this tired, that he could feel like this and still walk through his day. The four of them sit quietly in the living room, watch Hendrick sleep on a blanket on the sofa. It's mid-August. School starts in two weeks and Beth's off for the semester, maternity leave. Jack can't quite conceive of going back to school, but in a way, he needs it, needs something predictable in his life. Lectures, papers, tests. A knowable pattern.

In the evenings, he'll go in there and watch Hen sleep. He can't wrap his head around the notion of having another person in the house. They have made him. Three years ago he was standing on a porch in Chapel Hill drinking beers with sixteen other grad students. Now he's a *father*, for Christ's sake. The two mandatory parenting classes at the hospital were nowhere near enough. Don't shake the baby. Don't bathe him in scalding water. OK. But then what? Does he start saving all his quarters to pay for college? Is the house big enough? Do they have enough rooms? What do babies eat once they stop nursing? He stands in the baby food aisle at the grocery and looks at all the jars lined up like paint chips. Peas and Carrots. Prunes. Pears. Right next to all that, the diapers. He puts Hendrick in the papoose carrier and leashes up Yul Brynner and walks them both around the neighborhood, explaining what he knows to Hendrick, suburban sprawl and watersheds and cul-de-sacs and bridges and why kitchens in postwar homes are so tiny, how we thought we'd never cook again, how everything would come frozen, how we had defeated food.

All fall, Canavan comes over with burgers to throw on the grill, and he and Jack watch the end of the baseball season, the playoffs, the World Series. Hendrick, two months old, three, generally falls asleep for good by the second inning, either in his little motorized swing or in a folding crib Jack keeps behind the sofa. Beth gets to go to bed, and Jack does the night feeding. Hen's already, for the most part, sleeping through the night. Jack and Canavan cheer for both teams, cheer for the Series to run on longer, talk about the infield fly rule, four-seam fastballs, the Texas steal. About the women in Jack's classes, about how Canavan drives through the college between tree jobs just to see the girls walking the sidewalks. Every other weekend or so, the four of them—the five of them—have dinner. Jack's classes go fine. Hendrick slowly catches up to most of the benchmarks in the baby books. Eye contact. Smiles when talked to. Responds to his name. Jack turns in his grades and he and Beth get their spring schedules worked out to where she'll teach mornings, he'll teach afternoons. Someone always home with Hen. No day care. They can't afford it, anyway. Christmas with his parents in Atlanta, New Year's back home, eight-dollar champagne, the two of them trying to stay up long enough to watch Dick Clark make the ball drop in New York. Spring semester, summer, Hen's first birthday: There's a sheet cake Beth cuts into the rough shape of a dog, ices to look like Yul Brynner. Photos of Yul Brynner with his own piece, icing all over his face, photos of Yul Brynner and Hendrick looking like long-lost brothers.

When does it happen? It's another World Series, so it's October, just into November. On television, the pitchers blow into their cupped hands to keep them warm. Hen's almost sixteen months old. He gets quieter, at first, seems a little withdrawn. Like he's maybe considering something. Then he quits trying to talk. For a week he doesn't make any noise at all, doesn't acknowledge their presence, even, except to watch them. He stops making facial expressions. Jack and Beth take him to a restaurant, get him into a high chair. This is new, taking him out, but because he's so damn *still*, they can. In his high chair, he doesn't move, does not fuss or complain. He slumps down a little and ignores the beads that slide across the bar in front of him. He doesn't chew his blanket. *Your son is so well behaved*, the waitress says. *He's so serious.* Jack thanks her. Another half-week goes by, and then there's one long Wednesday where he does make noise again, finally, but he makes all of it, all at once, everything he's been saving up. He screams for hours. No tears. Just noise. They're worried he can't breathe, or that he won't. His face goes red, the skin of his arms hot and dry to the touch. Now they've got to ask somebody. Now they've got to take him in. On the phone, when he calls to make the appointment, Jack describes the symptoms. *First he was quiet. Now we can't get him to stop screaming.* They get an appointment for that day.

The week collapses into a cycle of appointments. It's cold out, Carolina late fall, everything gray and brown. *Could still be nothing,* that first doctor says. *Could still be nothing.* But even in the way he says it, there's an undertow. Still. Could still. The second doctor, Dr. Kriedle, draws blood, does some reflex tests. She picks him up and holds him upside down, and he curls up, a shrimp. *Look at that,* Beth says. *No*, Dr. Kriedle says. *That's not right. He should be hanging down. Like a pendulum.* She sends them on to another doctor, the one who tells them it could be anything, everything, asks them to sit down, says, *I want you to hear me out and ask questions whenever you like,* says *late onset* and *spectrum disorder* and *it's too early to tell* and *regular intensive therapies.* They sit there and look at her and Jack says, *I have to finish classes. I have to give finals in a month. We're going to Beth's mother's for Thanksgiving.* They go back to Dr. Kriedle, and she says, *I don't think we're talking about institutionalization here. But this is the long haul.* Jack remembers that so clearly, remembers the way her mouth looked when she said *long haul.*

After that appointment, Jack drops Beth and Hen off at home, goes to the bookstore, gets the clear feeling that he's falling through himself. He buys every book they have on the subject—*The Autistic*

Child. Boy in a Box. My Life with Samuel. The man working the register
looks at him like he's buying books about autistic children. They
get pamphlets from the doctors, get support group flyers in the
mail. Jack reads everything he can find. *Autistic children are usually
boys. Autism can strike anywhere between birth and six years. These children
often have little sense of themselves. Our Christopher was a gift from God. Sensitivity to light. To loud noises. To sudden movement. The autistic child has little
understanding of his body in space.*

*The autistic child has little to no object permanence.* Jack had to look that
up. He bought a medical dictionary, made space for it on the shelf
in the den. Object permanence: Remembering something exists
after it's removed from one's field of vision. Jack wonders if he
himself has any object permanence. What now, what next? Doctors. Endlessly. Diets and physical therapy—Hendrick's stopped
moving himself around, stopped doing much of anything. Forget
about benchmarks: He's just quit. They get a huge canvas beach
ball from Dr. Kriedle, roll him around on it, trying to teach him
balance. When he does sit up again, he's six months behind. And
when language comes back—he's two and a half, so it's another
full year, a bizarrely silent year—it's the complete text of a *News-
week* article on the decline of Amtrak. Beth and Jack are standing in
the kitchen, grazing in the fridge for leftovers, for anything they
can cobble together for a late dinner, and Hendrick, clear as anything, says *George Santos, regional line manager for Amtrak, notes that rider-
ship is down, and that he's not sure how to get it back. Safety violations pose a
problem, too.* Beth and Jack sneak into the room behind him, just out
of his line of sight, and listen to him. He's been playing with books,
with newspapers, but they had no idea he could read. At two and
a half, he can read. But it's not even that: These are the first words
of any kind he's strung together in almost a year, the first time he's
done anything, really, besides point at what he wants—Pop-Tarts,
pretzels—and grunt. It is like someone has plugged him back in,
but to the wrong socket.

The therapist—at least their seventh or eighth—tells them the only way they'll be able to potty-train him is to sit there with him, to literally move him into the bathroom except for sleeping. They'll try anything: Hen has taken to smearing his shit across the walls of his room. It takes the better part of two weeks. It's March. Jack sets the little TV up in there and sits on the edge of the tub, Hen on the toilet, and they watch spring training games on cable. On St. Patrick's Day, all the teams wear green versions of their uniforms, and Hendrick loves that. He repeats, word-for-word, the commercials, what the announcers say. He's a faucet turned on, an open valve. *Jim, I'll tell you, if this kid can get that circle change figured out, he'll make this club. And not just make it. He'll be a contributor.* The way he's able to get hold of words. Holy hell. They watch the games and every fifteen minutes or so they go through the flashcards the therapist gave them, these insane squatting stick figures pissing and shitting. This is Jack's life now—to somehow supply for Hendrick the notion that his ass is part of his body, too.

Once they do get him potty-trained, he spends forever in the bathroom. He'll go in, forget why he's there, and read or spin the toilet paper roll and just disappear. The first few times, Jack jimmied the lock with a coat hanger, found him sitting there. He wasn't drowning, wasn't having seizures. He was just sitting there, happy as he ever got. Now they'll stand at the door, call in to him. *Hen, buddy, are you alright? What are you doing in there?* Silence at first, and then, if they're lucky, one time out of five, or ten, he'll say, *I am making a poop.* What makes him respond sometimes and not others, they don't know. They never know. None of the books know. Most often he just picks up mid-sentence in whatever he's reading. Like they've switched on the audio feed. *We are experiencing technical difficulties. Please stand by.*

That spring, the spring Hen is almost three, Jack's teaching two sections of GenHum II. His third class, a gift from his chair, is a 300-level seminar on westward expansion. The Donner Party.

Custer. Bloody Kansas. The Golden Spike. It is not a generally pretty history, and this freaks the kids out. Any criticism of anything is unpatriotic, is un-American. No, he tells them. It isn't. *We did do these things.* He works them through how anyone who fails to understand history etcetera, and their eyes roll back in their heads, their ball caps come further down. But he's got a few smart ones in there, kids he likes, a little group of eight or ten juniors and seniors who do the readings, ask good questions, hold the class together. Kids who don't need PowerPoint slides of everything, kids who seem to believe in actual books with actual pages. It's those kids who stay after class, who email him, who ask him about Beth, about his life. *So you and the other Professor Lang are married.* The girls want to see pictures of Hendrick, of Yul Brynner. It's those kids who invite him out for beers that May, after they hand in their final papers, and he goes, asking each of them if they're old enough. They are, or they lie to him, and it doesn't matter, really. Why shouldn't he go? They end up at a place far enough off campus to where he's reasonably sure he won't be seen by that many people anyway, a little pizza and beer place in Burlington. Gubbio's. They drink a few pitchers around, eat pizza, ask Jack questions about his weekends, his house, where he went to school. He's a zoo animal to them. Teacher in the wild. They're trying to get hold of him as an actual person with an actual life, as someone who does not simply materialize in front of them every Tuesday and Thursday at 2:10. He is a person who has a vegetable garden. They have never even thought about growing such a thing as a zucchini. This is what their parents do. But he's still young enough to seem like one of them, or for them to think he is, or could be. They probe. He does not tell them much about Hendrick, doesn't tell them he's autistic. That belongs to him. That is what he doesn't share.

The students straggle out of Gubbio's in little clumps until finally and somehow it's just the one girl left, his favorite, Sarah Cody. He realizes what's happening while it's happening, but can't do much about it, or doesn't want to. He didn't do this. They did. The kids invited him out, he said yes. It's only nine o'clock. Sarah orders them one more pitcher. *Oh, come on, Jack. Just one more.* He likes that she says his name. She smokes. The waitress comes by and clears the table, looks at them a little longer than she needs to. He wonders how much older than Sarah he looks. The booths are red plastic. The floor is a wood floor. An oversized TV on the wall is playing the Braves at the Mets. It's drizzling in New York, cold. Here it's beautiful, May, the end of the school year, warm afternoons. Sarah tells him about her family in Philadelphia, about her sister's wedding, about how she's going to be the maid of honor, how she has to find a stripper for the bachelorette party. Her final paper was not great, was adequate, a surface exploration of what it means for the western states to have used longitudinal borders instead of geographical ones. She's bright enough, tries hard, just isn't exactly committed to the idea of being a student all the time. But she's his favorite anyway, has been all term. He likes the way she'll get excited about certain ideas, likes that she'll talk without raising her hand. He looks forward to seeing her. She wears T-shirts and jeans, T-shirts and little plain brown shorts. No makeup. Brown hair. Brown eyes.

Halfway through the last pitcher Jack's a little drunk, and she is, too, telling him about her other sister, who's older than she is by ten years. *She's retarded,* she says. *She goes to work at a place that makes lightbulbs. It's sad. She lives in a home. She comes over on holidays. Last year she gave us 60-watt bulbs for Christmas.* As much as anything that's going on here, Jack's relieved to be out of his own house, to be away from the flashcards and the beach ball and how completely tired they are by the time Hendrick's in bed. He registers this in little washes of guilt, but still: It's like he's been living a different life altogether since Hendrick was born, and a second and parallel one on top of that since he was diagnosed. He and Beth move through the house in occasionally intersecting orbits, but he's got the TV, got his baseball and weather and shows on PBS about the history of Tupperware, and she's got her little studio, the back bedroom, where she revises her dissertation when she can, still hoping for her book. Jack doesn't write at all any more, hasn't answered a string of emails from Dr. Dunst about when he might resume his dissertation hours. They grade papers over red wine at the dining room table, share bad lines, go to sleep.

Sarah Cody sits across the table from him in Gubbio's and tugs at the neck of her shirt, looks at him. She's someone who is maybe aware of her effect on the world, someone who is almost certainly *aware of her body in space.* Also, she's clearly in love with another kid in their little gang. Greg Alessa. When she came in to conference about her paper a few weeks ago, Jack had been amazed to find out they weren't dating. He'd even called him her boyfriend. *Oh, no way,* she said, laughing. *That would never work.* Since then he's seen Greg with the girlfriend, the typical Kinnett girl: Shiny hair, idiotic boots, thousand-dollar pants. He wonders when the last day was that Sarah didn't smoke pot, didn't get drunk. She is rough-edged. She's a little like a version of himself he wishes had existed in another universe, or in this one: He doesn't so much want her as want to *be* her. To take on her life for a while. He drinks his beer. Beth's at home, Hendrick's down for the night. She's probably asleep on the sofa. He's at Gubbio's with Sarah Cody, listening to her stories about how once she passed out on a city bus in Philly, how some girl she knows got arrested in February for selling a mashup of Vicodin and Ritalin mixed into Gatorade, how *my mom wanted to give me a boob job for my birthday.* And what in the hell is he supposed to say back to that? "I think you're doing fine in that department," he says.

She smiles, gives him a raspy giggle, looks away, lights another cigarette. "I probably have to go pretty soon," she says. "You know?"

"Yeah," he says. "Me too."

He signals the waitress, pays their bill, walks her out to her car, a brand new BMW. The money these kids have. She says, "Thanks for coming out with us."

"Thanks for inviting me."

"Yeah," she says. "It was cool." And then she puts her hand on his arm, leans into him a little bit, and he does, in fact, see it coming, sees the whole thing, sees how this is easily the dumbest thing he could possibly do, but sees at the same time how it might also be free, how maybe nothing would come of it, how maybe no one would ever have to know anything about it. Because there's no way he's getting ready to get in his car and follow her home. There's no way she's getting ready to ask him to do that. This is nothing other than a little blip on the radar, something that will happen right here and only right here, a tiny footnoted moment of time. And she knows what she's doing, for sure: She's had her share of the beer, but this is a girl who does not do something like this accidentally. You can read that much on her. For Sarah Cody, this will be like kissing a friend at a party. He should not do this, should not, and he does it anyway. In the fluorescent light from the Gubbio's sign, in the parking lot, in Burlington, North Carolina, the cars whipping by out on the highway, she wraps her hand around to the small of his back and then there he is, kissing Sarah Cody, twenty-one years old, his student. She tastes like cigarette smoke and something sweet. He can smell her deodorant, can smell her sweat a little bit through that. He puts a hand in her hair, something he's wanted to do since he called her name on the roll. Sarah Cody. Her tongue hits his lip and she presses her hips against him for as long as it takes the light up at the intersection to change, then pulls away. She smiles, looks at the ground, looks through her car keys. "Yeah," she says. "OK." He can see she's already working on it, scripting it for her friends. *We were pretty drunk. It was hilarious.*

He doesn't know what to do next. He can hear his own blood moving through his head. She gets her car door open, and he steps back. She says, "Well, you drive safely there, Jack."

He says, "You too." He says, "Are you OK to drive?"

"Sure I am." Her eyes are bright.

"Good," he says. "I was just checking."

"Thanks, Dad," she says, trying to make a joke out of it, but it comes out heavily, makes everything stranger, and she gets in the car, backs it out of the space, rolls the window down and waves at him. "See ya," she says, and laughs, shakes her head, and pulls out of the lot. Like that, she's gone. He's a letch, a coward. But it was worth it. It was. That's what he tells himself on the way home, holding the speedometer steady at 45, driving as straight as anyone has ever driven. It was worth it. He can still taste her. He finds 1100 on the AM out of Cleveland and listens to their postgame show. He puts both hands on the wheel. Ten and two. He drives home. He's a fool. Sarah Cody. Gum and smoke.

❦ ❦ ❦

Rena and Jack drink both bottles of wine, and he wakes up with a pretty good headache. And late. The clock blinks at him. They've lost power sometime during the night. No storms, but this happens: Old neighborhood, old electric. On and off. The angle of the sun on the floor means it has to be at least 9:30. He pulls on a pair of shorts, a T-shirt, hurries down the hall.

Hen's in front of his cabinet: Not new. What is new is Rena lying on the sofa under a blanket, the green thing they keep in the closet for picnics. Pieces of last night slide back into focus, ambling conversations about old girlfriends and religion and a man she'd been engaged to before she met Canavan. She's got a Ziploc bag of ice on her forehead. The wine glasses are on the counter, and Jack picks them up on his way to the coffeemaker, sets them next to the two empty bottles. *Let's drink all this wine.* Yul Brynner's on the floor, on his side, belly up against the couch, front legs out in front of him like he's flying sideways through the world. He thumps his tail. "Jesus, shit," Rena says.

Jack nods *yes*. His head's heavy, full of sand. Everything on this side of the kitchen is plugged into extension cords that run into the hallway. When he knocked the wall out, he had to cut the circuit to the outlets in the kitchen. One more thing for Beth to mark down in the ledger. Jack sits next to Hendrick once he's got the coffee going. The tile is cool on the backs of his legs. He rubs Hen's back. Closed. Forehead. Open. "How long's he been up?" he asks.

"Not long," says Rena. "When I woke up, he was still asleep."

"Really?"

"Or just hanging out in his room," she says. "I don't know." She watches him do the cabinet. "That doesn't hurt him?"

"Not usually." Jack reaches for him anyway, though, takes his chances, puts his hand flat on the cabinet in front of Hen's head. "Hendrick," he says. "Buddy. You're making my head hurt, OK?"

Hen makes a few noises, looks at him.

"Your head," Jack says. "Not today, OK? That hurts."

Hendrick sits up straighter, knocks his knuckles together, then digs at his nose, wipes his finger on the tile. He says, "The Greensboro Grasshoppers: They're Hoppin' Fun."

"They are?" Jack asks him. After they got through the wine, he remembers now, they moved on to whiskey.

"Call today to book your Family Fun Package," Hen says. He's getting himself cranked up.

"Would you flick on the weather?" Jack asks Rena.

"What?"

"The weather. The TV. Would you turn it on?"

She does, and the sound comes pouring out, huge in the room: LET'S GO NOW TO THE TROPICAL UPDATE. She shrinks back from it into the sofa, winces, holds the remote out at arm's length, turning it down. Hen gets up immediately, goes and sits on his knees in front of the screen. He rocks back and forth while a pregnant woman in a blue shirt explains that most June tropical storms originate in the Gulf and the Caribbean. There are pulsing kidney-shaped areas showing where the storms begin, animated arrows showing where they tend to go after that: To Texas, to Kentucky, to Nova Scotia. Rena wads up the blanket, leans against it. She's on his sofa. His life feels half-cooked. Jack reaches for the phone, to call the yard. Ernesto picks up after a couple of rings. "Hey, Ernesto," Jack says. "It's me."

"Yes," says Ernesto.

"Everything OK over there? Just checking in."

"Everything is fine," he says. "Butner will probably want the truck. Eventually."

"No problem," Jack says. "I'll bring it in about an hour." Ernesto says nothing. "Tell him I'll bring it in about an hour."

"OK." He hears one of the loaders get louder, then cut off. Ernesto shouts, then gets back on the phone. "I told him," he says.

"Is everything else OK?"

"Everything else is OK. We haven't knocked anything over today."

"Great."

"Terry Canavan cut off his foot, Butner says."

"Almost."

"*Castigo.*"

"What?" Jack asks.

"It's nothing. It's a figure of speech."

"What's it mean?"

"Something like, 'That's what happens.'"

"Right."

"Listen," says Ernesto. "We have customers. I should go."

"Oh," Jack says. "Sorry."

"It's OK," Ernesto says. "*Adiós,*"

"*Adiós*," says Jack, and hangs up. On TV, there's a green blob spinning off the coast of Cuba, and a graphic comes up that says *First Named Storm of the Atlantic Season*. He pours himself a cup of coffee, pours one for Rena. "Headed this way?" he asks her.

"They don't seem to know."

The blue-shirt woman sends it over to a guy in a suit, who keeps talking about the tropics. A new graphic runs the storm name across the bottom of the frame: *Tropical Storm Ashley*. "Ashley," Jack says. It doesn't sound fierce enough. It sounds like a baby-sitter.

Hendrick says, "Here are your tropical storm names for the season. Ashley. Bruce. Claudette. Diego. Eliza. Frederick. Grace." He keeps going through to the end of the list, Wanda, then starts over, runs it again.

"I take it you boys watch a little weather around here," says Rena.

"A little bit," Jack says. "We like knowing what's coming."

"That's sound." She tilts her head back, puts the Ziploc on her forehead. "I'm wounded," she says.

"Me too."

"Red wine," she says. "Not your friend."

"Tell that to the Italians."

"It was French," she says. "I couldn't believe your quickie mart had French."

"They're good down there."

"That wine wasn't," says Rena. "French or not."

"Yeah," Jack says.

"We should go down there and warn them. We should tell them something's wrong with their wine. Tell them it's broken."

"I'm right behind you," Jack says. "Just let me finish this coffee."

"Check." She gets up, readjusts her ice, walks to the sliding glass doors, looks out at his yard. On the TV, the blue woman is back, has given up on the tropics, is talking about thunderstorms in up-state New York. "Thanks for letting me stay the night," Rena says.

"Neither one of us could have driven you home."

"I know, but still. Thanks."

"You're welcome."

She taps on the glass. "No offense, but for you being a land-scaper, your back yard kind of looks like shit."

"I'm not a landscaper."

"I mean, I like those flowers over there, in the back, those are nice—"

"The daylilies?"

"Is that was those are? The orange ones? I never know. I like those. But the rest of the yard pretty much sucks, doesn't it?"

There's a skinny run of grass out to the left-hand side, but the rest is mainly weeds. He hasn't cut it in a couple of weeks. Every-thing's long. The fence is covered over in some vine. There's a big patch where there's only bare ground right behind the house. "I hit the water doing the kitchen wall," he says. "There was a flood. It took out a lot of the grass."

"Yeah," she says. "The kitchen." She walks around the island, knocks on the plywood wall. She's inspecting the premises. "Did I ask you about this last night? About what it is you're up to?"

"I was going to surprise her. I was going to put in a breakfast nook. A little sunroom."

"Surprise," she says. "Holy shit, right?"

"I know."

"Sorry," she says. "I think it'll be nice when you get it all fin-ished." She's wearing her same clothes, the Ore-Ida T-shirt, the worn-out jeans. Her blue hair is like what would be left over the next day from some Halloween costume. She keeps stretching her toes, laying them back down on the floor one by one. "I like the tile," she says.

"It's discontinued. I can't find any more."

"Well, it's still pretty. What's here is, anyway."

"Thanks," he says. "At least you think so."

"Beth doesn't like it?"

"She didn't tell you about all this?"

"She talks about it in kind of vague, grand terms. She says 'renovation' a lot."

"She's pretty pissed off."

"And now she's with Terry," Rena says. "Which is pretty fucked up, if I do say so myself."

"I'm sorry I didn't tell you," he says.

"You're sorry? What would you have said? Who needs to be sorry—and I feel pretty sure about this—is not us. I don't know if either one of us owes anybody sorry right about now."

"Yeah," Jack says. He watches her work her toes along a line of grout. Her toenails are painted brown. Outside, an engine starts up. A lawn mower, or something bigger. Probably the neighbor, Frank, doing something to his yard. "Do you want some breakfast or anything?" he asks. He should have asked her before, been a better host.

"I don't eat it."

"OK."

"I mean," she says, "sometimes leftovers. I like having coffee and Chinese. I like the sound the spoon makes on those takeaway Styrofoam boxes, you know? But not regular cereal or anything like that. I don't believe in cereal."

"How do you not believe in cereal?"

"I just don't. Anyway. About our good friends Beth and Terry." She puts her mug down on the counter. "This has been going on a week and a half, right?"

He counts it up. "I guess so."

"And you're doing nothing?"

"What are you doing?"

She checks her watch. "Hang on, alright? I've known for eleven hours. But you," she says. "You've known for eleven days. I don't get it. What's your plan?"

"I'm waiting it out," he says. "I'm seeing what happens."

"That's your plan?"

"I guess so," he says.

"That is not a plan."

"It's the one I have."

"It's shitty," she says. "It's nothing."

"What's yours, then?" he asks.

"Give me eleven days, and I'd have something."

"OK," he says.

"I just can't believe you're not doing anything."

"You started this," he says. "She wouldn't be over there if you were still there."

"Nope," she says, holding a finger out at him. "I don't think we're going to allow that. That doesn't make any sense."

"It makes more sense than you not believing in cereal, or whatever you just said."

"We're not talking about me." She looks around. "Except, you know what it feels like in here? In your kitchen? It feels like I'm making out with my boyfriend. You know that feeling? Like your top's off and now you're just listening out for the sound of the garage door opener so you can frantically look around for your bra and get dressed again before your parents make it inside?"

"Sure," he says. She says things like this at dinner sometimes. He'll catch Beth's eye across the table, she'll shrug her shoulders.

"I mean, except for all the making out and everything. Do you know what I mean?"

He does not know. "Sure," he says again.

"I wore a training bra until I was in ninth grade," she says.

"I never wore one."

"Good, Jackson. That's good." She blows on her coffee, takes a sip, makes a face. "Too hot," she says.

"Do you want an ice cube?"

"No," she says, "God no," and slides past him out into the living room again. She's a little strange. He's always liked her fine, but she's always been a little strange, a little loud, a little sudden. Still, he can't help but think of what she'd look like frantically searching for her bra, and then somehow he's imagining the two of them in high school, except they're in his actual high school girlfriend's bedroom, the light blue carpet, the pink and yellow bed, the window seat, the vaulted ceiling. Right over the garage. His eyes are starting to hurt. He's going to need a Coke or something. Sugar. Liquids. Maybe a cheeseburger.

"Don't you have to go in to work?" asks Rena.

"Not right this minute," he says.

"I heard you on the phone. You have to bring something in."

"They need the truck," he says. "For deliveries."

"So shouldn't you go in?"

"What are you, the Better Business Bureau?"

"I am not, in fact. I'm just looking after your well-being. Your professionalism."

"As long as I get it there in time for Butner to fill it up and for somebody to drive it wherever it's supposed to go, it doesn't matter. One of the perks of being the boss."

"The Patriot of Patriot Mulch & Tree?"

"Something like that," he says. He walks down the hall to check on Hendrick, who's gone to the bathroom. Behind the door, he can hear him saying *We're back live at The Weather Channel, at Hurricane Central. For the latest on Ashley, let's go to Dr. Steve Lyons in the Forecast Center. Thanks, Jeanetta. Let's check those latest coordinates from the National Weather Service.* The TV in the other room is saying basically the same thing. The engine noise from next door cycles up and down, loud and soft, loud and soft.

When he comes back to the kitchen, Rena's sliding one shoe off and on her foot. "I don't think we have any Chinese food," he says. "I might have some carrots you can drag through soy sauce if you want."

"No, thanks."

"Just offering you breakfast," he says. "Which you don't eat."

"Thanks, though," she says, and smiles at him. She says, "I'm glad you didn't kiss me goodnight."

"What?"

"Yeah," she says, getting the shoe on, reaching out with her foot for her other one. "It would have been too soon. Or too weird. Best just to tuck me in, leave me on the sofa. You were a perfect gentleman."

"Thank you?" he says, because now he has no idea what's going on, has no idea what to say, even though he feels like there's probably a right and wrong answer here, feels like when she's talking there might always be a right and wrong answer. He can't quite keep up with her. She's making him nervous, like those light-up tote boards on buildings that keep track of the national debt or tons of carbon dioxide emitted into the air per second or per minute. The numbers just keep ticking up and up.

"Don't freak out," she says. "I'm just fucking with you. We're not riding off into the sunset together or anything, OK? We're not riding off anywhere. Don't worry. Safety first. On belay, or whatever they say when they've got you all tied in."

"What?"

"Rappelling? Like when they've got you tied into the thing, and you have to say *on belay*, and the person on the ground who's got you says *belay on*?"

"I think I remember something like that," he says.

"Good," says Rena. "See? This is not that hard." Outside, the engine noise gets a lot louder. "I didn't mean to scare you," she says. "I'm sorry. Let's not talk about this. Let's go see what your neighbor's doing with that plane or whatever it is instead." She heads for the front door, and he follows her, because what else is he going to do? He takes his headache out onto the front porch, where their two whiskey glasses are still sitting on the rail, wilted mint leaves in the bottom. There's a breeze, but there's heat in it. Next door, Frank is standing in his grass, and he's got a pressure washer going, pressure-washing the boulder that sits in the corner of his front yard. The sun is very, very bright. Jack needs The Duck. When Frank pulls the trigger, when he's washing, the engine whines upward. When he stops, it drops back down again. It's loud. Motorcycle loud. He's wearing a button-down shirt, and he's wearing leather deck shoes, and he's out there with his pressure washer, pressure-washing his boulder. He's pretty much destroying the flowers he's got planted at the base of it. Jack's never seen anybody wash a rock before.

"Outstanding," Rena says, and turns around and goes back inside. Frank works on a corner of the boulder. When Rena comes back out, she's got Hen with her, has got her coffee, and the three of them stand out on the porch while Frank works in thin stripes across the face of the rock. When he finishes that, he starts in on the seams in his driveway, blowing dirt and weeds and everything else that's down in there ten, twelve feet in the air. He's getting mud on his deck shoes, on his shorts. In between seams, he looks up and waves. They all wave back, even Hendrick. Jack wonders who Frank might think Rena is.

"So this is how it goes in the suburbs," Rena says.

"Some days," says Jack.

"It's good to get out and see this again," she says.

"Because you've been in the big city too long?"

"Don't knock those condos," she says. "Very fancy down there. Very. The building next to mine is five whole stories tall."

"My head hurts," he says.

"Mine, too," says Rena. Frank's working the edges of his driveway. She says, "You should go to work."

"What are you going to do?"

"I don't know," she says. Her car's out on the curb.

"Do you want to have lunch or something?" he asks.

"What for?" she says.

"I don't know." He feels stupid. "To eat lunch. If you believe in lunch."

"Today?"

"Sure," he says. "Or some day. We could plan."

"I don't know, Jackson," she says. "Let me think that over."

"OK," he says.

"Great," she says.

"You can stay here a while if you want to," he says, flailing. "Finish your coffee. Take a shower if you want. There are towels in there. Take whatever you want to wear if you want to change clothes. I've got T-shirts on a shelf in the closet."

"OK," she says, looking at him like he's making a speech.

"And I can go in to work."

"Super," she says. "You've got it all figured out. That sounds great."

"Yeah." He feels like probably he shouldn't have to feel like he doesn't belong on his own front porch, but there it is. Or maybe that's not quite it. Maybe it's that he feels like he doesn't know where to stand, doesn't know where his feet should go. "I'm going to get him ready," he says. "Hendrick. To go."

"Good idea," she says. "I like it."

So that's what he does. He takes him in, finds the catalog, grabs him a package of Pop-Tarts from the cabinet, puts his shoes on him. Do what you say you're going to do. *Your word is your bond.* Something his grandfather said to him one summer—there had been a lie about a pocketknife. By the time Jack gets back outside, Rena's set up in a different spot on the railing, is tucked up into herself like a bird. Frank's pressure-washing his chain-link fence. "See you later," Jack says. "Have a good rest of your morning."

She smiles. Her teeth are very small. "You too," she says. "Thanks."

"There's a key in the bowl on the kitchen counter. You can just leave it in the mailbox."

"OK," she says. "I will."

Jack takes a deep breath, nods for a while, and then he walks Hendrick down to the truck, gets him all belted in. The problem is, he likes her up there on the railing, crazy and all. Likes it from here, anyway. He tries not to think about it any more than that. He's bird-watching. That's all. On his way down the driveway, Jack waves at her through the windshield. She waves back. He rolls the windows down. Fresh air. He leaves her there at his house, on his porch.

On the way in to PM&T, Jack works on what it is she's likely to do next. She'll sit out there, finish her coffee, watch Frank wash the fence, wash the wheelwells of his cars. Then: Go inside, maybe take a shower, definitely look through all their drawers and cabinets. That's what he'd do. Look for medicine bottles, dead bodies. After that, who knows? Maybe she'll eat bowls of porridge, lie down on all the beds.

Hendrick flips through his catalog some, then yanks the glove compartment open, looks in there, says, "Nobody beats Carolina Kia. Nobody."

"One-ninety-nine down," Jack says, and before he can even finish, Hen says, right over the top of him, "And one-ninety-nine a month." Jack flicks his blinker on, drifts into the far right lane, turns on the radio. *And now, Traffic and Weather Together with Dave Arbussy in the SkyTracker chopper,* the radio says. Hendrick says, *The Triad's Eye in the Sky.* Jack pulls the visor down, shields himself from the sun coming up off the hood. Hell of a way to start things off. He counts the traffic lights on 70, aims for the yard.

❧ ❧ ❧

Both loaders are right-side-up, nobody's hurt, nothing's on fire, no blood, no ambulances. Score all of that for the good guys. He bumps the truck through the low spots and pulls up next to the cypress pile, turns around neatly, leaves it there for Butner, for the delivery. A yellow scooter is parked over by the office, with a matching yellow trailer the size of a desk hooked up to the back of it. There's a man with a yellow helmet under his arm watching Butner and Ernesto load big slabs of bluestone onto the trailer one by one. After they get each one on, the man leans over, checks the tires on the trailer. Jack hangs back. The man leans over again, nods, hands Butner some money, and drives away, the scooter sounding like Frank's pressure washer. Jack walks Hen over to the office.

"Little man, what do you say?" Butner asks Hendrick.

Hen says, "Tropical Storm Ashley is the first named storm of the Atlantic season."

"That so?"

"Tropical Storm Ashley is churning off the coast of Cuba, and may make landfall in Florida by the weekend."

"You're a regular weatherman," Butner says.

"Jacksonville Tampa St. Petersburg Safety Harbor," says Hendrick.

"Goddamn right," says Butner. He hands Jack a wad of cash. "Eighty bucks for eight rocks. I figured that was fair. It was from the broken pallet, anyway. He said he'd be back for more. He didn't want to overload whatever the hell that thing was, that little trailer. You ever seen a trailer on a scooter before?"

"No," Jack says.

"Me neither." Butner leans in close. "You call over to Canavan's this morning? See how he is?"

"No."

"Good for you, man. Good for you." He runs something out

from underneath his thumbnail, squints in the sunlight. "Well, anyway, we called. He's fine."

"You called? What for?"

"I thought it'd be good. Like a call from the business, you know? A 'How the hell are you, how the hell's your fucked-up leg?' call."

Ernesto says, "Why is it that you have to curse so much in front of the boy?"

"I don't have to, Paco, I just do."

"If you don't stop calling me that, I won't cure your tomatoes."

"What's wrong with the tomatoes?" Jack asks.

"It's nothing," says Butner. "It's the goddamned yellow death. Always happens. Just a little early this year. But Paco here—" The phone rings, and Butner tosses it to Ernesto. "Paco says it's a fungus, says he's got some kind of magic potion."

"It's a disease," Ernesto says. "Nothing more. You need to use *habañero* and baking soda. In a spray. Also, vinegar will work sometimes. Fix it in a week. Two weeks at the most." He stares at Butner. "A spray, you know?" He makes a hand motion like he's spraying. Then he answers the phone. "Patriot Mulch & Tree?"

Hendrick follows Ernesto inside, trailing him, a shadow. Jack says, "You didn't really call over there, did you?"

"Sure we did."

"We did?"

"I did."

"Who answered?" He can't help it, even though neither answer can make him happy.

Butner scratches his cheek, doesn't answer, exactly. "Fucknut said he might be up and around in a week. Said to keep sending business his way." He turns to him. "Why didn't you call, if you're so interested?"

"I was busy this morning," Jack says. Part of him wants to tell

Butner about the possibility that Rena's in his shower right now, washing her blue hair. Part of him doesn't.

"You did go last night, though. To the hospital."

"Yes." What he remembers: The vending machine, the pirate in the fish tank, Beth standing in the automatic doors, looking out at him.

"How was he?"

"I didn't see him."

"Why not?"

"So Beth answered, right?"

"Hey, man, settle down. I think it was a nice middle ground, the phone call. From the guys. You went to the hospital, for chrissakes. And didn't see him?"

"They asked me if I was family. I told them no."

"You always tell them yes," Butner says. "That's easy." A couple of cars pull into the Shell. Two boys in white T-shirts get out, stand there at the pumps and smoke. Butner says, "Last night, after you left, I went on and shredded everything he bled on. Put it in the compost."

"Thanks," Jack says. He looks around, runs a quick mental inventory of the rest of the lot. Hardwood's low. Pine bark's fine. Shredded is fine. The air shimmers in the heat. It's summer, like someone's thrown a lever. He can smell the sweet in the air, can smell the bark and wood rotting into itself. And then he gets himself convinced he can smell Canavan's blood over the top of it, sweeter. He's slipping. There's got to be a pill he can take for this. An empty flatbed bangs by on the highway, brakes for the light. It's ten-thirty. Beth'll be through most of a pot of coffee by now, maybe prepping for class. Maybe changing Canavan's bandage. Maybe bringing him breakfast, ice chips, whatever spectacular meds they give you when you saw halfway through your shin. And Rena—

"You in there?" Butner asks.

"Yeah," he says. "Sorry."

"Come on, *jefe*. Help me water the plants. You need a job."

"I have a job."

"You need a busier one." Butner goes to turn the hose on.

"You didn't water yet?"

"We were covered up right at first. Three trucks in line when I got here. Then we dicked around a while, and then the scooter guy showed up. Just now getting back to the regular same old. Here." He hands Jack the sprayer. "I'll hold, you water. Don't water the birds."

"I'm not going to water the birds."

"OK, but we think the wren hatched hers last night. She's been back and forth a lot. So proceed with caution, know what I'm saying?"

Jack knows what he's saying. He proceeds with caution. His head throbs, a kind of low dull background noise. Wine and whiskey, Rena and Beth. Butner talks, Jack waters, and he's more than happy enough not to have to do anything else but hold the hose at the right angle and listen to Butner screed on about tomato fungus, about varieties of heirloom tomatoes, about blood, about Canavan, about how he was *bleeding like a motherfucking cut-open hog. Didn't you think he was motherfucking bleeding like a hog? I mean goddamn.* They get through almost all of the plants, and they're out at the roses and maples, Butner holding the other end of the hose off the plants and arguing with himself about how many pints of blood a person holds, when Bethany pulls the wagon onto the lot, which can't be right. She's way too early for lunch with Hen. Her being here feels like some magic trick, the tablecloth out from underneath the china. She parks next to a stack of halved barrels they've got up front.

Butner looks up. "Oh shit," he says. "What'd you do now?"

"Nothing," says Jack. "Shut up."

"Must have done something, man," Butner says. Then he says, whispering, "Remember: She's just as afraid of you as you are of her."

"That can't possibly be true."

"It isn't," says Butner. "I was just trying to cheer you up." He takes the hose from Jack, gives him a big, happy smile, says, "See ya," and heads off to finish the watering.

He has no idea what she's doing here. Could be anything: Canavan has died. An intense allergic reaction to the drugs. Or Canavan is miraculously and totally healed. The grinning face of Jesus Christ is in the bloody bandage. Across the lot, Hen comes out of the office, looks both ways, then starts taking laps around the shed. He's not wearing pants, but he's got his shirt and socks and shoes on, and a paper crown, like the kind from Burger King. Ernesto must have brought that to him. Jack shields his eyes with his hand. The sun might be getting brighter. Beth is out of the wagon, walking toward him. He could run. Where he'd run to, he's not sure, but he could run.

"How are you?" she asks. There's a kind of forced shine to her voice. Not good.

"I'm fine," he says.

"Good," she says. "That's really good." Hen comes around the building, the half-naked king. He stops, touches the spigot for the hose, touches his mouth, starts again. "And how's Hen doing?" she says. "He looks terrific. That's a good look for him."

"He's great," Jack says, watching him disappear around the back of the office, materialize again on the other side.

"It's hot," she says.

"It is."

"I didn't think it was supposed to get hot yet."

"There's a tropical storm coming," he tells her.

"Really?"

"Maybe. It was on the weather."

"You were watching the weather."

"Yes."

"Shocking." Beth pushes her hair out of her face, squints. "Guess what?" she says. "Rena called this morning. Checking on Terry."

"That was good of her," Jack says, readying himself for disaster. "So did Butner, he tells me. You're gonna need an answering service over there."

She ignores that. "It was funny, though. About Rena? She was at our house. Our house. Yours and mine."

The breeze picks up, dies back down. "Yeah," he says. "She would have been."

"Perhaps you'd like to tell me why that is?"

"She came by last night," he says. "After she found out about Canavan." She doesn't say anything back to that, so he clarifies. "About you and Canavan."

"Well, isn't that just perfect." She watches Hen. "And now she's staying with you?"

"She's not staying with me. She stayed last night. She turned up at the door."

"That must be a lot of fun for you, Jack."

"Is that why you're here?"

"Why do you think I'm here?"

"I don't know why you're here," he says. "Maybe you need a couple of yards of pine bark. I have no idea. I can get Butner to cut you a deal." Butner looks up, waves.

"What the hell was she doing at our house?"

"You really want to do this?" he says. "I mean, we can do this if you want to."

"Is she there now?"

"I don't know where she is," he says. "I have no idea in the world."

"But she was at our house."

"Yes," he says. "She was." He hasn't done anything wrong here, he reminds himself. He's not the one fucking Canavan. He can ride this out. "How's the patient?" he asks.

"He's in a lot of pain," she says. "Or what seems like a lot of it, anyway."

"You think he's faking?"

"That's not what I meant, of course."

"It's all an elaborate ruse," Jack says. "He didn't even cut himself. It's all special effects. Smoke and mirrors. CGI."

She takes a deep breath. "Try not to be a complete asshole, OK?"

"OK."

"We're supposed to go to the doctor tomorrow to get the bandages changed. To make sure he's not getting infected."

"We are?"

"He is. I'm taking him."

"Oh," Jack says. "That 'we.'"

"Don't talk like that."

"Like what?"

"Well, who's supposed to take him, Jack? He can't drive himself."

"Is that your reason for being over there now? Your new reason?"

"What's she doing in our house, Jack? What's going on with you?"

"Nothing's going on," he says. "She's not doing anything in our house. No one is. She turned up and got drunk and slept on the sofa. We both did. Get drunk, I mean. I didn't sleep on the sofa." Butner's coiling the hose back up. "And besides, what if there was something going on? Who would you be to ask me about it?"

"I'm your wife. I can ask you anything I want to."

They stand out there and look at each other. He doesn't understand what this argument is supposed to be about. Or any argument. Or anything else. He keeps ending up feeling half-insane, or pissed off, or confused. That more than anything else: She confuses the hell out of him.

Ernesto comes out of the office holding Hendrick's pants, intercepts him mid-lap, somehow gets him to put them back on, and Hen takes off running again. Jack says, "So you just came over here to get to the bottom of things? Reconnoiter?"

"Yes," she says.

"Outstanding."

"Oh, shut up," she says.

"Maybe I don't get it," he says. "What is it I've done to you this time?"

"Shut up, Jack, OK? Don't talk. Don't. Let's just stand here and don't talk for a minute. Let's just try that."

Hen comes back around the office. "Here," Jack says. He knows this is a mistake, but he's doing it anyway. He's got to find something to hold onto somewhere. "You'll like this."

"I thought we weren't talking."

"We're not. But you'll like this. This is good." He takes a breath. "Ernesto's been teaching Hen to speak Spanish," he says.

She waits a while before she answers. The wind picks up from off the back of the yard. "Speak Spanish how?" she says.

"He speaks a little Spanish now, is all." He hangs onto it a little bit. "He knows the words for things. He talks to Ernesto."

"He talks to Ernesto in what way?"

"He just does."

"Don't screw around, Jack. That's not funny."

"I'm not. He does. It's impressive."

"He speaks Spanish."

"Yes."

"Hen speaks Spanish."

"That's what I'm telling you."

"No," she says. "No. Don't tell me. Show me." She takes him by the arm, pulls him toward Hen and Ernesto. "Show me right now."

"OK."

"Right now."

"OK," he says, letting her drag him over. Hen comes around the shed again. "Ernesto," Jack says. "Beth would like to hear some of Hen's Spanish, please. If you wouldn't mind."

"Absolutely," Ernesto says.

"This isn't funny, Jack," she says. "You're being mean."

Ernesto catches Hen the next time he comes by, and holds him out at arm's length. He gets him to look at him, says, "*Hola, Hen.*" Hen says nothing. He's out of breath.

"*¿Hen, qué es eso?*" Ernesto asks, pointing to Hen's shirt. Hendrick still doesn't say anything. Beth stands still, and Jack can tell she wants to believe. Hell, he still wants to believe, too, even though he's seen it, even though he already believes it. Ernesto takes hold of the shirt, holds it out in front of him. "*Eso, Hen,*" he says. "*¿Qué es eso?*"

Hen makes a small popping sound, then says, precisely, "*Es una camisa.*" His cheeks are flushed.

"*Bueno, hombre. ¿Qué color?*"

"*Azul,*" Hen says, very quietly.

Jack's ears ring some, and Beth says, "Oh, no," hand in front of her mouth, and then she says, "Oh my God."

"*¿Y qué son esos?*" Ernesto asks him, pointing to Hen's feet.

"*Son mis zapatos,*" Hen says.

"Is he conjugating?" Beth asks. "Is he conjugating his verbs?"

"Not always," Ernesto says.

"Oh, God," she says, sitting down on the ground now, holding onto her head. "When did this happen?" she asks.

"Yesterday," Jack says, then corrects himself: "It's been going on a while. I found out yesterday."

"You didn't tell me. At the hospital, you didn't tell me. I can't believe you didn't tell me."

"I forgot."

"Bullshit."

"We were busy."

"Fuck you," she says. "My God, fuck you. How could you not have told me?" She reaches out for Hendrick. "Do another one," she says. "*Otro*."

"*¿Hablas Español?*" Ernesto asks her.

"*Sí, un poco,*" she says, and then she's off and talking to Ernesto in Spanish, longer questions and answers Jack can only barely get the gist of. Beth took Spanish all through grad school. Hendrick's listening to Beth and Ernesto like he might be ready to correct their grammar. Two police cars roar by out on the road, lights but no sirens, and Ernesto points.

"*Policia,*" Hen says. "*Hay una emergencia.*"

Beth looks at Jack. "How are you not amazed?"

"I'm amazed," he says. "I am. Plenty." He holds his hand out to Hendrick, says, "Come on, buddy."

"Wait," she says, standing up. "Where are you going? I thought maybe I'd go on and take him, find an early lunch somewhere, or a snack or something."

"Sorry," Jack says. He wants to take this back now, take it away—it's not that he wants to hurt her so much as that he'd just like to remind her that he exists. "We've got to go," he says. "We've got deliveries, and Hen rides the truck now."

"*Entregas,*" Hen says.

"Wait," she says again. "Hang on, OK? Please. Just for a minute. How much has he been talking?"

"Like this," he says. "This much. Not much more than this." He wants badly to be able to lie, to tell her it's been whole sentences, paragraphs, the full texts of Franco's early speeches. But he doesn't.

"We should take him to the doctor," she says.

"No way. Not today. The Beanbags can wait."

"But—"

"You know what?" he says. She's the one who showed up all full of questions and accusations. "You go back to Canavan. Go check on him, make sure he's comfortable. Make sure he's got enough pillows. We can go see the Beanbags next week."

"But what if he's not doing it any more next week?"

"Then he's not doing it next week. I don't care. We'll tell them that he could do it, and that then he couldn't any more. We'll see what they say to that. Either way, that ought to be our money's worth. Or theirs."

"Jack, you can't just—"

"I can't just what?" he asks her. "What is it I can't do?"

She looks like she's working on a long list. But she says, "Nothing." She looks away from him, looks out at the road. The wind blows her hair into her face. "Do whatever you want," she says.

"Yeah," he says. "I will." He turns, takes Hen across the lot, gets him into the truck. Laying this on her like this is probably one better than what he did to Canavan's yard. He knows that. But he can't help it. Butner hops up in one of the skids and starts loading the cypress into the truck. When he's done, he passes a clipboard through the window to Jack, and Jack starts the truck up, full load, and pulls past Beth, who's walking back toward the wagon, dust and dirt on her ass from where she sat down on the ground. None of this is fair right now. Not any of it. But she can't hold him entirely responsible. Here's what he knows how to do, he wants to tell her: Get up, eat, go back to sleep. Get Hendrick dressed, keep him dressed for as long as he can. That's what he's grown expert in. Do whatever it is he needs to do, see what's left standing after he's done it. Fix it then, if it can be fixed. If it can't, let somebody else sort it all out.

She stares at them as they come by. Hendrick adjusts his crown on his head, tugging at it until he gets it perfect, until he gets it right.

≈≈ ≈≈ ≈≈

Hen's got a ballpoint pen Ernesto's given him, so the ride is punctuated by the slow click of the pen in and out of the barrel. Jack feels light-headed. Just off the teacup ride at the amusement park. Things are surely seeming less fine now. He puts on the news. Bombings in Iraq, bombings in Indonesia, a car bomb in Chechnya. Things are less fine everywhere, which makes him feel a little less alone. The market is down thirty points. A congressman resigns from Ways & Means. Tonight it will drop down into the mid-60s. Tomorrow will be the hottest day of the year so far, 90 with thunderstorms. The forecast track for Ashley has shifted a little bit, the radio woman says, and rain from that storm could be here by the weekend. He loves her voice. She's British, or South African. Her vowels are beautiful. While she talks, he wonders what would happen if he let the truck slide off the road, let it ride out across the tobacco fields and the scrub, let them coast to wherever it is they'd stop.

Hen says, from nowhere, "I like Ernesto. I think he is my friend."

"What?" Yet one more miracle.

"I think Ernesto is my friend."

He sounds so *sure.* "Why do you think that?"

Hen says, "Why do you think that?"

Jack says, "I think he's nice to you."

"I think he's nice to *you*," Hendrick says, and Jack can't tell any more whether this is a conversation, a real conversation, or if Hen's just playing with the way the words sound.

"He is nice to me," says Jack.

"*Que bueno,*" Hen says. "*Que bueno, que bueno, que bueno.*" He repeats it for a while, barely audible, touching his finger to his thumb for each syllable.

Jack tries something. "Hen, what's this?" He points at the door of the truck.

"*La puerta,*" he says, "*y la ventana.*" Then he goes back to *que bueno, que bueno.* Jack's pretty sure that's right, *puerta* and *ventana,* pretty sure he remembers those words. What he's got left from high school is basically low-end language-lab-tape ability. Where is the library? *¿Donde esta la biblioteca?* Or is it *el biblioteca?* He could start a band under that name. He and Rena could start it up, maybe put Butner on bass. Ernesto on rhythm guitar. Beth and Canavan on backup vocals, on shiny matching tambourines. Hendrick on endless repeating triangle, or ballpoint pen. They'll tour the country. Get a bus. *Good evening, Pasadena. Please give a warm welcome to El Biblioteca.* And the crowd goes wild.

About halfway to Mebane—they're taking the cypress to Mebane—they pass a man standing on the concrete median, beating a yield sign with a chain. *Que bueno,* Hen whispers. This is precisely, exactly what Jack's life looks like these days. He should hire someone to follow him around, take pictures of everything, document all the signs and signals.

What happens to him at Kinnett College is this: Somehow it gets back to his chair, Alan Sherrill, that he has kissed his student Sarah Cody in the parking lot at Gubbio's. One of Alan's advisees is Sarah's roommate. No one else, apparently, knows, but the roommate has told Alan for reasons that escape everyone. Because she's pissed off, because it offends her religion, because she's twenty-one and bored and wants to rattle shit around. Jack sits in Alan's office, which is full of maps of the Pacific Ocean—his gig is Naval Warfare—and listens while Alan says, *You know, Jack, even absent these, ah, revelations, you haven't got your doctorate, and you've taught the four years full-time. Wouldn't it just be easier, really, for everybody, if.* The conversation is about how they wouldn't have had a place for him anyway, how they'd only have been able to give him one more year, tops, about how Jack shouldn't worry, how Alan intends to be discreet and professional about all of this. Jack watches it happen to him like he's watching it happen to someone else.

That night, after the meeting, when he tells Beth that—but not why—they're not renewing his contract, she's not surprised. They've been at enough department meetings, heard enough times what the hiring situation would look like long-term. And she's been on him lately to get back to his degree, worried that it would catch up to him eventually. *Take the year,* she says, *finish your dissertation, and then look for something local for a year or two.* They can live, she thinks, for the next year at least, on her salary, their savings. Hen will still have insurance through her, through the school. Jack can find *something.* Community college. High school. When and if her tenure decision gets made, they can talk about going on the market together. She's not planning on staying at Kinnett forever. If she's tenured here, she's more attractive somewhere else. This will be good for him. Send him back into his book about the Viaduct and the New Jersey Turnpike and the Ted Williams Tunnel under the Boston harbor. Possible titles: *Great Conveyances of the East.* Or: *Life Is a Highway.* They'll be fine, they'll be OK. And right in that first moment, he believes her, believes he could take the year, pick it all back up again. That this might all wash off. They make Hen some dinner, get him into bed. Beth finds some junk on the TV and says she's going to wind down for a little while. Jack pours himself a big drink, takes Yul Brynner out onto the porch—the rented house in Burlington, their old front porch—and sits on the steps, a man with no job and a busted son, somebody guilty of standing in a parking lot and kissing a kid. He comes pretty quickly back to the idea that things might not, actually, be all that OK. He's never been fired before. It feels like a medical procedure gone wrong. *Sir, while we were in there, we found something else.* He sits there with the dog and drinks his drink and works on just what it is he might be supposed to do with himself now.

Hendrick flicks the pen. They drive toward Mebane. Canavan's in bandages up to his hip. Jack's got six yards of cypress behind him. His entire life, just about, is sliding around underneath him. It's been eleven days. He has no plan. He reaches out the window to pick at the edge of the magnetic sign on the door, PATRIOT MULCH & TREE, just to make sure it's still there.

〜 〜 〜

Hen loves the hydraulic lift on the truck. Always has. Loves the sound, loves to see the bed lift off the frame, loves to see the gravel or dirt or mulch come spilling out the back into a neat pile. He stands off to the side while Jack dumps the cypress in a bare spot of lawn directly behind the basketball goal. Nobody's home. He's called back to the yard three times, has waited half an hour in the driveway—the woman called that morning, told them please not to dump it without speaking to her husband first about where he wants it—but no one's home. The number she left for them in case her husband wasn't there, Butner says, calling Jack back, turns out to be a science museum in Raleigh. There's no one who works there with the name she gave. But they're paid up, in cash, and Butner says into the phone, *I swear, boss man, I'd just find somewhere out of the way to drop it and come on back.* If they weren't paid, Jack wouldn't put it down—customers angry about eight-foot mulch pyramids in their driveways tend not to pay—but it's past noon and getting hotter and Hen needs lunch and Jack's head still hurts and he's getting hungry, too, so: What the hell. He gets the back of the bed just past the goal, gets Hen out of the way, works the control levers on the box on the side of the truck. Hen claps and lifts his right leg up and down in time to who knows what piece of music it is that's strung through his head right now.

It's always a little ghostly delivering to houses where nobody's home. Signs of life everywhere: Basketball goal, a basketball or two in the grass behind. There's mail in the mailbox to the right of the door, flowers on the patio with puddles of water underneath, a piece of a bicycle leaned up against the garage. And a bicycle pump. Coffee mugs on a glass-topped table on the deck out back. A dog-house, a couple of chew toys in the grass. It's as though the house itself might be alive, as though it's the house that has carelessly left these things out. The family has been whisked away, winked into another time. There's a shovel next to the A/C compressor, and Jack takes that, sticks it in the mulch pile, tapes the invoice to the handle. That'll do. "Hen," he says. "You want to come bring the bed back down?" With the bed up in the air, the truck looks like Yul Brynner trying to take a shit.

Hen walks over, saying, "The Sleep Number Bed, so you can choose your mattress preference, your Sleep Number."

Jack hands him the control box. "That one right there," he says, pointing out the right button. "Remember?"

Hen says, "Remember?" He takes the box, which looks huge in his little hand. He holds his index finger out, but can't quite figure out how to work the buttons and hold the box at the same time. He keeps dropping it. It bangs down onto the driveway, chipping a fingernail-sized piece up off the concrete.

"Here," Jack says, trying to hold it for him, but that's no good. Hen starts making his noises, thinking Jack's trying to take it from him. "No," Jack says. "Look. We're doing it together." Which makes it worse. Hen lets go of the box completely, starts screaming and hitting himself in the head with the heel of his hand. "Come on, buddy," Jack says, trying to calm him, "please now, come on. Let's do it together." Hen's turning in circles, grunting, hitting himself. Jack gets behind him, gets both his arms circled around him, holds the control box right in front of Hen's face. "Here we go," he says.

"OK? Look. Look." And Hen bangs his face so hard into the box that even before he checks, Jack knows there's going to be blood.

The impact stops him cold, though: No more circles, no yelling, no hitting. A trickle of blood starts down and out from his left eyebrow. Jack holds onto him, holds onto the box, pulls the hem of his shirt up to pat Hen's face dry. Hendrick reaches one finger out, pushes the green button, holds it a second, lets it go. The bed comes down a foot, maybe less, stops. Hen pushes the button again, and the bed bounces down a few inches more. He laughs. He laughs while he's bleeding from his goddamned face. He pushes the button a third time, a fourth, and the bed comes down a little more, a little more. Jack holds his shirt against the cut. Put this in *Extraordinary Parent Magazine*. One of Beth's subscriptions, one of the Bibles from which the scripture readings come. He'll send in a letter. *Our child really tends to come around when he concusses himself. Sharp edges seem to work best.*

It can't be good for the truck hydraulics, dropping the bed down a foot at a time, but what the hell. Butner can fix that, too. Jack holds onto Hen, can feel the warmth of his little body through his shirt while he pushes the button, pushes the button. A car pulls in behind him, a diesel. Mercedes, from the sound of it. Low metallic rumble. This is the woman, or her husband. Has to be. He dabs at Hen's eyebrow again: It's a tiny cut, nothing more than a puncture from the control box. It's putting out enough blood, though. The truck shudders every time the bed drops down.

It's the husband. He gets out, stands in his driveway, looks at his pile of mulch. "We'll be out of your way in a minute," Jack says. Hen bleeds.

The guy's wearing a coat and tie. "I guess that's as good a place as any," he says.

Jack says, "We tried to pick some place out of the way."

"I'm gonna put it along the house, here, up front," the man says. People are forever telling Jack what they're going to do with the mulch, like it's some kind of test they have to pass with him. They'll stand on the yard at PM&T, let a handful of mini nuggets slide through their fingers, and they'll say, I think this'll probably do for underneath the swingset out back. Right? They need their choices ratified by experts. People tend to look desperate around mulch.

The bed whines its way finally down onto the frame, and the man stands behind them, watching. It hits with a hollow bang. Jack takes the control box, fits it in its spot on the back of the cab. Hen's got a thin stripe of blood running down his jaw, like war paint. He says, "Sawtooth Oak."

The man says, "Do you guys need a bandage or something? Is he OK?"

"I've got Band-Aids in the truck," Jack says, knowing Hen'll never let him put one on. He hates sticky things. "It's just a little nick in his eyebrow. He bumped his head on the box." Jack points at the box. He's got to look like some sort of child abuser here, like someone should be called about this, but the man just nods.

"OK," he says, and loosens his tie.

"Sawtooth Oak," Hen says again, and the man takes a handkerchief out of his pocket, wipes Hendrick's face. He lets him. Another rule that's null and void, apparently.

"You like trees?" the man asks.

"Sawtooth Oak," says Hen.

"Switchback Oak," says the man. "One of my all-time favorites."

"Chestnut Oak," Hen says.

"Another good one," the man says. "Chestnut Oak. That's great." He turns to Jack. "Great kid. Smart."

"Thank you."

"You know I've got one already looking at colleges? Wants me to take her to see Cornell this summer. Have you seen what tuition looks like these days?"

"No," Jack says, even though he has.

"It's a fortune," he says. "It's another mortgage. Southern White Oak," the man says to Hen.

"Pin Oak."

"That's right," the man says. "Absolutely. The Pin Oak."

"Well," Jack says, touching Hen on his shoulder just to let him know where he is. "We better head on."

"My wife paid you already, I guess."

"In full," Jack says.

"She's been wanting to put in a bank of hydrangeas there by the road," he says. "Maybe this fall. You think hydrangeas would go in up there?"

"I do," Jack tells him, checking to see which spot he means. "Come see us when you get ready to plant. We'll give you a good price."

"I'll do that," he says. "I will." Then he reaches into his pocket, gets the handkerchief out again, gives it to Jack. "Here," he says. "You better hang onto this."

The stripe is back along the side of Hen's face. Jack takes the handkerchief, wipes him off. "Thanks," he says. There are initials embroidered into one corner.

"I've got dozens," the man says. "Keep it. She gives them to me for every holiday."

"They're nice," Jack says.

"I never use them. Almost never. But it makes her happy."

Jack wonders what the man would say if he asked him if he wanted to ride along for the rest of the day. For the week. Or maybe to come set up camp with them, maybe move into the house across the street. He hefts Hen into the cab, fires up the engine, cuts the brake loose.

"Thanks again," the man says.

"No problem," says Jack. "Thanks for this." He waves the handkerchief at him, like he's leaving on a transatlantic voyage. "Have a good day."

"You bet," the man says, and Jack drives away, wondering if they'll ever take Hen to look at colleges, wondering if the Lone Oak catalog will last them that long.

❧ ❧ ❧

They drive through for burgers. The girl at the window's got braces, the space station walkie-talkie headset thing. Brown and yellow employee vest. She drops Jack's Coke on the ground. She says, *Shit, y'all, excuse me,* and her manager, a boy maybe fifteen minutes older than she is, swoops in, pulls another drink, hands it to Jack, all apologies for the mistake. Then he tells the girl quietly, urgently, that *Your language just that minute ago was not very Christlike.* She apologizes. Everyone at the drive-through is wearing rubber wristbands. Live Strong. Save Something. These are people with purpose in their lives. Jack bumps the back right wheels over the landscaping on his way out.

For Jack: A double with fries. For Hen: Two plain hamburgers, two slices of cheese on the side, a stack of lettuce leaves, a handful of ketchup packets, a milkshake. Vanilla. He shreds his lettuce into dime-sized pieces and dips each one in the ketchup. Then he eats the burger patties, then the buns, then the cheese. They don't eat fast food much because of his diet, but when they do, it's this every time. Doesn't matter what place. Always the lettuce, then the two small burgers, then the buns and cheese at the end. Then the milkshake, after it's melted. He plays with it in the straw, pulls it up and down. It used to make Jack insane to watch him do it. Now it's the most normal thing in the world. Comforting, almost. Hen's is a life of ritual, like anyone else's, give or take the ability to name the British Colonies alphabetically—though it occurs to Jack, suddenly, that he has no idea if Hen eats like this when he rides with Ernesto. Maybe not. Maybe they order straight off the menu. *The gentleman will have the Number Four.*

He could be in a chair, in a helmet, could drool on himself all day long. He could have Down's. He could have died at thirty months from MS or MD. He could be manic. Schizophrenic. A dwarf or a giant. He could have stage four pediatric leukemia. He could have an enlarged heart, a failing heart, a hole in his heart. He could have one lung. One foot. He could have Lou Gehrig's or sickle cell or AIDS. A conjoined twin. He could be deaf, blind. When he's quiet, like he was in the drive-through, no one knows. When he climbs to the ceiling on the shoe racks at the Stride Rite, everybody sees everything there is.

Jack's pretty sure that he's not that great a father, that he's not in line for any parenting awards or special commendations. He's not even sure he always tries as hard as he can. He's maybe not Living quite Strong enough. Hen is, after all, sitting next to him, having only stopped bleeding from the head about fifteen minutes ago. But what he's always liked about fatherhood, about Hendrick, is his company, his physical presence, even from the first day they brought him home from the hospital. It's what surprised him most—not the overpowering love all the books required that he feel for his child—just that he simply liked being around him. And even with the diagnosis, or even since, there's something a little joyous, alongside all the disaster, about living with Hendrick. Some feeling he gets about being in better or closer contact with the things we need, the things we want. I want to run the controls on the dump truck. I want to touch the faucet. I want to open the drawer three hundred times in a row. Because who doesn't want that from time to time? To fall deeper in? Who doesn't do it? Some mornings Jack taps his own spoon a few extra times on the rim of the cereal bowl just for the sheer pleasure of it, and then he'll wonder what the space really is, after all, between tic and illness. Where biting your fingernails falls on the spectrum. Ticking the button on the emergency brake. Ordering salad dressing on the side, having a song stuck in your head, watching a ball game on mute.

Everybody wants him to plan. Butner wants the sprinkler system. Ernesto wants the second greenhouse. Beth wants him to *think things all the way through, goddamnit, Jack, why don't you.* Even Rena, this morning. Jack doesn't always want that. Often enough, here's his plan: Not to. Today is maybe not a great example of the screaming success of a life lived like that, and maybe this week isn't, either, these two weeks, but he knows it can work. So Hendrick's bleeding from his face. He can speak Spanish now, can explain all about his *dolor de cabeza.* Still: Maybe Rena was right, standing on the tile. He might need something new.

He goes by the lot to see if they need the truck, and they don't. It's empty. Butner and Ernesto are sitting up on the pallets of decorative stone, tossing pebbles into an empty five-gallon bucket, keeping score. *I'm up big,* Butner says. *He's up,* says Ernesto. *But it's close.*

*Take off, boss man,* Butner says. *Take a day. Do what you need to do. We'll call if we need the truck.* So he does. He is the P of PM&T, after all. He heads for home, for his house, to see what the street looks like, the yard, to see if Rena's still there, to see if Frank's pressure-washing the azaleas. To give the whole thing a good looking at. He checks the church signs on his way by. The First Whitsett says THE BIGGEST ROOM IS THE ROOM FOR IMPROVEMENT. And the Holy Redeemer's is better: IS PRAYER YOUR STEERING WHEEL OR YOUR SPARE TIRE? Jack's not sure which to choose, which the correct answer might be. Prayer is more of a jackhammer, he thinks. Or a water leak. He should go in there and tell them they've got it all wrong. Instead, he crosses himself, muscle memory left over from growing up Episcopalian, sends up good wishes to whoever might be listening in. First-time caller, long-time listener. He starts in one more time making a list of the things Beth has been wanting him to do.

❧   ❧   ❧

Rena's not there, of course. But there's a note: *Went home. Thanks for taking in a stray. Maybe drinks some time? I'll call you—* Jack reads the

note a couple times over in his bombed-out kitchen, then gets Hen
set up in front of the TV. Maybe drinks some time. Sure. Absolutely.
They can sit on the porch and sip Mai Tais. He'll hire a bartender.
*What's she doing in our house? What's going on?* Excellent questions. Hen
flips through the channels, settles on a financial news show. Stock
prices scroll in both directions across the bottom of the screen.
Soon they'll be millionaires. Aluminum's a good bet. The guy on
the screen is screaming about aluminum.

Hole in the window where he put the beer can through. Hole in
the back wall. Hole in the floor where the rest of the tile needs to
go. Hole in Hen's face and hole in the truck where the bumper
used to hang and probably yes some kind of hole developing in his
own head, and Jack starts thinking he might need to get out of here
for a night, or a couple of nights, maybe, gets a clear and present
notion of what it could have been to be in Beth's head the last few
months or weeks, or that last afternoon when she said she had to
go somewhere. He feels like knocking his own forehead into the
dump truck's control box a couple of times, see if that maybe
straightens him out some. He's got the handkerchief for it.

He's not losing his shit. He knows that. There aren't talking birds
in the microwave telling him he's got to kill the school board. He's
just home in the middle of the afternoon and his wife's moved out
on him and shacked up with basically his only friend, and he
doesn't feel right about much of anything, can't get comfortable.
*Aluminum*, the guy on the TV yells out at the world. *Aluminum.* Jack
stands in his open front door and looks out. *Abierto, cerrado, que bueno.*
What he needs is a change of scenery. He needs a room for improvement, a spare tire. He needs a bracelet to tell him what to do.
Yellow scooter, diesel Mercedes. These were men with tasks to
complete. Rocks and piles of mulch. So he'll get his own, he figures, looking at his other house. He will get his own. He'll move
his operation over there for a little while. Simple as that. Walk his
whole life across the street and just see how that feels. Same house,

different direction. Pointing the other way. And in doing so, make it look, to anybody who might be looking, like somebody lives there.

It makes a certain kind of sense: He'd be right there, so he could spend a few weeks fixing it up, get it out on the market before the summer's over. Might not even take that long. And he'd be out of this house, with its monuments to Beth, to what she says he's done to her, to them. The house over there has some of that, but maybe not as much. The evenings might be easier. Quicker. At least the walls are different colors. At least the kitchen's got all its walls.

He doesn't spend a lot of time weighing pros and cons—Beth isn't here to force him into some kind of list-making exercise—so he just starts in on it, packs a few changes of clothes for himself into a duffel bag and gets going on Hen's clothes before he realizes that the easier thing to do, probably, would be just to carry Hen's whole dresser across the street, which he does, drawer by drawer. He looks both ways each time. He doesn't need to be run down in the road by a trash truck, dresser drawer splintered into the street, little T-shirts everywhere, the pajamas Hen refuses to wear. The floor plan is nearly identical over there. The hallway's a little narrower. He sets the dresser up in what would be Hen's same room, on the same wall, because if this is going to work, for Hen, anyway, he'll need to replicate his room as much as he can, bring all the furniture over, put it in the same formation. He won't be fooling him. Hen doesn't get fooled. Jack just wants to try to keep him as comfortable as he can.

He comes back across the street and Hendrick's standing in the center of the den, watching TV, watching Jack, now, too. "Don't worry," Jack says. "We're going to like this fine."

"Aluminum has fallen to near historic lows," Hen tells him.

"OK," Jack says. "That's enough TV for now, isn't it? Hang on. I'll be right back." He goes across the street, gets a Pittsburgh phone directory he found in one of the kitchen drawers. What it was

doing there, he has no idea, but it doesn't matter. What matters is
that when he comes back, when he presents it to Hen, it is received
like an archeological wonder: Hen spins around, sits down on the
floor with his back to the television, flips immediately to the blue
government section. He drags his finger down the columns of city
and county services. He's whispering. Soon enough, he'll have garbage pickup for most of Western Pennsylvania figured out. Motor
vehicle taxes. Jack should get him on building permits. Hen turns
another page. He's a happy child.

Jack goes down the hall, starts taking Hen's room apart. He tries
to make as little noise as possible. He gets the bed frame, the mattress, the half-sized desk they bought him last year. Trips and trips
across the street. Head running about two speeds too fast. *But why
would you want to move across the street?* she'll want to know. *Wouldn't it
have been easier to do the work the other way?* He gets boxes down from
the attic, packs Hen's nightlight, adds a few toys that he'll never pay
any attention to. He unhooks the space shuttle replica that hangs
off the ceiling fan. Thank God there's already a ceiling fan across
the street. It's brown, but it'll do. He gets his little desk chair. He
gets his red rug. He gets the poster of the periodic table Bethany
brought home from some friend in the chemistry department,
pulls the pushpins, hangs it back up next to the window in his new
same room.

On to his own necessaries: He packs a box of towels and sheets,
unplugs the TV from the guest room, carries that across. He takes
the mattress from the guest bed, puts it on his back and walks it
over. Cars slow down in the street. A neighbor two doors down
watches from her stoop. He puts a few things from the fridge into
a cooler. Across the street, he pulls items from the garage, things
left over from the auction—a card table, some plastic Adirondack
chairs, huge brass lamps—and sets up a kind of dining room, a
living room. He uses boxes for coffee tables, end tables. Three
chairs right next to each other for a sofa. He goes back out to the

garage, finds a green ceramic bowl, blows the dust out of it, sets it on one of his liquor-box end tables. Decoration. He stands in his new house, his new rooms, has a look at his progress: He likes the living room this way—likes the brown carpet, likes how aggressively temporary it all seems. He's sweating. He could use a glass of water. They're going to need glasses. He goes back across the street.

A bag of encyclopedias. The plastic McDonald's cup Hen likes. A sack of plastic plates and cups, a box of plastic forks and knives. There are plenty of pots and pans left over from the auction, so no problem there. Dog food. A radio. He loads all that into the back of the dump truck, in boxes and lawn and leaf bags, and he gets Hen and Yul Brynner up and out and ready, locks the door behind him, backs the thirty yards down his driveway and up his other driveway. It's working, at least so far. He takes Hen inside, telling him they're *on an adventure, an adventure*. Hen's still holding the phone book. He walks the entirety of the house, doesn't say a word. When he makes it back to the den, he looks at Jack a long time, and then he sets the book on one of the boxes, sits down in front of it. He opens it to the white pages, looks up at Jack, says, "Granger." He looks back down, finds his place. "Granget," he says. "Grangetsky. John R. Grangetsky, 709 Fairmont Lane, 15216." Hendrick reads out the names of Pittsburghians circa 1970, and Jack listens to the cadences of his voice, his exactness, how he never stumbles, never sounds anything out, just gets it right the first time. This is working out fine. Pittsburgh should keep him occupied for a while. It's almost four-thirty. Jack decides to go out to the porch, sets himself up in a spot where he can see Hen through the window. He brings Yul Brynner out with him, ties him off to the porch railing, cracks open a beer. He plugs a radio in and tunes it to the news, listens to that a while. Relaxes. He views his new view. Scrub yard, roots from the trees coming up through the grass. Dead boxwood down by the mailbox, which is still leaning well over from where he clipped it last week. A long story comes on the radio about after-school programs in Connecticut. The guy being interviewed is talking about funding, keeps mentioning the need for his kids, the kids in his program, to get *a head start. A leg up.* Jack sips his beer, thinks about Beth watching him pull out of the lot this morning, about Hen speaking Spanish. *How could you not tell me?* But that's what he does, she says. His M.O. He doesn't talk. Like the baby, like when she'd wanted to talk about another baby—when they'd talked about it last, in March, or April, between seasons, before the auction, Beth said she'd been thinking she might want a second one. But Hen's already six, Jack said. And he's already two or three other things, he didn't say. She shook her head. *We've still got all the baby clothes upstairs,* she reminded him. They'd never thrown any of it away. *Bibs, overalls, onesies. There are rattles up there. Bath books. Saved.* She said sometimes she thought she could see them with a second baby.

*What if it was a girl?* he wanted to know.

*We could go a year or so on what we have. Or we could buy one or two really pink little outfits in case we want to take her to the store and we're worried about somebody mistaking her for a boy. We can put eyeliner on her from the beginning, if you want. We can pierce her ears. She can wear pearls.*

*That's not what I meant.*

*Well, Jack, what did you mean?*

He hadn't even been sure he wanted the first baby. He was twenty-nine. She was thirty. People do these things when they're too young to know what they're doing, too dumb or too blindly hopeful to know any better. So they'd already waited too long. But she wanted a child, and he thought he might, or would eventually, so they started trying to get pregnant. By the second month, they were. Jokes about how virile he was, how fertile she was. The Fertile Crescent. He beat on his chest. Make a big enough show out of it and it gets fun, maybe, or at least funny. They had friends who were pregnant, or who already had babies, a few friends, anyway, and Beth started inviting them over to dinner more often. They'd pass wine around, a half a glass for Beth, and she'd be at them about time between contractions or what kinds of exercises they'd done or how she'd read at some point that toward the end some women would eat soap, would get a craving and stand at the washer and eat laundry soap out of the box. Once, Jack got up from the sofa, went into the bathroom, dipped his finger in the box of Tide and ate what came up. It tasted clean.

Their friends who were pregnant looked frightened. The ones who already had kids looked like something had run them over, backed up, hit them again. Toddlers wandered Jack's shelves, pulling books down, putting candles in their mouths. Yul Brynner hid in the back when they had kids over. In her third month, Beth decided the smell of coffee made her nauseous. Jack moved the coffeemaker to the back porch, made coffee outside in the cold. At seven months she told him he could bring it back inside, but by then it was June and warm again.

Beth sits there and tells him she's not saying for sure that she wants to try again. She just wants to think about it, is all. Talk about it with him. They're on their porch, a couple of months ago, the house she hates, Hendrick through his paces and down for the night. But Jack can't do it, can't even discuss it, says he doesn't want to. Next door, Frank rolls his garbage cans to the curb, plastic wheels sounding like stone on the driveway. Beth and Jack watch him lining up the recycling can in perfect formation with the green garbage cans. Everything Frank does is in perfect formation. He will sometimes come out of his house, jingling a big handful of keys, and rearrange the three cars he's got in his driveway.

*I just thought we could talk about it,* she says, sounding sad, frustrated with him. *It's something we have to think about. I'll be thirty-seven this fall.*

He tells her he knows how old they are. He knows he should be telling her something else. He sits on the porch steps. He bites at his thumbnail. Big thick silence. He should touch her, at least, reach for her shoulder. Eventually, she gets up and goes in. And a little fissure opens up between them.

On the radio, the after-school program guy is talking about pulling kids off the streets. Jack works on his beer, leans his chair a little further back against the wall of the house, of this house, and waits. He's moved across the street. The light's different over here. This ought to count for something.

☙ ☙ ☙

Rena calls him on the cell, and he explains it to her. "You did not," she says.

"I did."

"I'm impressed," she says. "That's impressive. I'm coming over."

"OK," he says. "But we don't have much over here."

"I'll bring supplies."

It's Rena's idea to move to the back yard. She says there's something that doesn't taste right about sitting on the front porch, watching for something to happen, waiting, maybe, for Beth to come by. Says wouldn't the back yard be a nice, fine middle ground, instead. Rena as the voice of reason: There's one way to measure. So he drags a couple more deck chairs out from the garage—there are twenty or thirty in there, fake plastic wood grain pressed into them, stacked up like a pool party might at any moment break out—and they're set up out back now, the little radio tuned into the rock station. *It's a No Repeat Work Week on 104.7, The Wolf.* Hen's inside, reading his phone book and watching television. Jack brought the TV over, tried the cable for the hell of it, and it was still hooked up. A little miracle. Hen's watching the Dead Dog Channel, which is what Jack and Beth call the local access show put on by the animal shelter. Hendrick loves it. Loves it. It comes on basically every day, but at different times. They can never figure out what the schedule is, so when they're flipping through and it comes up, it feels like a gift. Fade in to the same guy, every time, standing in a beat-down grassy run with, say, Cleo. Female voice-over: *Cleo is a lab mix, happy and playful. She's great with kids. She needs some room to run. If you're interested in Cleo, mention number 476C when you come to the shelter.* Fade out and in again, and it's the same man, same weather, same angle of the sun: It's five minutes later. They've leashed Cleo, taken her back to her pen, brought out the next one. *Shasta is a mature dog, so she's calm and likes to lie down with her toys.* Shot of some ruined red stuffed animal in Shasta's mouth, shot of Shasta wagging. *She loves to have her belly rubbed. If Shasta seems like the perfect companion for you, call about number 556A.* Next up are two German Shepherd–mix puppies named for sodas and chips. Frito and Pringle. They run out of names at the pound.

He figures there's at least another half-hour of the Dead Dog Channel to go, and Jack refills their drinks from a small cooler they've got between their chairs. Rena brought it. Ice, bottle of gin, a couple of liters of tonic, a lime they're mauling into pieces with a box cutter he found in the truck.

Rena says, "So he'll just sit in there? He won't get into anything?"

"Like what?"

"Like he won't stick his head in the toaster or anything?"

"I didn't bring a toaster over," Jack says. "But no, I don't think so. He seems OK." Somebody down the street is getting a little work done, maybe roofing. The percussion of hammers, a crew working late. "He's good as long as the show's on, anyway."

"It's a little morbid, don't you think?"

"What's that?"

"Calling it the Dead Dog Channel?"

"Isn't that what it is?"

"I thought the shelter out there was a no-kill."

"I don't know," Jack says. "Maybe that's right."

"It's the High Point one, right? I think that one's a no-kill."

"So what do you want me to call it—the Indefinitely Imprisoned Dog Channel?"

"That seems better, at least."

"Doesn't have the same ring to it," he says. "It'll never sell."

Yul Brynner's lying in the dirt beside them, basically settled into his new digs. Jack found him a straight-sided metal dish, one more thing from the treasure trove in the garage, filled it up with water. Rena's running her foot back and forth across the dog's side. "So what made you do it?" she wants to know.

"What, the moving?"

"Hell yes, the moving."

"I'm not sure," he says. "It just kind of happened."

"That's bullshit," she says. "I'm saying that's bullshit."

"I needed a change of scenery," he says. "I needed to shake things up."

"Who even says that? Who shakes things up?"

"I do," he says.

"Well, you've shaken it." She licks her thumb, rubs something off the arm of her chair. "This'll make her foam at the mouth, you know."

"You think?"

"Oh, absolutely," she says. "Not a doubt in the world. But you don't need me to tell you that." She rattles her ice. "Right?"

"I guess not."

"Are you hungry?" she says. "I brought over some crackers. Want me to go get them?"

Jack can just barely touch the ground if he lets his arms hang. Maybe Beth would like it over here. Maybe Rena's got it wrong. "I'll go," he says. "I need to check on Hen, anyway."

"They're on the kitchen counter," she tells him. It's like she's lived here six months. He leaves her there in the yard, walks up the back steps into the house. Hen's sitting up right in front of the television, saying the names of the dogs over and over until a new name flashes up. *Ritz Ritz Ritz Ritz Ritz Ritz Ritz. Fanta Fanta Fanta Fanta.* Jack musses his hair, and he groans. He wants to be left alone, so Jack leaves him alone. Sleeping dogs and boys. He finds the crackers, opens up a cabinet, looks at what else he's brought from across the street. A jar of peanut butter. Some mustard. He's got half a gallon of milk in the fridge and a bag of ground coffee. He could use a grocery run. How unprepared he is for whatever he's doing is starting to dawn on him. He needs shampoo. He needs a book, or some magazines. He takes the peanut butter and the crackers back outside.

"Hi," she says, taking the crackers, opening the box up.

"Hi."

"Is he still watching the dying dogs?"

"He is."

She digs a cracker into the peanut butter, looks up at him. "Then would it be alright if I asked you some questions?"

"Whatever you want," he says. "Sure."

"Cool," she says. "I like that. So Beth just walked out one day?"

"Basically," he says.

"Not unprovoked," she says.

"No. I helped."

She nods. "And she moved in over there."

"Basically."

"With your best friend," she says. He looks around the yard, at the few flowers the old man had going, a couple of moldering bird feeders. The hedges are going to need some work. There's poison ivy all in the fence. "All I did was move downtown," says Rena. "I think we have a winner. I think she wins."

"Why's that?"

"Come on. It could have been anyone, right?"

"I guess so."

"But no," she says. "It's Terry. It's an impressive move. You have to give her credit."

"I do?"

"I think so," she says. "I think we both do."

"OK."

"You're taking it well," she says, grinning. "Or maybe you're not taking it at all. Doesn't matter. Let's keep going."

"Hang on," he says. "Can we talk about how you're taking it? Can we talk about you and Canavan? I mean—"

"More on that later, folks," she says. "I'm not finished yet. I have more questions."

"Why don't you have to talk about your part?"

"I'll talk about it. Here: He made me very sad. More than once. Now. My questions."

"You'll tell me?"

"When I'm finished, OK?"

"OK," he says.

"Alright, then." She smiles. "Promise you won't get mad."

"About what?"

"About what I'm going to ask." He feels like he's on a game show. "Because what we don't want is you getting all pissed off," she says.

"I won't get all pissed off."

"Are you sure?"

"It depends," he says. "What are you asking?"

She takes a long sip of her drink. "I want to know why they fired you," she says. "I always have. Tell me the real reason."

"There's no real reason," he says, right away. "They just weren't going to have classes for me."

She points a cracker at him. "That's also bullshit. Isn't it? It has to be. They love Beth. They could have made space for you."

"I didn't have my degree. I wasn't going to finish."

"Bullshit again," she says. "You could have finished. And plus they would've hired you anyway. Andy Baumbartener's got a job, for fuck's sake, and he's only got an MA."

"They wouldn't have hired me. Alan was clear about that. I needed the PhD in hand."

"Jack. Earth to Jack." She waves at him, snaps her fingers. "It's me. Your best friend's girlfriend. Like in the song. I have slept on your sofa, deeply inebriated. You have refused and/or failed to take advantage of me. Your wife is half an hour away from where we're sitting, running some kind of X-rated nursing clinic for my shitbag boyfriend. You can tell me why they ran you off." She's talking with her mouth full. "Because they did run you off, right?"

He's never told anyone. Not one person in three years. He's never discussed any part of it with anyone but Alan Sherrill. But what the hell. He's now sitting in his auxiliary back yard. With Rena. *Pepsi is a Dachshund-Poodle cross who loves to have her ears rubbed.* "They didn't run me off," he says.

"What'd they do, then?"

"I kissed a kid," he says.

"What?"

He says it again. "I kissed a kid." It sounds very plain like that.

"No shit," she says.

"No shit."

"That's fantastic."

"Not really."

"What, you're not proud of it?"

"No," he says. "I'm not."

"Are you embarrassed?"

"I probably should be," he says. "But no. I'm not that, either." He's nothing about it. He never has been. It's always just been something that happened, like accidentally dropping a plate.

"This is great," she says. "This is genuinely outstanding. You have to tell me who it was. Did I have her?"

"You didn't have her."

"How do you know? I could have had her." She's excited about the possibility.

"Sarah Cody," he says.

She frowns. "I don't think I had her."

"See?"

"When was this?"

"Three years ago."

"I don't think I had her," she says again. "Aren't they all named Sarah Cody, though?"

"They're all named Meghan," says Jack.

"They *are* all named Meghan," she says. "Perfect. OK. Follow-up question. Did you fuck her?"

"What? No, I didn't fuck her."

"Listen," she says. "Don't get all high and mighty with me. I'm not the one who felt up Sarah Doty."

"Cody."

"Right. More importantly, how did you achieve this? Tell me everything. Did you take her somewhere for the weekend? Or did you just both get hall passes at the same time and meet in the stairwell?"

"It was in the parking lot at Gubbio's," he says.

"Gubbio's?"

"A pizza place out there. In Burlington. Some kids from a seminar I taught took me there at the end of class, once it was over. Her seminar."

"What was it?"

"The history of political boundaries, that kind of thing."

"You kissed a kid you had in a seminar on boundaries?"

"We were a little drunk."

"That makes it much better," she says, holding her cup out. "Cheers."

"Cheers," he says.

"So what happened? She fell in love with you, and then made some kind of complaint when you didn't love her back?"

"No," he says. "It was just bad luck. Her roommate was Alan Sherrill's advisee."

"No shit."

"No shit."

"That is bad luck."

"I know."

"Though, for the record, ladies and gentlemen, and all the ships at sea, he did kiss the boundaries kid in the parking lot of wherever-the-fuck."

"Gubbio's," he says.

"Maybe I have heard of that place. Is there a kids' slide out front? Or one of those big bins of plastic balls to jump in?"

"Gubbio's just has TVs and beer. No slides."

"Video games?" she asks.

"I think so."

"Like a little piece-of-shit college dive."

"Sort of," he says. "Yeah."

"I love those places," she says. She leans over, picks up a pine-cone. "So what did Beth say about Little Miss Sarah Cody?" By her tone of voice, he knows she already knows what the answer is.

"Nothing," he says.

She aims the pinecone at him. "Because you didn't tell her."

"I didn't," he says.

"Yeah. She would have told me."

"She would have?"

"Of course," says Rena. "We talk, you know? To each other?"

"Not all the time, apparently."

"Yeah," she says. "I suppose not." She reaches in the cooler, gets more ice. "You want?" she asks.

"Thanks." He hands her his cup.

She says, "You know what the saddest thing I ever saw was?"

"No."

"One of my profs in grad school got divorced the first year I was there. Salima Baker. Expert in Coptic Greek. We were close, sort of. There was a group of us who'd have a few glasses of wine from time to time, Salima and another professor whose name I can't ever remember and a few of the grad students. It was like a little salon. We thought we were hot shit." A dog starts barking, and Yul Brynner picks his head up to listen. She says, "Anyway, her marriage came apart. Salima's. She asked a few of us to help her move out, and on the day she moved, we got there, to her house, and she wasn't even packed. No boxes. We had to pack her stuff for her. Her husband sat on the back deck the whole time drinking coffee. The only thing she'd done was get her books tied up in stacks. With twine. She had all these books stacked up and tied off in sets of ten or twelve. One of the guys, some boy, I don't know, had a pickup, and we filled it up with the books, and like one wicker sofa and some clothes. And she had a fish. That was it. That was all she moved out with. Into this awful studio apartment she rented over by where we all lived."

The dog stops barking. Up the street, the hammering's stopped, too.

Rena says, "So that's why I moved out on Terry. Why I moved out of the house."

"What's why?" He's lost.

"Because I'm not ending up like that. I don't want my books in stacks."

"What are you talking about?"

"I'm telling you. I don't want to end up like her. Like that. The whole thing was just so deeply unhappy."

"But that's why you moved out?"

"It's what you and Beth are doing, right? It's what Beth's doing, anyway. And it must be what you're doing over here. It's an off-season. You're both taking deep breaths. You're looking at me like I'm crazy. I'm not crazy."

"I know," he says.

"I'm not."

"I didn't even know she was moving in with him until she called," he says. "She just said she needed to get out for a while. Two weeks now."

"Fuck that," she says. "Two weeks is nothing. Two weeks is easy. You guys are fine. We're all fine."

"How is it you're so OK with this?" he wants to know. "You didn't seem OK last night, all full of wine."

"I'm not OK, you asswipe, and I'm not the only one who got full of wine. What are you, from the forest?" She gets up. "You're not getting it. Here's how I see it, OK? This is what's going on right now. All this, right? We go with it. We live here, all four of us, in this little bit of time. The two of us can live right here in your back yard, if you want. We'll set up a tent. Jack Lang East, or whatever you decide to call it. And Beth and Terry will do whatever it is they do. Maybe she can move them in across the street. We'll bake them something, welcome them to the neighborhood. A pie. Toad-in-the-Hole. We'll all be grown-ups. All of this will be extremely grown-up."

"There's no way any of that's happening."

"Why not?" she says. "How would that be any worse?"

"I trenched your yard," Jack says.

She turns around. "That's about right," she says. "When?"

"The night before he chainsawed himself."

"Good," she says.

"Beth was fairly pissed."

"That's good for her. Healthy."

"I took the tomatoes out. By the mailbox."

"You're a cold-blooded killer, Jack Lang."

He looks at her. "It's just—"

"Just what?"

"It's all wrong," he says. "You know? Everything. It feels like I'm doing everything wrong. I feel like I should feel—I don't know. What'd you say? He made you sad? I feel like I should feel sadder."

"And you don't?"

"I guess not."

"Well, fuck, Jack, get sad! Be sad. That's what this is for. Look at you. You've moved across the street. This is a step in the right direction. Listen to what I'm telling you: Unhappy is bad news. Unhappy is different. That's a kind of permanent condition. We don't want you getting unhappy. But be sad, OK? Take another week or two here and get sad. Bail out on your boys over there at Mulch City. They can run the show without you for a while. How hard can it be? You dump mulch into people's trucks, right? Let them do that for a while." She pours her drink out on the dirt, sets her cup on the cooler. "You know what? Track down Sarah Cody, wherever she is. Call her up. Tell her you want to see her. Old times and all that. Meet her at some interstate exit halfway between here and Maryland and buy her dinner in an Outback Steakhouse and fuck her brains out in some Econolodge. Get the room with two king beds and fuck her once or twice on each of them. Alternate between the two. What is she by now, twenty-four? Twenty-five? She's probably still never been with anybody who doesn't shoot his wad in ninety seconds. You'll be a hero."

"I've never fucked anybody in an Econolodge," he says.

"See? You're missing out. This is your big chance."

Jack gets up, walks to the fence, opens and closes the gate to the side yard. He's not convinced. Of anything. He says, "Why aren't you mad at Beth?"

"I'm mad," she says. "Who says I'm not? I'm plenty mad. Aren't you mad at Terry?"

"Of course," he says. "But it's like I'm not mad enough at either of them, you know?"

"Not really, but maybe we can work on that."

One of the windowsills on the side of the house looks like it's rotten. He'll have to get at that. He lives here now. He says, "How about we order food? You and me. We can rent a movie." It's a ridiculous move.

"No way," she says, smiling. "Not tonight. No movies for me. I'm having one more drink, and then I'm going home. I think I ought to let you gentlemen settle into your new digs."

"OK," he says, relieved and disappointed at the same time.

"Don't take it so hard," she says. She gets the bottle of gin out of the cooler, waves it at him. "Come here. Sit down with me for the rest of the Dog Death Show. Pour me one last drink. Give me some conversation. Make a half-honest woman out of me. Tell me all about all the other teenagers you've gotten to throw themselves at you."

"She wasn't a teenager," he says, sitting back down, handing her his cup. "She was twenty-one." Rena is a small brushfire somebody's set in the corner of his head.

"Twenty-one?"

"Yes."

She pats his knee. "Well, see? That makes all the difference."

❧ ❧ ❧

Two days go like this: Jack gets up early, earlier than usual, because Hen's up early—he's not used to the way the light works over here, and his dresser is too far away from the wall. Once Jack gets that figured out, though, things go better. They haven't been back across the street. They're making a go of it. And overall, it's been fine, has been better than Jack really could have hoped for: Hen's found the faucets over here, has eaten the fish sticks Jack's made him, has been deep into his new phone book. Jack sits up in the evenings, gets used to a whole new set of sounds.

He goes in to the yard both days, makes sure to meet Beth there, lets her take Hen on errands, lets her take him to lunch. He's not sure that he wants her to know he's moved out. He's doesn't know what he'd say to her about it. She'd have questions. *You've just got lawn furniture everywhere?* Rena shows up at the house unannounced a couple of times, brings a poster for a bike race in Durham, hangs it on the wall in the living room. *You need some kind of color in here somewhere,* she tells him. Jack brings home catalogs from work, tears out pictures of shrubs, hangs them on Hen's wall.

PM&T grinds along under its own power. Butner and Ernesto work the vegetable gardens, and when he's in, Jack drives the loader back and forth, sets rows of boulders along the front of the lot, in between the flags. Butner's idea. He's got it in his head that a boulder might be an impulse buy. They get another truckload of roses in, all in bloom, run a special: Three for the price of two. They move pretty well. Butner's got a second dry-erase board going in the office now, a gridded schedule of incoming and outgoing. Hen likes to touch his thumb to the ink, leaves little thumbprints all through Butner's tallies of cubic yards of crush rock. They sell out of petunias. A woman wearing an accountant's visor buys the last few four-packs.

Hendrick finds a closet full of old *National Geographics* in the back bedroom, and they spend all of Thursday night looking at the rivers of Zaire, dugout canoes in Greenland, humpback whales off the shores of the Aleutian Islands. There are large maps of the Cherokee Nation, of the Sea of Tranquility. Hen loves the maps, folds them and unfolds them, runs his fingers along the thin red topographical lines. Jack hangs a couple up next to the bike race poster.

Friday late afternoon Jack takes Hen outside, gets him set up with November 1989: The Colorado River, the Urals, the Bay of Bengal. Jack's got a project: He's replacing the mailbox, finally. He digs it out, resets it in a new hole, pours in a bag of concrete mix and soaks that down with the hose. Frank comes down his driveway to retrieve his trash cans, waves at Jack, face full of questions. Jack waves back, squats down to see if the mailbox looks plumb and level. Frank rolls the bins back up to his house one at a time. Jack pulls a can of marking spray paint out of the truck, starts drawing in big ovaled flowerbeds in his new front yard. He's trying things out. He's planning.

Rena arrives that night with another sleeve of crackers. They drink gin and tonic. She wants to know things—wants him to show her what he's thinking of doing to the house, what colors he's going to paint everything. She asks him how he was able to buy it in the first place, how he got the cash for the down payment, how much he thinks he might make when he sells it, how soon that might be. She makes him tell her the Sarah Cody story again, asks him more questions. *Was she smart? Who kissed who?* They have another drink. Before she leaves, she stands in his kitchen, says, "I think I want two things from you, OK?"

"OK," he says, looking at the pale hair on her arms.

"One: I want us to go to yard sales some day soon. I've been feeling like buying some useless shit."

"I can do that," he says. "We can go to yard sales."

"We need lamps with no cords," she says. "I want a pasta bowl and a Salad Shooter."

"Good," Jack says, feeling like he's fallen off of something. "That sounds good to me."

"And second," says Rena, holding up two fingers.

"Second," Jack says, feeling like, for once, he knows what's coming.

"Take me on a date, Jackson. It's time, I think. Isn't it? I think it is. I want you to take me to Gubbio's."

&#8667;  &#8667;  &#8667;

SATURDAY'S ARE KARAOKE NIGHT'S AT GUBBIO'S! is what the sign says
outside, big lightbulb arrow running across the top of it. Jack works
on apostrophes and possessives while he gets the dump truck
wedged backwards into a space next to the Dumpster. Hendrick's
riding between them, tuning the radio in to station after station.
He does not get easily babysat, so he's along for the ride. Rena in-
sisted, anyway. *It wouldn't be right without him. You two are like some kind
of package deal.* And Hen will eat pizza: Plain cheese, and you have to
blot the grease off with a paper towel, but he'll eat it. Jack's wearing a pair of jeans he bought this afternoon specifically for the
occasion. He's pretty sure he's headed for catastrophe. He just
doesn't know precisely what sort.

They sit over on the side, away from the bar. The music's not
going yet, but there's a folding table with a karaoke machine and
a huge white three-ring binder set up in the corner, a couple of
microphones and speakers next to that. A banner hanging off
the wall says JEFF AND AARON! KARAOKE, and then under that,
WEDDINGS-PARTIES-ANYTIME. There's no sign of Jeff or Aaron. The
restaurant is about half full, mostly families and couples. No
students, it looks like. There are a couple of tables of kids about
the right age, but they look like locals. Jack's only been back
here once or twice. It does not feel like the scene of the crime,
does not feel charged with anything like import. There is Carolina Panthers paraphernalia all over the walls, plus NASCAR
posters and beer company banners of bikini-wearing volleyball
girls. Drink specials. Pitchers are four dollars. Hendrick starts in
on lining up the sugar packets in rank and file across the table.
A girl at the bar puts down her cigarette, comes to take their
order. She's wearing a black T-shirt that shows off a good stripe
of her stomach. She's thin, fit. "What can I get you?" she asks
them.

"What kind of ice do you have?" Jack asks.

"Huh?"

"Is it cubes, or is it the little crunchy kind?"

"Isn't it the same thing?" The girl's lipstick has glitter in it.

"Is it big pieces or little pieces?" he asks her.

"Do you mean the turd ice?" she says. "Like at the movies?"

"Yes," he says. "Yes."

"No. Our kind is square, with, like, little belly buttons in them."

"Then he'll have whatever you've got that's diet, no ice," Jack says, nodding at Hen. "He can be choosy."

"That is choosy," she says. Hen looks up at her, blinks. "Diet Coke or Diet Sprite?" she asks.

"Diet Coke or Diet Sprite?" Hen says right back.

She says, "Diet Sprite, if you ask me."

Hendrick says, "A sprite is a mythical woodland creature." He says it very seriously, and Rena laughs out loud.

"Cute," says the girl. "What about for y'all?"

"We'll take the pitcher special," Jack says.

"They're four dollars," she says. "All of them."

"Whatever's coldest," Jack says.

"They're all cold."

"Bud," says Rena, interrupting. "Jesus. We'll be here all night if you let him decide. Bud."

"Pitcher of Bud and a Diet Sprite," the waitress says. "Y'all want menus?"

Jack says, "Two slices of cheese and a large—" he looks at Rena. "Pepperoni?"

"And sausage," she says. "Make it pepperoni and sausage."

"We got good sausage," the girl says.

"Great," Rena says. "Perfect." The girl walks over to the bar, writes up a ticket, hangs it on a wheel in the window through to the kitchen. She comes back with the pitcher, with Hen's soda.

"She's about your speed, right?" Rena asks, after she's sitting back down at the bar again. "About the right age?"

"She doesn't strike me as a big reader," he says, pouring the beer.

"That's what you'd want her to do to you? Read?"

"Here," Jack says, handing her a glass. "Drink this. Leave me alone."

She smiles at him, clinks her beer against his. "To Gubbio's," she says. "To you and Hendrick." She takes a long sip, wipes the foam off her mouth with her wrist. Hendrick stacks the sugar packets in a little rampart around his Sprite glass. Here's what's wrong, or what isn't: They feel like a family. It doesn't feel anything like a date. It just feels easy. "Tell me where you and the world-famous Sarah Cody sat," says Rena.

"Over there." He points out a row of tables underneath a map of Italy. "It was a bunch of us. We pulled the tables together."

"I don't care about anybody else," she says. "Everybody else is ancillary. Tell me what she was wearing. What she looked like. If she kept leaning over so you could see her tits."

"Tits," says Hen.

"Sorry," Rena says.

"Sorry," Hen says back.

"I don't know what she was wearing," says Jack.

"That's a complete load of shit," she says.

"That's a complete load of shit," says Hen, leaning his catalog up against the wall, putting it on display. Then he says, "Lone Oak Tree Farms can deliver in as little as forty-eight hours. All trees, if installed by Lone Oak certified arborists, are guaranteed for one full year."

"Is it OK for me to curse in front of him?" Rena asks. "I won't do that any more."

"It's OK," Jack says. "I do. Butner does."

"What kind of name is that, anyway? Butner?"

"A family name, he says."

"What about Hendrick?"

"Also family. Beth's grandmother. Her maiden name."

Mentioning Beth makes everything squeeze down for a minute, but Rena saves them, bangs her fist on the table, says, "Come on. Tell me what she was wearing. Explain to me, in detail, the outfit of Sarah Cody."

"Jeans," he says.

"Tight jeans?"

"Just plain jeans." He runs his thumb over the logo painted on the side of his glass. The Bud Racing Team, it says. "Holes in the knees," says Jack. He remembers being able to see her knees, remembers that mattering very much.

"And?"

"And I don't know, something white, I think. A white tank top. Jeans and a white tank top."

"What color is her hair?"

"Brown."

"Is it long and perfect?"

He smiles. "It is sort of long and perfect, or at least it was. Probably she's chopped it all off now, and she's dating some singer in a band. Or the drummer."

"No," she says. "She's not dating anybody in a band. No way. She's all settled down. She's with a tax attorney. Or an anesthesiologist." A couple of boys are playing a Ms. Pac-Man game in the corner, and one of them yells at it, kicks it. The waitress shouts at them from the bar: *Y'all treat that thing right or I'm unplugging it, OK?* Rena says, "Tell me why you didn't go home with her. I would have gone home with her, I think."

"You would have?"

"Sure," she says. "Twenty-one? If I was you? Come on."

"What does that mean, 'if I was you'?"

"Just that. If I was you, I'd have done it. I mean, you'd already kissed her. You were already fucked. No pun intended."

"She didn't ask me to."

"But you would have, right?"

"No," he says. "No."

"Why not?"

"I couldn't see it."

"Couldn't see it how?"

"I couldn't see me waking up there. Couldn't figure out how it would work, or what we'd talk about. Or what I'd tell Beth."

"First of all, you don't wake up there, obviously. You leave that night. Do you have no idea how to do this?"

"What are you talking about? Do you know how to do this?"

"I know how I would do it." She pulls a couple of napkins from the dispenser. "I'm just surprised you had it that well thought out, is all. You had that all planned, anyway."

"I didn't have it planned," he says. "I was planning not to."

"That's still planning, isn't it?"

The boys' game ends, and they feed Ms. Pac-Man more quarters. Somebody's phone rings. The girl from the bar brings their pizza, sets some plates down hard on the table. She says, "Here y'all go. I'm going on break. Yell for Tommy if you need anything."

"Who's Tommy?" Rena asks.

"Cook," she says, and points at the man in the kitchen window. He pulls another ticket off the wheel, waves it at them. They wave back.

Rena takes a slice, puts it on her plate, starts blotting at it with napkins, the same as Hendrick. "You've got to be kidding me," Jack says. Both of them are going through exactly the same motions.

"What?"

"You both do that," he says.

Rena looks at Hen, nods her approval. "Great minds, and all, I guess," she says. She lifts her greasy napkin off her pizza, puts it in a little defeated pile on top of a clean one, gives him a triumphant smile, starts eating. She takes tiny, delicate bites. Grease shines at the corners of her mouth. Jack tries not to look at her too often.

The karaoke guys—Jeff and Aaron—show up during dinner, start setting up. They're wearing T-shirts with the sleeves cut off, and one of them has on a black leather cowboy hat. They've got tight jeans, cowboy boots, big belt buckles that say JEFF and AARON, respectively. They look like they go to the gym often enough—overmuscled, shirts one size too small, veins showing in their arms. They seem proud of themselves, of the whole JEFF AND AARON! KARAOKE situation. The one with the cowboy hat, Aaron, lights a cigarette from a crushed pack he pulls out of his front pocket. They run wires back and forth, plug things in, move the microphones to where they want them. *Test one,* Jeff says. *Test two.* Aaron tries out the mikes for himself. He leans in, says, *Hey, hey?* Then he answers himself: *Hey, hey.*

Rena says, "Mother of God."

"*Madre de Diós,*" Hen says, around a mouthful of crust. Jack stares at him.

Aaron signals to the cook, Tommy, and then he flicks a switch on a console on the table. A row of blue and red lights comes on behind the microphones. A projector throws a pale square of light up onto the wall, and JEFF AND AARON! KARAOKE flashes up in cursive, the color of the lettering shifting from red to green and back again. Then the graphic flips up on its end and starts spinning, quickly at first, and then slowing down and finally falling over, like a quarter on a table top. Jeff and Aaron have put some time into this.

Aaron flicks another switch and music starts coming through the big box speakers they've got on stands on either side of the table, something Jack recognizes from the call-in show he listens to with the dog, something they seem to play most nights. Synthesizers, drums. And then Aaron walks around the front of the table, holding the microphone with both hands, closes his eyes, and starts singing. *You should've seen by the look in my eyes, baby/There was somethin' missin'.* He holds the n out in missin' a long time. Rena leans across the table, whispering. She says, "What song is this?"

"You know it," he says.

"I do?"

"Just wait."

Aaron's voice sounds like a record played slightly faster than it's meant to be, thin and high. Like he's under water, or a long way away. He isn't bad. He's just not great. He's almost certainly singing on the biggest stage he'll ever see. When he gets to the chorus, Jeff comes out from behind the table, a move they've clearly choreographed, and sings backup. "Holy, holy shit," Rena says. Jeff and Aaron are right on the verge of harmonizing. *And I'm gonna keep on loving you/'Cause it's the only thing I wanna do.* Hen's completely taken in by Jeff and Aaron, is watching everything, recording it. Rena stares, her mouth a little open. Jack can tell she's trying not to laugh. There are plenty of things he likes about her, but it comes to him that maybe what he's starting to like best is that when she's around, these last couple days, anyway—he can't quite remember if it was like this before, if she was like this before— what he likes is that the universe seems tilted partway off its axis, and she finds ways to enjoy that, finds ways to make him enjoy it, too. Jeff and Aaron sing the whole song. Neither of them looks at the words on the screen. They've got it memorized. This is their act, their gig. This is what Jeff and Aaron are all about. They finish, Jeff hanging on to a high note, and the place goes kind of bonkers for them, the kids over in the corner, especially. Jeff and Aaron are stars inside Gubbio's. Jack looks over at the tables of locals. The girls are trying a little harder than he'd noticed at first, miniskirts and tight jeans and little halter tops. They've maybe put on more perfume than normal for tonight. *Amber, let me have some of that.* One of them gets up, goes over to the table, starts flipping through the white binder. Thin green skirt, a too-tight pink

T-shirt that says CUTIE in sequins. There are two dimples in the small of her back, right above her ass. She keeps smiling at Jeff and Aaron, hooking her hair behind her ear. Jeff and Aaron start up another song, a country song Jack recognizes from the radio, something about bull fighting and Rocky Mountain climbing. The whole bar claps and cheers, and Aaron tips his hat to the crowd, a move that looks easy when he does it. The CUTIE chooses something out of the notebook, puts her card on top of the machine, steps back, and cocks her hip out and watches them from over on one side.

"This might be the most important thing that has ever happened to me," Rena says. "Is it always like this in here?"

"I don't know," he says.

"We may never leave," she says. She gets up, takes their empty pitcher to the bar, comes back with a full one, and sets it down. Then she walks up toward the table, says something to the CUTIE, and the two of them flip through the book together. Jack pours their glasses, checks Hen's Diet Sprite to make sure he's got enough left. Hen takes the red plastic cup back from him without once looking away from Jeff and Aaron. He's mouthing the words to the song they're singing. He may well know the words to every song ever recorded.

Rena sits back down at the table. "I signed us up for one," she says. "Do you sing?"

"No," Jack says. He's terrible.

"Come on," she says.

"I can't do it," he says. "I'm sorry."

"What about Hen?"

"I don't think he'll—"

She looks at Hendrick. "Would you like to sing with me?"

"Yes," he says.

"See?" says Rena, looking at Jack.

"*Quiero cantar una canción,*" he says.

"Holy crap," she says.

Jack squeezes his eyes shut for a second, then opens them again. *Well, Oprah, we always knew he was a genius. We just didn't know which kind.*

A new song starts, and four girls run up to the front, cluster around one of the microphones, start shouting along. Jeff and Aaron sing into the other microphone. Jeff gets his arm around one of the girls, then around a different one. More people come in. Gubbio's is filling up. There's a line at the binder of people waiting to sign up for songs. Jeff and Aaron are huge. Rena says, "Seriously: We can stay for a while, right?"

"We can stay as long as you want," he says.

She reaches across the table for his hand, takes it, lets it go. The song ends, and the girls sit back down. Aaron says into the microphone, "Rena Soluski. Rena, you out there?"

She says, "Last chance, champ. Sure you don't want to try it?"

"You don't want me up there," says Jack. "I'm telling you."

"If you say so." She stands up, holds her hand out for Hendrick. "You ready?" she asks him. "Do you still want to go sing with me?"

"Yes," he says, and works his way out of the booth. He takes her hand—of course he does—and they walk up to the microphone, and the place gets pretty loud. Here's this six-year-old boy getting ready to sing. Everybody's clapping, whistling. The local girls think he's just the sweetest thing in the whole world. Jack sips his beer, tries to wrap his head around the idea of his son standing up there in front of all these people. Hen's got his feet together, and he's looking down at his shoes—galoshes, red with yellow striping, the only shoes he'd let Jack put on him before they left. Rena whispers something to him. He shakes his head a couple of times, marches a little bit. Rena hands a microphone to him, gets another one for herself. The song comes on, and Jack knows it right away: His father owned this record, played it endlessly when he was a kid. Kenny and Dolly. "Islands in the Stream."

For a long time, Jack thought the chorus was *Olives in the street*. Because when he was eight, that made as much sense as anything else. *That is what we are.* The music comes around and Rena sings the first verse alone, her voice soft, not quite on key. Hen stares at his microphone. The bar stares at Hendrick. Rena sings. *Baby when I met you there was peace unknown/I set out to get you with a fine-tooth comb.* A little red ball bounces above the lyrics on the screen. She makes it through the first chorus. She's enjoying herself, he can tell, getting into it a little bit as she goes along. The lights move through their sequence. Rena goes blue, then green, then red. When Hen joins in on the next chorus, the hair on the back of Jack's neck stands up. Beth would love this. Or she'd say they were making a spectacle of him. One or the other. The crowd's cheering. Hen's mostly speaking instead of singing, but it doesn't matter. He's doing it. He's actually doing it.

Rena's dancing now, sliding her hips back and forth. Hen's a statue, microphone out in front of him like it's some injured bird he's picked up. *Sail away with me/To another world.* Hendrick sings *And we'll rely on each other/uh-huh*, and the whole place screams. Rena reaches out to pull him closer, but he sidesteps her, keeps singing. Another verse, the bridge, another chorus. *No one in between/How could we go wrong?* The song doesn't end, Jack remembers now. It just repeats the chorus until it fades out. Hen keeps right on going, knows the words already, starts the chorus over one more time even as the music fades. And then, suddenly, it's just Hendrick alone, singing a capella. The music stops completely. Gubbio's is dead silent. Hendrick sings. *Islands in the stream/That is what we are.* When he finishes—and there's a moment where Jack thinks he might not stop, that he might sing "Islands in the Stream" for the rest of his waking life—there's a long beat before the crowd goes jackshit insane, everyone shouting for his son, for Rena, for the two of them. Rena takes a big bow. Hen puts the microphone down on the table, and the contact bangs through the PA. This is one

more thing that can't be happening, something else that is not possible. The Beanbags would need video evidence. Jack almost needs
video evidence. Everyone keeps clapping until the two of them are
sitting back down in the booth again, and then Aaron says into the
microphone, "Let's hear it for that kid one more time," and the
place goes electric all over again.

Soon enough another song starts up, the local girls again. Rena
grins at him, touches his leg with hers under the table. He can't tell
if she did it on purpose. "So this is Gubbio's," she says.

"Yeah," Jack says. He can't quite hear right. His tongue's thick in
his mouth. His teeth taste like rocks. Hendrick's stacking the sugar
back up again, back to his old self, singing along with the girls.

"I like it here," Rena says. "This is a good place."

❧ ❧ ❧

About a week before Beth leaves, Jack wakes up in the middle of
the night to a kind of scratching sound. That's what registers first.
He wakes up and his eyes adjust to the thin sulfured half-glare of
the streetlight coming in from Frank's yard next door, the streetlight Frank badgered the power company into hanging this past
spring. *I'll tell you, Jack,* he said, standing there in the strip of weeds
between their driveways, *got to do something to keep a certain element from
wanting to come up to your property. You know what I mean?* The light
streams into their bedroom all night long now, no matter how Jack
angles the blinds. He's been to look at privacy shades, but the things
cost a damned fortune.

The scratching is still going. He lies there on his back, blinks.
The ceiling fan's noisy, too, broken or breaking, ball bearings
scraping in there on whatever ball bearings scrape on. Plus there's
a ticking. Something has definitely gone wrong with the fan. Pretty
soon, it will probably go ahead and cut fully loose from the ceiling
and fall directly on his forehead in the middle of the night, and it
will kill him, or at least give him a concussion. But that's not the

noise. It's something else, something out in the hall, scratching. Jack works through his options: Burglars? Terrorists undeterred by the streetlight? Hendrick?

Not Hen. Can't be. Hen still and always sleeps through the night. So: Terrorists or burglars. Or just one burglar, even. But burglars don't stand in your hall and scratch things. Burglars sneak past security systems, over laser beams, steal the diamond necklace. Jack and Beth have neither lasers nor diamonds. They have the silver tea service in the hutch out front, a wedding present from her mom. Why they have it, how they'd use it—he has no idea. He's not sure he's had a cup of tea since they've been married, much less a service of tea. He gets out of bed, bangs the living shit out of his toe on his way around, sees in all sorts of colors, swallows sentences. For a second he thinks he'll throw up, but that passes. He reaches down to touch the toe, to make sure he hasn't knocked it off, or bent it out at some awful angle. He's off to a bold start.

First he checks Hen's room, the official fatherly thing to do, stand completely naked in the hall and check on your son in the middle of the night. He's sleeping, of course. Stock still. Face down and turned just to the side so he can breathe, arms behind him, palms up. He's a rocketship. At first, after he was diagnosed, after it all set in for good, he'd sleep so still they'd wake him up to make sure he was still alive, stand over him, watch him fall back asleep. Then she'd want to wake him up again. *Even if he is dead, what will we do?* Jack wanted to know.

*But if we're there when he stops breathing—*

*He's not going to stop breathing.*

*But what if he does?*

*We'd have to sit here all night, every night—*

And at first, she did. The first week or so. But soon enough she was too tired. Amazing what being tired will do to your ideas about how you'll raise your kids. Hen on a leash at the mulch yard. The two of them giving in whole hog to the faucet-toothbrush thing, instead of trying to do anything about it. *Engage in various be-havior modification techniques.* When was the last time he wasn't tired? Jack can't quite remember.

He stands in the dark of his house, waits. Hears it again. The scratching. He's pretty sure it's in the closet, whatever it is. He stands still to make sure he's right. Yes. The closet. He walks over there, carefully, *don't creak the floorboards*, turns the knob as slowly as possible, opens the door. The sound stops, starts again. Jack reaches up for the pull chain for the light. He pulls it and squints in the sudden brightness and the noise stops altogether. Jack waits, counts to ten. To fifty. And the noise starts back up. It's down in the cor-ner, by the baseboard. He moves a box. The noise stops, starts. And then he sees it: Two paws hanging over the top of the baseboard, a nose sticking up over the top of a chewed hole that runs between the baseboard and the bottom of the wall. It's a rat. There is a god-damned rat in his house. Furry, pink nose. Like a pet store rat. Chewing on his house. Right at first he can't quite process it. He stands there and watches it chew. There'd been noises in the attic last month, Beth after him: *What if it's a raccoon?* she'd said. *Or a pos-sum? I don't want a possum in my house.*

*It isn't a raccoon. Or a possum.*

*How do you know?*

*It'd be heavier.*

*How much heavier?*

*Heavier. It's squirrels or something, in through the roof vents, probably. No big deal. I'll set a trap up there.*

She'd looked at him like he would never set a trap. He never set a trap. And now it isn't squirrels. It's a rat. Can you even have one rat? It's probably seventeen. A rat in his closet chewing a hole in his house, and sixteen more in the attic, down through the walls, cheering him on. *Go for it! Let us know what it's like on the inside!* Jack stands there in his hallway and tries to figure out what to do. The house is still except for the chewing, the ceiling fan, a few other creaks and groans as it settles down and down into its foundation. The whole place will fall in on them in the morning. He picks up the first heavy thing he can find, the wok that's in the closet now, along with most of the pots and pans, because of his fine work on the kitchen. He takes the top off of the wok—thinks it through enough to get the top off—and gets a good hold on the handle with his right hand, grabs the edge of the rim with his left, leans into the closet and just starts banging away at the wall, at the rat. It makes a hell of a noise, the wok ringing like a bell against the wall and the wood floor. He hits again and again, grunting each time with the effort. The rat disappears and Jack stops, stays like he is for a minute, peering down into the hole. It's pitch black in there. The closet light throws out weird shadows all around him. He is naked and tilted headfirst into a closet, looking into a hole that leads into the crawlspace, hitting a rat with a wok. He stands back up. His hurt toe is throbbing, maybe broken. But the rat's gone. He has run the rat off. He's a conquering hero. And then there's Beth, standing in the bedroom doorway, wearing a long T-shirt, his, something she's pulled on. She folds her arms. "What are you doing?" she asks him.

Jack does try to guess at what she sees. Her naked husband, wok in one hand and rubbing at his face with the other, two weeks without shaving, half-assed beard coming in around his jaw. He sucks his stomach in. He's not fat. He's just not twenty-one. He stands straighter, squares his shoulders. Here stands the brave warrior, etcetera.

"What are you doing?" she says again.

"There was a rat," he says, pointing at the closet with the wok.

"A rat?"

"Yes."

"A rat."

"In there," he says.

"In the *house*?"

"In the closet." It seems like an important distinction.

"Great," she says. "Perfect." She looks at Hen's doorway. "He didn't wake up, right?"

"I don't think so," he says.

"I mean, while you were dealing with the rat in our house. In our *closet*."

"I got rid of it," he tells her. "It left."

"You used that?"

"It was what I could find."

"You're going to wash it, right?"

"Sure," he says.

"Jesus Christ, Jack," she says. She pulls at her hair, at a knot. "I mean, this is just like you, isn't it?" She turns around, heads back for their bedroom. "This is just exactly like you."

He stands there in the hall after she closes the door. He turns around and puts the wok back on its shelf, turns out the light, scratches himself. She's right, is the thing. She always is.

❧   ❧   ❧

Jack and Rena eat what they can of the rest of the pizza and watch the girls sing songs for each other, for their skinny boyfriends, for Jeff and Aaron. Jeff and Aaron sing a few more by themselves. When Jack and Hen and Rena leave, the place is jammed full, more kids, more girls, plus a few older men, standing at the bar, leering at the girls, looking at their asses. These men sing, too, Jimmy Buffet songs, spill their beers on the ground in front of the microphones, down the fronts of their tucked-in golf shirts. Jack pays the bill, and they go out to the parking lot, where the noise is damped down to the dull thump of the bass line, muted screams when the crowd recognizes another song. Hen's tired, a little overloaded, but he's basically fine. Jack gets him belted into his booster seat. In the parking lot, under the green and red cursive Gubbio's sign, under SATURDAY'S ARE KARAOKE NIGHT'S AT

GUBBIO'S!, Rena pushes Jack up against the door of the truck, leans in, kisses him on the neck. He's surprised enough, the requisite amount, the amount he's always been when someone's been willing to touch him on purpose. But what did he think they were doing, anyway? Pizza, karaoke, drinks in the new back yard, *Take me to Gubbio's*—he's let it happen, or asked for it, or both. He's able to look behind her at the parking lot, at the cars all lined up, at cars running east and west out on the highway. The glow of the mall a half-mile up the road lights the horizon blue-white. Jack wonders if Hen's watching, if anybody else is, what this looks like to somebody who isn't him. She moves to his mouth. She smells like pizza. Even if he was aiming toward this, he knew, too, that she would have to be the one to come to him, knew he wasn't capable of doing it. Rena pulls back from him, says, "You're not kissing me back."

"I'm sorry," Jack says.

"Kiss me back, you fucker," she says, and he does what she asks. Her mouth is small. Her teeth click against his. She reaches behind his head, takes hold of his neck. She feels like something metal, something stretched, bent. She pulls away again, sniffs. She says, "I'm not crying."

"I know," he says.

"This is not good behavior," she says. "This is not the behavior of model citizens."

"I know," he says. "But it's OK." He wants her to keep making decisions. More than anything, that's what he wants.

"Take me to Mulch City," she says. "Stop off somewhere and buy us something to drink and take us to Mulch City."

"It's not called that," he says.

"I know," she says. "Take us there anyway."

He checks his watch. Not eleven yet. The Shell should still be open next door. He opens the door for her on her side, belts her in, too, and then walks around the front of the cab, running his hand

along the hood. It's a warm night. The weather pattern's changed.
Things have shifted. He's kissed her back. He takes her to PM&T.

❧ ❧ ❧

Here's one set of things he knows for sure: Hardwood. And shredded pallets, red-dyed or black. The black isn't quite black. It's more
dark brown. Pine nuggets, mini and regular. Cedar for dog runs,
or for keeping the bugs down. Cypress won't float. Wheat straw,
pine straw. A live snake once came out of a bale Butner was pulling
for delivery. He kicked it out of the truck with the toe of his boot,
said, *Goddamn snake in the pine straw. You see that son of a bitch? Ought to
charge extra for the petting zoo.* Top soil. Compost. Shredded leaves. Regular shredded, a composite mix of everything Canavan and all the
other tree guys bring in. For general use. Gravel, river rock, stones,
boulders. No rubber mulch. He'll never carry it. The dyed shredded pallets look fake enough. Rubber mulch is shit.

Here's another: He knows, now, part of what must have been
running through Beth's mind when she drove to Canavan's that
night, rang his doorbell, stood out on his porch, waiting. He knows
what Canavan must have thought when he opened the door and
there she was, when he saw what kind of trouble he might be getting himself into. It doesn't make anything any easier, doesn't make
it make any more sense, but now he knows.

❧ ❧ ❧

Cherry, in the Shell, gives him a serious look when he buys the
beer, a twelve pack, one of the long skinny boxes that's supposed
to fit in the refrigerator better. He also buys a bag of ice and a five-
dollar Styrofoam cooler and a *Junior Big Ol' Bucks* lottery ticket,
which he scratches off right there. Nothing. By the time he gets
back out to Rena, she's found a few towels behind the seat of the
truck, has made Hen a bed in the front seat. "He was freaking out
a little bit," she says. "He wanted to get down, so I let him, and all

he did was run over there to the hose thing and touch his forehead to it a few times. Then he came right back."

Jack says, "How'd you get him to lie down?" The cooler squeaks against his leg.

"I didn't, really. He did it on his own. He's got that tree book underneath him."

"Good." Jack puts the cooler on the hood of the truck, looks in at Hendrick, who's not asleep. He's lying on his side, eyes wide open, picking with one finger at the fabric of the seat.

"You know I've never actually been here?" says Rena. "I mean, I've driven by plenty of times, and I beep at you guys, but I've never actually been in here." She looks around. "It's kind of cool."

"You've never come over with Canavan when he's dropping shit off?"

She lets out a long breath. "You know what he smells like at the end of the day?"

"Basically," he says, "I do."

"Like gasoline," she says. "Like a lawn mower, actually. Like my dad." She's got her back to him, arm on the hood. "He smells like my dad would smell Saturday afternoons when he cut the grass. We had a big lawn. He'd stop in the middle, have lunch, and make the whole kitchen smell like lawn mower and sweat. Then he'd come back in when he was done and drink a beer and sit in his chair and watch golf on TV. During the week, before he'd come home from work, I'd sit in that chair and smell him. I mean, I love that smell." She kicks at the gravel. A big semi turns left through the traffic light, and then there's quiet again. "Like that first week in spring when suddenly everything smells like cut grass and lawn mowers again? But it's my dad's smell. I don't need my boyfriend smelling like that, too. So I wait for him to come home. I wait for him to shower."

He wants her to tell him other things. He wants to know about her dance recitals, her failed tryouts for the soccer team and the school play, her broken arms. All of a sudden, he wants to know everything. He says, "How did you end up here, anyway?"

"Here where?"

"Here in North Carolina. At Kinnett. With Canavan."

"We never told you guys any of that before?"

"I don't know," he says. "Tell me again."

"Can we go up on one of these piles first? I want to sit up there. It feels like we're at some ancient ruins or something, all these mounds everywhere."

"Sure," he says.

She points at the pine bark. "How about that one?"

"Ants live in it," he says. "Let's do the cedar."

"Ants?"

"They nest in it."

"What do you tell people who buy it?"

"Wear gloves," he says. "Plus it's just black ants. It's not fire ants or anything." He walks over to the cedar, then up in it, carrying the cooler, his feet sinking in to the tops of his shoes. He makes it to the top, ten feet off the ground, and turns around to help Rena, who's scrabbling up after him on all fours. She's got another towel from the truck slung over her shoulder. They get set up, spread the towel out, and he gets beers for each of them.

"You can see a lot more from up here," she says.

"Yeah," he says. "The inside of the dump truck, the roof of the office, the satellite dish over there on the Shell—"

"I think it's pretty up here. Don't ruin it."

"Who says I don't like looking at the bed of the truck?"

"Just don't fuck it up, OK?"

"I'm trying not to," he says.

"Good," she says. "Keep at that."

From up here he can see Butner's tomatoes all lit up by the light they've got hung up on the pole, their only security measure. It's all an enormous tangle, vines on top of vines. There might be fruit in there already, little blotches of red in all that green. Soon enough they'll get the tables set up out front, sell them for two bucks a pound. Drag the big plywood sign back out from behind the office: TOMS. Jack wonders how much Butner might have stashed away in coffee cans in his back yard, under his mattress. Thousands.

Rena says, "The market wasn't great, and my research wasn't great. And I didn't care much about being at an R-1."

"What?"

"You asked how I got here. I applied, and they hired me. Same as Beth." She leans back on her elbows. Her shirt bunches up around her sides. "And as for Terry, we met in a plain, dumb way. Over sandwiches at this place that's not even there any more. We were in line, ordered the same thing, and he asked if I wanted to share a table. He turned out to be funny. I'd given up on finding anybody at Kinnett. Everybody's either already married, or they're sociopaths. One of the two. Do you know Stephen Budbill, in Accounting?"

"I don't think so," he says.

"I dated Stephen Budbill for a few months. Then he wanted me to go on this trip with him, to Chattanooga, to some conference thing where people dress up like wizards and cast spells on each other and pretend to stab each other in the woods." She shakes her head. "My boyfriend was a wizard. And not even. A pretend wizard. He had a purple cape. He showed it to me."

"Did you go to Chattanooga?"

"No. But he made me go to some local thing in Raleigh one weekend. There were these guys there, in the parking lot of this branch library, hitting each other with swords. Real swords. And they'd made their own chain mail. Stephen knew them. After that I broke up with him. So Terry seemed—I don't know. Normal. Not a wizard. That's all I'm looking for, really," she says. "Give me a guy who's not a wizard, and I'm fine."

"I'm not a wizard."

"I know. I looked all over your house for the pointy hat."

Moths are circling in the lights at the Shell. A car rides by on 61, music blaring out the windows, bass rattling the trunk. She yawns, and he watches her neck go tight, loosen again. "How long do you think this whole thing might go on?" he says. He's asking her, he realizes, because he thinks she might know the answer.

"That depends on what you mean."

"How long do you think Beth'll live with Canavan?"

"I have no idea," she says. "I don't know whether him cutting his leg off will make this go on longer or not." She picks at the cooler. "What about you? How long are you planning on living in your dollhouse?"

"I like it over there," he says. "I like the lawn furniture."

"That's because you're still just playing at it," she says.

"Maybe so."

"You want to be able to set your shit up wherever you decide."

"I like sitting in the plastic chairs and watching TV," he says.

"You seem to, anyway," says Rena.

"How long are you going to stay in the condo?"

"At least as long as Beth's living with Terry," she says. "So we're back to the beginning."

"What the hell's happening here?" he says.

She digs a toe into the cedar. "You ask too many questions."

"Beth says the opposite."

"Beth isn't here," she says. "And by the way, I'm not coming on to you. That's not what this is. This is two grown adults having a little beer at the end of the night. There may be some physical contact between us before we're all done. But I think the situation warrants all of that. I think we've got some leeway."

"I'm still not sad," he says. "Just so you know."

"Oh," she says. "You're sad. Look at your fucking house."

"I don't know," he says.

A car pulls into the Shell, up to the air and vacuum. "Why'd you kiss Sarah Cody?" she asks.

A man gets out, puts money in the air machine. Jack can hear the coins landing in the bottom of the canister. The compressor kicks on, and he works on his left front tire. "I kissed Sarah Cody because she was cute, and because she kissed me."

"So why'd you kiss me?" she asks him. "Same reason?"

"That," he says, "and I enjoy your company." And other reasons he's having trouble naming.

The tire guy leaves, and the highway goes still. No cars, no trucks. She says, "Alright. Here's what I propose we do." It is hugely quiet. "We are going to sit up here and finish our beers," she says. "And we're going to wait until one more car comes into the gas station." She sips, wipes her mouth. "And after that, I think I'm going to throw myself at you, and we'll just see what it is that happens next."

"That seems a little dramatic," he says.

She holds up a handful of cedar. "I'm sitting on the world's largest hamster cage," she says. "My boyfriend tried to maim himself, and your wife is over there washing his socks. We have been to Gubbio's. We are now right here at Mulch City. The situation calls for drama, Jack."

"You think so."

"I do think so," she says.

Three cars go by, all in a row. None of them stop at the Shell. Jack drinks his beer, looks down at the dump truck. "Do you think he's actually asleep in there?"

"Let's say he is," says Rena. "As an indication of his faith in all of this."

"His faith in this?"

"Yep," she says.

There's a little bit of wind. It's hazy. A red pickup, an old one,
Toyota or Datsun, pulls into the Shell, pulls up to a gas pump. A
girl gets out, tall, pulls the nozzle down off the thing and starts
filling up. Jack didn't see her take the gas cap off, didn't see her
open the little door on the side of the truck. They both must be
missing. She's smoking. Everybody smokes over there. Cherry's got
a tin of cigarettes on the counter, sells them for ten cents each. Jack
imagines the whole thing going up in flames, imagines running
down there with the towel, or a blanket, trying heroically to put
her out. *There was nothing we could do. And then the whole thing just blew up.*
She pulls the nozzle back out of the truck, hangs it up again, digs
in her pocket, comes out with money. She walks into the store and
the bell rings against the glass door. Rena moves toward him. His
heartbeat speeds up. He can't right now remember the last time he
kissed Beth. He remembers touching the back of her neck while
she sat at the kitchen table, remembers bringing her another cup of
coffee. The girl comes back out again, bell bouncing. She gets in
the truck and pulls her door shut—she left it open the whole
time—and drives back out onto the highway, a cloud of bluish
smoke behind her. Jack has a good sense of where each bone might
be inside his body, gets an idea of his vertebrae stacked one on top
of the next. His hair itches. His mouth goes dry. Rena comes at
him on her hands and knees, straddles him, is on top of him,
pushes him down into the mulch. Even though this will untie his
entire life, it feels familiar, like he knows how to do it, or like he
could learn, and she's kissing him, and she may be crying again, or
she may just be sniffling because of the cedar—and he reaches for
her, reaches for her shirt, pulls it up in the back. He's touching her
skin, feeling out the plane of her shoulder blade, moving back
down to the waist of her jeans, slipping his hand under, one finger
finding the last of her backbone in the cleft of her ass. She's a rubber band. A spring. She kisses his ears, his neck, his chest through

his shirt. He works his hand around to her hip, feels the outcrop of bone there, pushes against her, wraps a leg around hers. She's tiny. He feels something starting to shift underneath him, feels them moving an inch or two, then a little more, and realizes too late that what's going on is that the whole mulch pile is getting ready to give, and all at once they're sliding down the back of it, a little avalanche, the smell of closets, of pet stores, and when they hit the wooden wall at the bottom, the cooler hits right after them, cracks open, spills ice and cans of beer everywhere. Rena's already laughing and trying to stand, and Jack gets himself upright, sits up, trying to figure out exactly what happened, what's happening. The cedar chips keep coming down the pile in a little trickle. Mulch is everywhere: In the cooler, in their hair, in his shirt.

He says, "Are you OK?"

"I hit my head," she says, still laughing.

"Are you hurt?"

"I don't think so," she says. "You?"

"No," he says. "I'm good."

"I've got wood chips down my pants," she says.

"I'm sorry."

"Don't apologize. It's not your fault." She unzips her jeans, pulls them down to her knees and shakes them out. She pulls on the waistband of her underwear, looks in there. "Nope," she says. "I'm unscathed." He stands up, too, shakes cedar out of his sleeves. There's dust in his nose, in his throat. She leans over, runs her hands through her hair, shakes it out. Her jeans are still down around her knees. He looks at her in the half-light. When she stands back up straight, she says, "Stop staring at me."

"I'm not staring," he says. "Just looking."

"You're staring." She pulls her jeans up, rebuckles her belt. "Shit," she says. "Maybe it's a sign."

"It's not a sign," he says.

"Everything's a sign," says Rena. "From one god or another. We're just lucky they're not down here raping us any more."

His heart's still going hard. He's sweating. And he'd like to take her home, which can only be one more misstep in a long, long line, but it's still what he wants. "Let's get out of here," he says.

She looks at him. "Oh, yeah?"

"Let's go home, take a shower, and go to bed." He's got clean sheets on the mattress. He put clean sheets on this afternoon, felt like an idiot doing it, did it anyway.

She stands there. Another car pulls into the Shell, a white Ford. She says, "OK, Jack. Let's go home."

And without saying anything more about it, they climb around the cedar pile, leaving the broken cooler and the beer where it is. When they get to the truck, for a minute Jack's afraid Hendrick won't be there, that he'll be standing across the highway, hands at his sides, repeating safety tips. *Only You Can Prevent Forest Fires. Stop, Drop and Roll.* But he's fine. He's right there, on the bench seat, asleep, face down and ass up in the air. Jack gets Rena up into the cab, shuts the door as quietly as he can. When he starts the engine, Hen moves around a little, but doesn't fully wake up. The air smells like rain. Jack pulls out onto 70, makes the familiar set of turns that take him back into Greensboro.

He thinks about Bethany standing in their kitchen, back from Chicago, looking at the back wall, trying to understand it, trying, possibly, for ways to tell him that it would be beautiful if he ever finished it. Thinks of her standing in Canavan's front hall, waiting for him to drop Hen off. Thinks about what it is that he might be doing here with Rena in the cab of his truck, what they might talk about tomorrow. When they get home, Yul Brynner greets them with the full show. Jack gets Hen put to bed, gets the door open the right number of inches, gets the nightlight shining in the correct manner. They shower, one at a time. Rena's waiting for him when he's done. Yul Brynner's already asleep again on the floor by the TV. He takes her into the bedroom. She laughs at him, takes off her towel, takes off his. He reaches for her. Her hips feel like golf balls, like limes. She bites at his shoulder, locks an ankle behind his. She is in my house, he keeps thinking. She is in my house.

# THREE

# Backyard
# Sidewalk
# Tricycle Racetrack

Jack comes up out of a dream where he's wearing blue coveralls with his name stitched in cursive over the pocket, and the coveralls feel kind of tight on him, and he's riding an escalator down into a stark white room filled with hundreds of wooden tables holding flat after flat after flat of impatiens, all colors, the foliage looking really healthy, which is what he's noticing in the dream, how good the foliage looks on all these impatiens, that these are the healthiest plants he's ever seen, but the phone's ringing, his work phone, and his bed's in the wrong place, because he's in the wrong house, and the light's gray outside, cloudy, and Rena's there in the bed, turned away from him, sleeping, and he gets up, finds the phone out in the den on the arm of one of the Adirondack chairs, looks for a minute at a *National Geographic* map of the Prince Albert Islands he's hung on the wall. It's a little crooked. The phone's still ringing. He answers it. It's Beth.

"What the hell?" she says.

He says, "What do you mean?"

"Where are you?"

"What?" He's still half in his dream. He goes to check on Hendrick, who's still sleeping.

"We said I'd take Hen out for pancakes. I'm parked in our god-damn driveway. Your truck is across the street. Rena's car is across the street. I'm standing here looking at them. Nobody's home over here. So what I want to know is, where the hell are you?"

He looks out the window. She's standing in their front yard, by the lamppost. He can't remember anything about pancakes. Doesn't matter. Here she is. "I'm over here," he says.

"Where's over here?"

"In the house," he says.

"In the house." She looks over. "In that house?"

"Yes."

"With her?"

"Yes."

"And Hendrick?"

"Yes."

"OK," she says. "Guess what? I'm coming over."

"Wait," he says.

"For what?"

"I need to make some coffee."

"You want me to wait while you make coffee."

"Please," he says. "Yes."

"What am I supposed to do?"

"Just give me five minutes," he says. "Let me get Hen up. Let me make coffee."

"He's not up?"

"No."

"He never sleeps this late."

"I know that," he says.

She stands in the yard. It's strange, seeing her out there and hearing her on the phone. "Fuck you, OK, Jack?" she says. "What is this?"

"I'm sorry," he says.

"Five minutes. Get him up. I'm still taking him out for pancakes. Whatever you've got going on over there doesn't change that."

"OK," he says. "Thanks."

"Fuck you," she says again, quietly. And she hangs up, puts her phone in her pocket, turns around, and walks up into their house. Jack measures a few breaths in and out. He thinks about grabbing Hen, grabbing whatever else he can carry, driving to Mexico. Mexico might work. They could hide out down there for a decade or so, let this all blow over. Instead, he makes himself go to the kitchen to get coffee started. Grounds and water. The pot sizzles on its metal plate. Rena comes out, her hair bent at funny angles. "Hello," she says.

"Hi," he says.

"Who was on the phone?"

"Beth. She's across the street."

"She's what?"

"Across the street."

"Like *here* across the street?" She goes to the front door. "Holy shit, Jack, her car's here."

"I know," he says. "That's what I'm telling you."

"This is bad," she says.

"It's not that bad." He hears himself say that. *It's not that bad.* He doesn't believe it.

"It's pretty fucking bad."

"I know," he says.

"Did you tell her I was here?"

"She sort of knew already."

"Oh, great."

"I didn't go into any detail."

"What do you mean, detail?"

"I mean I didn't say anything other than that you were here."

"Maybe we can still make this OK," she says. "Maybe there's still something we could do."

"I don't think there's anything we can do," he says. "We're here. You're here. She knows."

And what happens is that Rena starts laughing. She covers her mouth at first, tries to keep it in, but she gives up on that soon enough, gives over to a kind of whole-body silent laughing. She's shaking, holding a hand out toward him, making some signal to tell him, he thinks, to leave her be, that she's OK, and then she's laughing harder, making noise now, and he just stands there and watches her go. Finally she takes a huge breath, gets an I'm sorry out, turns both hands out at him, palms flat.

"Are you OK?" he says, and that starts her up again. She's bent over at the waist. She keeps making these high-pitched wails. He has no idea what to do. "It's not that funny," he says.

"Oh, God, I know," she says, still laughing, sliding down the wall until she's sitting on the front hall floor. "Oh, no," she says.

"Why are you doing that?"

"Because," she says. "This is what happens. I'm sorry. I'm sorry." She catches her breath, slows down. "Oh, fuck, Jack, she's going to kill us. She's going to kill me, anyway." She wipes her eyes, keeps laughing a little bit. "I laugh when I'm nervous," she says.

"It's not funny," he says again.

"It is," she says. "A little bit. It has to be." She looks up at him. "What do you think you're going to tell her?"

He pours them some coffee. "What should I tell her?"

"It better be something good," she says, and giggles.

"Maybe I won't tell her anything," he says.

"Maybe she won't ask," Rena says.

"She'll ask," he says. "You would."

"You could tell her—" She stands back up, sniffs. "I know. Tell her I cut my leg, and you're just here to help out. I hear that one works." She opens the front door, and they both look at Beth's wagon in the driveway over there. Rena pushes the screen door open a few inches, lets it fall back. The throw clicks in the latch. "You could tell her I need a kidney and you're the only match." She pushes the door open again. "We could say there was a gas leak in my condo," she says. "Or a bomb scare. A baby in a well."

"Those are good." He expects Beth to walk across the street at any moment. The low light makes everything on the street look greener, somehow. "Those are all good." Frank's cat is curled up in the driveway under the wheel of his Cadillac.

"Listen," she says. "I'm still glad I'm here, OK? I just want to say that. I mean, I'm not sorry about what happened. Whatever she's getting ready to do to us, I'm not sorry."

"Me, too," he says. Except that he is sorry, or he's some version of it, guilty enough about having done this, because surely this is not what you do. He's just not so sorry he wishes it hadn't happened. He's in the damn middle. He doesn't feel like he's gotten even, or like he's exacted any kind of revenge. Mainly what he feels like is that he's gone to bed with Rena, something that had never occurred to him was really possible in any kind of actual way, and so it didn't exist. Now it feels bizarre. It's not that he wants to take it back. It's that he's been awake five minutes, and everything that was wrong with him yesterday is still and completely wrong with him today, and it all might be getting much worse. He wonders if you can drive past Mexico. If you can drive over the Panama Canal and all the way down to Chile. To Uruguay. To Argentina. "I've got to wake Hen up," he says. "I told her I'd get him up."

"Go ahead," she says, and sits down in one of the chairs. "I'm good."

"You can sit in the back if you want to," he says. "You can hide out somewhere."

"Maybe I will when she gets here," says Rena. "But go ahead. Do your thing."

He leaves her there in the living room, in his living room, goes in and stands over Hendrick, who's awake now, staring at the ceiling. "Hey, buddy," he says. Hen's whispering the song to the

Allgood Construction commercial. *The smartest way to do your home work is Allgood.* If Hen could understand it—if he could explain it to him—what is it he'd say? *Honey, Mommy's coming over in a few minutes, and she may be a little bit upset.* He gets out some clothes. It already smells the same over here, or mostly the same. There's a new dust smell, the smell of this air conditioner instead of theirs, but Hen's room smells like Hen's room, the odor of a little boy sleeping, a cereal smell. What to tell Beth: That he needed a change of scenery, same as she did. That he and Rena went out for some pizza. That after that they went to Mulch City and made an enormous mistake on purpose. He gets Hen into a pair of jeans, some socks, a Spider-Man shirt at least one size too big for him. He won't wear any shoes, keeps kicking his feet away, so Jack just hands him his sneakers, and Hen takes them with him out into the den.

"Good morning," Hen says to Rena, like he's any kid in any house.

"Good morning," she says back.

"Today I will be carrying my shoes." Full sentences. More and more he speaks in full, relevant sentences.

"OK," Rena tells Hen. "I think that's just fine."

The doorbell rings. Yul Brynner flies down the hall, barking, announcing imminent attack.

Hen turns to Jack. "Daddy, someone is at the door," he says, leaving space between each word.

"Do you want to get it?" Jack asks him, trying to act like Hen acting normal is normal.

"WFMY News 2 is the name you can trust," Hen says. "When news breaks in the Triad, turn to News 2."

Jack wishes he had something good to say to Rena, one last thing, but he doesn't. The dog's still barking. He goes to the door with Jack, wags like hell when he sees it's Beth. "Hi," Jack says, because the only other thing he can think to say is absurd: *Welcome to our home.*

"Give him to me," she says, looking him right in the eye.

"Hang on," he says. There's a wren in a tree in the yard, screeching at them.

"Give him to me."

"I'm going to. I just want to—"

"I'll bring him back, Jack, goddamnit. That's not what I'm saying. Just give him to me so I don't have to stand here and look like—whatever I look like right now. I'll bring him back in a little while, and we can deal with whatever else there is then, OK?"

"Fine," he says.

"Where is she?"

"Rena?"

"Who do you think I mean?"

"She's here. In here."

"Don't think this has anything to do with you," Beth calls into the house.

"OK," Rena says, from her chair.

Beth takes a step inside. "You're right there," she says.

"Yeah." She doesn't say anything else, doesn't apologize.

"How the hell are you right there?"

"It's hard to say, exactly," Rena says.

"You're not embarrassed?"

"I am," she says. "Plenty."

"You seem more relaxed than embarrassed."

Rena doesn't answer. They stare at each other. "Hello," Hendrick says, still holding his shoes. Jack feels like his brain is evaporating through his eyes.

"Hi, sweetie," Beth says, bending down.

"¿Como estás?" he says.

She puts a hand on his cheek. "Perfecta," she says. "¿Y tú?"

"Perfecto," he says. "Perfecto." He holds onto the word, says it syllable by syllable.

Beth looks around, takes in the house, the plastic chairs, the TV on its box. She stands back up. "What is it you two think you're doing with the furniture in here?"

Jack says, "It was in the garage."

"This is how you live now?"

"I guess so," he says.

"You know what?" She picks up a chair by the arm, sets it back down. "I don't know who's crazier. You, for doing this, or you," she says, turning hard on Rena, "for dating him."

"I'm not dating him," she says.

"You like this?" Beth asks her.

"I'm here," she says. "I'm just here."

"You're not just here. You don't get to be just here."

It's all sliding somewhere, slipping. He says, "What if, instead—"

"I'm talking," Beth says. "OK? I'm talking to Rena."

"Sure," he says.

She looks at the wall. "What is that a map of?" She's not talking to Rena.

"Canada," he tells her. "Some islands in Canada."

"Show me his room."

"It's the same one."

She pushes past him into the hall, opens his door, stops in the doorway. "It's the same," she says.

"I know."

"I saw it over there. I saw it empty, I mean, so I figured you'd done this."

"I did."

"But I wanted to see it," she says. "It looks the same. Exactly the same."

"I know."

"I like the pictures of the plants."

"Shrubs," he says. "From a catalog."

"The catalog? You cut it up?"

"A different one."

She flicks the overhead light on, then off. "He's eating, right?"

"Yes."

"He's sleeping? You're putting him to bed on time?"

"I'm trying to," he says.

"Any more criminal activity, Jack? Have you painted your name on the water tower?"

"No," he says, but that's an idea. Maybe he should paint something up there. A blanket apology, an admission of guilt. Or just PLEASE SEND HELP.

She turns around, lowers her voice. "I don't get it," she says. It almost sounds like she's pleading with him.

"Get what?"

"What are you doing? What's she doing here?"

"What are you doing?" he asks her right back, whispering. "Isn't it the same?"

"It's not the same," she says. "It's not the same at all." She reaches for a picture hook in the wall, spins it around. It's all starting to press down on him. He can't believe he's really done this. He thinks he might cry, standing there, Rena in the other room and Beth right here. And he thinks Beth might, too, from the look on her face. Maybe he has done the one thing he could not do. Maybe the rules are different for him than they are for her.

"He's still speaking Spanish," she says.

"He is."

"That's good, right? That has to be good."

"Yeah," Jack says. "It is."

"I can't be in here with her here," she says, looking at the floor.

"I'm sorry," he says.

"You fuck off," she says, her voice small.

"I didn't—"

"You didn't what?"

He doesn't answer. He can't tell what he's supposed to say.

"I'm leaving," she says. "We're going. We have to go." She slides around him, back into the front room. She's in a hurry now, getting angry again. He can't blame her. And angry's better, easier. "When do you want him back?" she says.

"Whenever you like," he says. "Pick a time."

She checks her watch. "Maybe I'll take him to the park afterwards," she says.

"It's supposed to rain."

"I'll take him before it rains," she says.

"OK."

"So, two o'clock, then? Does that fit your schedule?"

"Two's good," he says.

"Fine." She tries to get Hen's shoes on him, but he won't let her do it, either. "It looks like a fucking frat house in here," she says. "Except even those boys would have real furniture."

"This is what was here already," he says.

"Terry's doing fine, by the way," says Beth, not looking at Rena, still working on Hen's shoes. "He's doing great. In case you want to know."

"Good," Rena says.

"You want me to tell him anything from you?"

"No," Rena says. "I don't think so."

"This doesn't have anything to do with you," she tells her again.

"Maybe not," says Rena.

"The both of you are a couple of goddamn fools," she says.

"Goddamn," says Hen.

She gives up on the shoes, takes Hen's hand. "How does it all end up, do you think, Jack?" she asks.

He doesn't answer her.

"What about you?" she asks Rena. "Do you have this figured out?"

"I don't have any of it figured out yet," Rena says.

"Yet? So we should just wait until you understand it all? Will there be some kind of announcement? A briefing?"

"You're still with Canavan," Jack says.

She spins around. "This cannot possibly be your way of keeping score."

"No," he says.

"So what is it, then?"

It's karaoke night. It's Gubbio's. It's whatever snapped free in his head when he bought this house. "I don't know," he says. "Maybe we could talk about it some time."

"What?" she says. She stares at him, or past him. "Forget it," she says. "I'm going. I'll bring him back at two."

"We'll be here," he says, but then he changes it: "I'll be here," he says.

She turns to Rena. "Do you have any tricks for getting him to wear his shoes?"

"I don't," she says.

"Good," says Beth. "Don't get any." She puts her hand on Hen's head. "And how about you?" she asks him, trying, Jack can tell, to make her voice bright. "Are you ready?"

"¿Listo?" he says.

"Sí," she says. "Vamanos."

"Kernersville Chrysler Dodge is the Triad's Price Leader," he says.

"Yes," she says. "I know." And she walks him out the door, leaves it standing open behind her. They cross the street. She loads him into the wagon. Jack follows her out. It's the same as watching her back out of the driveway the day she left, except now she's got Hen with her, which makes it not the same at all.

He sits down on the steps, tries to figure out what it is they might be attempting to do to each other now. He takes a few long breaths. Rena comes out, brings him his coffee. "Thank you," he says, watching Beth stop at the end of the street, watching her blinker flash, watching her turn and pull away. He dips his finger in his mug to see if he can feel temperature, to make sure some or any of this is actually happening.

"You're welcome," Rena says. She cracks her neck. "Well."

"Yeah."

"That could have been worse, don't you think?" she says.

"I guess so," says Jack. Then he says, "I don't know how."

"Nobody got killed. There's that." She sits down next to him. "May I sit here?"

"Sure," he says.

"We could have been at my place. That would have been worse."

"How?"

"It would have been," she says. "Believe me." Jack looks at his yard, at his truck in this driveway. A couple of delivery vans drive past. He's keenly aware of Rena being there next to him, of her having slept next to him. It's like she's some radio tower, blinking away above the tree line. He wants Beth to come driving back down the street. He wants to go back to bed with Rena. "I feel like something bad is coming," he says.

Rena smiles at him, puts her hand on him. He stares at her knuckles. "Nope," she says. "Not something bad. Just something."

Three kids skateboard by in the street. They're fourteen or fifteen, skinny, tall, not caught up to their own bodies yet. They look like puppets. The skateboards on the asphalt sound like marbles in a wooden box. Jack thinks about Hendrick at breakfast, how he'll space his twelve silver dollar pancakes equally around the edge of his plate, like a clock. The cement step is warm underneath him. Rena's warm next to him. He used to teach his kids about the importance of mapping expeditions in the frontier west, about how much it meant for the next people to go to have even a badly drawn approximation of what they might find. He works on the difference between something and something bad. He works on what new kinds of trouble might be headed his way now.

❧   ❧   ❧

A dinner, a year and a half ago, winter, Canavan's back patio, Canavan's birthday: The two of them out there, freezing, Canavan pushing a few logs around the bowl of a new copper firepit Rena'd given him. Beth and Rena had come outside with them at first, but when Canavan stoked the fire back up for one more round they said they'd had enough, said they were cold, went in to work on the end of the bottle of wine. *You boys stay out here and play as long as you want,* Beth said. Canavan and Jack were drinking scotch, a bottle Jack had brought him. Jack dropped his first glass on the ground while Canavan was fooling with lighting the fire. *It's OK, it's OK,* Canavan told him. *Those are cheap glasses. I need to replace them anyway.*

*Well, what about the scotch?* Jack asked.

*That part's the tragedy,* he said. And he poured him another one.

Canavan was feeling it, was talking about turning thirty-three. *My Jesus year,* he kept saying, poking at the fire, sparks up into the sky. Jack listened, nodded, made noise when Canavan paused so he'd know he was still following along. *Time for me to do something big,* Canavan was saying. *Right?*

*Like what?*

*Like I don't know. Something big. Sell the house and buy a camper and get one of those maps for it where you add stickers for every state. See the country.*

*It's not time for you to do that.*

*Why the hell not?*

*Because your life's here,* Jack said.

*So's yours.*

*Yeah.*

*And that's OK with you?* Canavan had wanted to know. *I mean, all the time?*

Jack was looking in through the sliding glass doors at Beth, at Rena, thinking about how he was maybe pretty lucky, thinking about Canavan being lucky, thinking that having a life here wasn't such a bad thing, that he'd done fine for himself, that Canavan had done just fine, too. That was the scotch, probably, but still. *It is*, Jack said. *It's OK with me.*

*Me too, then*, Canavan said, topping his own glass off, topping up Jack's. *You sold me. No campers.* He leaned back, looked at the sky. *You know what I think?*

*What?*

*I think this spot right here is the navel of the universe.*

*You're drunk*, Jack said. Inside, Beth said something, and Rena laughed.

*Still*, said Canavan, throwing another log on. *You listen to what I'm telling you, OK? This is the fucking navel of the universe. The dead damn center.*

&#x1F33F; &#x1F33F; &#x1F33F;

They're getting a thin rain now, from the storm, Ashley, and he runs the wipers back and forth on the way to PM&T. Rena's following in her car so he can drop the truck off with Butner and Ernesto, who are in for a Sunday delivery, a big job. Twenty yards of hardwood. Two trips. Jack's thinking hard about Beth calling him on the phone from their own front yard. About what he might say this afternoon when she brings Hen back. He keeps looking in the rearview to make sure Rena's still with him. This all feels like it's happening to someone else. At the yard, in the shed, Butner's telling Ernesto about a strip club in Alamance County called The Parasite.

"Why are you always talking about things like this?" Ernesto says when Jack comes in the door. Rena's waiting in the car.

"Shit, man, it's OK," Butner says. "Right, boss man?"

"Where's Hendrick?" Ernesto wants to know.

"It's a long story," Jack says.

"Anyway," says Butner, pulling Jack into the conversation. "Here. Come on. You'll like this, too. They've got this one girl there with one leg shorter than the other one. She's a hell of a pole dancer."

"OK," Jack says. "Maybe—"

"And she was going around the pole, and she kept sort of looking at everybody sideways, kept covering up her one side, and my buddy kept asking me what was up, and then when she turned around, she had a goddamned colostomy bag on!"

Ernesto says something Jack doesn't understand, shakes his head like he feels sorry for them, walks out into the rain.

"She was fantastic," Butner says. "Really talented. She had this move she did with her good leg? Amazing stuff."

"The Parasite? It can't be called that."

"I'll take you out there."

"Thanks," Jack says. "But no."

Butner watches Ernesto move a couple of trees around. "Too much for Paco's virgin ears, I guess."

"I guess."

"So where is the little man, anyway?"

"With Beth. For a few hours."

Butner looks at Rena waiting in the car, looks back at Jack. "Who's in the car?"

He feels caught. Or diagnosed. "Rena," he says.

"Who's Rena?"

"She's Canavan's girlfriend."

"You're shitting me."

"It's true," Jack says.

Butner picks his nose, grins. "Canavan's girlfriend," he says. "Goddamn." He waves to Rena. She waves back. "Nice job," he says. "I mean, this'll all end in violence, but nice job."

"Violence, how?"

"Somebody will definitely end up fucking you up."

"Why me?"

"Look at you," Butner says. "It'll be you." Then he says, "Shit, I don't know. Maybe you'll get lucky. I'm impressed, anyway." He picks up a marker off the desk. "But be sure to call me up after all y'all go out and purchase handguns and slingshots and Japanese army swords, OK? I want to watch."

"I think maybe I've screwed up here," Jack says.

Butner says, "But are you having fun?"

"A little bit," Jack says.

"Enough fun?"

"I think so." He's always liked being around her. Turns out he likes sitting in the back yard with her, eating crackers. He liked last night just fine. He has not liked this morning that much.

"You didn't start this, man," Butner says. "Remember that."

"Yeah."

"So."

Jack's not sure what he means, so he doesn't say anything. Butner looks at him. "What?" Jack says.

"So give me the damn keys to the truck and go do whatever it is you're planning to do."

"OK," Jack says, and hands him the keys. They're on a boat key-chain, a blue floatable puff that says AAMCO.

"You wrapping that thing up?" Butner wants to know, pointing at Jack's pants with the keychain.

"I'm not sure that's really—"

"Wrap that motherfucker up," he says. "This has been a public service announcement. Wrap up your peckers out there, germs and gents. Do not get warts on your dicks."

"I appreciate your advice," Jack says.

"I'm here to help," Butner says, and he hangs the keys off a corner of the whiteboard. Jack tries to figure out what else he could

say, if there's any advice he could ask for, but there's nothing. Butner says, "What are you waiting for?"

"Nothing."

"So go," Butner says, and he does. He walks back through the
rain to the car, gets in. Her car smells clean. "What were you talking about in there?" she wants to know.

"Strippers," he tells her. "With colostomy bags."

"No, you weren't."

"It's true," he says.

"Do you want to go see them?"

"See who?"

"The strippers."

"No," he says. "No."

"Just offering," she says, and pulls out onto the highway. It's
warm in the car. The windshield's fogging over. She runs the wipers, and that makes no difference. She wipes a stripe clear with her
hand. "Where do you want to go, then?"

"Let's just drive," he says.

"We should find somewhere to eat," she says. "Do you want to?"

"Sure."

"Can we find one of those places with the green plastic trays
with the dividers? And metal forks?"

He says, "We can find any place you want."

"I like those places," she says. At the light, she turns south on 61,
takes it over the interstate, keeps driving. Jack counts years back
since he's had breakfast with someone he's just gone to bed with
for the first time. That math's easy. It's Beth, of course. He tries to
make himself think about something else.

∽  ∽  ∽

They drive by a place that may be called Family Dining. That's all
the sign says, FAMILY DINING, in red block capitals. "Perfect," Rena
says, stepping hard on the brakes. "That's our place." It looks like it

may have once been a gas station. Inside, there's a long steam table
with women behind it serving white beans, chicken quarters,
cornbread pancakes. They've already switched over to lunch. While
they stand in line, Jack starts to feel like there's something he
should be doing or saying, some grand speech he could be delivering. At the cash register, a man hands them each a Styrofoam cup
of iced tea, a napkin, some silverware. Jack follows Rena to a table
by the wall.

"You're thinking about this too hard," she says, once they're sitting down. "That's your problem."

"I'm trying not to think about it at all," he says.

"Well, it's definitely one or the other."

"The thing is, you were right," he says.

"Yeah?"

"What you were talking about last night. I don't have any idea
how to do this."

She takes a bite of beans. "How do you mean?"

"I mean, what Beth asked. How it ends. That's what I've been
working on all morning."

"God," she says. "Just eat your lunch. You *are* terrible at this."

"Aren't I supposed to be?"

"I guess so," she says. "But, what, I'm supposed to tell you how
it all goes?"

"That's not what I'm saying."

"Doesn't seem fair. I don't get to be the scorned woman or the
lovesick kid."

"You can be both of those, if you want," he says.

"It's alright," she says. "I'll be those in a minute. First I'll clean
up your mess. Our mess, really." She wipes her mouth with her
napkin. "Here: Let's figure this out. When do you take Hen to the
doctor next?"

"What?"

"Straightforward question. Hendrick. Doctor. Next appointment."

He looks around the restaurant, at all the families dressed for church, the kids looking uncomfortable, unhappy, like they'd rather be anywhere else. "She'll want to go this week," he says. "She'll want to show them all of—whatever this is. Whatever he's doing."

"Well, then, that's it right there."

"What is?"

"You haven't been to the doctor since she left, right?"

"Right."

"Yeah—that'll definitely be it. She'll come over, pick you up, and the three of you will ride to the doctor together." Jack tries to interrupt her, but she stops him. "Listen. You'll be sitting there in the waiting room, full of its little choo-choo trains, all that wooden Brio toy shit, and something will happen, and you'll laugh about how ridiculous all this has been, how all of this has been some huge mistake, and that'll be it. The veil will lift. All this will be over."

"What veil?"

"I'm just telling you the truth, Jack. We need some kind of out here, anyway. So that'll be it."

"We need an out?"

"All of us do. All four of us. Or would you rather we just keep things set up the way they are?"

"I sat with her in the hospital," he says, trying to slow this down, whatever it is. "Nothing happened then. She comes to get him for lunch. You saw her this morning."

"Oh, come on. This morning doesn't count."

"Why not?"

"For sixteen different reasons." She takes another bite, leans back in her chair. "Stop playing helpless. You must have thought about this. All of us have, I hope. It's just nobody's doing anything about it yet."

He says, "OK."

"Here's my version," she says. "Yours might be a little different, but basically, it goes like this: You guys go to the doctor, whenever, later this week. Let's say Thursday." She shrugs. "For whatever reason. Because Hendrick talks now. Or talks some. It's all very exciting."

"It is exciting," he says.

"I'm not saying it isn't. You two have your little moment there in the waiting room. Your epiphany. You get back home, and you look around at the house, realize that it looks like what it looks like, and you decide to move back across the street at some point, because that's the only thing that makes sense. And it'll make you look sane, which will help. Then, once she's got Terry to where he can get up and around for himself, she moves back in with you."

"What about you?" he asks.

"What about me? I stay at the condo in Greensboro for a week or two, just to let him sweat it out a little more. I don't want to come off like I'm too needy. Maybe I drink a little too much wine and bump into the doorjambs for a while, but eventually I give up and move back home, too."

Jack says, "I'm not sure—"

"Here's the best part," she says. "All four of us wait a few months in our own houses before everyone decides that not talking to each other is stupid, that we should all find some way to put this behind us, or whatever the hell people say about this kind of thing, if there even is something people say about this kind of thing." She takes a deep breath. "And then we'll all go out for Mexican somewhere, and what will happen is we'll laugh about all this. About our little fling. Flings. We'll make miserable small talk. It will be horrible. Awful. Terry and I will ask you if you've sold the house yet. You'll say no, you haven't, but you've got plans to repaint the doors or something. You'll tell us all about the mortgage payments, how it's tough, but how you've figured you can make it a few more months if you have to. Beth will give somebody a knowing smile. Maybe it'll be me. She'll forget the rules. Eventually she and I can start trying to talk about school, and you and Terry can talk about whatever it is that you talk about—" She makes a motion with her hand. "Hockey and wood chippers and boobs. And then everybody goes back home to their respective original houses and you fuck Beth's brains out, some fancy position you picked up from me, or that you remember from some college girlfriend, or something you dreamed of doing with the elusive and lovely Sarah Cody, and I service old Terry, the same old same old, only everybody imagines it's really the other person they're fucking. For maximum fucked-upedness."

She's putting on a performance. The old men at the next table are staring. There's a sign on the wall that says NO CURSING NO FOUL LANGUAGE. Jack folds his napkin down into a thick square. "That's your ending?" he asks her.

"That is my ending," she says. She digs her thumbnail into her Styrofoam cup, little runes one after another. "That, or everybody ends up in court suing the shit out of each other."

Jack runs his finger along the edge of the table. He can see the four of them in some little booth at La Bamba, ordering Combination #6, nobody really looking anybody else in the eye. That's her ending. His feet feel spiked to the ground. He could maybe sit here in Family Dining for the rest of his life, try to hold things still. Because what he's starting to think is that he might not want an ending. Surely he doesn't want that one. Rena gets up, gets a refill for her tea, takes a cobbler. She waves at him from over by the steam tables, does a kind of elaborate curtsey. She is a creature from a completely different world.

They finish lunch and it's still raining, a little harder now. Rena drives them back toward home, taking surface streets, taking her time. Jack's losing basic track of the way things are supposed to work. He wonders: Can people do a thing like this and then come out the other side unscathed? Or scathed, but not too badly? He feels like one of those kids back in the restaurant, dressed in itchy clothes, kicking their chairs. Or maybe he feels more like an infant: A baby cries because he's not getting exactly what he wants right then. You're the person you are when you're six months old for the rest of your life, Jack thinks. We never change, never get much further along than that. We're always teething.

He's got more questions for Rena, but he's not asking them. They ride north for a while until she picks out a new road, turns, drives through a long stretch of tobacco. Nothing out the windows but fields and the occasional little house where they've put in something like sliding glass doors across where the garage door used to be. Cars and trucks for sale at the end of driveways. The county's got huge concrete pipes lined up in a ditch along the roadway, brand new fire hydrants every few hundred yards with orange bags tied over the tops. They must be getting ready to bring the sewer out from somewhere. They pass churches, a school, a post office. The post office looks too small for its parking lot, looks like a kid's toy. The flagpole out front dwarfs it. Whoever works there is growing vegetables out front, and the yellow of a squash flower flashes as they drive by. That would be an OK life. Stamp letters, grow squash. That would be an alphabet you could understand. Rena slows for a stop sign. TOPENBOTTEM ROAD, the sign says. Off to the right, down in a little swale, is something called the Carolina Flea Market and Undersea Adventures Mini-Golf. The booths for the flea market are set back, and the golf course is up front. The holes have blue Astroturf instead of green. The top of the mini-golf sign is cut to look like waves, and there are painted blue bubbles going up between the words. A posterboard is tacked to it that says MINI-GOLF CLOSED——FOR SALE, and there are For Sale signs hung around the necks of the various fiberglass undersea creatures set up in little scenes between the holes. There's an octopus, a lobster, a shrimp wearing sunglasses and a ball cap that says HOLE IN ONE! There's a catfish with an eye patch. Jack stares at them out his side of the car. "Pull over," he says.

She's already through the stop sign. "What?"

"Take us back to that putt-putt place. I want to take a look at it."

"Why?"

"I just want to get out and look around."

"It didn't look like they were open."

"I want to look at that catfish," he says.

"I don't think we have room for it in the car," she says, joking.

He's not joking. He's jerked around in his seat, looking back behind them. It's like some kind of lunatic sign. You do not pass this and not stop. "I just want to see it," he says.

"OK," she says, and turns the car around. She pulls into the lot, and he's out of the car before she's even got it fully stopped. It's still raining. He walks right up to the fence. His head's sparking on him. *This is not the behavior of model citizens.* The catfish is eight feet tall. Maybe a little more than that. It's standing on its tail, and has its flippers folded across what would be its chest. In addition to the eye patch, it's wearing a painted-on button-up Hawaiian shirt. Underneath the paint, which is flaking off in fingernail-sized pieces, the fiberglass is a grayish white. Rena walks up behind him, holds an umbrella over them both. "Is it smoking?" she asks him. It is, in fact, holding a cigarette in one of its flippers. It looks like there's glass in the end of the cigarette, maybe for a red light, for the glowing ember. Rena says, "I don't think they should let him be smoking in front of the kids."

"We should go get Hen," he says. "He would love this."

"OK," she says.

"Do you know where we are?" he asks. "Do you know how to get back here?"

"Sort of," she says, looking back at the road, frowning.

"We have to bring him back here, maybe play a round or something."

"I'm pretty sure they're closed," she says. "Like, permanently."

There's a trailer hunched off to the side of the course, to the side of the parking lot. It's blue. All the stripes in the parking lot are blue. There's a car out front of the trailer, an old Buick, fabric top peeling back, but he doesn't see anybody. Pine trees are growing up through wide cracks in the asphalt. The putt-putt's a mess, pine needles and leaves and plastic bags all over the course. The undersea creatures are for sale: It's never occurred to him that anybody would have to do anything with the animals when a putt-putt closes down. Or that putt-putts even close down at all. But of course they would, like anything else. Maybe there's some huge warehouse somewhere full of elephants and giraffes and rhinos. Zebras. Maybe they've got them all grouped together, all the rhinos in one room, all the giraffes in another. "We have to bring him back here," he says.

"Has he got a thing about fish?"

"No," Jack says, except that he's sort of got a thing about everything. Depending. A part of Jack is sorry he saw this first, without him. He wonders what they'd want for the whole set, for the catfish and the octopus and everything else.

"So let's go get him," she says.

"Yeah," he says. "Let's do that." With his good eye, the non-eye-patched eye, the catfish is looking at something off in the distance. He's having a smoke, thinking about what to do with himself. He's working on personal matters.

They get back in the car. Rena shoves the umbrella behind his seat. She says, "Why the catfish? Why that one, specifically?"

"I just know it's something he'd want to see," says Jack. "That's all." And he already knows he's going to have to buy the catfish, knows he needs it. Hen needs it. What he doesn't know yet is where he could put it. At the yard, maybe, up front, by the sign. Butner would surely be on board with something like that. They could have it out by the road, slow people down, bring them in. Or he could donate it to Hen's school, see if they wanted to put it on the playground, adopt it as a mascot. Or, he thinks, he could drive that thing over to Canavan's ruined front lawn and install it next to the driveway, bury it up to the base of its tail—a sure signal he'd be sending up to Bethany, to all of them, a smoking putt-putt catfish planted there, the flag of his nation.

&#8766; &#8766; &#8766;

Rena drops Jack off at the house, says it's probably best if she's not there when Beth brings Hen back, says she'll come back later. Jack tells her that'll be fine. He sits in the living room and thinks about putting one undersea creature in each room in the house, naming the rooms that way. The Jellyfish Room. Like some kind of bed and breakfast. He waits for Beth. She comes back right on time, but won't come in. It's pouring now. She stands in the door, huddled half under the little roof, ushers Hen inside, says, "Where is she?"

"She's not here."

"Good," Beth says.

"Look—"

"Don't," she says. "Don't tell me about how you're sorry. Don't tell me anything."

"But what if—"

"I mean it, Jack, goddamnit, OK?"

"Alright," he says.

"I can't talk to you right now." She squeezes closer to the door, trying to stay out of the rain. "I'm getting soaked," she says.

"Do you want a towel?"

"Have you even got one over here?"

He doesn't. Not an extra one, anyway. "I can find something," he says.

"Jesus Christ, Jack," she says.

He says, "What do you want me to do?" And at first it looks like she might actually answer him, might even step inside to discuss the matter, which would be fine—somehow it all weighs about the same today. Besides the prospect of buying the catfish, he can't hold a whole idea in his head for any length of time. Maybe she reads that on him, because instead of saying anything else, she turns around, runs through the rain to the wagon, leaves. He's found another way to disappoint her, a new way, and he's not even sure what it is.

"Jesus Christ, Jack," Hendrick says, and he's probably right, too. Jack gets him set up with the *National Geographics* and the TV. It's raining too hard to go back to see the undersea creatures. He wouldn't even be able to get Hen out of the car. He's not huge for standing in the rain, generally. They'll have to go tomorrow. Jack's disappointed—he wants to go now, right now. A dog on a TV commercial barks and Yul Brynner comes in to see what it was, then settles down in the hall. Their day winds itself through. He feels trapped in the house. He wants out, wants something to do. Hen's fine. Jack marches up and down. Late afternoon, Rena shows up with wet bags of groceries: Cornish game hens, bell peppers, expensive cheese, bottles of wine. She's got a recipe. A project. She's got projects for him, too: She takes over the kitchen, digs a cutting board out of some drawer, hands him a knife and a pepper, says *julienne.* Jack slivers peppers. They drink wine. It rains.

All this is associated with Tropical Storm Ashley, says the TV, which over the course of the last couple of days has gone ragged out in the Gulf and half-fallen apart despite the breathless cataclysmic predictions—*first named storm of the season and it could be a monster, folks, you'll want to keep it tuned right here*—and it comes ashore as just that, a tropical storm, not a hurricane, in Florida, does nothing, really, but rain and blow the live weather reporters around some. During the afternoon and evening the storm sprints through

Georgia and into the Carolinas. Live from Augusta and Greenville. White guys in yellow and blue slickers stand in the rain and talk about how there's really not that much damage. They use phrases like *dodged a bullet* and *Mother Nature's wrath* and *agricultural concerns.* The storm stalls out and spins.

Jack gets Hen put to bed, and he and Rena sit up a while, watching the TV, watching it rain. Across the street, Jack's yard is a lake. Over here it's a lake, too. A woman looks into the camera and tells everybody watching at home not to drive into standing water, not to drown. She says that. *Do not drown.* Hendrick ate Rena's dinner, ate the game hens, the peppers, everything. He said *gracias*, said *que bueno.* It's possible he might be starting to crack open a little, Jack thinks, just enough for somebody to be able to see inside. Though he's trying hard not to hope for anything. If Hen wants to eat game hen, let him. Don't make it a thing. Let him be himself, and see what might happen after that. *At this point, Ashley is mainly a rain event. There may be some embedded thunderstorms overnight.* Jack stands at the window and looks out at his driveways, waits for alligators, for pairs of alligators, for some dude to ride by, lean out of the ark, explain that *at seven years old you may see some signs of change. You may see some improvement.* No doctor would say that to them. None ever has. Hen's birthday is in a month.

"What would you do with it, anyway?" Rena asks him. She's finishing a glass of wine, sitting sideways in one of the plastic chairs.

"With what?" he asks.

"With that catfish. That's what you're thinking about, right?"

"Maybe," he says. The radar spins across the screen. He worries about the undersea creatures out there in all the rain, then remembers: They're fiberglass. And fish.

"So what would you do with it?"

"Put it out front of PM&T? Set up some kind of little playground over there or something? I don't know." He keeps glancing over at her just to make sure she's still there. It's like she's a planet, like she's got her own moons. He's one of them.

"What does a catfish have to do with mulch?" she asks.

"Probably nothing," he says.

"You could change the name to 'Catfish Mulch.' "

"I could get Butner to paint an American flag T-shirt on him."

"You want a catfish wearing a T-shirt out front of your store?"

"People would stop to see that, don't you think?"

"And then think to themselves, 'I could really use some mulch'?"

"Maybe," he says.

She gets up, puts her glass in the sink. "This is probably the part of you I like best," she says.

"What?"

"A catfish in a T-shirt. I like that best. You've got big, stupid plans."

"Bethany is not so fond of that part."

"She's got to live with it," Rena says. "I get to just look at it."

"What part do you like least?" he asks her, only half-wanting to know.

"God, I don't know," she says, standing behind him now, hands on his shoulders. "Can we go to bed?"

"You're staying?"

"Why not?" she says.

He can think of plenty of reasons why not, but he lets her take the remote from him and she flicks the TV off, the screen fizzing, the weather gone. The room goes dark but for Frank's streetlight finding its way in. It's late. She takes his hand, leads him down the hall. It still doesn't entirely feel like he's doing anything wrong. Or: There's nothing left for him to do wrong. He's done it all. They don't talk. They take off their own clothes, climb down into opposite sides of the bed. He kisses her, kisses her neck, gets his face buried in her hair. She smells like pine needles. She's smaller than Beth is, slighter, more like rope. Her breasts are small. He keeps kissing her, tries to think about technique instead of anything else, about where his mouth is supposed to go, where his arms go, and somehow she gets up on top of him, gets her hands dug into his back, his side, and she pushes against him, down onto him, and as he pushes back she rocks her hips against him once, then twice, and that's it, he can't stop himself, grabs her, comes right then, right away, way too fast. There was one thing left to do wrong. He feels like a complete jackass. He's sweating. They both are. She rolls away from him, says, "Well."

"Sorry," he says, whispering. Like if he talks out loud it'll make it worse. "Give me a few minutes. We'll try again."

"You're fine," she says. "Don't worry about it. That was fun. Like it was your first time."

"I'm sorry," he says again.

She puts her hand on his belly. "You seemed kind of desperate. I liked that."

"I am kind of desperate," he says, because it seems true.

They lie there on the mattress. The room feels bigger than the one across the street, even though he knows it isn't. He's measured. Maybe it's because he's got no furniture in it. He feels lonely in here and happy all at once. He's almost comfortable, absurdly. Almost calm. The A/C kicks on, a whole different set of bangs and wheezes in this house. She says, "Are you OK?"

"Sure," he says.

"You're not OK."

"I'm fine," he says. "I'll be fine."

"You don't want to talk about it."

"Not right now," he says, and hopes she'll let him get away with that.

"Can we talk about something else, then?"

"Like what?"

"Like anything," she says. "I don't know. I'm awake. Tell me about your first time. Tell me who it was."

"Come on," he says.

"I'm serious. I want to know."

He folds his pillow in half. "Lesley Wofford," he says.

"Yeah?"

He says, "She played trombone."

"How was she?"

"She was OK. She was the only girl trombone player, so everyone kind of liked her."

"I meant in bed."

"Oh. She was fine."

"Fine?"

"I was fifteen. She was amazing, for all I knew."

She turns on her side, facing him. "You want to hear about mine?"

He doesn't, in his dumbass swashbuckling way, but he knows enough not to say so. "Sure," he says.

"Bobby Theroux," she says. "We were seventeen. His parents were divorced. We did it at his dad's place." She scratches at the inside of her thigh. "His dad worked late all the time, and we fucked on the living room floor, right in front of this huge aquarium. The whole time I just kept watching these yellow and black angelfish swimming back and forth. I was trying to figure out if they could see us through the glass. If they were watching me, too. We broke up a week later."

"Why?"

"Because it was the end of the school year, and he was moving to Dallas. We were trying to be grown-ups about it, so we just broke up."

"That's a sad story," he says.

"It's not supposed to be," she says. "It was actually really good.

I got to figure out what sex was, and I didn't have to be in love with him. Bobby Theroux. Everyone should get it that way."

"I was in love with Lesley," he says.

"Of course you were," she says.

"What does that mean?"

"Nothing," she says. "It's a compliment."

It doesn't feel like one, but he lets that wash past. The wind pushes against the roof of the house, against the windows in their frames. "What do you think they're doing right now?" he asks her.

"Who, Lesley Whoever and Bobby Theroux?"

"Or Beth and Terry," he says. "Either way."

"I'll tell you," she says. "Lesley went on to become a concert trombonist, and Bobby owns a Ford dealership. A big one."

"That's great for them."

"I know, I know. Great news. A couple of great kids." She rests one leg over his. "Beth and Terry," she says, "since you didn't ask, are probably sitting up watching movies. *Cannonball Run. Cannonball Run II.* Terry likes Burt Reynolds movies."

"He does?"

"Yeah, but I have no idea why." Jack listens for Yul Brynner, for Hendrick. Nothing. "She's not fucking him any more, by the way," Rena says. "In case you're wondering."

"Burt Reynolds?"

"Don't be stupid," she says. "You know it, too. Beth's not fucking Terry any more."

"She's not?"

"I could see it on her right when she came through the door. Plus he's crippled now, anyway."

"Why are we talking about this?"

"Because if you're going to lie here in bed with me, then we both need to say we know that she's stopped fucking him."

"OK," he says. "Fine."

"Say it," she says, serious.

"We said it."

"I said it."

He says, "She stopped."

"Yeah?"

"Yeah."

"And you're OK with that."

He doesn't know what it would mean if he were or weren't. "Yes," he says.

"And now you're going to buy a giant catfish."

He knows the answer to this one. "Yes," he says.

"And the rest of them, too, right? You're going to buy them all?"

"Maybe," he says. "Probably so."

"Who is it you're trying to impress?" she asks.

"You, aren't I?"

"It's working," she says. "Some." She puts her hand flat on his chest. "Who else?"

"Nobody," he says.

"Everybody's a safer answer," she says.

"Fine, then," he says. "Everybody."

❧   ❧   ❧

To take Hendrick to see them. To take himself again. Because every stray should have a good home. He's got his reasons. When they arrive, he's happy to find it's all still blue. The flea market tables and metal roofs are blue. The trailer is blue. The Buick parked out front of it, same car as yesterday, is blue. Jack gets Hen out of Rena's car, and Rena takes Yul Brynner over to the side of the lot, lets him pee. Hendrick stares up at the undersea creatures. It rained all night, all morning, but the remnants of *Ashley* have pulled north and out to sea, are spinning off toward Philadelphia and New York and Massachusetts. There are a few high, thin clouds left, but there's sun, and it's hot. Like they're in a greenhouse. Jack leans on the wet wooden fence and the top rail gives way, crumbles and half-implodes. Hendrick picks up one of the splinters and holds it out. "Thank you," Jack says.

"You are very welcome," says Hendrick.

The trailer door opens up and a woman comes out, smoking. She's so slight that at first Jack thinks she's a girl, a twelve-year-old girl. Up close, though, her face is creased. She's fifty, maybe older. She could not weigh a hundred pounds. Jack wipes his hands on his jeans. "Sorry about your fence," he says.

"It's rotted to shit," she says, her voice high, porcelain. "Don't sweat it. We're closed."

"When are you open?" Rena asks, back with the dog.

"We're not," says the woman. "My husband runs the flea market. He's in the hospital. We'll open that back up when he's out. But the golf's closed permanent." She waves the hand with the cigarette at the undersea creatures. "Don't make enough money to keep it going. His stupid idea. Wanted a soda stand and some mini-golf. Donald loves the ocean. When he said he wanted the holes in blue, I said, No, people want their mini-golf green. But he wanted blue." She drags on her cigarette, ashes it down onto her shoe. "And look where that got him. We got a cooler-freezer for sale, too, if y'all could use one. I'm selling whatever I can while he's in."

"I'm sorry," Rena says. Jack looks at the catfish, wonders how many people it might take to move it.

"Don't be," the woman says. "Best thing for him. Only thing for him, really. Doctors told him to lay off, and he kept right on drinking. Had a heart attack, and when the paramedics came, they found fifteen bottles of wine behind our headboard. I didn't even know they were there. Now he's drying out. He'll be all dried out when he comes home. Like a raisin. Then we can go on a trip. Maybe to see the Grand Canyon. I've never been west of Tennessee."

"That'll be nice," Rena says.

"Nicer than Donald falling off the back porch at three in the morning and spraining his ankle. Which he did the week before he had his heart attack."

"Wow," says Rena.

"Wow is right," the woman says. "I tell you what. Don't marry a boozer. More trouble than it's worth. First few months are fun, like it's all some long party, but then it's bad news and worse. Listen," she says, looking out at the blue holes. "You want to play a round? It's all wet, and it ain't been sweeped out or nothing in months, but you can probably play through the leaves and all that. Never mind what I said about being closed. Come on. I'll give it to you free."

"Absolutely," Jack says. He loves this woman, her drunk husband, loves the Carolina Flea Market and Undersea Adventures Mini-Golf. There's something here, finally, that seems correct. Broken, but correct.

"What about Hendrick?" Rena says. "And Yul Brynner?"

"You know who loves the mini-golf?" the woman asks. "Kids love the mini-golf. He's free, too. And you can let that dog run loose in there. It's all fenced in. Keeps the deer and raccoons out. Donald says we'll get bears in here soon enough, with the way they're cutting all the forest out to put in these goddamn houses. I tell him if we get bears then I'm moving someplace else. Anyway. Just cut the dog loose. I don't care if he shits the place up. Holes aren't for sale, anyway. Can't be. It's all poured concrete, and that turf is glued right to it. They're probably there forever. Be there after we have nuclear war. Just the animals and all the putters and balls and scorecards is what we got for sale."

Jack checks the low chicken wire that runs around the perimeter of the mini-golf. It'll be fine for Yul Brynner. He says, "Do you have a cigarette I could have?"

"You don't smoke," Rena says.

"Sure, honey," says the woman. "But they're menthols. I hope that's OK." She shakes a long skinny cigarette out of the pack for him.

"You don't smoke," Rena says again.

The woman hands over a lighter and Jack gets it going. It tastes awful, but he keeps at it, blows a cloud of smoke out of his mouth. He says, "I just feel like it."

"That's what I always tell people," the woman says.

Rena looks at him, blinks. "You're freaking out," she says.

"I'm not freaking out," he says.

"You are. I get it. That's what this is."

The woman looks at each of them. "Tell you what," she says. "I'll go get your scorecards out and get the putters lined up. Y'all come on up to the window when you're ready."

"OK," says Jack.

"It's fine if you're freaking out," Rena says, after the woman has walked back up to the blue trailer. The border covering up the base of the trailer is light blue, cut into the shape of waves, like the sign. The woman goes inside, bangs the door shut behind her. "You should be," Rena says. "You're due."

Jack looks down the hill at all the empty tables, imagines what the market must look like going full bore, old photographs and Coke bottle glassware and stick pistols. Hendrick's playing with the rotted fence rail, probably trying to piece it back together. If she knew he was here—if Beth knew he was thinking about carting the catfish back home, or to the yard, Rena aside—she'd go pretty apeshit. *You've got to be kidding me*, she'd say. *But I'm not kidding*, he'd tell her. *That's the thing with me.* He can't let the undersea creatures end up out front of some knock-off burger place. It wouldn't be right. "I'm not freaking out," he tells Rena. "I just want to play a round. That's all. It seems like it'd be fun."

"That's not all," she says, squinting at him.

He makes a golf swing in the air, smiles at her.

She looks out at the course. "What's that supposed to be over there, do you think?" She's pointing at a lumpy pink cave.

"A coral reef," he says. He smokes some more.

"A coral reef?"

"What else would it be?"

"Give me that," she says, and takes the cigarette from him, puffs on it. "How can you stand this?" she says. "Goddamn."

"I've come a long way, baby," he says.

"Don't call me baby," she says, and drops the cigarette on the ground, crushes it out.

"Hey—"

"No. If I have to play mini-golf, you're not smoking. Or calling me baby. OK?"

"OK."

They stand there and look at each other. Hendrick pushes his forehead against a fence post. It holds. She says, "So are we going to play, or what?"

Jack lets Yul Brynner out onto the course, and the dog sprints the edges first, checking the perimeter, then starts sniffing everything, drinking rainwater out of the holes. He barks at a smaller fiberglass something, what looks like it's probably supposed to be a clam. It's got a big toothy grin and eyes on top of its shell. The shell opening is the mouth. It's a good thing to bark at. The woman opens up a window in the side of the trailer, and she gets five or six putters lined up, and six golf balls, all varying shades of blue and blue-green. She says, "Donald had to order from four different companies to get enough kinds of blue. I told him people would get confused, but he had to have everything blue. Said it all had to match up. He'd joke with the pretty girls about blue balls. It's a wonder he didn't get arrested. No one could tell them apart at night, under the lights. We'd get high school kids out here shoving each other around about whose was whose. And grown men, too."

"I like it," Jack says. "I mean, I can see where you'd have trouble, but I like the idea." He picks up a turquoise ball.

"Men," the woman says to Rena.

"I'm Rena," she says, holding her hand out.

"Lovely Rena, meter maid," says the woman. "Or something like that. I'm Zel."

"Short for Zelda?"

"Just Zel, honey," she says. She holds up a glass with something frozen in it. "I'm gonna have a daiquiri while you all play, if that's OK."

Rena says, "Fine by me."

"Can I get either of you anything? Or a Coke for the young man? We got bottles."

"No, thanks," Jack says. "None for me, anyway." Though the daiquiri looks good to him. Blue like everything else.

"I'm good, too," Rena says.

"Suit yourselves," says Zel. "I'm right here if you change your minds. With the blender. Just give the high sign. Here's your score-cards." She hands them across. "Now. Lemme give you the run-down. We got two courses. Twelve holes each. Don't ask. It was something to do with space. He ran out of room at twenty-four. Was going to add the last six to each of them eventually. In the back there. Clear some more trees out." She sucks at the straw in her drink. "Anyway. Two courses. Guess what they're called." She waits for them to guess, but not long enough. "Never mind. It's Atlantic and Pacific. Pacific's better, I always said. Got better holes. But play 'em both and see what you think."

Jack chooses a short putter for Hendrick, chooses one the same size for himself. He leans way over, pretends to putt.

"You've got a funny one there," Zel says.

"Yeah," Rena says. "Class clown. One in a million."

"Keep him," says Zel. "He seems nice enough."

"Oh, shit," Rena says. "Maybe I will."

Hendrick walks over to the gate, lets himself in, throws his golf ball for Yul Brynner, who runs after it, brings it back. Jack and Rena stand at the window, watching.

"Good-looking kid," Zel says.

"Thanks," Jack and Rena say, at the same time.

≈ ≈ ≈

Sometimes he thinks of his life like everything that's happened to him has been something he's at least half-fallen into: History because it was easy, mulch because it was even easier. Butner appeared as if Jack had rubbed a lamp right and been granted some wish. *Here's how it needs to be done*, is what Butner's saying every time he opens his mouth. Not that way. This way. Like Jack is some kind of protectorate in Butner's empire. And there was no HELP WANTED sign in the window when Ernesto arrived: He just arrived, was standing in the doorway of the office one day asking if they needed someone five days a week. Beth teases him about it: *Good things happen to Jack Lang.* Sort it all out another way, a more likely way, and Jack's standing alone out there on the lot for six months hemorrhaging money, piles of mulch around him, nobody buying a single thing. But he's been lucky, has tried to make a habit of often enough finding the low spot in the valley, watching the water come to him.

*You can't just let everything happen to you,* Beth tells him. *You can't always just wait.* Except this: When he's the one reaching, when he tears out his kitchen or buys the house across the street, it's that he's tearing out his kitchen or buying another house. It's the grand, flailing gesture, or it's nothing. He thinks of it like ballast, sometimes. A good day on the yard mitigated by trying to fix the shower handles, and breaking them off in the wall in the process. He's not hapless. He just makes certain of his calculations incorrectly. Gets excited. Forgets to carry the two.

He knows there's more required of him than this. That he cannot just ride along, and that he also can't just reach for whatever he wants. He thought marrying Beth might do it, or thought becoming a father might, but each of those things just made him more the way he already was. Those nights before Rena turned up at the door, he looked out his windows, thought about what Beth was saying when she left. *I can't do this any more. Not like this.* Maybe it's in what they ask Hen when he's clicking his teeth or shaking his head or popping his lips: *Hen, buddy, why are you doing that?* Jack knows *what* he's doing. He always knows. Auctioneer spooling off prices, his hand going up in the air. He knew *what* that was. But when Beth wanted to know *why* he'd done it, he had nothing good for her, or nothing good enough.

If he asked her—if he took a shower and buttoned his shirt and drove over there and asked her again why she'd moved in with Canavan—he knows she'd have an answer, or that she could find one. If she asked him, though, what he was doing out here getting ready to buy an oversized catfish off a blue golf course on a Monday afternoon with Rena, what would he be able to tell her that she didn't already know? Would he be able to convince her that the undersea creatures might be something new, something else? Something that could land them somewhere between the two kinds of mistakes he knows how to make?

❧ ❧ ❧

They're in the coral reef, almost halfway through Pacific. Rena beat him by three strokes on Atlantic. Hen's out on the other side of the course with the dog. The way he's playing is to hit the ball about ten inches at a time, then hit it another ten inches. He scored a thirty on the first hole, a thirty-seven on the second. He is an exceedingly careful player. They can see him from everywhere, just about, so they've left him to play his own way. Yul Brynner sits while he putts, like he's Hen's caddie. Zel's been watching them out the window the whole time, and when Jack hit a hole-in-one at the far end of Atlantic, Zel clapped. It was a thin sound coming across all the concrete.

Jack tees up, putts his ball, bangs it off a dented metal triangle in the center of the Astroturf, and it veers toward what looks like a real shark jaw sitting in some sand. They have actual sand traps here at the Undersea Adventures Mini-Golf. It would be an impressive layout, actually, with a coat of paint, some pressure washing, somebody to mow the parking lot.

Rena sets her ball down—navy blue—in the little rubber square, lines up her putt. She hits to the far side of the triangle, up and around it on a little hill, and her ball coasts back down toward the hole itself, which has a wooden fish arched over it, blue with white and black stripes. It looks homemade, like maybe Donald made it himself. Its smile is crooked. Her ball bounces off a fin and stops right in front of the hole. "Hell, yes," she says. "Would you look at that?"

"I'm looking," he says, looking instead at Hen, who's tapping his putter six times on the ground before every shot. One, two, three, four, five, six.

"You're not," Rena says.

He turns back to her. "Sorry," he says.

"You go off on your own a lot."

"What?"

"There are just times when you're not really in there, you know? Where you're not really talking to people? Not all the time, but there are times."

He goes over to his ball, knocks it out of the sand. It rolls almost up to the hole, up next to hers. He putts his in, putts hers in, too. "I talk," he says.

"Beth says you don't. She says you don't talk to anybody, really.

I didn't ever believe her, but now I think I might see what she means."

"That's not fair," he says. "We talk. Beth and I talk. You and I have been talking all day. We were talking just now."

"Not really," she says.

"Yes we were."

"Well, then, do it again," she says. "Go."

"What do you mean, go? You can't just tell somebody to go."

"Sure you can." She picks up the golf balls, walks out the other end of the coral reef, toward the next hole. "You can talk about anything. I don't care. It doesn't have to be hilarious. It doesn't have to feature you kissing some child. Just talk to me."

He checks Hen again. He's leaning over, forehead on the end of his putter. A still shot from a dizzy bat race. It's hot. *Go.* "OK," he says. "Here. Last Fourth of July, we took Hen to the parade downtown. In Greensboro."

"See?" she says. "That's all I need. A parade story. You're doing fine. Baby steps."

"He likes parades," Jack says. "But he's not supposed to."

"Not supposed to, how?"

"The doctors are all the time telling us things he won't be able to do. And then he does them. Like he's not supposed to like crowds, but he likes parades." He shakes his head. "When they find out he can speak Spanish, the Beanbags will lose their shit."

"The Beanbags?"

"His therapists."

"Why are they called that?"

"I call them that. They have beanbag chairs."

"Oh."

"We had a doctor one time tell us to think about putting him in a home. He told us we'd be lucky if he ever fed himself," Jack says.

"What'd you do?"

"It was Beth," he says. "She was on the ceiling—we both were—but she scheduled an appointment with someone else, and that was the woman who told us not to make our minds up about anything yet, that we should just ride along and see what happened. She was one of the first ones I liked. She seemed human. She was the first one to tell us about food, about making his diet right."

"And that worked?" she says.

"It did," he says. "Some."

The wind picks up, blows oak leaves and slips of paper around. "Do they know how he'll be?" Rena asks. "I mean, if he'll get better?" She scratches her leg with her putter. "Can he get better?"

"Nobody knows anything," he says. "It's all bullshit. The books are bullshit. Nobody knows what the hell they're talking about."

"Is that true?"

"No," he says. "Not always."

They're both watching Hen now, watching Yul Brynner watch him. "What's it like?" she asks him.

"What is what like?"

"All of it. Raising him. Having him."

"You and Beth never talked about this?"

"We talked about it."

"What did she say?"

"I'm asking you, Jack."

He rubs his nose. "It's like it's always happening, every minute," he says. "It's like you're never, never not doing it."

"You're tired."

"Fuck yes," he says. "Very. All the time."

"And Beth."

"She's tired, too."

Rena sits down on a bench. It's shaped like a dolphin except for the part where she's sitting, which is flattened out. "You two aren't that pissed off at each other," she says.

"I think she's pretty pissed."

"Yeah, but that's not what this is."

"Maybe not," he says.

"Terry and I've talked about it. We talk about it some."

"About Hendrick?"

"More about just having kids," she says. "Whether we should."

"Do you want them?"

"I have no idea," she says. "Some days I do, some days not at all."

Jack says, "That doesn't ever really change."

She looks up at him from the dolphin bench. "Tell me the rest of the parade," she says.

He watches a jet fly across the sky, long white contrail tracing out behind it. "These trash trucks came by right at the end," he says. "These spit-shined, gleaming trash trucks. They were running the robotic arms on the sides up and down, running the arm on the front that picks up Dumpsters up and down. The trash guys were walking out to the side in brand new yellow T-shirts, and everything looked so—*clean*. Like the trucks were the cleanest things that had ever been." He chews his thumbnail. "And then Hendrick ran out into the goddamn parade—I wasn't holding onto him, and he ran right out in the street, and he got up in this one trash guy's arms, and the guy carried him for the rest of the parade." Hendrick's doing something complicated now with his putter and what looks like a newspaper circular. "He's not supposed to like strangers," Jack says. "But he sat up in the guy's arms and waved at people. He had a blast." Hen tears a piece off the circular, puts that underneath his putter. The dog watches, learning. "At the end," says Jack, "they even let him work the controls a little bit. He loved that."

She gets up off the bench, reaches out for his arm. "See?" she says. "It turns out you can talk. You and Hendrick both." She sets her ball down, putts it into a puddle. She says, "Maybe you're both getting better."

"Maybe."

"Let's finish up and go see Zel and buy however many of these things you're going to buy," she says.

"OK," he says.

She hits again. "Maybe you could load them up in your truck and hire them out to seafood restaurants or something," she says. "Drive them around."

"We don't really have that many seafood restaurants."

"You could open one. Patriot Mulch & Seafood."

"You mean like a market? Like we'd sell fresh fish?"

"No," she says. "Like a restaurant. The whole thing: Tablecloths and hush puppies and the metal napkin holders on the tables. Little pretty high school girls as waitresses. You'd like that, right? We'll do it together. We'll be proprietors. It'll be great. We'll smell like fried fish for the rest of our lives."

Hush puppies. He could live that way, too. He watches her while she finishes the hole, picks her ball up, puts it in her pocket. "Why is it easy for you?" he wants to know.

"It isn't," she says. "I just make it look that way. Smoke and mirrors."

"I'm going to miss this," he says.

"I'm going to miss it, too, Jackson," she says, and she looks at him. "And you. I'm going to miss you." She makes a face. "But let's not turn this into some kind of scene. I don't want to be crying and wearing a T-shirt you gave me and planning out some mix tape for you while your parents drive you away from camp in your dad's Corolla, OK? None of that."

"OK," he says. "Sure."

"So long as we've got that straight." She walks to the next hole. He stares at her, watches her line up her next putt. She holds her thumb out in the air to measure something—slope, distance. He's already trying to remember all of this as best he can.

❧ ❧ ❧

Zel tells him he can have as many as he can take away for a thousand dollars, but she's keeping the clam. It's always been her favorite, she says. She likes the way he looks at you. Also, there is, yes, supposed to be a light in the end of the catfish's cigarette, but the wiring's gone bad and only Donald knows how to fix it. *When he gets out, if he stays dry, I'll send him to see you. Maybe you two can get it squared away. He is some kind of electronical genius.*

Rena drives and Jack looks out the window, watches while the landscape works itself back toward Greensboro. He's arranged it with Zel: He'll come pick up the undersea creatures tomorrow. He'll bring Butner and Ernesto, bring the truck and maybe a trailer. And cash. Zel would prefer cash. *It's nothing to do with me not trusting you, just so you know. You're good people. I can tell just by seeing you here. You two make a real nice-looking couple.* Rena smiled and got in the car. Jack shook Zel's hand one more time. Zel dumped what was left of her blue daiquiri into the parking lot and waved at them with her empty glass as they pulled away.

On the way home, they pass a man screaming at a telephone pole. They pass two dead deer. Closer in to town, they pass a church with a sign out front that says FORGOT SO LOVED THE WORLD.

Rena bumps into PM&T and coasts to a stop in front of the pile of cedar. Butner and Ernesto are not out front. No one's over at the Shell, either. The lot's empty except for the dump truck and a jacked-up Nissan pickup past the office. It's that kid's, Jack thinks, Butner's friend from the overturned loader. The kitten tattoos. The office says OPEN, but the door's shut. Almost the entire front of the lot is under water from yesterday's rain. No customers. There's a gunshot. "What the hell was that?" Rena asks.

"I think it was a gun," Jack says. He gets out of the car. He says, "Stay here."

Rena says, "What, are you crazy?"

"I don't want anybody getting hurt," Jack says.

"Why are you talking like that?"

"Like what?"

"For fuck's sake," she says, and gets out. She opens the door, lets Hen and Yul Brynner out. The dog's ears are flat back on his head. He hates loud noises. Rena takes Hen by the hand and Yul Brynner snugs up close to her leg and she starts walking all of them back in the direction of the mulch bays.

"What are you doing?" he asks her, following behind.

"We are going over here," Hen says, over his shoulder. Jack can't get used to these outbursts. Each one's a flashbulb going off. Maybe the doctors will tell them that he's pulling himself into sharper focus, like some kind of eye exam: This? Or this? This? Or this? There's another gunshot, a thin, sharp crack that comes echoing off the bricks of the Shell station. The dog bellies down onto the ground, tail between his legs, then slinks under the pickup, curls up under a front tire and hides. Hen lets go of Rena, covers his ears, turns in a circle. Jack tries to decide whether or not he should throw his body in front of him, whether or not anybody should be hitting the deck. He feels like he should be in slow motion. Slow motion shot of pigeons scattering up out of the parking lot. Off the telephone wire. Up from the piazza. Rena shouts out, "Hey!"

From behind the mulch piles, Butner and Ernesto shout Hey back. Ernesto comes around the retaining wall, smiles when he sees Hen, heads right for him. "Hola," says Hendrick.

"¿Como estás, jefecito?" Ernesto holds his hand out for Hendrick to give him five.

Hen puts his fist into his hand instead. There's something solemn about it. He repeats it: "¿Como estás, jefecito?" Then he says, "Estoy bien." His accent is even getting pretty good.

Ernesto looks at Jack. "We found rats in the tomatoes."

"You're shooting rats?" Rena asks.

Butner walks out, the tattoo kid with him. They're both grinning. It's the kid who's got the gun, a rifle, on his shoulder. "Two already," Butner says. "Big ones. Randy, you remember Jack Lang, and his son, Hendrick. And this is—"

"Rena," she says.

"This is Randy Troxler," Butner says, meaning the kid. Rena shakes his hand. "He works the kitchen at Sandy's, over by Kinnett. You probably know the place. And he helps us out sometimes."

"Not just the kitchen," Randy says. "I've been saving up. As soon as I can afford some speakers, Sandy's gonna let me DJ on the weekends."

"That's cool," Rena says.

"I'm a good DJ," Randy says.

"You guys want a shot?" Butner says.

"You bet," says Rena, and holds her hand out for the gun.

"Fantastic," says Butner. He smiles big at Jack. Randy hands her the rifle without asking her if she knows how to shoot one. Back behind the bays, they've got the lawn chairs set up facing the tomatoes, a cooler full of beer. Rena sits down, and Butner and Ernesto and Randy stand behind her. Ernesto's got Hendrick, holds him by the shoulders. Jack says, "You guys are really back here shooting rats?"

"Found 'em while we were tying everything back up after the rain," Butner says. "Saw one walking along the caging with a cherry tomato in his mouth like he was just going home to share it around. Bright goddamned red tomato, little black motherfucking rat."

"Where are they?" Rena asks, sighting down the rifle.

"They've been back in there, on the left," Butner says, leaning over and steering the barrel toward the far end of the garden. The gun goes off.

"Oops," Rena says. "Fuck."

"Don't worry," says Butner. "It's only a pellet gun. You can't really hurt anybody unless you're trying."

"How do I reload?"

"Like this." Butner slides the bolt out and back, and pulls a pellet from his pocket, chambers it. Pellet gun or not, all this seems terribly unsafe. Yul Brynner's curled up even smaller under the tire.

Rena says, "I don't see anything in there."

"Maybe they got them all already," Jack says, hoping.

"No," Ernesto says. "There are always more. *Siempre.*"

"*Siempre,*" says Hen, serious.

"Are they gray?" Rena wants to know.

"Those are squirrels," Butner says.

"Please do not shoot the squirrels," Hendrick says.

"Yeah," says Randy. "I like those guys."

"Eastern gray squirrels breed twice a year, typically," Hendrick says. Jack just looks at him.

"What?" says Rena, and the gun goes off again. Everybody jumps and Rena says, "Shit. Sorry." A couple of vines lean over at the far end of the garden. She hands the gun to Butner. "I'm a menace with this thing. You take it."

"Suit yourself," Butner says, and takes it, takes her seat. He puts his left foot up on one arm of the chair, steadies the gun across his raised leg. He waits. He says, "Tell us more about the Eastern gray squirrel, little man."

Hen says, "Eastern gray squirrels are the most frequently seen mammal in our area. They are members of the rodent family, and spend most of their lives in trees."

"That kid's like a computer or something," Randy says.

"That was nothing," Butner tells him. Ernesto says *Bueno, hombre,* and Jack reaches out to touch Hen, make sure he's still real. *The fruit is, of course, the acorn.*

"You should tell them about your giant catfish," Rena says to Jack.

"Your giant what?" asks Butner.

"Tell them," she says.

"I bought a catfish," Jack says. "I'm going to. Tomorrow. We found this putt-putt with all the animals for sale. So I'm buying them."

"You are?" Butner asks.

"I am."

"What the hell for?" Butner says.

"Is a catfish an animal?" Randy wants to know.

"A catfish is a fish," Hen says.

"I'm pretty sure a catfish is an animal," says Randy. Hendrick doesn't say anything back to that.

"What are you planning on?" asks Butner. "Building him a putt-putt?"

"I don't think so," Jack says, waiting for whatever's going to come out of Hen's mouth next. "That seems like a lot."

"You could put it here in the parking lot, man," says Butner, looking around. "That would be sweet. A whole putt-putt. Give us something to do."

"We have something to do," Ernesto says.

"I don't want to build a putt-putt," says Jack.

"Why not?"

"That's what went out of business in the first place."

Butner sights the rifle back into the tomatoes. "You got me there, I guess," he says.

Randy rolls up one sleeve, flexes his bicep, looks at it a while. He's got a new-looking tattoo, the skin red around its edges. It's a footprint. Butner holds one hand up for everybody to be quiet, goes very still. "I got one," he whispers. He takes a long breath, lets it out. Hen puts his hands over his ears. This is either more or less crazy than anything else. Less, maybe. Butner fires, works the bolt, reloads, fires again. He makes a kind of whoop, gets up, lays the gun across the arms of the lawn chair and walks into the tomato patch, his feet crunching gravel down into the wet mud. Jack notices for the first time that they've used the skid steer to dig a shallow moat around the garden, pull some of the water away from it. It looks to be working pretty well. Butner leans over into the vines, then stands back up, holding what looks like a huge mouse. "Shit," he says. "It's a baby possum." And then it comes back to life, and Butner jumps back, screams, drops it, and starts stomping it, his leg and foot hidden by the tomatoes. It had just been stunned. Or wounded. "Gross," says Rena.

Randy and Ernesto are laughing, and Hen laughs too, along with them, but it's a forced laugh. This is probably not the kind of thing Jack should let him watch, but he's not sure what to do. There's no way he'll let him cover his eyes. Butner leans down into the vines again, picks up the possum, finds his way out of the tomatoes. He tosses the body into the Dumpster on his way back. He's got his hand wrapped into his shirt, and he's squeezing it. "Motherfucker fucking bit me," he says, sitting back down.

"Gross," Rena says again.

"It was a possum?" Jack asks, because somehow the taxonomy seems to matter.

"Yeah, I mean, I feel bad, but they're no better, right?"

"They get big," Randy says. "My brother says the problem with your average baby possum is that it grows up into a possum possum." He leans over, looks at Butner's hand. "You up on your shots?" he asks.

"They give dogs rabies shots," Butner says. "Not people."

"What do they give people?" asks Randy.

"Shots," Ernesto says. "In the stomach."

"You think that thing had rabies?" Butner asks. He squeezes his hand harder, then looks at it. "I'm fine," he says. He picks up his beer, drinks it down in a few swallows, crushes the can and tosses it on the ground. "I'm still gonna be fine for playing putt-putt," he says. "List me as day-to-day."

"I'm not building a putt-putt," Jack says.

"I think it'd work," says Randy.

"Actually, I was thinking of building a racetrack," Jack says. "For Hendrick." He hasn't been thinking that at all. It just comes out of his mouth.

"A what?" Butner asks.

"I don't know," he says. "Something like a loop, maybe, for Big Wheels. Or bicycles. That kind of thing."

"Oh," Butner says. "Sure. I can see that." He squats down next to Hendrick. "You think you'd like that, little man?"

Hen pops his lips together once, twice. He says, "I do not know if I would like that or not."

"That's fair," Butner says. He looks at Jack. "Kid's thinking it over," he says. "He's working shit out."

"Working shit out," says Hendrick.

"There you go, man," Butner says. "There you go."

Ernesto says, "Where would you build it?"

"In my yard," Jack says. It's coming to him all at once, like a kind of vision. It could be a sidewalk. He could pour Hen a sidewalk in the back yard, set in all the undersea creatures around that. There's room back there. What kid wouldn't like something like that?

"Your front yard?" Ernesto asks.

"No," says Jack. "The back."

"Yeah," Randy says. "Front yard would be crazy."

Butner picks the rifle up, clicks the safety on, sets it back down. He pulls on his chin. "Are we talking about like some kind of asphalt situation?"

Jack says, "What about concrete? Like a sidewalk?"

"Cool," Butner says. "I know a guy we can call. Concrete guy. I'll call him in the morning."

"Hang on," Jack says. "I didn't say I was going to do it. All I said was I was thinking about it."

"No man, you gotta do it," Butner says. "It's done. You gotta do it."

"I like it," Rena says.

"When are you going to get them?" Butner asks. "The putt-putt things?"

"Tomorrow."

"I'll definitely call my buddy, then."

"Just don't commit to anything," Jack says. "I need to think about this."

"What's there to think about?" Butner wants to know. "We could cut it in with the skid. In and out. Bang."

"What's that?" Randy asks, pointing into the tomato vines, and they all look. Ernesto takes the rifle. It's his turn. Hen sits down on the ground in front of the pickup, and Yul Brynner slides out, puts his chin in Hen's lap. Hendrick lays both his hands on the dog's head. Jack goes and sits, too. The ground is wet. A few clouds are coming across the sky south to north, and the light seems half-finished, like there's something not entirely right with it. Rena brings Jack a beer, brings a lawn chair over. Ernesto mutters something else, sights down the rifle, but then leans back, relaxes. Butner holds his bitten hand in his shirt. Rena says, under her breath, "A racetrack? Really?"

"Why not?" Jack says.

"No reason," she says.

Butner points out into the garden, and Ernesto sights again, then shakes his head, rests the gun across his knees. Randy flexes his tattoo until Ernesto gives in and asks him about it. Randy gets all excited, rolls his sleeve up further, says, It's my baby girl. Her footprint, from the hospital, you know? From the birth certificate? Randy seems nowhere near old enough to have a girl of any age. Jack works on what a sidewalk racetrack might look like, how it might operate.

Bicycles, Big Wheels, tricycles. He's going to need some tricycles. Red ones. A catfish with an eye patch. Ernesto leans in to get a closer look at the footprint, says, *When did you get it done?*

*Last week*, the kid says. *It was her second birthday. It hurt like hell, too.* Ernesto picks the gun back up, aims once more into the tomatoes. They wait. They all wait.

❧ ❧ ❧

FREE TRIP TO HEAVEN. DETAILS INSIDE. That's what the sign says this morning out front of the Holy Redeemer, and Jack gives the metal building a half-salute as he drives by. Rena's gone back to the condo *to take care of one or two things*. She stayed last night, but they slept in their clothes. Something's lighter between them. She snored. Jack doesn't even remember dreaming. He rolls his window down further and reaches around Hen, scratches Yul Brynner between the ears. The dog's along for the ride. Seemed right to bring him.

Butner's called him already, said the concrete guys could drop in the sidewalk in a day. *In an afternoon, really*, he said, *man. One afternoon. Those guys are some fucking pros, I'll tell you that.*

*How much?* Jack wanted to know.

*Guy owes me a favor. We'll deal with the fine print later.*

So there it is. His plan. Undersea creatures and a backyard sidewalk tricycle racetrack. For his son, who, if Jack's going to be honest about all this, may never actually set foot on the thing. Bethany gave him a Batman Big Wheel for Christmas two years ago and all he ever did was move the adjustable seat up and back. Then again, it's possible Hendrick might sketch out tensile strength schematics for the sidewalk on the back of a receipt by the time they get out to see Zel. Or just engage in some casual cocktail party conversation. No way of telling how it all might go.

At the lot, three orange NCDOT dump trucks are in line by the topsoil pile. One's towing a huge bulldozer. Butner's leaning against the fender of the lead truck, and Ernesto's standing next to him. Four or five NCDOT guys are out there, standing around, tan NCDOT shirts stretched over their bellies, orange NCDOT baseball caps. Everything looks like it's on the verge of being very official.

Butner waves Jack over. He's looking a little less official, wearing a black T-shirt that says CHEVROGODDAMNLET. There's a cartoon of an old Camaro giving a toothy snarl underneath the lettering. Maybe Jack ought to order them some PM&T shirts. That would look pretty sharp. American flags and an embroidered pile of pine bark. A tomato. A half-dead stomped baby possum. Butner says, "This is Jack Lang, our COO. Jack, these gentlemen would like to purchase some of our topsoil. I told them we could probably make them a deal."

Ernesto takes Hendrick over to show him the big dozer, lifts him up into the cab. One of the NCDOT guys, a little skinnier than the others, holds his hand out, says, "Kenny Trimble. We'd like to take about forty yards."

"Have we got forty yards?" Jack asks.

Butner doesn't even look at the pile. "I said we'd give him what's sitting here, see if we could take delivery off the farm this afternoon, and finish him up that way."

Jack says, "Doesn't the state normally—"

"They're working off the clock today," says Butner, cutting him off.

Kenny Trimble looks embarrassed. "We're adding a turn lane back at 100," he says. "And we're a little stalled, waiting on more equipment. Road digger, paint guys, that sort of thing. They're held up." He nods back up the road. "But the Reverend down at the church there said if we'd scrape his property and put topsoil down, he'd pay five grand."

"What, at the Redeemer?" Jack says. "We'd have done it for that."

"They've got the heavy machinery," Butner says, meaning the

bulldozer. Hendrick looks tiny up there in the huge seat, surrounded by yellow caging and levers. The bulldozer's blade gleams along the edge where it's been cut clean of paint. It's at least five times as big as either of their skid steers, makes them look like toys sitting there by the mulch. "I went on and quoted them fifty a yard," Butner says, letting a little smile show.

"Fifty?" Jack looks over at the office door. Butner's taken down the sign advertising their per-yard prices. They charge twenty-four for topsoil.

"They're willing to pay a premium for our discretion."

"We'd ask you to keep it fairly quiet," Kenny says. "Not sure the home office would understand. But we'd just be sitting idle all morning otherwise."

"It's kind of a win-win," Butner says.

Jack squints at the Holy Redeemer. The lot out front is nothing but scrub, clay showing through the weeds in spots. It would take him days to do it with their little skid. It'll take these guys a morning. He does some quick math. Twenty-six extra dollars per yard times forty yards is right at a thousand over and above what they'd normally get. A mortgage payment. The cost of the undersea creatures. He looks a while at the bulldozer trailer. He says, "Would that trailer hook up to our truck?"

Kenny eyes the hitch on Jack's bumper. "It'd hook on," he says. "You need it?"

"How about I give you forty yards at forty-five, and borrow your trailer for the morning? After you get the bulldozer off it down at the church?"

Kenny looks at the rest of the NCDOT guys, and there's a round of shrugging. Butner says, "We were fine at fifty, I think, boss man."

"I need the trailer," Jack tells him.

"What for?"

"For the undersea creatures," Hendrick says, from the cab of the bulldozer. Jack looks up there, at his son, who's cataloguing the world.

"Oh, shit," Butner says. "I got a trailer for that."

"What's it for?" Kenny wants to know.

"Oversized animals," Jack says. "Fiberglass. Big."

"How big?" Butner asks.

"Big," Jack says. "Like that trailer big. They're like putt-putt elephants, only they're fish. There's an octopus, too. And a shrimp. I bought them yesterday," he tells Kenny. "Or I agreed to, anyway."

"OK," Kenny says, looking at him like he might need medication.

"You really think we need a trailer this big?" Butner asks.

"I'm gonna put them in my back yard," Jack tells Kenny. "Around a racetrack. A sidewalk. For my son." He points up at Hen in the bulldozer. As he explains this to Kenny Trimble of the NCDOT, he starts to get an idea of what it'll be like to explain it to Beth. Or anybody who's not Butner or Ernesto. Or Rena.

"I got it," Kenny Trimble says. "You want a putt-putt in your yard."

"Kind of," Jack says.

"That's cool," says Kenny. "I got a daughter. I bet she'd like something like that."

"Bring her by," Jack says, feeling friendly. "You guys going to be out here tomorrow?"

"She lives in Wilmington. With her mom."

"Oh," he says. "Well, if she's ever in town——"

Butner pulls them back toward the deal. "OK, fellas. Forty-five and the trailer and we're all good, right? We're agreed?"

Kenny nods, picks at his palm. "If we take it back up to fifty," he says, "could we use one of your small skids to get into the corners, up around the building, places like that?"

"Absolutely," Butner says. He's got his deal back.

Jack says, "Let me call my guy before we go too much further.

We might be able to get you forty yards dropped down there this morning. That way you could get the whole thing at once."

"Sounds good," Kenny says.

"Great." Jack walks over to the office, and Butner follows him. The NCDOT guys huddle around the front of their dump truck. Ernesto gets Hen down out of the bulldozer and they head for the office, too.

"Is all this above-board?" Jack asks Butner, once they're inside.

"Sure, man. They pocket three grand and we get one. They'd just be sitting on their asses all morning otherwise. Everybody wins."

"But you're sure it's not illegal?"

"I mean, it's probably not legal. But I wouldn't call it illegal. They do a job, they get paid. And we get paid. Your tax dollars at work for you. Think of it like a refund."

"A refund," Jack says.

"Yeah," Butner says. He tosses the phone to Ernesto, so he can call the soil guy. "See if he can bring us a full truck," he tells him. "That way he can dump forty down there for the government, and fill us up here while he's at it." Ernesto starts punching numbers in, steps outside to make the call. Butner opens the fridge, gets himself a beer. "You want one?" he asks Jack.

"It's nine in the morning."

"Five o'clock somewhere. You want one?"

"No," Jack says. Then he says, "Sure." Why the hell not: This has got to be the day for it.

Butner grins, hands his over, gets himself another. He makes a little show out of sitting up on the desk and popping it open. "So," he says.

"So."

"What is it that's going on in your life, boss man, where you've ended up with a giant mini-golf catfish?"

"Nothing," he tells him. "We were just at this putt-putt yesterday—"

"You and Fucknut's girlfriend."

"Fucknut," Hen says.

"—and I saw them, and I liked them."

Butner takes a long swallow, says, "You belong on TV or something, don't you?"

"Probably," Jack says. He drinks his beer. It tastes like he's drinking beer at nine in the morning.

"I'm impressed."

"Thanks."

"This racetrack, though," Butner says. "That's good. That's the best of all of it."

Jack says, "You're going to help, right?"

"I'm your fucking project manager, my man. I called my guy. He'll be ready about noon. We'll go get your figurines, come back and pick up the other skid to carve the sidewalk in with, close up shop for the afternoon, and we'll have the whole thing in by tonight."

"Really?"

"Really. These guys drop in sidewalks in their sleep."

"OK," Jack says.

"Just make sure you really do want to do it before we do it. Easier to put a sidewalk in than take one out. Those fuckers get heavy."

"Right."

Ernesto comes back in, says their farmer can bring them the soil. "By ten-thirty," he says. He gives the phone to Hendrick, who begins pressing each number, counting in Spanish. "*Ocho*," he says. "*Siete*."

"Kid's getting to where he can talk about as good as you, Paco," Butner says.

Jack picks up stacks of paper on the desk, sets them back down. It's Tuesday in his life. Hen's on the sofa, calling Guatemala. Beth's been gone however many days. Seventeen. He sips his beer. "The catfish is smoking," Jack says. Maybe if he explains it one small piece at a time, that'll work. He says, "He's smoking a cigarette."

Butner says, "He's doing what?"

"He's smoking. He's got a cigarette in one flipper."

"But he's a catfish, right?"

"Right."

Butner rubs at his hand, the one that got bitten. He's got it bandaged up. "OK. How's he smoking under water?"

Jack hadn't thought of that. "I don't know."

"That's a problem," Butner says.

"The cigarette is supposed to light up on the end."

"I mean, I get it," Butner says. "But the whole underwater thing is still there."

"You'll like it," Jack tells him. "You'll still like it."

"Yeah, I probably will," he says. He walks out the door, onto the lot, turns around, looks back in at Jack. He says, "You know what? I like it well enough so far."

"Thanks," Jack says.

Butner raises his beer at him. "You're welcome," he says.

☞  ☞  ☞

If there's an eight-foot catfish standing over a sidewalk racetrack by the end of the day, then that's one kind of success. Jack works on that idea while Ernesto takes Hendrick through the subtleties of verb tense. The three of them are in the cab, plus Yul Brynner. Butner's riding the trailer. He couldn't be talked out of it. *I'll be fine, boss man, I'll be fine.* He's got one of the lawn chairs strapped down to it, and he's strapped himself into the lawn chair. He'd be crushed to death if Jack flipped the thing, but other than that, all this seems about as safe as anybody could hope for. Ernesto keeps turning around in his seat, looking through the little metal rectangle of mesh holes in the dump bed right behind the back window, checking on Butner. In the rearview, Butner's hair blows in the wind.

It's ten in the morning and with the windows down, with Hen and Ernesto and Butner and Yul Brynner with him, Jack feels like he's on some kind of mission. He almost feels good. He thinks of Rena, checking her mail, maybe watering a few plants. He thinks of Bethany. What he feels like he knows, now: Rena will have to go back to her house, whichever house that ends up being, and Beth's got to live in hers, whichever one that ends up being. What happens to Canavan, or to him, after that, Jack doesn't know, but it's Canavan who's had the worst of it, Jack decides, changing lanes, letting himself smile at that. Canavan's got fifty-four staples in his leg, the fucker. Fifty-four. Jack imagines the gleam of the stainless steel. He thinks about the chainsaw finding bone, the luck of it kicking back out instead of digging the rest of the way through.

He knows there's more to it, of course. He knows they don't just get to rinse this clean. There's the easy picture of Bethany in bed with Canavan, for one thing, and the just-as-easy picture of Rena in his plastic chairs, unraveling the universe for him. But he aims, for now, at least, toward the better feeling, tries to choose it, tries to do not much more than listen to the hum of the truck tires on the macadam, a word the NCDOT guys would use. *Macadam.* He listens to Ernesto and Hen. *En Español, claro.* Which way to the train station, the language lab voice would ask Jack. *¿Donde está la estación de tren?* Over and over in those headphones. *¿Listo?* Ernesto's asking Hendrick now, and Hen's saying *listo* back to him. *Listo.* Ready. They pass a cop sitting in the median and Jack keeps checking his mirrors, waiting for the blue lights, for him to pull them over, walk up to the window, eye the dog, Butner, say *Sir, could you please step away from the vehicle?* But the cop doesn't move. The cruiser looks like a giant bug there in the grass. He's getting away with it. Jack almost feels good.

Zel is sitting in the open window of the mini-golf trailer when they get there, up on the putter counter. It occurs to him that she probably lives in it. There's nothing else on the property that looks like it could house anybody. She kicks her legs at them and raises another blue drink, same tall glass, in salute. Jack taps the horn at her, and she sets her drink down on the blue Astroturf that covers the counter and waves crazily with both hands. *Welcome, welcome.* He slows on the gravel lot and pulls the truck and trailer as close as he can to the fence, to the undersea creatures, and cuts the engine. Butner's singing something back there, something Jack feels like he knows the words to. They get out of the cab, Ernesto reaching back in and hefting Hen down. Butner's filling in the parts he doesn't know with blank syllables, vowel sounds. *Hie, hie, hie, hey, hey.* Then he goes into a guitar solo, and strapped into the lawn chair like that, he looks like he's the one they've come to take away, that they've just tied him, chair and all, to the trailer, and now they're going to take him back to the institution. He shakes his hair all over the place during the solo, finishes his song. They all stand next to the trailer, looking at him, and he says, "What?"

Hendrick adjusts The Duck. "The greatest hits of yesterday and today," he says.

"Goddamn right," Butner says, and unstraps himself. "This is the place?" he asks. "These are the undersea creatures?"

"Yes," Jack says. "This is the place."

"Cool," Butner says. "Cool, cool, cool."

There's a flat heat, flat blue sky to go with it. The catfish looks like he wouldn't want his cigarette relit just now. Jack sweats down his spine. Butner hops the fence, goes up to the catfish, knocks on it. He gets a hollowed ring back. He gets down on one knee, looks at the fins, at the base, says, "Did you bring a socket set?"

"There's one in the glove," Jack tells him.

"Toss me the wrench, and I'll get at these bolts."

He hadn't really thought about them being attached to anything, but it makes sense, of course. They'd blow over. Or get stolen. You'd need an NCDOT trailer to do it, but still. He hands the socket set over the fence to Butner, and then heads for Zel, who's still sitting up in the window.

"You're back," she says.

"I am."

"Donald called here last night," she tells him. "They let him make a call. He earned it, he said. Some kind of points system they have them on." She sips her drink. "I told him about you buying his fishies. He said he was glad they were going to a good home."

"They are," Jack says.

"That's what I told him. A nice young couple and a beautiful little boy, I said."

"Thank you."

"Where's your wife today?"

Jack considers all the possible answers. He says, "I brought these guys instead."

"Fair enough," she says. They watch Hendrick leading Ernesto around, pointing things out to him. Explaining. Every now and then, Ernesto reaches out, takes a bolt from Butner, but mainly he's letting Hendrick show him the secrets of the golf course. Jack wonders whether Hen's talking to him—really talking—or if he's giving him last night's newscast.

Zel says, "So what are you going to do with them?"

Jack smiles. "It's a little out there."

"As out there as all this?" Zel waves her glass at the Carolina Flea Market and Undersea Adventures Mini-Golf.

"You see the guy working on the bolts?"

"Sure."

"He's going to get a friend of his to pour a big sidewalk in our yard. Like a Big Wheel racetrack."

"Yep," says Zel, like she's got a tricycle racetrack in her back yard, too, like everybody does.

"I've been thinking maybe a figure eight. And I thought maybe they could all go in the middle of it. In the holes of the eight. Or out around the edge."

"See? That sounds perfect," she says. "Just perfect. Donald will like that. I'll tell him that the next time he earns himself a phone call." She pulls a piece of hair out of her mouth, examines it. "Would you like to know where we got them?"

"Yes," he says.

"From a catalog. You get all these mailings when you start up a mini-golf. Like you wouldn't believe. And not just golf stuff. We'd get these catalogs with go-carts in them, where if you bought thirty go-carts, you got some kind of discount. Also batting cages. You know we could have bought a batting cage with three pitching machines for ten thousand dollars?"

"I did not."

"Plus the chain-link fencing and the ball return and the machines for tokens. The whole thing. You're talking about pouring concrete, right? All we'd have had to do was hire someone to come pour us a mile or so of concrete to get everything to slant back towards the machines. All those catalogs. You name it, they make it." Out on the course, Butner and Ernesto have worked out a system, and they're already lowering the shrimp to the ground. Hendrick is sitting on the tee box of Atlantic #3. "People don't think about where things like that come from," she says.

"That's true," Jack says. He's wishing Rena were here for this, to see Zel one more time.

"They don't just come from nowhere." She gets down off the window. "You know what I always thought would be nice out here?"

"What's that?"

"One of those waterfalls. A little river running through the whole place, and then over there, right out next to the octopus, a waterfall. Right between the two courses."

"That would have been nice," Jack says.

"It would have given them something to look at," she says, and Jack's not sure if she means the people who came to play golf, or the undersea creatures. He gets his cash out of his pocket, crisp new bills from the bank, counts them out. Ten hundreds. "You've got to be going, probably," Zel says.

"Probably," he says, and hands her the money.

She folds it in half, holds it. She says, "Do you want to know what he told me right before he hung up?"

"Sure."

"He said he wanted us to walk across the whole country. On foot. He wants to start in Seattle and finish in Miami. Top left to bottom right. He kept saying that: 'Top left to bottom right.' And he kept saying how we were going to need all these pairs of shoes, because we'd wear them through so quickly. He's getting it all planned out. He says we'll mail shoes to ourselves all across the country, and they'll just be there waiting for us when we get to Montana and Missouri and Georgia." She lights a cigarette. "Does that sound like something a person could do?"

"I think it does," Jack says.

"That's what I keep thinking, too." Butner and Ernesto pick up the catfish, walk it over to the trailer. "I told you his cigarette has a light in it, right?"

"Yes ma'am," Jack says.

"I'm not your mother," she says. "Don't call me ma'am."

"OK."

"Call me Zel."

"OK, Zel."

"Go load up the fishies and take your boy back home to play with them," she says.

"OK, Zel."

"I like you," she says.

"Thank you."

"I can tell you've got a good heart," she says, and reaches out and pats him on the chest. She stands there, putters on the wall behind her and golf balls in eight shades of blue stacked up in wire bins. She says, "You need anything else?"

"I don't think so."

"Then I guess we're done." She looks out at Butner and Ernesto, shields her eyes so she can see better. "Look," she says, "that catfish is heavier than it seems, if I remember right."

"Thank you," he says.

She says, "You're welcome," but she says it a little quickly, like she might want to be somewhere else right then. He's about to ask her if she wants to rethink all this, if she maybe doesn't want to sell after all, but she disappears into the trailer, shuts the door, doesn't come back out. Jack waits for her, but she's gone. Maybe he should knock. Butner calls for him, wants to know if he can maybe *give us a hand over here a minute.* They're having trouble getting the catfish over the fence. Jack leaves Zel in the trailer, goes to help.

Hendrick's touching his fingers to his thumb one by one, working on the long version of the Kernersville Chrysler Dodge commercial, complete with the description of their *zero percent financing and Employee Pricing, Kelly, that's right, EP, they'll pay the same price we would on this brand new Durango, the country's hottest SUV. Perfect for tailgating.* Jack and Ernesto and Butner get the creatures loaded up onto the trailer, into the bed of the truck. Jack leaves the clam, Zel's favorite, where it is, out by Pacific #6. Butner straps his lawn chair back down, straps himself back in. He's facing sideways this time, riding between the catfish, which they laid down on its side, and the octopus, which is sitting upright, its tentacles reaching out for Butner. The shrimp, the two jellyfish, and a small gray whale wearing what might be an Olympic medal are stacked into the bed of the dump truck. Jack and Ernesto and Hen get back in the cab. Zel does not come back out of the trailer. The mini-golf window is still open, the signboard telling everybody they get a fourth game free

when they pay for three. Jack pulls the truck slowly out of the lot
and beeps the horn for Zel, wherever she is in there. *Just drive slow,*
Butner told him, *and we'll be alright.* They didn't have quite enough
tie-downs, Jack thought, but Butner reassured him. *Just drive slow.*
Jack drives slow.

Everyone in every car that passes them on the way back north
stares. It must be a hell of a picture they make, Jack thinks, holding
the speedometer between 35 and 40. He's got the hazards on. The
trailer lights aren't hooked up. He's just hoping, keeps looking for
cops in the medians. So far, so good. Ernesto says something Jack
doesn't hear. "What?" he says.

"*El imperfecto,*" he says. "I'm explaining past tense."

"Oh," Jack says. "Good."

"*Hablaba,*" Ernesto says.

"*Hablama,*" Hen says back.

"No. *Hablaba.*"

"*Hablaba,*" Hen says.

"Good," says Ernesto. "*Perfecto.*"

"How's he doing?" Jack asks.

"He's doing great. Really great," Ernesto says.

"Thank you," Jack says. "Thanks for teaching him."

"It's nothing at all," Ernesto says. "I enjoy it. He does, too."

Jack checks Butner in the side mirror. He can just see him. He's
got his head leaned over the back of the chair, and he's turning his
face into the wind. All pleasure. Everything for pleasure. The thing
for the sake of the thing itself. Butner and Yul Brynner and Hendrick are all the damn same. Jack rolls down the window a little
further. "Let me ask you a question," he says to Ernesto.

"Of course."

"What if I put these in at the new house, instead? Do you think
that would work?"

"The racetrack and the whole thing?"

"The whole thing," Jack says. "Why not?"

Ernesto looks at Hen, then at Jack. "I think it would work the same anywhere you put it."

"Yeah," says Jack. "That's what I was thinking." Across the street. Because that's where something like this belongs. He feels as sure now about that as he does about anything else. He checks his mirror one more time. Across the street. The new house. When they get back to the lot, he'll tell Butner to tell his guys.

❦ ❦ ❦

They stop back by PM&T to pick up the skid and to check in down the street on the NCDOT guys, make sure their soil arrived. It did, and Kenny's all smiles. Jack can keep the trailer all day if he needs to. Jack explains to Butner about the shift in venue, and Butner doesn't ask him anything about why, which is good. Butner makes a few phone calls and says he'll head over to wait for the concrete, get everything started. *I'm on every part of this, boss man.* By the time Jack gets there an hour later—he stops for lunch for Hen, because he can't remember when he's supposed to meet Beth, or if he's already missed it, or if they'd even had anything set up for today—there's a cement mixer sitting in his driveway, big drum on the back of it spinning around. It reminds him of an old record player, of old wax cylinder recordings. RANDOLPH & SONS CONCRETE is painted on the side of the drum. The lettering looks like they did it themselves. There's a guy laying down boards in his side yard, rolling out an enormous rubber mat over the top of them, and Butner's backing the skid down off its little trailer, which he's towed over off the back of his car. Jack parks out front, along the curb. The sun throws bright noontime shadows off everything. Rena's standing in the driveway. She comes over, leans in the open window. "You're back," he says.

"I couldn't miss this," she says.

"Me neither," he says.

She says, "I talked to Butner."

"Yeah?"

"You're really going to do it over here?"

"Yes," he says.

"This is going to be a little like an eclipse," says Rena. And before he can ask her exactly what she means, she walks away, follows Butner as he drives the skid over the rubber mat and into the back yard.

Beth's entire head will come off her body. She'll *at the very goddamn least* want to know why he put it over here, instead of at their house. *How in the hell do you expect to sell it now, with the yard like that?* And he's got a ready answer for that. This is what came to him riding back home. He doesn't expect to sell it any more, he'll say. He's got a whole new plan. This is all for her. For them. They can move over here. This thing with Rena's all but done. That much is sure. So they'll move over here, and what he'll do is find some way of finishing the kitchen off over there, and that one, with its walls already knocked through, with paint up on the walls, mostly, can be the one they sell. 3BR. 2BA. BRAND NEW KITCHEN. She never liked that house, anyway. He'll start in on the attic over here, get their little room put in over here. There's already a good floor up there from where the old man had his workbench, from where he'd loaded up all his shotgun shells, getting himself ready. They'll drop a new stove in this kitchen and be done with it. Leave the walls where they are for now. Nothing fancy. No demolition. A plain, simple house. Small rooms. More like their old rental in Burlington. Get everything back down to how it was. They can sit out back in the evenings, talk about whether they'll ever get Hen to try out for something like Little League, look at the ground lights lit up around the sidewalk racetrack. He's going to need some ground lights.

It'll all work out, he thinks, even though he knows it can't, or probably won't, if he keeps going, if he gives the sign, tells Butner to go ahead and drop the blade in, start cutting the bed for the racetrack. But it could. It could. What he needs is some oversight, some kind of overarching intervention, a benevolent presence, a blessing. He needs a patron saint of lost causes, or damaged ones. Fatal flaws. Intentional missteps. Maybe it's Yul Brynner. Maybe the dog has been here all along to officiate at these kinds of occasions. Or maybe it's Hendrick. It really could be Hendrick. Jack's head is starting to feel overfull.

He gets Hen out of the truck, gets the dog, takes them both around to the back of the house, where there's mayhem. Butner's in the skid steer, and the blade's already in the ground, so none of it matters anyway, because go-ahead or not, he's already carving a miniature road into Jack's back yard. Another version of the to-mato moat. Ernesto's running a crew of three or four guys Jack's never seen before, directing them as they hammer metal stakes and guide boards into the cut Butner's leaving behind him. Another guy wheelbarrows a layer of gravel in over the bare ground. It's clear everyone's done this before, or something like it. Jack can't figure out where all these people have come from. Butner sees him, hollers, wants to know *Do you want it to curve around this way?* Jack puts Yul Brynner in the house, leaves Hen with Rena, says, *Will he be OK with you for a minute?* Rena's nodding *sure, sure,* and Jack walks out there, finds himself suddenly out in the middle of every-thing, pointing now to where he wants the racetrack to go, and Butner's yelling back, *Yeah man, yeah,* and he changes direction to where Jack's pointing, the skid giving off clouds of black smoke. It's happening much more quickly than he had it figured. It's like it's as simple as Butner said it was. Ernesto's over the top of his crew, saying *No, no, aquí, así,* and showing them where to run the forms out straight, where to pull them back around. The ground is red where Butner peels back the top layer of soil. Raw. Jack waves him down, meaning *over here, over here.* Butner shakes his head *yes,* puts the skid where Jack's aiming. The eight's already half-dug. It's happening.

Randolph, of Randolph & Sons, comes up, introduces himself. The man's given his business his first name. He wants to know if it's time yet, and Jack says he doesn't know. Randolph looks at Ernesto's guys, says, "It looks like it might be time."

"OK," Jack says.

"I'll call the rest of my boys. They're just down the street getting some lunch."

And soon enough there's another pickup out front, more people in the yard. There's a deeper rumble and the cement mixer backs out onto the street, turns around, rolls up onto the lawn, onto the wood and the rubber mat. The planking sinks down into the ground. Randolph's leaning out the driver's window and one of the Sons is motioning him back, saying *C'mon back, 'mon back*. All of them—Randolph and all the Sons—are sporting the same chubby necks. The Son gives a thumbs-up when Randolph's got the truck in the right place.

Hendrick gets free of Rena and walks out toward Ernesto, one foot in front of the other in measured heel-to-toe steps. Jack waves to Butner in the skid, and Butner nods back: *I see him*. Ernesto says something Jack can't hear, and hands Hen one of the hammers and a metal spike. Hen holds them by his sides a while, but then he leans over, hunches down, starts pounding the spike into the clay right in the middle of where the sidewalk will be. Jack's throat goes tight: Somehow it's this small, blunt, dumb thing that finally gets him. Hendrick is not touching the spike to each ear. He is not doing the cement guys' jobs better than they are. All he's doing in the world is knocking a spike into the mud, nothing more, which is beautiful in its own right, and now Jack's crying, watching him, this boy doing plain boy things, and he tries to hide it, tries to wipe his eyes before anybody can tell. The metal hammer on the metal spike rings out over the rest of the noise like a bird. Randolph gets down out of the mixer, gives a signal, and the Sons start pumping concrete into the far end of the eight.

Butner idles the skid, walks over, starts shouting and pointing. "That shed's kind of close to the edge of the track over there," he's saying into Jack's ear, so he can hear him. "Want me to take it out? We should probably take that out. It'll take five minutes with the loader. I mean, that fucker's ruined as it is, right?" It is. It's rotting into itself, leaning over ten or twenty degrees, made at least in part out of what looks like leftover fencing. There's nothing in it but a couple of rusting galvanized trash cans. Maybe a paint bucket or two. It needs taking out one way or the other. Jack wipes his eyes again. "Sure," he yells. "Go ahead. Whatever you want."

"I'll just pile it along the back there."

"Great," Jack says. "Fine."

Butner goes back to the skid, spins it around, picks the blade up into the air as high as it'll go, drives over and brings the blade back down, almost gently, on the shed roof. Everybody slows down to watch, all of them little boys now. Demolition. Hendrick marches in place. Jack sees Rena shake her head, laugh to herself. Butner brings the blade down further. The whole shed shifts. The loader throws out a column of black exhaust and the blade comes down a little more, and the structure gives in all at once, corner posts snapping and crumbling, the roof falling down through the center. Butner backs up, drops the blade down to the ground, then drives forward, pushing what's left of the building off its foundation. He cuts the skid off, gets out, walks up to the pile, pushes at a few pieces with his boot, peers down in there. Something's not right. While Jack's still trying to figure out what that might be, up and out of the rubble comes a thin spiral, a helix, a stream of smoke, something alive—let it be ants, he thinks, even though he already knows that it can't be, because that'd be too easy, that it's got to be termites, an indictment, finally, long overdue, of what he's doing here, a quick and easy reminder that no patron saint can save him from himself. There are so many, so fast. They're like water, like somebody's cut a hose on, thousands of termites flying out of the ruined shed, heading up into the air twenty or thirty feet and then getting pushed downwind, over the house and across the street, toward his and Frank's houses and out into the neighborhood. Hendrick clenches and unclenches his fists, blows air through his nose in short bursts. He's watching, for sure. Butner backs up until he's standing next to Hendrick. The termites keep coming. Millions, Jack thinks. Not thousands. This is what millions of anything looks like. His ears ring. Ernesto holds one hand up, stops his crew. Randolph & Sons are standing at the other side of the yard in a little knot, mixer shut down. Without the engine noise the yard's church-quiet. The termites keep on.

"What is it?" Rena asks, walking over.

"Termites," Jack says.

"*Coptotermes formosanus*," Hendrick says.

"What?" she says.

"*Coptotermes formosanus*," he says. "*Coptotermes formosanus*."

"What's he saying?" Butner asks.

"It's Latin," Jack says, tears in his eyes again, just like that, because there's his son, delivering species and genus name for the fucking termites. Next will be the declensions for numbers and kinds of girlfriends and wives. Jack wipes his nose, sniffs, takes stock of his half-destroyed back yard. "I think it's the Latin word for termites," he says. "The classification."

"Where the hell would he have learned that?" asks Butner.

"Magazines," Jack says. "We found some magazines."

"Seriously," Butner says. "You gotta get that kid on the news."

"OK," says Jack.

"You should call somebody."

"I know."

"I know a guy at Channel 14," Butner says.

They're landing on them, in their hair, their clothes. "Jesus," says Rena, slapping at her arms. "Can these things get into your house?"

"Probably," Jack says.

"Oh, shit yeah," says Butner. "Termites can get in anywhere."

Hen's got one on his finger, and he holds it out in front of him, looking at it. The wings look too fragile to function. Butner gets back on the loader, fires the engine, moves the pile a few feet farther away. He tries to cover them over, but that just makes the termites come faster than ever. "It's like locusts," Rena says. "Like a plague." Hen shakes the termite off his finger, holds it out, waits for another one to land on him.

Jack counts off the rest of the plagues: Boils, dead livestock, darkness. Firstborn sons. He can't remember what kind of blood you need for the door. Lamb. He's pretty sure it's lamb.

Randolph comes over, wants to know if they should keep going. *Yes*, Jack tells him, not even having to think about it, because even if he knows nothing else by now, he knows that what he absolutely cannot do is leave this half-finished. You can't have half a backyard sidewalk tricycle racetrack, termites or no. They're either in the house, too, or they're not. They'll get in or they won't. Finish things. He's supposed to finish things. *Swarm.* He thinks about the word *swarm.* He tells Randolph OK. *Do it*, he says. And Randolph goes back to the Sons, and they go back to pumping cement into the forms. Butner brings the skid back from the shed, back to the cut, starts going over some of the high spots to get them flatter. He's almost got the eight finished. The noise of the cement mixer and the noise of the skid cover everything over again. Ernesto gets his guys back in behind Butner, laying in the last of the forms around the edge. Rena stands with Hen, and Jack can smell the cement as it hits the ground, a kind of cold smell of fire, of burning, of sand and water. Two Sons in rubber boots stand in the forms, raking the slurry where they want it to go. Jack hopes Frank's not watching from inside his house, wondering what the hell he's got going in the back yard over here, wondering if the Neighborhood Association ought to be called. Or the health department. The ter-

mites keep coming, keep coming, and finally Jack leaves his post
there near where the sidewalk will eventually cross itself at the
middle of the eight, walks up into the side yard to see if he can tell
how far the termites might be flying, if they're landing on any of
the houses, if there's anything he could do about it if they were—
and while he's trying to figure that out, while he's looking at what
he's done, Beth pulls the wagon into the driveway across the street,
parks. She sits there in the drive, brake lights lit red, and here it
comes. Here is what he's wanted since she left. Here comes, after
all this time, what's next.

❧   ❧   ❧

And even though he tries to push it away, what he thinks about is
Sarah Cody. She just appears. In his head, she's married, like Rena
said, to some anesthesiologist. They're rich. They have a media
room. They have two good cars. They do not have a backyard sidewalk tricycle racetrack. There are not termites in their lawn.

She's twenty-six. He's a couple of years older, fresh out of med
school. If they have a kid, she's perfectly normal. One normal baby.
Sophie. They buy her ruffled hats and tiny socks and they feed her
apricots and put her to bed right at eight-thirty every night and sit
on their expensive sofa and watch their expensive TV and think
about the little family they've started, think about their good fortune. The baby monitor hisses quiet static from the end table. They
do not fight about how to calm Sophie when she's crying. They do
not worry yet about whether they'll have another child. They do
not have affairs with their closest friends. *The craziest thing she ever
did*—that's what their friends want to know at dinner parties, other
friends with brand new babies, too, the bottle of wine going
around the table one more time, everybody half-tired, half-
celebrating their deeply functional lives. *I don't know*, she says. *Come
on*, they say. *You must have done something.*

OK, she tells them. *Once, in college, I kissed my professor in a parking lot. We'd had some beer.* It's a good story to tell, lasts a couple of minutes, everybody laughing, asking questions, wanting to know what else happened. *Nothing,* she says. *That was it. That was all.* And then surely somebody else in the room has something wilder, a trump card, sex in the back of a moving pickup in an ice storm, and she can settle down into the comfort of deferring to somebody else's story. She's had her turn. She's exactly wild enough. She's been thinking of going back to school when the baby's old enough—maybe architecture, maybe public administration. Who knows. Soon enough, they think, the baby will be walking.

*I was going through a phase,* she probably tells people. *I wanted to see what would happen.* Jack's been wanting to see what would happen his whole life.

❧ ❧ ❧

Beth walks across the street, headed right for him, and he can guess pretty well at what she's seeing, because he can see it, too: Pickups all along the curb and the nose of the cement mixer sticking out from behind the house and the long NCDOT trailer carrying his green octopus and the shrimp and the catfish. Cloud of termites headed back her way. Rena's car in the driveway again. The planks and the rubber mat, dirt and mud everywhere, Butner and Ernesto and their crew and Randolph & Sons all in the back yard, Hen out in the middle of all of it. She walks up into the side yard, stands next to him. Things he'd like to tell her: That he's got everything under control. That he knows what's going on. That if she'd seen the undersea creatures there at the Carolina Flea Market and Undersea Adventures Mini-Golf, she would have bought them, too. Or that he wishes she would have.

"Jack," she says. She's calm.

"Hi."

She takes a long breath. "Whatever this is, you can't be doing it." She's wearing work clothes, clothes she teaches in, pants instead of jeans.

"Maybe not," he says.

"But you are."

He still doesn't know how much he owes for the concrete. "I guess so."

"What is it?" she says.

"It's a backyard sidewalk tricycle racetrack," he says.

She tries to say several things before she says, "I don't have any idea what that means."

"It's a sidewalk," he tells her. "For tricycles. For Hen."

"We don't have any tricycles."

"He's got his Big Wheel," says Jack.

"He doesn't use it."

"He might."

"But he didn't," she says. "Before, I mean."

"We didn't have this before."

She folds her arms across her chest like she's wanting to fold her whole body in on itself. "No," she says. "We didn't." Down in the yard, Randolph & Sons have almost finished pouring the bottom loop of the eight. It's taking shape. The wet concrete shines. A couple of Ernesto's guys are pulling a 2x4 across the top of the forms, shimmying down the concrete, leveling everything. "Who are all these people?" she asks him.

"Most of them are from the cement truck," he says.

"The cement truck," she says. He points it out to her, but she pushes his hand back down. "I see it, Jack. I haven't gone blind."

"OK," he says.

"Except, my God, I kind of wish I had."

Now that she's here, all this feels a little realer than it did with Butner riding the trailer, with Zel drinking her blue drink and wishing him luck. This is probably not the same as the kitchen. This is probably different.

"Are people going to be able to see this from the street?" she wants to know.

"I don't know," he says. "We'll know when it's finished."

"When will that be?"

"Today, I think."

"How will it be finished today?"

"They say it will be."

"The cement truck people?"

"And Butner."

"Butner," she says. "Wonderful." She turns to him. "What is it," she says, "that you want me to say to something like this?"

He thinks about that. "I don't," he says, finally.

"You don't what?"

"I don't think I want you to say anything to it," he says. "That's not what I had in mind."

"Do you ever have anything in mind?" she says.

"Yes," he says. "I do. A lot."

"Just not this time."

"That's not true," he says. "I wanted to buy him the catfish."

"Is that what's in the trailer?"

"Yes."

"Where did you get it?"

"The trailer?"

"The catfish," she says.

"It came from a mini-golf that was closing."

"What?"

"A mini-golf," he says. "And I wanted to buy it for him, so I did."

"I don't understand, Jack."

"There isn't anything to understand," he says. "We just thought of it."

"We."

"I just thought of it. It came to me."

"And now you've got nine people in the yard making a—a whatever this is?"

"Backyard sidewalk—"

"Don't," she says. She's got a pair of cheap sunglasses on her head, and she pulls them down onto her face, a simple thing, something she's done ten times a day every day he's known her, and it's that little motion that makes his body hurt. He probably doesn't get to want his racetrack and then miss her at the same time, but there it is. "Why is it always like this?" she says.

"It isn't," he says. "It's only like this sometimes."

"This is insane."

"It's not insane," he says. "Maybe it's a little crazy, but it's not insane."

"What's the difference?" she asks, her voice pinched. "What does it matter?"

"It matters," he says. He needs her to see it the way he does. Or try to. "I mean, it's fine. You can think it's crazy. But can't you like it, too?" Butner parks the skid by what's left of the shed. "Look at it," Jack says.

"What the hell do you think I'm looking at?"

"But how can you not like it even a little bit? How is this not a little bit fantastic? I'm not saying it isn't out there, Bethany, and I'm not saying everybody would have done it—"

"Who would have done this?" she says. "Who else in the world would have done this?"

"But can't you just—"

"What are you asking me?" she says. "How can you be asking me why I don't like it? How about this: How are you not sorry right now? How is it even *possible* you're not apologizing for this?"

"I'm sorry, OK?" he says. "I can be sorry. I can apologize, if that's what you want. I can apologize for all of it. Everything. But that doesn't make it not here, right?"

"Is everybody else on board with this?" she says. "Butner and Ernesto and all those guys down there? Is Rena?"

"I think so," he says. "They're here. They like it."

"God, that's even worse." She pushes hard at one eyebrow. "You're all completely nuts, you know that? All of you." She's sweating in the heat. She says, "I'm not the freak job here, OK? You don't get to make it out like I'm some kind of bad guy just because I don't think you and your sidekicks putting a theme park in the back yard is a good idea."

"I'm not saying that. I'm not. All I'm saying is—"

"What, Jack? What?"

He has no idea what he's saying. He's still got Canavan's coffee cup in the glove compartment of the truck. He still owes him some tomatoes, some azaleas. As of this morning, Rena had a toothbrush in his bathroom. He says, "What if there are some days—not a lot of days, but some days—where maybe putting in a sidewalk isn't the worst possible thing that could happen?"

"What are you talking about?"

"What if there were some days where you let yourself get surprised?"

She stares at him. "What did you just say?"

He doesn't say anything.

She takes a couple of breaths. She says, "I'm plenty fucking surprised, Jack. You surprise me all the time. But I'm getting *tired* of being surprised, you know?" She looks out at the back yard. "Clearly you don't know." Jack checks to make sure Hen's still in the same place. He is. "You know what I'd like?" she says. "I'll tell you what I'd like. I'll tell you exactly. I'd like to come home, just once, one time, to the house being the same way I left it that morning. I'd like a dinner where you don't tell me that what you've got in mind is some kind of six-story observation tower you want to add on to the back of the living room. A kitchen floor that's a kitchen floor. A back yard without a cement truck in it. How is it you think that's so wrong?" she says. "How is that too much to ask?"

"It isn't," he says. "It's a fine amount to ask."

"Great," she says.

"Maybe it's like Hendrick," he says. "Maybe it's like—"

"That's it," she says, grabbing his arm. "Stop right there. It is like Hendrick. But that's not alright. This is the part you don't get." Her voice is getting quieter. "I love you," she says. "I do. OK? None of this was ever about that. But listen to me." She squeezes his arm tighter. "Listen. We already have one Hendrick. One is plenty. I can't have you being another one. You don't get to be another one." She's blinking a lot. "You don't," she says. "It isn't fair."

He's failing. He sees that. He's not explaining it well enough to her. "That's not what I meant," he says. "You're getting it wrong."

"I'm not," she says. "I'm not getting it wrong at all. That's the whole, whole thing." She lets go of his arm and starts to walk away.

He says, "I don't understand why you always get to decide what's OK."

She stops, turns, looks at him like if she could make him disappear, wink out of existence right here and now, she would. But she turns back around, leaves him there on the little hill, walks down into the back yard toward the racetrack, toward Hen. She comes up behind him, touches him on the back, tries, it looks like, to pick him up, but she's done it without letting him know she was there first, a rookie mistake, something she'd never do otherwise. Do not startle him. Rule number one. Hen never saw her coming. He crumples immediately down onto the ground, into the mud, starts kicking and rolling, and just like that, it's like old times. No Spanish now, no Latinate National Geographic trivia answers. She tries to hold him, to get him to slow down, to stop, but he's too far gone already. It's a full-blown meltdown, up out of almost nowhere. He loses The Duck, which only makes it worse. Jack stands in the side yard. Ernesto tries to help her, but something's wound too tight in her head, or more than one thing, and she swings at Ernesto, actually swings, hits him with the back of her arm. He holds both hands up in the air, backs up, shaking his head. *I'm sorry*, Jack can see him saying. He can't believe she hit him. Ernesto keeps moving back, away. It's a silent movie down there, all the human noise drowned out by the cement mixer. Randolph & Sons are still at it, pumping concrete into the racetrack. She's crying, rubbing at her cheeks, at her neck. She swings again, this time at nothing. Ernesto stays well out of reach. Hen's facedown in the mud. Butner stands up in the skid, locks eyes with Jack. Jack looks away. What he can't do is take this back. They're already almost finished with the cement. It's all but done. Like Butner said: *Make sure you want it in there before you do it.* Beth goes back to Hen, tries a couple more times to get him to be still, but eventually she gives up, leaves him there in his tantrum, walks away, toward the mixer, the wet edge of the sidewalk. Randolph gives a hand signal and they stop pumping. The engine noise drops down to a hum, just the lowered groan of the drum still turning on the truck. The 2x4 guys stand to the sides, their board dripping concrete off its bottom edge. Beth leans over, reaches down into the slurry, picks up a handful, lets it fall back down into the muck. It's the consistency of cake batter. There's something plastic about it, something viscous. Rena's looking at him now. Everybody else is looking at Bethany, watching her pick up another handful of concrete, but Rena's looking at him. *Do something*, she mouths at him. *Do something right now.*

He has to think about making his arms and legs move, has to think about taking the steps, but he does it, does as he's told. He goes to Hen first, picks The Duck up out of the mud, wipes the lenses on his shirt. They're not broken, thank God, not too badly scratched. He gets him to sit back up, his whole front red from the clay, and Jack gets The Duck back on him, gets the glasses square on his head, which slows him down some, even if he's still squirming, still pushing. Jack's always amazed by how strong he is. Hen's making his noises: *Bup-bup-bup-bup.* Jack says that back to him, and he calms down one notch more. Jack waits. Hendrick takes a few shallow breaths, grabs a spike, puts it to his mouth, and he talks— he says, very quietly, *Call today for your free brochure.* He's never come out of one of these talking before. He works the words out around the spike. Jack takes a few breaths of his own, says, *Operators are standing by,* just to try him out, and Hen says right back, *Pellegrino is a three-year-old terrier mix who loves to fetch his ball.* He's slowing, stopping. He's one of those prize wheels at the fair. Jack says, *You think Yul Brynner needs a friend?* Hendrick looks at Beth, and says, *I do not know the answer to that.* He says, *Yo no sé.* He puts the spike back down. *She is standing in the wrong place,* he tells Jack, and Jack says, *I know that.* He stays a minute with Hen to make sure it's really over. This is all new territory. State names, dinner that's not fish sticks. It's hard to say what weather might be off on the horizon.

He counts to ten. He's got to try Beth next. Explanation, apology, accountancy: The Beanbags' three rules of something—either conflict management or behavior modification. He can't remember which. Hen stays still. Jack says, "Can you wait right here a second?"

Hendrick sits up straight, adjusts The Duck, says, "That will be fine."

"You're OK?"

"I am OK."

"You sure?"

Hen doesn't answer him, and Jack stares at his son, tries to look him in the eye through those sunglasses, like if he looks long enough he'll figure out what it is that's happening in there. Hen stares back. Jack tells him again: *Wait right here.* Beth's still at the edge of the wet concrete, working what's left in her hand through her fingers. Randolph hangs the hose on the cement mixer, looks for somewhere else to look. The Sons stand by the fence. Ernesto and Butner pretend to fool with something on the loader. Hen adjusts and readjusts The Duck. He's got mud on his head. Rena holds her ground, across the yard, watching, hands in her pockets. Jack walks over to Beth, stands right next to her.

She says, after a while, "I don't."

"You don't what?" he says.

"I don't always get to decide."

"I know."

"Then why did you say that?" she says.

"I don't know," he says. "I'm sorry." She picks up more cement, lets it drop back onto the ground. "What are you doing?" he asks her.

"I'm not doing anything."

She's still crying. "Why are you crying?" he asks.

She says, "Are you kidding me?"

He holds his shirt out to her, lets her clean some of the cement off her hand.

"Thanks," she says.

"You're welcome."

She says, "You got him to calm down."

"Yeah," he says.

She runs the hand without concrete on it through her hair. Another familiar motion. "What's going on with him?" she says.

"I don't know," he says. There are still termites coming out of the pile of rotten shed. "I've been thinking maybe he's getting better."

"You always say we can't talk about it like that," says Beth.

"I know."

"You have rules, too," she says.

"I know."

"You're the one who says he can't get better."

"I know that," he says. "But now it feels like he might be."

"How could he be? What's happening?"

"I'm not really sure," Jack says. "He knows things. Not just memorized things. He really knows them."

"He's always known things."

"Not these things," he says. "And he talks to you now. Some."

"You should have come to get me," she says. "You should have come and gotten me and told me he was getting better."

"What would you have done?"

"You just should have come to get me," she says again.

Jack says, "I thought I did."

"We have to take him in," she says. "We have to go see what they say."

"I know."

"I don't even know how to be standing here with you," she says.

"I know," he says.

"No, you don't."

She pushes her toe into the edge of the sidewalk, and he watches her do it. "Why Canavan?" Jack asks, finally. Or again.

"Why not?" she says. "He was the same as anybody else."

"He wasn't," Jack says.

She sniffs. "Did Rena stay here last night?"

"Yes," he says.

She works her toe further into the concrete. "We have to stop this," she says. "We have to do something."

"You and me?"

"All of us," she says. "All four of us. We can't keep going like this."

"I know," he says.

"We need to sit down," she says.

"Sit down how?"

"All of us together," she says. "Soon. Tonight."

"Tonight?"

"Yes," she says. "Tonight. I'm done with this. We're done with this. We have to be. We're all going to figure out what we ought to do. Together."

"Hang on," he says. "What is it you think is going to happen if the four of us sit down?"

"I don't know," she says, "and I don't even know if I care." She shakes her head, looks around. "All I know is that we have to do something before you—what, before you buy a blimp and paint your face on it."

"What?"

"I'm worn out, Jack. I'm not saying I'm coming home. I'm not saying anything. I can't come home, anyway, because you don't live at home any more. Or alone, either. But we at least have to hate each other more if we're going to keep acting like this. We at least have to act like regular lunatics."

"Instead of what?"

"Instead of whatever we're doing now." She shakes her shoe free of the concrete. Yul Brynner's standing in the sliding doors, wagging at them. Beth says, "Finish all this up, and get rid of all these people, and I'll go home and get Terry, and we'll be back in a few hours."

"Here? Why here?"

"It's the closest thing to neutral territory there is," she says.

"It's the opposite of neutral territory," he says. He's standing under the falling safe, looking up at it. He can't figure out if he should run, or if he should spread his arms wide open and catch it.

"It's what we have. It's that or you come to Terry's."

"I don't want to come to Terry's," he says. He doesn't want to go anywhere.

"Well?"

"Are you crazy?" he asks her.

She smiles a bent smile, but a determined one. "I don't think it's really your turn to ask me that," she says. "You know?" She steps out from between the forms, doesn't say anything else to him, walks away. She tells Rena *See you tonight* on her way by. He can't tell if she's kidding or coming unglued. He can't tell if any of them are. But he seems to have agreed to this, somehow. Yet another self-inflicted wound. Jack stands there for a minute, but then he goes and picks Hendrick up—makes sure he sees him coming—and carries him over to the patio, puts him back down. "*Gracias*," Hen says. Rena wants to know what Beth meant, what *see you tonight* meant. *Like tonight? Where's she going?* Jack doesn't answer. He doesn't want to think about Beth, or anything else. He looks out at the men in his yard.

Randolph holds his hands out: *What now?* Jack takes one long breath and then runs his finger around in a cranking motion: *Go ahead.* Randolph gives a thumbs-up, walks to the mixer, throws the lever on the side of the truck, and the pump kicks back on. Everybody snaps into motion one more time. Jack stands with Rena, tries to figure out what Beth could possibly be hoping for, tries to figure out what the hell stories the four of them might tell each other tonight. She'll be back in a few hours. With Canavan. Jack doesn't understand how this could possibly go, how they'll ever land somewhere so that any of them could say *There was this one time when*.

✿ ✿ ✿

Randolph and his crew are gone by six. What's impressive is how fast it all goes, how simple a thing like a sidewalk is, finally. It's two guys pouring wet rocks into a form, two more guys smoothing it out. When they get it flat, one last guy drags a destroyed push broom across the surface, roughs it up in little lines. *Leave it perfectly smooth*, Randolph tells Jack when he asks, *and people'll slip and fall and break their asses. You don't want an insurance situation on your hands.* He pronounces the first syllable heavy. In-surance. Jack had never given much thought to sidewalks before. Now he knows.

They've unloaded the undersea creatures, and they're on their sides in the front yard. Butner took the trailer back to the NCDOT guys. Before he left, before any of them left, they all put their hands into the concrete, all in a row. Jack felt like that was important. Randolph and Butner and Ernesto, the Sons, Rena. They brought Yul Brynner out, pressed each paw in. He did not love that. Hen didn't want any part of putting his hands in, either, did not like seeing the cement get on everyone else's hands, but they convinced him, finally, to put his two pointer fingers in, so there's the row of hands, the paws, and then two small holes, little knuckle marks next to each. And right now, in the half-glow of the evening coming on, it looks good. Jack's sitting on the back patio, has been for a while. The yard's pretty well torn up from the cement mixer and the skid steer, but he'll get out here with some soil, some grass seed. Maybe he'll get the NCDOT to come by, turn the back yard into one of those State Wildflower Projects they've got all in the medians of the interstates and up the off ramps. Every now and then a leaf or a stick falls down onto the racetrack, and he gets up, walks over there, leans out over the wet cement, picks it out.

Beth and Canavan coming back is an unmitigated catastrophe. Rena's fine with it, of course, fine with all of it, said, *That's as good as anything else, Jackson, isn't it?* Didn't even flinch. She's inside, getting drinks. Hen's watching the weather. Some show called *If It Happened Again*. It's a re-imagining of historical weather disasters—the Chicago Blizzard of 1967 strikes again, that kind of thing. Bad graphics. Urgent narration.

Rena comes outside with two plastic cups. Jack takes one from her. It's a beer with some ice cubes in it. "Something's wrong with the fridge," she says. "It's getting kind of warm. Your freezer seems fine, though."

"Perfect," he says.

"Well," she says, "yeah."

They sit and drink their beers. These are the hours before the execution. This is his last meal. He looks down into his cup. "This is an elegant life we've got cooked up for ourselves," he says. "Beer on the rocks."

"Elegant enough," she says. "I'll take it."

He chases an ice cube around with his finger, pulls it out, tosses it into the yard. "I don't want to do this," he says.

"I know that."

"I'm not ready."

"How could you be ready? Ready for what?"

"For anything," he says. "To sit down with them. To ask Canavan how his leg is. To take Hen to the doctor to find out what's going on."

"To trade back," she says.

"This wasn't a trade," he says.

"Sure it was."

"How can you say it like that?"

"How can you say it any other way? She's with him, and I'm with you."

"But it wasn't—"

"Jack," she says, and spins her chair around so she's facing him. "It doesn't matter what you call it."

"Why not?"

"Call it whatever you want," she says. "I don't care. Fact remains, I'm still sitting here, with you, in your back yard, and she's in my house." She puts her feet up on his legs, leans back. "I'm not some kind of muse for you, you know," she says. "You keep wanting me to carry you through this, but that's not my job."

He has to ask her. "What is your job?"

"I don't have a job," she says. "People don't have to have jobs.

Your wife's in my house. I don't see why it has to be any more than that. That's plenty right there."

He puts a hand on one of her ankles, feels the warmth of her skin, and looks at the racetrack, at the two muddy holes of the eight, at the six square pads Randolph & Sons poured in around the edge for the undersea creatures. Butner and Ernesto sunk threaded bolts down into the concrete. Jack hadn't thought to do that. *How else we gonna get 'em to stay still?* Butner had wanted to know. *That's how the lady had 'em set up, anyway.* It's not finished. They have to wait for the concrete to set around the bolts to drop the creatures on. But the sidewalk's in. It's huge. It's taking up most of the back yard. The shed is still in a pile in the corner. The termites stopped coming out before everyone left. *Burn it,* Butner told him. *No sense in doing anything else. A few cups of kerosene, toss a match in.*

"Do you think it's too much?" he asks her.

"Do I think what's too much?"

"All this. The racetrack. The catfish."

"Absolutely."

"You do?"

"Of course," she says. "But in a good way," she says. "This is the good kind of too much. Wild excess. Crazy shit. You've done some crazy shit here. But it's the beautiful kind."

"Beth doesn't think so."

"She might," says Rena. "Eventually. Give her a while." She rattles the ice in her cup. "I think it's beautiful, at least. It's pretty fucking impressive."

"This house will never sell like this."

"You don't want it to."

"We'll be here forever," he says.

"Maybe so," she says. "But maybe that's not so bad, either."

"I don't know," he says. "I can't figure it out." He gets up, walks to the fence, checks the driveway, checks across the street. No wagon. The eave lights have flicked on over there, but they're on a timer. He looks back at Rena, sitting there in front of the racetrack. She moves through the world so much more easily than he does. "They're still not here," he says.

"Let them be late," she says.

"Where do you think they are?"

"Up in some tree somewhere," she says. "He's showing her an owl nest. Or a rare fungus."

"Yeah?"

"That's where I think we should look first, anyway."

It's over. He knows that. What he needs to do is figure out how to say that he's been happy these few days, that he's glad it happened, even with what's coming. That it's been worth it. Also, he wants to say, *Let's get in the car right now. We'll go anywhere you want. We'll pack up Yul Brynner and Hendrick and never come back.*

He wants it each way. Both ways. All the ways. He wants his marriage solved, and he wants to be out on the road with Rena, one of the undersea creatures strapped to the luggage rack, Yul Brynner with his head out the window, licking the air. He wants the Beanbags to smile, shake their heads, look at Hendrick's charts, tell them *We've never seen anything like this. It's a long road in front of you, but his chances for a normal life are. He may now be able to. We'd like to present his case this spring at the.* He wants to feel less lost. Rena sets her beer down, gets up, comes and stands behind him. He doesn't turn around. She wraps her arms around him. He doesn't move, doesn't want to do anything that would make her move. She presses her forehead into the center of his back, and that seems like it might be almost enough to keep them pinned exactly where they are. He wants to undo everything he's ever done. He wants to keep everything exactly as it is. He wants to stand in this back yard, the sidewalk almost finished, for the rest of the week, for the rest of his life. He wants to hold right here as long as he possibly can. His chest hurts. His face hurts. His whole body hurts. He wants to

sleep. He wants a shower. He wants to touch his lips to every faucet
in the house.

He can feel the earth wheeling underneath him. The sidewalk is
turning a mottled gray, lighter in the places where it's drying. The
sun drops a little lower in the sky. She pushes harder against him,
and inside Jack's head, circus music starts playing. Fairgrounds
music. At first, he can't remember what the thing is called, the
organ, the thing that plays while the merry-go-round turns, but
then he gets it. Calliope. It's quiet, but it's definitely playing. And he
can hear the barkers: *Step right up, folks. Step right up. Guess your weight
and age. Guess your birthdate. Fabulous prizes. You, sir. Yes, you. Why not win
a prize for the lovely lady?*

♋ ♋ ♋

Beth and Canavan show up, finally, and they've got a bottle of
white wine Canavan's saying is *nice, really nice,* the gift offered up
like they've arrived for some dinner party. Jack keeps drinking beer
on ice and tries to stay the hell out of the way while Rena stands in
the kitchen pouring the wine into teacups. The whole thing already feels right on the verge of disaster. Even Beth seems to think
so. She keeps looking at the walls, out the windows, anywhere but
at him or Rena or even Canavan. Nobody's talking much. Jack's
checking all the surfaces to make sure nothing fragile is too close
to an edge, but outside of the teacups, yet another garage find,
there isn't anything really breakable. At least there's that.

Hen and Yul Brynner are set up over by the TV, watching the
channel that previews what's on other channels. Hen's got a bowl
of peanuts, and the dog's waiting for him to drop one. On TV, the
red and black and green bars scroll by. It's Tuesday on television. It
must be Tuesday out here, too. The show they're running in the
half-screen above the scroll is also about what's going to be on TV.
Jack's head hums. Having everyone in the same room at the same
time is like having all the channels on at once.

Beth sits down, runs her finger around the top of her teacup, frowns, wipes it on her leg. Rena brings Canavan his wine, sets it on the arm of his chair. He's propped his leg up on a big box of Field & Stream Jack dragged out of one of the closets. It's the first time Jack's seen him since the accident. They've got his leg rigged so he can't bend it, in the kind of full brace they use for hyperextended knees. He's in bandages all the way down to his ankle. Jack's feeling like he's supposed to say something, but it's as though he's in the school play, and he's forgotten his lines.

Canavan saves him. He reaches for his wine, winces as he sits up.

"Still hurt you?" Jack asks. Easy enough: Inquire about the patient.

"He almost cut his leg off," Beth says. "Of course it hurts."

"I didn't, actually," Canavan says, pointing at his shin. "I only went about halfway through the bone. I have the X-rays. It's kind of cool. You want to see?"

"Sure," Jack says.

"They're out in the car," he says, and pushes himself up. "It's better at the doctor's office, with that light box they have. But you can see pretty well if you hold it up to a lamp, or against a window." He crutches over to the door.

"Terry," Beth says. "They said to stay still as much as possible."

"I am," he says.

"How is that staying still?"

He looks at Jack. "I'm getting better," he says. "I'll be up and around for real in a week or two. I'll be back on the job."

"That's great," Jack says. "That's terrific."

Canavan walks out the door, leaves it standing open. Jack goes and shuts it against the heat. "Does he take them everywhere?" Rena asks. Beth doesn't answer. "I bet he takes them everywhere," Rena says.

The TV runs through the listings. Beth drinks the rest of her teacup of wine. She looks around the room, says, "You guys hung up more maps."

"Hen loves the Craters of the Moon National Park one," Jack says.

"What else does he love?"

"He likes the Tennessee River," says Rena.

Beth goes to the window, looks out at Canavan, plays with the blinds. "He's supposed to be keeping his weight off it," she says. She turns around when Canavan comes back through the door. He leans his crutches against the wall. One falls, and she picks it back up.

"Here," he says. He's carrying a white envelope with green triangles all around the edges, holds it out to Jack. "Go ahead. Take a look." Beth closes the blinds, opens them back up, and then leaves the room, walks down the hall. Jack watches her go. Maybe they've been fighting. Maybe they fought on the way over here. Maybe it's any of a hundred other things. Jack takes the X-rays from Canavan, slides a film out of the envelope and holds it up so the light can shine through. It's dim, but he can make out a good-sized notch in what must be Canavan's shin, a rectangular piece missing, and a bunch of tiny white spots around the bone itself. It's shrapnel, he realizes. Chips of bone blasted out into the muscle. He listens out for Beth, doesn't hear anything. She could be in Hen's room. She could have climbed out the bathroom window in a daring escape. Jack looks closer at the interior of Canavan's knee, at his ankle, at literally how the man is put together.

"Cool, huh?" Canavan says.

"Yeah, actually," says Jack. It is.

"Didn't I buy you shinguards last year?" asks Rena.

"They're uncomfortable as shit," he says.

"More uncomfortable than this?"

"I know," he says. "I know."

"You have shinguards?" Jack asks Canavan. He hands Rena the X-ray, and she holds it out at arms' length, looks through it at him.

"Like for soccer, except that they're Kevlar. The saw would have bounced right off." He gets himself settled back into his chair, winces again. "I'd be up in Mrs. Jacobs' maples right now. We'd have firewood cut and stacked and drying by the end of the week."

"There's still plenty of time," Jack says. Somehow he feels like he's supposed to reassure him.

"I'll probably start wearing them now," Canavan says. "The shinguards. After this."

"You think?" Rena says.

The three of them fall back quiet. Rena reaches for the envelope, shuffles through the rest of the X-rays. They're waiting for Beth. Jack thinks about going to get her, decides against. On TV, the host is talking about What's Hot and What's Not in Tonight's Viewing Lineup. Hendrick seems to be mouthing what she's saying along with her, so he's either psychic now, too, or this is something they've played a few times already. As far as Jack's concerned, it might as well be either. If he turns up psychic, fine. Let the kid become some kind of shaman. Line people up around the block to hear what he knows. They can charge five dollars for him to touch people's foreheads.

Beth comes back down the hall, and she rounds the corner in a hurry, walks into the kitchen and opens the refrigerator door, opens up some cabinets, rattles and bangs things around. Eventually she arrives in the living room with a tumbler in one hand and their bottle of gin in the other, the tonic water crooked into her armpit. She sets all that down on the box Jack's been using for a coffee table, and says, "You know what? I think we should make this a party." She's a little loud, moving a little too quickly, like a small animal. Her eyes are red. Not the kind of red where she's been crying, but like she's been back there in the bathroom scrubbing her face, something she does when she's stressed. She mixes herself a strong drink, splashes tonic into her cup, spills some out onto the box. She's not using any ice. She says, "I mean, shouldn't this be a party?"

"What's wrong?" Canavan and Jack ask her, at the same time.

"Nothing at all," she says. "I'm having a drink. Does anyone else want one?"

"I'm fine," Jack says, and Canavan says he is, too.

Rena downs her wine, says, "I'll have one."

Beth nods at the box table. "Of course you will," she says. "Make it your fucking self."

The room goes quiet but for the TV. Everybody's looking at Beth. Rena says, "Maybe we should try this another night."

"Absolutely not," Beth says. "Why would you say that? Make yourself a drink. Make yourself ten drinks. Make yourself at home, which, of course, you've already done."

"Beth," Rena says, and something begins to tilt, however slightly, in the room. The air's getting thinner.

"You know what we need?" Beth says. "Hors d'oeuvres. Something to snack on. Some of Hen's peanuts, maybe." She goes back into the kitchen. "What do you guys have in here?" she asks. "I bet Rena's been making some fine meals for you two—you three. You three! Let's look in the cabinets." She's opening doors, reporting her finds. "Cheerios," she calls out. "Oregano."

"I'll get us some crackers," Jack says, trying to slow down whatever it is that's bubbling up. She seemed fine, or half-fine, ten minutes ago when they rang the doorbell. Now she's not, and it's all wrong: Beth's supposed to be the one sitting on the front porch after he trenches somebody's yard. She's not the one who does the trenching.

*How's the sidewalk?* she wanted to know, when they opened the door.

*It's really great,* he said. *You should see it.*

*Maybe later,* she said, looking behind him, through the glass doors.

*The undersea creatures go on in the morning,* Rena said. *When the concrete's dry.*

*You're pretty excited about all this,* Beth said.

*I just like it, is all.*

Beth chewed on her lip. *I bet you do,* she said. Then she recovered, gave them the bottle of wine, said *Let's sit down, I guess,* and Jack invited them in.

"Where are they?" Beth calls. "The crackers?" She's rummaging through more cabinets. "Wait. Here's some more cereal. Chex. Those'll be good." She rattles the box at them. "You have Chex, Jackie. I could make us some party mix. The recipe's right here on the side of the box. We're going to need butter. Do you have butter?"

Jack gets up, looks at Rena, who blinks, shakes her head. *I don't know.* He aims for Bethany, for the kitchen. She's opening drawers. She finds a box of plastic spoons. She opens the refrigerator again. "You don't have butter," she says, looking in.

"I know."

"This room's ugly as shit, by the way. I don't think I noticed it before." The linoleum, a pattern of red bricks, might be original. The walls are a dirty pink, dirtier behind the stove. The stove is green. There's a wallpaper border of ducks around the top of the wall. It's a museum of somebody else's life. Of somebody else's other life. "You know what we should do?" she says. She seems almost frantic. "Forget about the Chex mix. No Chex mix. We should go across the street and get our slides down from the attic. Wouldn't you like that? We can look at all our old pictures. The good old days. You remember those, right?" She drinks her drink. "Do we even have slides?"

"Maybe we could do this some other way," he says. "It would be fine if you wanted to do it another way."

"Have you got something to say?" she asks, stepping closer. "If you've got something to say, you should say it. By the way, I think your refrigerator is broken. It's hot in there."

"This was your idea," he says. "Tonight. The four of us. We can stop right now if you want. You and I can go get breakfast in the morning or something, instead."

"We could go get pancakes," she says. "We could bring our slides."

"Beth."

"What?"

He says, "This isn't good. We should do this another time."

"This isn't good? That's what you came in here to tell me?"

"No," he says.

"Because believe me, I know this isn't good. I can tell. I've got a good sense for things like that." She looks over his shoulder. "Terry," she calls into the living room. "Jack says things aren't going so well. Jack says we should do this tomorrow."

This is what he doesn't want. He doesn't want Beth and Canavan in here, which he knew all along, but he isn't even sure he wants Rena here any more. Not right now, anyway. He could use some quiet. A long empty evening. A baseball game on television. Watch the concrete dry. He leaves her in the kitchen, appeals to Canavan, of all people, says, "Help me out here, man, would you?" It's a mistake, something stupid, a little confederacy of men he reaches for. He should know better. Rena gives him a look that says as much.

"This ain't my show," Canavan says.

"Whose show is it?"

"It's not a show," Beth says, from the kitchen. "Don't call it that."

"What should we call it?" he asks.

"Jesus," Rena says. "Sit down, OK, Jack? Calm down."

"Me calm down? What about her?"

"What about her?" Beth asks.

He turns around. She's come out of the kitchen, is standing very close to him. He's not pissed off, but he's something like it. There are people in his house, undersea creatures on his lawn. He had it in mind a different way. "Maybe you should try some of Canavan's meds," he says to Beth. "That might do the trick."

"Do what trick?" she says.

"I don't know," he says. "It seems like you could use something."

She squares her body to him, and, holding her drink in her left hand, she slaps him full in the face with her right. Hendrick and Yul Brynner both turn around to look because of the noise. Jack's face feels very much in the present moment. And it hurts. The woman on TV keeps talking. *At nine o'clock, The History Channel turns its spotlight on Modern Marvels.*

"How's that?" she says. "Is that something? Does that do the trick?"

"You hit me," he says.

"Yes," she says.

"That's what you wanted to get us all together for? So you could fucking hit me?"

"No," she says.

"Why don't you tell me what you did want? What grand scheme you had in mind?"

"Me?" she says. "My grand scheme?"

"Yeah," he says.

"What is this, Jack?" she says. "What is all of this?"

"It turns out we should have charged them admission," Jack says, looking from Canavan to Rena. "We didn't need them at all. They're getting the whole act for free."

"What a complete bastard you are," Beth says.

"Yeah," Jack says. "That's me."

"A real piece of shit," she says.

"You know what?" he says. "Fuck off, OK? You're the one who walked in the door like this was some kind of a, what, I don't know—"

"Like what? Go ahead. Tell me how I walked in here."

"I don't know how you walked in," he says. "But since then you've been acting like a goddamn lunatic."

They stare at each other, and it's only right then that he really remembers Hen's in the room, that he processes the fact that they probably shouldn't do this right in front of him, but none of that much matters—he hears Canavan say *Wait*, and the room goes a little static, and there's a moment where Beth still isn't moving, but then there's one where she definitely is, a sprung coil, and she's coming at him, swinging again, closed fist this time. She hits him right in the eye, his left eye. He doesn't even have time to flinch. His entire universe goes green and red and black. Her motion carries her fully forward, off balance and onto him, takes the two of them down through the Adirondack chairs and onto the floor. Jack's trying to hold his head, his face. On his way down he kicks the coffee table box over, and Rena stands up just as the thing collapses, the gin and the tonic bottles and a couple of teacups falling off, rolling, breaking. One of the end tables falls over, too, and its lamp with it, the bulb exploding, glass everywhere. Everything everywhere. Plenty of noise. Beth's kneeling over him—they're on the floor, and she's hitting him in the chest, the arms, and she's screaming at him, and Rena's trying to get hold of her, pulling her off, yelling at her to *slow down, slow down*. Not stop, Jack notices. Just slow down. Like it's a critique of her form. Rena pulls her back further, harder, off him, but she swings at Rena, pushes her, gets free, and then somehow Canavan's in it, pulling Rena away from Beth, and Jack's thinking *keep your weight off it*, and Canavan's saying *leave them be, goddamnit*, and by then Beth's back at him, hard. They tumble up against the front door. He gets his leg tangled up in one of Canavan's crutches, gets that wedged into the corner such that he can't move, really, can't get out of the way. She hits him again, but he manages to get up onto his knees, get himself turned away from her, and she works his back, still yelling, crying, now, too, and he curls away, trying to wait it out, trying to let her wear herself down. He's in pain. He's holding his eye. Yul Brynner thinks it's all some game, is up and barking at them. Rena's yelling at Canavan, at Beth. Canavan's saying *hang on, hang on a second*. There's a lot going on. His eye. Fucking Christ. *Take a knee, Lang.* She stops hitting him, finally, sits back on her knees. He can hear her trying to catch her breath. He puts a hand on the ground in front of him, holds onto his face with his other hand. He gets one eye open. Rena's on the floor, leaning against the wall. Canavan's in a different chair, holding his other crutch out at Rena like a sword. Jack touches his eye, looks at his hand. He's bleeding. Not a lot, but some. Beth reaches for him, and he flinches, thinking she might be ready to start up again, but she's got her hand on his shoulder now, her mouth right up in his ear saying *I'm sorry*, saying she was aiming for his chest.

"What the hell are you doing?" he asks her. "What the hell was that?"

"I'm sorry," she says. "I am. I don't know why I did that. I was aiming for your chest."

"Which time?" he asks her. He presses the heel of his hand against his eye.

"One of the times," she says. "The first time."

"For fuck's sake, Beth," Rena says.

Jack sits up, gets his foot free of the crutch, and opens his good eye fully, the one that doesn't feel like it's been pushed back into his brain. Canavan picks up his X-rays, as if they might prove a point. The flipped-over Adirondack chairs look like something dead on the side of the road. At least one of them's cracked. They've knocked a plant over, too, broken the pot, spilled the soil out across the floor. The only plant he had in here. Rena gets Yul Brynner by the collar, gets him out of the way of the mess. Jack wipes his mouth on his sleeve. More blood. Hen's come over from the TV, is standing over the scene, presiding, a tiny pope. He says, "Only Coors Light is frost-brewed."

Beth looks at him. "Mommy is very sorry," she says. "She had an accident."

"Fuck," Rena says.

"It won't happen again," Beth says. She sounds like she believes it.

"The furniture has been knocked over," says Hen.

"Yes," Beth says. She's breathing hard. They all are.

"We have some fabulous deals at American Furniture Warehouse," Hen says. "Bedroom Suites for only $999." He takes a breath. "$999? $999."

Beth reaches for him, and he lets her take his hand. Her face is red. "That's a good price," she says.

Jack wills Hen to say it, wants him so fucking badly to say *We've gone C-R-A-Z-Y here at American Furniture Warehouse*. Instead, he touches his thumb to his pointer finger a few times. *A dust. I have got a dust.* Jack pulls his hand off his eye, blinks a few times, tries to get things to come into focus. Even moving his eyelid hurts, but he can see. He's a little disappointed. What it would have been for her to blind him. Something he'd have had forever. A trump card. An eye patch. Now all he's got is that she kicked his ass. "You OK?" he asks Rena.

"I bit my tongue," she says. "I'm fine."

"Are you bleeding?" Beth asks her.

"No," she says. She touches her finger to the end of her tongue. "Maybe."

Beth builds the lightbulb glass into a little pile. She pushes the

potting soil and the pot shards into a different pile, then moves
everything up against the wall. She's moving slowly, deliberately.
Rena lets Yul Brynner go once everything is out of the way, then
helps Beth turn the chairs right-side-up again. Jack's still down on
the floor, his eye throbbing. He can feel the blood under his skin
moving along in his veins and arteries. Beth takes his face in her
hand. "Let me see you," she says.

"I don't think so," he says, trying to push her away.

"Stop it and let me see you."

"Are you planning on hitting me again?"

"I wasn't planning on hitting you the first time."

Canavan laughs, and Rena tells him to shut up.

"Maybe we should get some ice," Beth says.

"I'll get it," Rena says.

"Thank you," Beth says, so quietly only Jack can hear. She pushes
at him with her thumb. "I think you're OK," she says.

"That's your professional opinion?"

"I think you're OK," she says again.

"Maybe you should put a steak on it," Canavan offers.

"Do you have any steaks?" Beth asks Jack.

"No," he says. "Not over here."

"Across the street?"

"I can't remember."

Rena comes back with the ice, and then they're both working on
him, Beth looking down into his face and Rena holding a towel
full of ice against his eye. He can feel the cubes shifting against
each other. "Careful," he says.

"I'm being careful," Rena says.

"Can we sit back down?" Jack asks. "I'd like to sit down."

"You are sitting down," Beth says.

"In a chair," he says, and takes the towel, picks his way across
the room, takes over his own first aid. He sits down. This is us, he
thinks. This is our family. He pats the dog, who still thinks there

might be a game in this somewhere. Hen's back down on his knees in front of one of the tipped-over boxes, lining up his peanuts. Yul Brynner stretches his neck out and eats one, very delicately. Rena touches her tongue again, wipes her finger on her leg.

"Everybody settled back down?" Canavan asks.

Rena says, "Terry, I'd hit you, too, if you weren't crippled."

He looks at her. "You can if you want," he says. "It's all the same to me."

"It probably is," she says.

"You're welcome to it," he says. "Do your worst."

Rena shakes her head. She picks up a teacup that survived, pours gin in it. "What the hell just happened?" she asks.

"I got mad," Beth says. "That's all."

"That's all?" says Rena.

The air conditioner kicks on outside. It's got a low grinding noise right as it starts up. He's going to have to replace it eventually. "What is that?" Canavan says.

"It's the air conditioner," Jack says. "The compressor."

"No," Canavan says. "Not that." He sniffs the air. "Do you smell that? Are you cooking something?"

"What are you talking about?" Jack asks.

"That," he says. "You don't smell that?"

"Yeah," Rena says. "I smell it, too. In the kitchen." She gets up, goes in. On the TV, a guy with a beard wants to know if they've been having problems with calcium deposits in their shower. "Oh, shit," Rena says, and then it sounds like she's moving things around.

"What?" Beth says.

"Somebody better come see this," she says.

Jack goes to see what could possibly be happening now, and Beth does, too, and it's that the kitchen is about half-filled with gray smoke. Rena's pulling at the fridge, trying to move it away from the wall. The smoke's coming from back there. She's swatting at the space behind the fridge with a towel. "I think you have a fire," she says.

"What kind of fire?" Beth says. Jack pushes the ice against his eye.

"An over here kind," she says. There aren't any flames. Just smoke. And the smell, a terrible, acrid smell, like a pile of hair on fire. Or bike tires. There's more smoke than he thinks seems right, and it's collecting up at the ceiling, and there is one last good long moment where everything's still alright, where Rena's on the job, and he and Beth are standing there watching her trying to move the refrigerator, a moment where Jack still thinks they might be able to paste everything back together and it all still might hold, but then the smoke detector in the hallway goes off, a shrill huge beeping that sends Yul Brynner fully into orbit, and the whole house erupts all over again. Hen gets up and comes in. Canavan's limping around. The dog whines, barks, ears straight back. He hates smoke alarms. It'll take all night to calm him back down. Hen should be berserk, too, but of course he's not. He's got his hands over his ears, and he's marching in place. He shouts something Jack can't hear. "What?" Jack asks him.

"We are having an emergency!" Hendrick yells.

"I know that!" Jack yells back, eye throbbing.

"Fix it, please!" Hen shouts. Rena's shoving at the fridge. The smoke alarm's going like it's inside Jack's own head. Yul Brynner's barking. It's all the noise in the world. Jack opens the sliding door to let the dog out the back of the house, and Yul Brynner goes through the screen before Jack can get that open, too, tears it off its runners, and he runs for the racetrack, runs through it, leaves paw prints all the way across one end of the eight. "Call the fire department!" Hendrick yells.

"No," Jack says. "It's OK. We don't have to do that. There's not a fire."

Beth gets one of Canavan's crutches, jabs at the smoke alarm until she knocks it down, and then she crushes it on the floor. It stops beeping. "What do you mean, there's not a fire?" she asks. "Isn't that a fire?"

"It's an electrical fire," Jack says. "Probably. The fridge's been acting up. We just have to unplug it."

"I think it's a real fire," Rena says, and they all look, and the back wall is on fire right around the socket.

"Holy shit," Canavan says.

"Call the fire department!" Hen screams again, and Rena picks up the phone, looks at Jack, and he nods at her, *yes*, because that is what you do in an emergency. You call the fire department. Hen had it right all along. Rena dials.

"Do you have an extinguisher?" Canavan asks.

"Maybe in the garage," says Jack. Canavan heads that way. Jack can't remember if it's baking soda for a grease fire or an electrical fire. It doesn't matter, because he's got no baking soda over here. He turns the faucet on, pulls the sprayer out, and sprays the wall, which makes it much worse. Now it's certainly a fire department fire. The flames jump up higher on the wall, and there's fire coming out from underneath the refrigerator now, too, like some obscene cartoon rocket. He can't understand what would even be burning under there. Hendrick walks up to the fridge, transfixed, and before Beth can stop him, before Jack can, Hen reaches out— Jack can't believe he's watching him do it—he reaches out and tries to take hold of the flames, tries to grab one, to touch one. Jack knows he knows better than that, knows he does, but there he is doing it anyway, and there's nothing he can do to stop him. Hen screams right away and pulls his hands back, but he loses his balance and falls forward onto the fridge, into the fire, and Canavan's back now with an extinguisher, running, limping on his braced leg, and he puts the whole thing out immediately, so fast that Jack can't even tell if Hendrick was ever on fire, or if his clothes were. The extinguisher sounds like radio static. You're supposed to put butter on a burn. They don't have any butter. Canavan covers Hen in powder, and Hen's screaming, screaming, ash-white from the extinguisher, and Beth picks him up, runs him to the sink, tries to fit his whole body under the faucet, but he's too big, so she carries him down the hall toward the bathroom. Jack follows her. Rena's saying his address into the phone, is saying fire, is saying *we may have an injury, we may have somebody burned.* Beth's got Hen in the shower by the time Jack gets in there, and she's in under the water with him, asking him what hurts, what hurts. He's still screaming, but now it's a breathless, noiseless scream, no real sound coming out any more, just air. *Where,* Beth's asking him, *where, honey,* and he's not saying anything. His mouth's wide open. No tears. *Where,* Beth's saying, more and more insistently, and the water's running out of the shower, pooling on the floor, seeping into the hall. She's soaked. Hen gets a breath, starts again, a horrible, impossible sound, a sound that's not any kind of sound at all. Jack does the only thing he can think to do, which is to get in there with them, to wrap his arms around Hendrick, around Bethany, to stand with them in the freezing water in his clothes and shoes with his eye throbbing and his house on fire and try to figure out what to do to get Hen to take another breath, to try to find out where he's burned and how badly, to try to be there with him so that even if he can't ever tell them anything at all, he'll still know they were both of them in there, together, trying every way they could to hear him.

ଶ ଶ ଶ

The night they first bring him home from the hospital, they set him in the center of the floor in his carrier, stare at him. The house is stone quiet. They're afraid even to move. Beth's in pain, exhausted. Jack isn't sure what to do with himself. They've got a book on swaddling, on how to wrap him up so he doesn't cut himself with his fingernails. He's come equipped to do himself harm right from the start. Every now and then he moves, blinks, stretches. Mostly he stays still.

The room they've got set up as a nursery seems ridiculous, somehow. The dresser full of diapers. The crib. The changing table. The mobile hanging in the corner. Jack doesn't know what they're going to do with any of that. He sanded down the corners of the top of the dresser a couple of weeks back. Beth had asked him to. *He won't be tall enough to hit his head on the corner for years*, he told her.

*Even so, though, right? I mean, why not do it anyway?*

So he did it. Sandpaper, sanding block. He repainted each rounder corner white. The dresser's white. The mobile is cats, something Beth picked out, all these wildly colored cats, sitting, smiling. Pink. Yellow. Blue. Jack hangs a wind chime outside Hen's window. Two weeks later, after it keeps waking him up, he takes it down, moves it to the back yard.

Jack sits there on the sofa with her looking down at him, feels like he'll never be ready to be a father, never know what to say to this creature to solve the world for him. He already doesn't know how to solve the world for Beth, keeps trying to even though she tells him he doesn't need to, that she needs him to do other things, different things. *What things?* he'll ask her. *You'll know*, she'll say. But he doesn't know, or he hasn't. They watch him. Maybe it's nothing more than this, he thinks. Maybe it's nothing more, after all of it, than sitting in some rented house on a thrift-store sofa with your infant son at your feet, his mother beside you, and it's not, finally, that you're supposed to try to survive each day until evening, but instead that you're supposed to survive each night, looking all the time for ways to make it to the next day as whole as possible.

❦ ❦ ❦

Firemen get them out of the shower and take them to the ambulance, which is parked on the front lawn, near the undersea creatures. Three fire engines are out in the street, lights turning, flashing red on his house, his other house, his neighbors' houses. It certainly looks like an emergency. A few more firemen come jogging past, axes in hand, saying *get back, get back, get back.* The inside of the ambulance is lit up. Everything is very white: White sheets, white towels, white gauze, white uniforms on the EMTs, who want to know if Beth or Jack are hurt, too, and they're saying *no, no.* The EMTs have got Hen sitting up on the stretcher in the back. He's breathing more regularly now, at least. But he's silent. He hasn't said anything since the kitchen. Somebody brings them blankets, and Jack uses his like a towel, dries Hen's hair, then his own. The EMTs are wearing latex gloves, are working every inch of Hen's body. Nothing. They're finding nothing.

Jack keeps looking back at the house, at the roof, keeps waiting for flames to come shooting out the windows. He's seen houses on fire in movies, on television. This does not look like that. It looks like a training exercise. They've got everything but the fire. Another fire truck arrives, sits at the end of the street, engine idling. The neighbors are out of their houses. Frank's standing on his porch. Jack's life is on full display. Nobody's hooking hoses up to the hydrant yet. That has to be good. The EMTs scissor Hendrick's shirt and pants off him, saying *This is just a precaution.* Jack looks. Still nothing. Hen's clicking his tongue against the roof of his mouth. *Where's he hurt?* Beth wants to know. *Is he OK?*

*I don't see anything yet,* one of the EMTs says. *So far, so good.* It comes to Jack that there might be too many ambulances and fire trucks in his life of late. *Wait,* another EMT says. *Here.* They've worked his entire body over and come back to his hands. Hen's got his left hand balled into a fist, and they pry it open, and inside is a little constellation of blisters, white and red, a palm full of raw skin. Jack reaches up for him, takes his arm, and the EMTs push him back, saying *Please, sir,* and he wants to say *No, you don't understand,* wants to explain it all to them, wants to tell them that one easy mistake could land Hendrick sprinting back into the fire, if there even is a fire, but it doesn't matter: Hen's not paying any attention to what they're doing to him. He's watching the lights on top of the nearest engine. His legs hanging over the stretcher don't make it anywhere near the floor of the ambulance. He's a doll, a toy. *It doesn't look so bad*, the EMT says. He shows Jack and Beth. *I think we can deal with this right here.* Beth's blinking a lot, and she picks up Hen's cut shirt, holds onto it. *Hand me a burn box*, the EMT says to his partner, and she does, opens a drawer and takes out a kit wrapped in plastic. She pulls the wrapping free and gives it to him, and he opens the box, opens a tube, squeezes some kind of gel onto Hen's hand. *This ought to cool things down*, he says to Hendrick, who ignores him, lets him do it, stares out at the yard, the trucks, the street.

"Is he OK?" Beth asks Jack.

"I think so," he says.

Canavan and Rena are across the lawn. They've got Yul Brynner on a leash Jack's never seen before. Maybe a neighbor brought it. Maybe Rena keeps leashes in her car for emergencies. Canavan doesn't have his crutches. They must still be in the house, Jack figures, and he's thinking about what else is in there, what he'd lose if the roof did suddenly collapse in a hail of sparks and fire. Beth's shaking his arm, pushing at him. "Listen," she's saying. "Listen."

"What?"

He turns and it's the EMT who wants to talk to him, to both of them. He's got Hen's hand wrapped up already. His thumb's just barely sticking out. "OK, folks," he says. "We can take him in if you like, but it's really not a serious burn, and that's an expensive ride, if you want my opinion. It'd probably be just as good if you just keep an eye on him, change his bandage out in the morning."

"OK," Jack says.

"But if he loses any significant amount of skin, you should see a doctor."

"What's a significant amount?" Beth says.

"Anything bigger than a quarter," he says.

"Oh my God," she says, wrapping and unwrapping his shirt around her own hand.

"That shouldn't happen," the EMT says. "It really shouldn't." He reaches behind him, into another drawer on the other side of the ambulance. "If he's in any pain," he says, "give him these." He hands Jack some little packets.

"What is that?" Beth wants to know.

"Headache powders," the EMT says. "We've got other stuff on the truck, if you want, but that works the best. If he won't drink it in water, put it in peanut butter."

"Like he's a dog?" she says.

The EMT smiles. "I just always figure whatever works."

"You can put it on ice cream, too," his partner says.

"So he's OK?" Beth wants to know. "He's fine?"

"Yeah," the EMT says, and pats Hen on the back. Hen flinches away a little. "He's real brave."

"Thanks," Jack says.

"What happened in there?" the EMT asks.

"The refrigerator was on fire," says Jack. "He was reaching for it."

"Reaching?"

"I don't know what he was doing," Jack says. "I don't know why he did that."

"Kids do some things that don't make sense," the EMT says, and wraps a blanket around Hendrick's shoulders. Hen shrugs it right off.

"How did it catch on fire?" Beth asks.

Jack says, "It just did."

"Can that happen?" she asks him. She turns to the EMT. "Can that even happen?"

The EMT says, "Ma'am, I wouldn't know about anything like

that." He shakes his head. "But I've never heard of a refrigerator being on fire."

The firemen come back out of the house, finally, coats open, carrying their helmets. Walking. They walk back to the truck, hang their coats in one little compartment, their axes in another. Two of them sit down on a step on the truck, and the other one walks over to Rena and Canavan, who shake their heads, point Jack out. The fireman crosses the lawn to the ambulance. "Captain Gary Arnold," he says, introducing himself. "Everybody OK here?" Hendrick stares at Captain Gary Arnold like he's some kind of god.

"I think so," says Jack. "I think we are."

"Good," he says. "Whose home is this?"

"It's mine," Jack says.

Captain Arnold nods. "I'm afraid we had to make a little bit of a mess of your kitchen," he says. "But the fire's under control. We took care of that."

"Good," Jack says. "Thank you."

"What kind of a mess?" Beth asks.

"The fire was in the wall," Captain Arnold says. "We had to go into the wall."

Another firefighter goes inside, carrying what looks like a video camera.

"What's he doing?" Jack says.

"That's a heat sensor. We cut the circuit to the refrigerator, but he's gonna check to make sure the fire didn't spread any further. Standard procedure," he says. "Just precautionary."

Beth looks at him. "Spread where?"

"Through the electric into another wall."

"So the walls could be on fire?"

"That's pretty rare, ma'am," says the captain. "But that's why we do the heat imaging. Infrared. To make sure."

"How rare?"

"They're checking," Jack tells her. "That's why they're checking."

"We won't let you go back in there until it's all clear, ma'am."

"How did it happen?" Jack asks.

Captain Arnold shrugs. "You know," he says, "the wiring fails, gets hot, starts a fire. Simple as that," he says. "People forget how dangerous electric can be."

"It was the fridge, then?"

"That, and the outlet," he says.

"So it wasn't anything we did."

"Not unless you put that receptacle in. The connections looked a little screwy, if you know what I mean."

"I didn't," he says. "I didn't do anything to the electric," he tells Beth. She nods, and Jack thinks she might believe him.

Captain Arnold holds his hand out to Hen, who's still staring. "Pleased to meet you, young man," he says.

Hendrick doesn't say anything, but he reaches out his right hand, the one that's not bandaged, shakes Captain Arnold's hand.

"He's a little shy," Jack says, explaining.

"Doesn't seem shy to me," he says. "How is he?" he asks the EMT.

"First-degree," he says. "Maybe second. Small, though. Pretty good, considering."

"Nobody else injured?" Captain Arnold asks.

"Nope," says the EMT.

"Good enough," the captain says. He looks across the yard, at the catfish, the octopus. "What are those things, anyway?" he asks.

"They're from a putt-putt," Jack says, a kind of exhaustion coming over him now. Hen's OK. None of the rest of it makes any difference at all.

The captain looks a little closer at Jack, squints at him, and from the way he's doing it, Jack can tell he must have a pretty good shiner already. "Y'all been in some sort of accident?" he asks.

"Yes," Jack says, but doesn't explain what kind. Captain Gary

Arnold doesn't ask any more questions after that. A small, important kindness. The captain looks at Hen in the ambulance, and at Beth, who's up there with him now, stroking his face, his hair, whispering to him. It seems like the captain knows. It seems like he knows every piece of it. He tells Jack *Have a good night, now, sir, be safe,* and he goes back to his truck, to his men. Jack looks for Rena, who's sitting over by the mailbox. She's still got Yul Brynner. Canavan's limped over to talk to the firemen out in the street. There's not much more Jack can do except to wait here with Beth and Hendrick for the last fireman to come out of the house, wait for somebody to tell them they can go back in. Hen's watching the firemen put all their gear back away in all the open doors on the side of the engine. Jack stands on his auctioned front yard, fire truck lights spinning. This is all mine, he thinks. My house, my marriage, this mess of my own making. Whatever all this is, whatever else it is, it's his. It belongs to him. He's done it, he's made it, he's punched holes in it, he's dug it up, he's lit it on fire. It's his. It has to be. A radio on the fire truck Canavan's standing next to kicks on, announces somebody else's fire, somewhere else. There's a string of numbers that must mean what kind of fire it is. Jack's going to need more ice for his eye. Canavan backs up, and the fire truck edges forward, pulls away, turns the siren on at the end of the block. Jack waits. The red lights run right to left across the fronts of the houses. All of this, Jack thinks. All of it mine.

❦ ❦ ❦

Hendrick's still not talking, and the kitchen is torn to shit. There's foam and powder everywhere, footprints through all of it, and it's tracked back to the front door. The refrigerator's well out into the room, and from the hole in the wall behind it, it looks like the firemen went after it with the axes. The wire running to the outlet's been cut. The wallboard and the studs are scorched. The bottom of

the fridge is black. It smells like fire. It smells like cigarettes, actually, like wet ashtrays. It'll be at least a weeklong job to put it all
back together. Hendrick's playing with the foam, pulling his good
hand through it. Jack wonders if this is the same stuff they spray
runways down with for crashing jetliners. Beth comes in the door
with Yul Brynner, walks up behind them. "Don't put that in your
mouth," she tells Hendrick. He looks at her, doesn't talk.

"Are Rena and Canavan still out there?" asks Jack.

"Yes," she says.

"Did he find his crutches?"

"No."

"Should we be looking for them?"

"No," she says. She reaches for Hendrick, pulls him gently back
away from the foam. "I don't think so." Hen's wearing sneakers
and his underwear. Beth's holding his ruined clothes. "We need to
get him dressed," she says.

"OK," says Jack.

"You brought his clothes over, I guess."

"Yeah," Jack says. "In his room. In his dresser."

"Right." Beth walks around the corner, flicks on the light in
Hendrick's bedroom. "Does he have any new favorites?" she calls.

"It's all the same," Jack says. She's opening drawers. Jack holds
his hand out for Hen, takes him in there. Beth's got shorts and a
kid-sized Kinnett College T-shirt laid out for him. They sit Hen up
on the bed, and he lets them take off his shoes, put the shorts on,
pull the shirt down over his head. His bandaged hand is like a mit-
ten. He won't let them put his shoes back on, which Jack takes for
a good sign, a sign that he's OK.

"Why isn't he talking?" Beth asks.

"He'll talk," Jack says. "Right, buddy?" Hen looks at him, makes
a popping noise with his lips.

"He's not talking," she says. She sits down in his half-size desk
chair.

"He will," Jack says. "I promise."

She says, "You said nothing ever happened to him."

"He's fine," Jack says. "You heard the ambulance guy."

She points at his hand. "He's not fine."

"He'll be fine," Jack says.

She stands up, and then she sits back down. The chair spins a little to the side. "Your eye looks bad," she says.

"It does?"

"Go look at yourself," she says.

He goes into the bathroom, looks in the mirror. He looks like she hit him with a baseball bat. Or a bulldozer. His left eye is swollen half-shut. There are blue bruises in moons above and below it, and on the side of his nose. "You did a good job," he says. He touches it, and it hurts like hell.

"I'm sorry," she says. "I didn't mean to."

"Yes, you did," he says.

"I'm still sorry. I didn't mean to do *that*."

"It's OK," he says, turning the bathroom light back off. "I'll live." He stands in the half-dark, looks at the outline of his head in the mirror. The air conditioner kicks on again. He can hear cicadas out the window.

"I'm done with Terry," she says, from the other room. "I'm finished with that."

He walks back down the hall, stands in Hen's doorway. "What?"

She says, "I'm finished."

"We're talking about it?" he says. "Now?"

"I thought you should know," she says. "That you'd want to know."

"Why?" he asks.

"What do you mean?"

"I mean, why now? Why are you finished?"

"I just am," she says. "I have been."

"No other reason?"

"I had reasons," she says. "We can talk about them."

"I don't know if I want to," he says.

"People don't do this," she says. "I didn't want to do this any more." She gets up, pulls the pushpins out of the periodic table on one side, straightens it. She pushes the pins back in.

"Why'd you do it in the first place?" he says.

She says, "I had to, Jack."

"You had to?"

"Well, what about you? What about you and Rena?"

He thought they were all going to have to sit in some circle in the living room and confess things to each other. He did not think she'd hit him, did not think he'd light the house on fire. He did not think she'd sit in Hen's chair and tell him plainly that whatever all this was is done. *What about you and Rena?* What is it he's supposed to tell her? That in some other version of his life, he could have ended up with somebody like Rena? He knows he could have lived a slightly louder life. The life Rena kept wanting him to have. But the life he wants, the life he's grown to know, is this one, and he knows that he'd rather choose this one, that he needs to, that a life with Rena would be one where no one ever said *are you sure,* or *wait a minute*—she'd be cheering him on, endlessly, cheering them both on. They'd end up owning an ostrich farm, or they'd be owner-operators of a plane-banner advertising concern, or they'd become acrobats, or they'd be like his uncle and aunt, who built a house that sat on its point, a square turned diagonally, tilted up, because the county taxed property by the square footage of the home's footprint. They hung an addition from steel cables off a tree. When they were kids, they called it the Crazy House. *Are we going to the Crazy House this summer?* He knows he needs Beth to save him from his crazier angels, or try to, and he knows, too, or hopes, that she needs him to try to save her from her plainer ones. "Rena's over, too," he says.

"Are you sure?"

"Yes," he says.

"I'm not coming back yet," she says. "You can say no if you want to."

"What if I had said no?"

"I wouldn't have come home then, either, you idiot," she says.

"What're you going to do, then?" he says. "Stay with Canavan?"

She says, "I'm not sure." Then she says, "I was thinking I might move back in across the street. To our house." She slides Hen's desk light over some. "I thought maybe we could try that for a while. We could be neighbors."

"Neighbors?"

"We've got to be something, Jack."

"I know," he says.

"Something else," she says.

"I know that, too."

"I miss you," she says. "I did the whole time."

"I miss you, too," he says. He looks at the ceiling, at the ceiling fan, at the model space shuttle hanging there. He did, at least, do a good job in here. It looks almost exactly like Hen's old room. It's finished, complete. It's a room. "I want to ask you something," he says.

"What?"

"Come outside," he says. "I want to show you the racetrack. I want to show you how it turned out."

"Oh, Jack, I don't think so, OK? Not right now."

"Come on," he says. "Five minutes. Just come see it."

"Now? Really?"

"Yes," he says. "Really."

"What about Hendrick?"

Hen looks at her, and then, holding his left hand, his burned hand, above his head, he gets up, walks out of the room. They follow him. He installs himself in front of the television, and the dog lies down almost on top of him while Hen flicks from one channel to another. He can't quite settle on anything. They stand behind him, watch with him for a while, watch until he's cycled through all the channels three or four times. "Come outside," Jack says, quietly. "Please."

"Do you think his hand's OK?" she asks.

"No," he says. "But it will be. He'll be fine." She looks at Hendrick once more. "He will," Jack says, and he can see she's not sure, but she nods OK anyway, follows him out the broken sliding door.

In the weird wash from Frank's streetlight he can see well enough to take her around the outside of the racetrack, show her where all the creatures will go, show her the ridges in the concrete the push broom left. She's let him take her outside. He's surprised, but he keeps going. He tells her about how he wants to plant something in the middle—wildflowers, possibly—and tries to tell her about Kenny Trimble and the NCDOT. He tells her how at first it was going to be a loop, how then he thought of the eight. He tells her about Randolph, and the Sons. He tests the concrete in a few spots, and it feels dry, or almost dry. "See these posts?" he asks her, showing her the bolts sticking up out of one of the concrete pads. "They get bolted down to these."

"What do?"

"The undersea creatures."

"Are you kidding me?"

He straightens up. "No," he says. "Why?"

"I just thought somebody should ask you that."

She's orange in the streetlight. They both are, and so's the ground, the sidewalk, the sky above them partly clouded over and throwing back Frank's light, the light of the rest of the city. "Why don't we put one up?" he says.

"I don't know," she says.

"A small one," he says. "A small one."

"Are they heavy?"

"Sort of," he says.

She shifts all her weight to her right foot, then her left. She looks at him. He can see her trying different answers out in her head. "One," she says. "I'll help you do one."

The undersea creatures on their sides in the front yard look like some kind of marine biology project gone badly wrong. He tries the catfish, just to say he did, but it's too heavy for the two of them, so he settles on one of the jellyfish, the maroon one. It's got a bow tie and a pocket watch. No pocket. They pick it up, and he gets them spun around to where he's walking backwards, so it'll be easier for her. He tells her about how he left the clam for Zel. She wants to know who Zel is, and he tries to explain while they carry the jellyfish around the back and look for the right pad, the one with the right configuration of bolts. Once they find it, they get it on there pretty easily. Butner and Ernesto did a nice job. It's a good fit, and it's three feet tall. At least. It seems bigger here than at the Undersea Adventures Mini-Golf, but he likes that, likes the way the scale changes, likes how it feels like it doesn't quite entirely belong here. That's the appeal, after all. The surprise of it. They stand back and he says, "What do you think?"

She looks at him, at the house, at the racetrack. "Jesus, Jack," she says.

"What?"

"I still don't know what you want me to say."

"You don't have to say anything," he says.

"It's a lot," she says. "That's all."

He knows there's more, knows that's not all, but when he takes her hand, she lets him, and he pulls them a couple of steps farther back, so they can look across the street. The house is all lit up over there. Either the lights timed on, or Canavan and Rena went in there to fight, to apologize, to shake hands and part ways, to stab each other with steak knives, to try to figure out what might happen to them now. He can't see anybody. All he can see is the light through the windows, the cardboarded-over hole where he put the beer can through. He needs to get on that. Get a pane of glass cut. Beth lets go of him, walks back to the jellyfish, puts her hand on its head, like it might be another child they have. She leans over, puts her forehead on it. He's fairly sure she's crying. He can hear her breathing. He can hear himself breathing. He walks down to her, stands behind her, is reaching for her, is about to put his hand—where? on her back? her shoulder?—and then there's Hen in the doorway, the back door, Yul Brynner next to him, the two of them silhouetted against the lamps in the living room. Hen's taken his clothes back off, is completely naked. He's taken his bandage off, too. He's not marching, not singing, not speaking Spanish. He is not reciting constitutional amendments or the entirety of the Yellow Pages. He's not doing anything to make them think he's any better or any worse. He stands there and looks out at them, at his racetrack, at his jellyfish. He reaches for the door. More than anything else, Jack thinks, he looks like he's been born once more, new, into this world.

# Acknowledgments

I am deeply grateful to Lisa Kopel-Hubal for finding this book, and forever in debt to Peter Steinberg for taking such good and thoughtful care of it, and of me, from there on out. Thanks always to Paul Slovak at Viking for taking a chance on a story full of mulch, but more importantly, for pushing to make all parts of it, even those pages without pine bark, so much more like what they were supposed to be. Thanks to Paul Buckley, Sharon Gonzalez, and Kate Lloyd at Viking for their excellent assistance along the way. Early readers of this book—Sarah Cox, Jane Kitchen—thank you for your encouragement and advice. Thank you Terry Kennedy for details large and small; thank you Jon Baker for knowing it wasn't ready, and for saying so.

Thank you Jim Clark and Julie Funderburk and the faculty of the UNC–Greensboro MFA program—Fred Chappell, Stuart Dischell, Lee Zacharias—for providing a home it turns out I'd never really leave, and thanks especially to Michael Parker for pulling me so often from flowerbeds both real and perceived. Thanks to Elon University for its support, to Kevin Boyle and Cassie Kircher in particular, and to my students for reminding me, with some frequency, what matters and why. Many thanks, of course, to Jason

Wright at American Mulch Supply in Whitsett, North Carolina, for humoring my request for a brief internship. Thanks to Jeff Towne for the forgiven rent.

My parents raised my brothers and me in a house full of books—among so many other things, they taught us to read. Thank you Judy and Tom, Neil and Josh. Thank you Piver. Thank you Jane and Walter, Sally and Jack, and Nancy.

Tita: Without you, no home to come home to. No story, either. Thank you, thank you.